THE FINAL CONFESSION
OF
SAINT AUGUSTINE

Dedicated to Professor Klaus Jankofsky
who posed the questions:

ubi sunt?

and

"où sont les nieges d'antan?"
François Villon

which sparked my interest in lives
already lived.

Works by Tim Jollymore

Listener in the Snow

Observation Hill
a novel of class and murder

The Advent of Elizabeth

Lake Stories and Other Tales

People You've Been Before

The Final Confession
of
Saint Augustine

Contents

THE FINAL CONFESSION
OF
SAINT AUGUSTINE

an historical novel by

Tim Jollymore

FINNS WAY BOOKS

Author's Note

There is little use to say of how I got hold of this story, whether it was found in a desert jar after centuries, whether it was bought through a dealer in antiquities in Carthage who did not know its worth, or whether it fluttered in through the window onto my Sicilian writing desk on a gentle April breeze cooling the beach at Letojanni.

Any story I could tell about its origin you would not likely believe even if it were true. So, there let this history's beginnings rest and be thankful.

T.J.

Printed in the United States of America. For information, address Finns Way Books™, 2244 Lakeshore Avenue, Suite 4, Oakland, California 94606; or contact www.finnswaybooks.com.

The Final Confession of Saint Augustine is a work of historical fiction grounded in recorded events and informed by circumstances and characters not recorded or not accurately recorded in the surviving histories.

Biblical quotations are from the Vulgate then known to Augustine and available in translation at www.vulgate.org.

The cover art is a digital restoration of a fresco depicting Terentius Neo and his wife found in the ruins of Pompeii, housed in Museo Archeologico Nazionale di Napoli. Photo and editing by Finns Way Books.

ISBN 978-0-9985288-7-8

June 14, 2022

THE FINAL CONFESSION
OF
SAINT AUGUSTINE

Foreword

I have, lacking authority all my weary life, long pled experience, but, even then, there is no full accounting for what I have here set down against anything that actually happened, for, though I have traveled extensively, I could not be and have not been everywhere to hear and see all that had transpired.

Much of the story of the-friend-of-my-youth, Aureleus Augustinus, onetime bishop of Hippo Regius, I tell from firsthand knowledge, having been at his side in youth and, again, in old age, both privately and in many of his public appearances. What I say of him I have seen or been told by those who know, including the bishop himself. For what I have been led to say that I do not truly know, I have relied on divining the habits and the natures of my fellows, Augustine included, and on the inherent verity of plain gossip.

When I was not present for events and was not informed later by those who were, I, loving a good bit of a story, added to what I knew that which I did not, according to my desire to make sense of all that occurred.

So to speak, I have stitched a sail of my own heavy canvas along with the tatters of others' spars and with the very wind that blew my vessel toward its port, bringing my readers, I hope, the satisfaction of knowing home.

I. Q.

1

Innomenatus and Augustine

I died without a name.

Now, returned from the dead, I call myself *Innomenatus*, the-one-without-name.

I've not since our passionate adolescence curried the favor of Aurelius Augustinus, now longtime Bishop of Hippo, the friend-of-my-youth, but strangely find myself here under his roof just the same.

It is to my own wide travels—Alexandria, Jerusalem, Dacia, Corinth, Rome, Gaul, and Hispania—that I owe my present position. It was not out of friendship that Augustine offered me work—at the time, thinking me dead, he did not know who I was, and only lately recognized me. I came on as but a tool in the wars of the episcopate, a translator to the Greek and, more rarely, to the Gothic tongues. In that way I play an unimportant role in the bishop's extensive writing, but mostly—until our chance meeting alone on an African hot summer's night—I labored in translating his letters to the East, since he failed miserably at and even ridiculed the Greek language from the time of our schooldays. Augustine, then as he does now, looks to Latin Rome more than to the bishoprics of Alexandria and Constantinople, or than to Jerusalem or Antioch. So, in his African scriptorium, I languished happily in the background, simply an occasional and particular scholar in Hippo Regius, but I am here, like Hannibal's elephant come home, perhaps to die again.

Aurelius Augustinus, *puer amicus*, friend-of-my-youth—should I say, "wild youth?" For that is exactly how we played then, fired by inexhaustible recklessness and together in a lust for life much greater than that to which he has made measly confession in his writing. Aurelius, I say, did not at first know me for who I am. I had died to him. After my second illness, I died *only* to him. In truth, I recovered from that second fever as well as the first, and my family, fearing more plague, sent me to Alexandria, where I continued to study Greek and Hebrew. Even after a half-century's travel intervening, I see the day clearly:

Aurelius sat on my bedside. He caressed my hand and kissed it.
"You have grown so thin, my brown boy." He laughed softly.
"Two bouts of fever cook you down, my love," I told him.
He kissed my cheek. "Oh my, you burn still."
"Always in your presence, *cupitus meum*, my lover."
"And when will you return to the school? Study and teaching are lonesome, truly loathsome without you there."
As my nurse brought in a basin of mint-water, "To cool you," she said, Aurelius leapt away and turned to the window.
"Later. Later, please," I said. She set the bowl on the night table and left. Then to Aurelius, "Lonely, even with Tizem[1] there?"
"She is no comfort for what I desire. I want you."
"Come, sit again, Aurel. I have news." He stood at the window but craned his lithe neck and set his swarthy countenance on me.
"What news?" He frowned.
I am sorry to say that in my excitement I broke it to him ungently, "I am to go to Alexandria to study."
"What? Now? You are still sick. You cannot travel."
His complexion took on an even darker sheen when he was angry. At that moment, he looked as black as the darkest desert-traveling Berber.
"Aurel, I will go. I sail in two weeks."
"No. You cannot sail! You hate the sea as much as do I." He stamped his foot. "You will not go. You must stay here with me. We will run away to Carthage again and live together there."
It was something Aurelius could not accept. The East, even Alexandria, was a place he could not go, tied as he was, married to the Latin world in Africa. So wedded was he to the West that he

---

1 I preferred her Berber name. Augustine had called her Sabina, always.

could not see it in himself and could not be himself without it. And I? I had survived my fevers. I had lived. So, I wanted not just Rome but the *whole* world.

"The empire is great and wide, my love. I must see it. I know that now."

He stuck out his jaw, glaring out the window.

From then until the time I left for Alexandria, Aurelius shunned me. He would never speak my name again. He'd called me dead, *Qui mortuus*, one who has died.[2] When much later, at the election of Innocent as Bishop of Rome, having lived in Antioch and Jerusalem for years, when I again turned west, the friend-of-my-youth wrote of my death, never mentioning my name, in his famous *Confessio*. It was at that time that I began to call myself *Innomenatus Quimortuus*, the dead man without a name. It was a travesty, but the shame was not mine.

I had grown old even before I returned to Africa, to Hippo in the second year of Valentinius III. By that young emperor's fifth year, I felt even more ancient. Although we lived sound in body, *eramus senem*, we, the Bishop and I, were age-old.

Untrue? I make it sound as if we were together. Not so. In those two years, I worked in the monastery but kept very much to myself. I did not desire the bishop's attention and had not revealed to him who I was or had been. That changed one wakeful African night, when during the few dark hours of summer, we both suffered, intimately, one of the infirmities of aged minds, sleeplessness. That night, hours before dawn, we—not just the bishop and I, but *puer amicus* and I— met again.[3]

---

2 He proclaimed it to his students and to our friends, too. And though it was only a period of a week before I left for Carthage to join my ship east, it was hurtful, especially when encountering friends who ran away from me thinking me a ghost!

3 For my part, at least, our 'meeting' jarred loose sensations I had not felt in decades. The curious attention the bishop paid to me at the time led me to believe that he also felt that very, involuntary swell of feeling under the fulsome moon. Later I confirmed it was true.

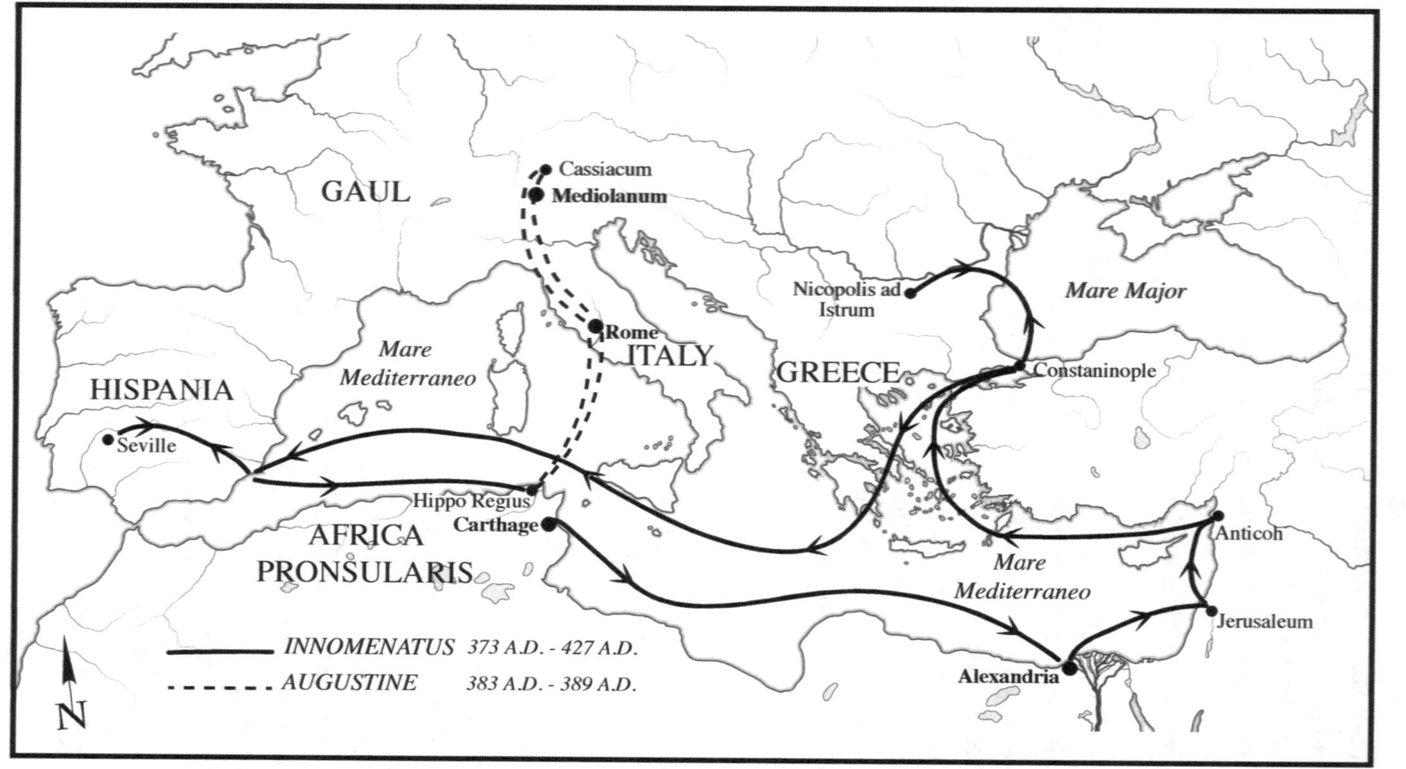

Travels of Augustine and of Innomenatus

It was nearing *fariae Agusti*, the mid-August Roman holiday, during the early harvest, and the weather was unbearably hot. Who could sleep? Certainly not the old. When reading or writing failed to exhaust me on such nights, I walked always without a torch, an extravagance for a poor scribe. In any case, the night I encountered the bishop was nearing the full moon and walking was pleasant and easy. A light breeze from the sea kept my garments from sticking to my body, drying them even as I perspired. I was, perhaps, in too much of a hurry, returning to my cell to seek sleep and, rounding the corner near the apse of the cathedral, I crashed into Augustine. So surprised I was that I addressed him in Greek, επίσκοπό μου, my bishop. Then in his Latin, *ignosce me*, forgive me. I thought he was hurt, for in my years of frequenting the kitchens of wealthy patrons, I had become, some said 'fat,' but, in any case, a much larger man by then, and he was still, as always, slight. He emitted a loud *ugh* as we collided, but I prevented his fall by my embrace.[4]

"Let me help, my lord. Please sit a moment, here on the footing." I unfurled my arms, took his elbow, "Permit me," and guided him to the seat to gather himself.

When Aurelius caught his breath, he looked at me in the moonlight. "I know you." He looked closer. "Are you from Carthage?" His voice quavered in the light wind.

Still not wishing, especially at that moment, to be recognized from our youth I said, "No, my lord, I am in your scriptorium." My deception was not a lie, I thought, since I worked there and was not from Carthage but of his own town, Thagaste.[5]

"Ah, the Greek."

I assented. "Yes, the Greek."

"Brother in Christ, I mistook you in this uncertain light for a man I knew in youth. Though he was much slimmer." Augustine paused and perhaps thought. To himself he murmured, "He had no beard."

"Forgive me for saying it, but our youth is so long ago that I myself

---

4 It was by that embrace that he recognized me, I believe.

5 Looking back now, I think it strange to have been secretive, but at the time, acknowledging our youth and our love meant opening a well of suffering and abandonment I had capped only by years of travel and absence. So, when we came so close that night, I shied away from admitting to my identity.

have forgotten much and many, too."

He sat in silence. I did not speak. Finally, he looked curiously at me again and said, "You have aged well, my brother. How many years have you?"

I trust it is not a mortal sin to speak an untruth to a bishop, especially about one's age. "*Sextaginta anni.* Sixty, I think. Perhaps sixty-two." Once slipping into falsehood, now I leapt further, "I was born in the reign of Gratian."

The bishop searched my face once more. "Yes," he muttered again as if talking to himself, "too young." He laid his hand on mine, paused there for just a minute, and then rose from the stone. "If our Lord wills it, I shall write now. In the name of Jesus, sleep." He bent to kiss my cheek and was gone.

He walked off toward the *scriptorium.* Likely he would rouse several scribes there and work them until long past dawn. All his words were taken down at once by several. I suppose that is my excuse for recording, even when he'd asked me to abstain, all he said and all that happened. Again, it was not out of friendship, neither his asking nor my writing.

Perhaps I deceive myself.

Truth be told, I was, all those three years as well as those just before returning to Africa, unsure of my reason for coming back or for seeking-out Augustine's employment. Surely, the hot coals of love had cooled, at least for my part. Neither was desire to inflict hurt nor to open old wounds in my nature. Certainly, I lack the temerity to have wanted to attempt saving the bishop from himself, though having known his writings and activities from afar, likely I should have tried. No. I could not divine my reasons for having arrived on his doorstep. Perhaps I simply wanted to see, to find out what would happen, and as an inveterate gossip—not perhaps my worst fault—to tell the tale.

Even so, I was relieved to sleep that night—perhaps the blessing of a bishop can work a miracle—and next, blessed my good fortune that I was called away the following morning.

"*Innomenatus Quimortuus?*" I recognized the commanding voice as a soldier's of Bonifacius who looked at me through the grating of my tiny room.

"Yes, the same. What do you want?"

"By order of *Comes* Bonifacius, Governor of *Africa Proconsularis*, you, Innomenatus are to accompany me into the presence of our Lord Count. He has use for you."

"What use?"

"That is not for us to discuss," the centurion told me.

"What have I done?"

"It is for what you can do, speaking and writing, that you are called, commanded to come."

Such is the place of the scribe in a great empire. I would go and be grateful. My confusion of the night before washed away in the flush of wakefulness after a sound sleep.[6] I would not have to appear before Augustine—much, perhaps, to the relief of us both—not as it turned out for several months.

The work Bonifacius had for me was sensitive to the state, bore great personal meaning to me, and interested me as an observer of politics and of the military as well. All of us living under Roman protection paid close attention to the political winds and the protecting legions of the Roman army, for good reason in the reign of a child-emperor.

Years before—I was in Antioch again—like everyone in the empire I had been shocked and frightened by the appearance of Visigoths in the north of Italy and soon after by the sack of Rome at their hands. The Eternal City was no longer forever impregnable. Long before it had thrice lost the name of capital—first to Constantinople, then to *Mediolanum*, and finally to Ravenna—but in the hearts of all living under what had been *pax romana*, Rome was still Rome. When it fell to barbarians, the dust of plunder blew throughout the empire and whirled over what was left of the West, including

---

6 I now confess a dream of the previous night. 'We were young, sun-drenched, and lustful, colliding in a catacomb of the Coliseum at Thuysdrus, where Africanus had been crowned. Our skins stunk of the vapors of local olive oil and of our desire. He ravished me.' That dream though intense and lurid did not, I think, wake me from the sleep to which my long-ago lover's benediction sent me.

Hippo Regius in Africa. It is certainly true that the trauma Rome's fall engendered, emboldened other tribes: Huns, Visigoths, and what became the Alan-Vandal[7] alliance. It was this last barbarian band that Bonifacius—to aid in never-ending civil war—now courted to help protect himself and Africa in his fights with the regent of Rome, Galla Placidia, mother to the young emperor.

For Augustine's part, the sack of Rome inspired the bishop of Hippo Regius to write his magnum opus, *De civitate Dei*, The City of God. The terror he felt, we all felt, pushed the friend-of-my-youth to rebuild an unconquerable, truly eternal city in the air of his philosophic, Platonic mind. If the worldly city could not hold, we must, he said, seek the one not of this world.

To the sack of Rome, the soldier, Bonifacius, responded with arms, the churchman, Augustine, with intellect. Neither, now twenty years after the event, could foretell what would come of Augustine's earthly little town, Hippo Regius, of the entirety of the African church headquartered there, nor of the New Jerusalem the bishop had raised in *De civitate Dei*. Even I, coming to know both men well and having observed recent Vandal history up close—I had tutored Gaiseric himself in Gaul and Hispania—could not guess.

Called to duty, traveling east from Augustine's ecclesiastical see toward Carthage and staying at the count's villa a day's march from town, always in the company of *Comes* Bonifacius, I was away from Hippo and from its bishop for months.

I was relieved.

Bonifacius would write during that time to the Vandal king, Gaiseric, and wanted to do so in that king's own language. Knowing and having translated into and out of Gothic—not as easily, I admit, as Greek or Hebrew—I seemed to be the only scholar in Numidia or Africa Proconsularis who could do the work. For what can a poor scribe be thankful, except for work and for an opportunity to take part in or, perhaps, bend a little the course of events? Adventures of that sort had given me the reason long before to travel, to leave

---

7 Even to my Vandal friend, Gaiseric, I apply the word *barbarian*, though not without nipping at my own tongue. Belying the infamy in that moniker, I had learned respect even for the Visigoths from my years of work under the Dacian bishop Ulfilas translating the gospel of Luke into Gothic.

Carthage and Augustine behind me. This new encounter did the same for me and was for Bonifacius a chance to save his title and his wealth in Africa.

A pact with *Comes Africae* would relieve my former pupil and friend, the Vandal king, Gaiseric, and his people from constant attack in Hispania at the hands of Sueves, Goths, and imperial legions. On his part, Gaiseric, even having traveled much and fought by siege many times, could not feel or truly understand the security of walls. Fortifying Seville, his capital, would not, I knew, have made him feel safe or alive. So, at the death of his half-brother King Gunderic, he quickly abandoned the walls and responded to Bonifacius's plea for help, taking to the very sea that most of his land-loving kinsmen feared.

I had known Gaiseric quite well—a friendship I now revealed to no one—and I understood that he would feel freer and safer even on the sea and afterward in the wide, ill-protected lands on the southern shores of *Mar Mediterraneo* than hunching behind stone walls in Hispania. But not even Gaiseric, the most practical and longsighted of warriors, could know what lay in store for his people in Africa.

I, though, when it came to pass, was not surprised.

2

Bonifacius and Augustine

Early that morning, while I, Innomenatus, slept, *Comes Africae*, Count Bonifacius, having interrupted Augustine's dictation, stood alone before the bishop who, sitting on his episcopal throne, looked up at his Roman protector. Even were he standing, Augustine would have barely reached the Count's shoulder. The bishop eyed the Roman soldier, waiting for him to speak first, a rarity in their long relations.

Despite the heat that had persisted all through the night, Bonifacius wore his *palundamentum*, his commander's mantel, draped over and across the back of his tunic and fixed at his right shoulder with a *fibula*, a marvelous gold pin in a gorgonish form. Augustine considered: *Tanit*? He wears a pagan brooch to meet me! Then the bishop regarded the soldier's bare legs—muscled and browned in leagues and leagues of marches—and looked up again, slowly sweeping his gaze over the tunic that stretched tightly over Bonifacius's waist and more tightly over his chest. He imagined himself rising, reaching out for the golden image of *Tanit*, releasing it and with it the soldier's robes to the floor. He stopped himself from acting on the frightful impulse, but fight the allure as he might, the bishop found it difficult not to imagine the body beneath the cloth. Augustine raised his eyes to his guest's and waited for the Count to start.

"I am sorry that this is not a visit to talk philosophy or theology," Bonifacius began. "I have come for counsel. Despite this uneasy truce, my troubles are compounded and seem to multiply by the day." He scanned the dark face of the aged bishop, looking for encouragement or disapproval. Finding neither, he continued. "I am trapped in Numidia. I have scant resources to draw on, nor do I seem able to build up an army to retake Carthage. There are rumors, as always, that the regent will send more troops to defeat me once and for all." He drew a long breath, expanding his chest and tightening his abdomen against his tunic. Augustine watched the general attentively, waiting for more. "With a small additional force, perhaps of 3,000 adding in more cavalry, I could withstand attack and maybe throw Sigisvultus out of Carthage on his ear. Of course, there will be a cost."

Augustine, already done listening, sat forward. "There are but two kinds of wars, I tell you. One type is the never-ending clatter of swords against shields and helms, raising shouts of victors, cries of anguished defeat and hatred, which is the variety that settles nothing but the lust for blood and booty"—the presbyter raised his thin finger, pointing at the Roman's chest— "such as that pagan pin you dare to wear in the presence of a bishop of God." Augustine seemed to consider some unmentioned topic and hesitated a moment. "Even so, that lust, like all temporal endeavors, is never satisfied, nor does it fulfill the soul." The bishop paused. "Such fleshly battles only drain life away and grind bones to dust to which Peter speaks: '*Carissimi obsecro tamquam advenas abstinere vos*, Dearly beloved, I beseech you as strangers and pilgrims, abstain from fleshly lusts, which war against the soul.'"

Bonifacius stood tall and burly, listening now. It would do no good trying to interrupt this line of talk, nor could one hurry the bishop during one of his arguments, as he had often proved in their discussions of philosophy or the gospels. It was now as it had often appeared before to the count, that Augustine's arguments seemed to wrestle not with him, the soldier, but within the bishop himself, trying to prove over and again some point of contention within the churchman's soul.

Augustine continued, "But by the unity of The Father and equality of The Son, our Lord Jesus Christ, and the harmony of the Holy Spirit, all one God, we come to know the other type of war which not only fulfills the destiny of a man who follows this battle but also fills and purifies the living, breathing spirit within us all, be it listened to but once, which is the kind of war the soul seeks to make upon the lustful body, to defeat the *mundial* wanting which drags us down and away from our appointed course, the road to everlasting life."

The bishop now spoke quickly, certainly, to his point. "So, the soul battles the body's needs and the mind's weaknesses to keep clear the path to The Father. It engages no physical battle, spills no blood, steals no plunder, procures no enslavement, nor breathes the air of concupiscence, but wars nonetheless, which is the fight you and your Arian wife might well take up and forget about Galla Placidia and her *Comes* Sigisvultus who holds an object of your desire, Carthage." Again, the bishop paused and resettled himself regally on his throne. "Desire it not, for as the psalmist says, 'For the wicked boasteth of his heart's desire.' You, my friend, have been a protector of our church, of our faith, of the whole of Numidia and Africa Proconsularis—for that you are owed great thanks—but what have your efforts brought but invitations to war and to more war? And now, it seems, yet another conflict is in the offing. May you survive another day while you purify your soul."

Now, Bonifacius waited to see that the bishop was done. He watched Augustine's eyes rove over him from his pin to his sandals and back again.

The bishop asked, "Who does Rome send now?"

"An envoy, and then, I suppose, another army."

"And what is *your* plan?"

"I could recruit Numidians who are good fighters but who without good pay can easily turn against a master. Are resources available?"

"Not from the church. We are but a poor lot here."

The Roman knew better but also understood that help must be offered, that it cannot be taken. So, he said, "The nearest help is in Hispania. The Vandal king Gaiseric could be useful."

The bishop rose and took one step on the dais toward Bonifacius. "*That* is your plan?"

"My *bucellarii*, my escorts—Augustine silently corrected the count, thinking, 'Your wife's royal guard, her *bucellarii*'—can control the barbarians."

The bishop shook his head. "Those biscuit eaters can barely control themselves, rampaging as they do through our countryside. No wonder no Numidian soldiers can be hired."

"It may be so. What more can I do in the absence of gold or silver?"

He brought his left hand to his heart and covered the brooch with his fingers as if to hide all his treasure.

Augustine began another lecture. "There are but two things, one fits the sin of despair . . ."

The count's hand left the *fibula,* and he pushed his palm out to halt the diatribe. "*Tempus fugit,* my bishop."

"Ah, well, then although I have not the money for war or for much else, I have an idea."

He again looked the Roman up and down, perhaps considering how much to tell the soldier. "I can offer only small aid." Bonifacius was forced to wait him out.

Augustine fidgeted on his seat, looking first left, then right, then down. Finally, he settled a matter obviously rounding his mind. "We have here a scribe, Innomenatus, who writes Latin and Greek, and who, it is said, also writes that Germanic gibberish, having assisted Ulfilas, they say, in translating *Luke* from Greek into Gothic. From his Latin, I can assure you that he has a charming tongue, and I am told he comes to us lately from Hispania and so must know something of those wild men. Perhaps he can persuade this Vandal king to come to your aid without much cost or danger to you or to my parish. The written word, as I have found over the course of the long life God has ordained me to live, can be most effective. Can that man read?"

"I believe the Vandal king can read or can certainly be read to. But how do you know this man, this Innomenatus? It is a strange name."

"To say it is a name is to contradict the name. He is named without-a-name. Ah well, he is in my scriptorium these last three years, translating from and to the Greek for me. I read him though I know him but slightly."

"Can he be trusted?"

"Have faith, my Roman friend. It would become you."

"Well, then, I shall send for him." Augustine was still. "Have I your permission, my bishop?"

Augustine set that thin finger to his lips and bore into Bonifacius with his eyes. "I understand your Arian wife is with child."

"Yes, it is so."

"I offer baptism to all. Shall you bring the child to me?"

What his wife, the daughter of a barbarian king, would say to this request, if that was what it was, Bonifacius did not know. But he needed the bishop's good will and could not turn down even this paltry offer. "My Lord, I shall."

"So be it. The child is to be consecrated in my church."

Comes Africae retreated and raised his right arm, "Vale." He backed out of the chamber bowing ever so slightly.

As Augustine watched him go and smoothing his robes over his legs he said, "*Abstinare*. Leave off, my flesh."

Surrounded by his Centurions, the Roman general strode away muttering to himself. "Always, always one loses the argument to that man. I have given up more than I have gained. A scribe! Well, what use I may have for him shall be revealed shortly." He spoke to his captain, "Find me the scribe Innomenatus who records for the Bishop of Hippo Regius. Escort him to my villa. He may bring what little he owns. It will be a long visit."

"*Faciam ut dicus*. I do as you say, my lord." The man and two centurions left the retinue. His group continued their march. Bonifacius continued his ruminations. "What can I offer the Vandal? Transport, certainly. A piece of land in Mauretania or better in Lilybaeum, safely across the sea in Sicilia. Best, when the barbarian had served his purpose, that he is sent to fight for his rights against the Roman legions far enough from Africa." The general knew firsthand that a great concentration of military might had grown in Hispania over the past ten years. Sueves, Alans, Goths, and Romans had swelled in conflict, sometimes annihilating whole tribes, so Bonifacius would not be surprised if Mauretania, just across the straits, appeared to Gaiseric safer than Hispania. Many of his Vandal people already were there, trading and keeping order. It was not the wisest of actions to let a barbarian into his realm, much less invite him, but Bonifacius, having fought three successive Roman invasions with no hope of regaining favor with the regent of Ravenna, was looking not for one of these Roman treaties, like the one which was presently in force, but for a decisive victory. Something told him Vandal help would finally unite the whole of Africa.

Augustine had watched his soldier-protector leave, finally, turning his back on the bishop, and followed him farther by the clatter of arms and the shields of the count's bodyguard, those same who would have been under Constantine the Great members of the Praetorian Guard, now long since disbanded. But this was Africa, and there was much here that remained as it had been a hundred years before and more. In Rome all changed too fast and much was lost in every altering wave—even before the sack of the city. Even when Augustine as a young man had been in Italy, Rome was not the western capital, had not been for two hundred years—and now all had moved to Ravenna. Rome was not everlasting. "Not so *Civitate Dei*, the Eternal City which would always endure," he thought. And perhaps his town, Hippo Regius, was a portal through which all would pass from grander cities and places on their way to the Father. "This thought is as vain as lust," he said. "*Abstinare.*"

Bonifacius and his men were gone. Augustine lingered in his reception chamber even though the urge to finish an argument he had begun, *De haeresibus ad Quodvultdeum*, "Heresies against God's Wishes," called him to the scriptorium. Too, he supervised the tedious labor on the corpus of his work, making sure the copies were accurate and sound. "I am growing no younger."

Yes, it was the influence of his Roman friend's body and the emergence of the name Innomenatus that caused him to loiter. At the inception of the general's requests, Augustine had had no intention to speak the name of him without-a-name but had suddenly and involuntarily connected the two whilst perusing the soldier's physique. "Perhaps it is the deep brown of the skin." Something uncontrollable, as if in a deep-sleeping dream, had, like a salacious oil, suddenly lubricated his tongue. He had uttered the name, and immediately, relief like waking from a turbulent sleep lay upon his brow. Sending Innomenatus away had freed him from a past he feared.

Now that his scribe was gone, he regretted the impulse. The man would be away, perhaps for months, traveling the countryside with the count's legions, reading, and writing for the Roman, rather than for *him* in the scriptorium. After the previous night's encounter, Augustine had found himself searching his mind for work that would bring Innomenatus closer to him, perhaps the unanswered letters to the east to which he owed replies in Greek. Too, the schism that the unruly son of Memorius had kicked up needed attention. He could use his scribe to write the Macedonian and Greek bishops who would be important in his condemnation of that raw but— Augustine nearly choked using the term—*brilliant* young man, Julian, who even now, he suspected, was infecting believers in his own hometown, Thagaste. "Well," muttered the bishop, "that brat and his Thagastan correspondent will have to wait. And so, too, can I for my scribe's return.

The bishop muttered to himself, "So now Julian's and this newly discovered heretic's destruction must wait. That delay, though, is not why you feel bereft." Augustine had spoken to the count and despite his misgivings would not now change his mind.

The retreat of Bonifacius's guard had left him in a silence not unlike that in the hot night before. Augustine felt again the bulk, solidity, and a certain familiarity of Innomenatus's body as it had pressed against his own. He recalled the other's protecting arms thrown around his almost-never-touched body. Then for a second and now in the new day, it felt like a loving embrace. Had the man held him? Augustine did not brook touch from any—human contact, he said, distracted him too much to bear—and it had been months, perhaps a year, since any had been so near to him outside the holy sacraments and baptism.

His spiritual duties remembered interceded on his bodily feelings. "Ah, baptism!" Yes, he would see to it that the child of Bonifacius was consecrated in *his* church, not among the heretical Arians to which the *comes's* wife cleaved. Those Arians outnumbered even Julian's Pelagian sect and were looming nearer. The bishop had exacted a promise, and Bonifacius would not betray his word. He was truly

Roman in that very way.

Augustine sighed. It was time to return to work. Although midday dictation was not as productive as that of the morning, it awaited his attendance. The old man rose and followed his duty like a draught horse, dragging his worried load that others might not sense his private shame.

3

Sabina, Called *Tizem*

At Sabina's convent in Hippo Regius, the previous day's heat had given way under a soothing breeze late that night, and now, just before sunrise and prayers, to the deepest cool of the new day. The full moon all night had spilled light over the convent garden where she, the mother superior, privately called *Tizem* by her familiars, had set her cot and slept. The near-dawn poured freshness into Sabina's deep well of faith. Wrens hopped and sang in the olive trees. Noisy gulls scraped the lightening sky and headed out over a fish-full sea. Both mixed with the soft sounds of her sisters stirring, readying the morning meal in company of quiet laughter over their baking, and, autumn now approaching, with the odor of the pomegranate flowers still blooming amongst the garden trees. To Sabina all spelled renewal and God's freely-given, unremitting grace.

The quiet of her mind accorded with her senses but as yet did not allow itself to move with the beginning of the day, keeping still, listening to her body's breath. Coolness inspired; a damp warmth flowed out, again and again, without thought, only appreciation of the goodness of God in this new day. Without hurry, with no wasted movements, she readied herself for the joys and sorrows of the work to come, and at the rising of the sun, ruby red at the horizon of the sea, she prayed in psalm:

> Lord, rebuke me not in thine anger, neither chasten me in Thy hot displeasure, . . .
> O Lord deliver my soul: oh, save me for Thy mercy's sake.

And in her own words, gleaned from Gospels other than the ones her Augustine knew—he less than a mile away through the winding streets of Hippo—she added to her prayer:

> Lord, as with your servant, Mary, guide our family to share in openness,

bringing your word—for Thy goodness's sake—to your multitudes.

She finished her songs and allowed daylight thoughts to stream into her mind: the coming grain harvest to the south, the sweet well that fed the gardens—the onions, carrots, and parsley all needed drink—and the coming afternoon in the shade of the walls where Ia and she would salt the early olives and prepare the brines and presses. Sabina slid her tunic over her torso, lightly caressing the skin with the cool fabric, running her hands down her sides, hugging her body in an embrace of praise for Christ's bounty bound in flesh. Then, she wrapped herself in the lightest and most modest garments, fixing the sewn hem just below her ankles, clipping the shoulder and waist each with a bronze cross, in *memorium nostri Dominus*, in memory of Jesus. Although she clothed herself in the light attire of sweetness and love, she was *Tizem*, the Berber lioness. At her center, like the rigid metal of the crosses, she raised a stalwart faith. Sabina moved quietly and steadily on her way to breakfast.

In the kitchen, the sisters were laughing, and her entrance did not reduce their merriment. Though Sabina ruled the house with a firm hand, she gloved it in amusement and gaiety. She gave her presence as a joy to them at the beginning of the workday. Sabina was their *materfamilias*, head of their house, its mighty spiritual center, but of the kindest, most inviting, and most gentle touch. Sabina smiled at their antics, hooking loaves from the oven with a long, crooked pole and ringing them around its shaft down to their breadbasket. It took skill and care to avoid getting burned by the hot loaf and that was the subject of the women's laughter.

Sabina clapped her hands, smiling and paraphrasing Job, said, "Let that which should be set on thy table be full of fatness." The women clasped each other and laughed more, then scurried to the table. They joined hands around the board.

"Ia, please lead us today," Sabina said.

Ia gave thanks to The Son not only for the food: the barley and emmer breads, the cheese from their goats, the fresh peas and parsnips wrapped with a little parsley, and the olives, of course. She gave thanks also for the *materfamilias*, the sisterhood of their house, and the wider believing community in both Numidia and Africa Proconsularis. In her prayer, Ia included the Berbers of the desert, some of whom still worshiped the ancient Punic goddess, Tanit, mentioned those Donatist Christians forever at odds with Hippo's Bishop, Augustine, and named the newly arrived Arians, both Goths, long-ago allies of Rome and, as was rumored, Vandals, now crossing from Hispania.

Sabina prompted her sister then. "Ia, please, don't forget our pagan citizens who yet worship their local spirits. May they amend their beliefs."

The good sister added these last and all said "Amen."

They ate quietly, but, after Sabina spoke of the day's chores, though there was hardly any purpose since each knew all that needed to be done, they began to jostle and laugh once more, poking the air at one another in jest about their work to come.

One of the youngest, then, asked, "And what shall our mother be doing this morning? The while we work?" The young woman blushed and added, "I mean no disrespect." They all tittered.

Sabina with gentle calmness told this sister that she had prayers to recite, reading to finish, garden planning to do, and letters to write.

"And what book do you read? And to whom do you write?" she asked. Having put this unsuspecting one up to the asking, some smiled kindly, some chuckled, and others, now a bit nervously, yet again laughed.

Sabina looked around at the expectant faces and brought her hand to the table to clasp the young woman's. She looked softly, perhaps, lovingly into her eyes while squeezing their palms together lightly, "I write to our presbyter, the Bishop Augustine, to discuss our needs and our lives here." Sabina furrowed her brow, remembering this girl's incident with spilt milk last Friday, even as she smiled and added, "but I will not mention your holey milking pail." Laughter rolled down the long table.

She continued in a serious tone, "What I read is also of our bishop, '*contra Donatistas*,' 'against the Donatists,' but only a part of it that came to me from the bishop of Carthage where the argument was delivered. I am not sure, she now laughed, but perhaps it concerns the lactation of goats!"

The sisters roared. Sabina let the woman's hands go and smiled at all the table. "So, we have prayed, have eaten, and have celebrated our Lord with kindness and laughter. Now, off to work. Shoo." Sabina took just a moment to kiss the little interrogator's cheek. "I love you," she said.

Soon, the morning grew hot. She took to the shade in the garden to read his marvelous arguments and to write her poor, short sentences filled with errors but also full of firm kindness and absent of regret. From within the walls of this house, within its gardens, and especially from the chapel, she would work to bend, if ever so slightly, the world—and in it, the iron will of her lost lover and bishop—to her chosen ways following Christ, an open practice to which she had dedicated her own and her daughter's lives.

She would that her bishop would have followed as she had the *christicolae*, seekers of the Son of Man. Augustine to much greater effect in the world had converted but had not followed her into the house of Christ. Nor, after his return to Africa, had he truly bound himself to the quiet, spiritual life. He had only appeared to precede her in faith, even after he had sent her ahead from Cassiciacum back to Africa, even after he arrived in Carthage again behind her, even after joining her there in that one error they committed during their sorrow over their dead son. So, he had followed her but not into the serenity of her fellow *Christicolae*.

And now, cloistered both, at work—he for God the Father in His anger and she herself for a loving Christ—they could not, would not touch again no matter who might reach out first, but only through a letter from her now and again which he might read and which and from which, also, he might burn again. And as in this present epistle, she spoke no shame. Nothing salacious was left in her, having been drained in the hurt of Augustine's shunting her off from Italy and having been washed again in pain of the death of their son, sweet and precocious Adeodatus. Their sins, committed over three days after Adeo's funeral, had brought no joy to him nor unto Sabina but for the happiness born later with Sequidei, the daughter of that tryst.

This letter told nothing of those days, nothing of longing, nothing of suffering the losses of life and love. No, that was far in the past for Sabina, teaching her each day to be gentle and kind, faithfully strong, admitting, and wise. She wrote to Augustine about the Donatists many of whom she knew from Leptis Minor and Sullectum, adherents to Christ first and to their sect after. These Donatists, even after being outlawed, hunted, and their churches destroyed, lived on in exile, continued their fierce, wild faith outside the protection of Augustine's Church.

"Of course, he will not like this," she said aloud, "he wants only capitulation or expungement."

She wrote to the Bishop of Hippo Regius in a mild spirit, disclosing nothing of her burning inside. In the face of the Donatist's fiery resistance to the bishop's even more strident attacks, Sabina saw neither side profiting from their war. "May my words be soft, O Jesus, and quell, a little, the flames in his heart. For Peter has said, 'But let it be the hidden man of the heart, in that which is not corruptible, even the ornament of a meek and quiet spirit, which is in the sight of God of great price.'"

Sabina raised her eyes from her work. Ia had come to sit with her.

"Are you troubled, sister?"

"Writing always troubles me. I was not born to it."

"You are of humble birth, *Tizem*, like our Lord. That is a blessing, but I see you are troubled."

"I was thinking of the danger to Sequia in her correspondence with Julian of Eclanum."

"It will likely become known. But there is little reason to worry, is there?

"No. I am only old and feel the weight of age firmly pressing me down. Still, my sisters and Our Lord Jesus lighten me."

"We had a good laugh this morning." Ia chuckled again.

"'Then was our mouth filled with laughter, and our tongue with singing,' says the Psalter, so it cannot be anything but good. And you were lovely."

Ia placed her hand on the old woman's arm. "I know Our Lord Jesus loves the kindness in your work. You will bring these church-wars to an end. Be at peace."

Sabina reached her free hand to Ia's, stroking it warmly. "I am done here, at least for today. Shall we layer the olives?"

"Yes, work is what we need. We can talk over our labors."

The two women left the garden and walked slowly to the shed where the olive harvest, so much as it was yet, was stored. In the pomegranate, two wrens hopped and sang at their passing.

The women, friends from the time Ia came into the house eight years past before Sabina had taken so much responsibility, worked together on the curing, one spreading the fruit on a deep tiled tray, the other sprinkling and packing the salt. Sabina moved from one tray to another, and when she finished one, Ia came behind her and Sabina moved back to the other spreading the next layer of olives over the salt Ia had packed down. Like the small birds they kept hopping from one position to another.

"It is getting close to the emmer harvest," Ia said. "Will *Tizem* be coming this year?"

Sabina tossed a small shovelful of fruit over the salt bed and raked them around with the implement. "I would like to this year. It has been two since I have seen Sequia. I keep her in my heart, but embracing her in body is much better, at least from time to time. She does as I do: studies, reads and writes."

"And she works what is left of that small plot of old Patricius's farm," Ia added. "Was it not given to you when Adeodatus died?"

"Yes, a generous gift seemingly out of kindness. That was before he took orders and became bishop. It has changed him. Responsibility changes us all. I feel it, but in my case, not being so public, it does not lead to frothing anger or intemperate jealousy. It just wearies me." She finished the tray and traded places with Ia. "Yes, after all, I will go to Thagaste to the harvest."

"Many will come out of the desert to hear you preach again. Word will travel fast."

Sabina glanced at her younger companion. "Yes. And news of Sequia's and Julian's letters may also speed to wary ears. I do not know how widely the missives are circulated. I expect trouble."

Sabina then turned the talk away. "Come with me, Ia."

"And who will tend the house? And watch the counsel," Ia looked at her friend, "and boss?" They laughed.

"There are many who will try to do that." Sabina smiled. "It is simple to announce our trip and watch those who stand forward to lead. That will give us the answer to your questions."

Their work grew hot but was soon finished. "I will return to my writing. Please see that the kitchen isn't in an uproar! The evening meal is not far off." Sabina touched her friend's cheek and drew her into an embrace. "Go with a light heart."

Sabina returned to the garden corner. The trip to Thagaste worried her. The town haunted her memories, going there could be trouble.

Even though Augustine disagreed with her work, he had and likely would forebear condemning her for it. Such was not necessarily the case with Sequia, of whom he knew little except as Sabina's daughter. A trip to Thagaste, preaching while there, and joining in with Sequia's parishioners, would likely draw the bishop's attention.

Her adherents and Sequidei, her daughter, would expect her to deliver a sermon. Sequia had carried on the work of melding one community with another much better than she herself could do. Still all wanted to listen to Sabina. And now there would come Arians to join their ecumenical worship. The others: Catholics, Donatists, and even Manicheans would accept the newcomers better with her blessings. Sabina knew that her years with Augustine and their one-time closeness lent power to her reputation, though she had never cultivated the notoriety but strove to stand on her own within Christ's ways. She hoped that all her admirers were followers of Jesus, a multitude of apostles each tied to one another through their Lord Christ in Word made flesh.

"Flesh," she said to herself. "Blessed and a trial as well."

4

Gaiseric

The September nights were cooling little in Hispania, but Gaiseric, the brother of the dead king, had bid that the Vandal council fire be lighted.

The blaze sent its smoke into the upper reaches of the long, low house, its heat wavering up into the ridge of the roof, then through the opening there whose wattle and daub sides already had been blackened by fire-smoke. The gathering of earls and retainers was named *alþingi*, and the flames were needed on the death of any leader. The circle of earls and strongest Vandal fighters gathered around the fire in rites and in talk. A new king must be found.

Gundaric was dead. The wounds the Nicene fighters had inflicted, as sneaks often do, from high walls above their city, *Hispalis*, Seville, had worsened day by day. Those arrow slashes had waxed green, then black, and Gundaric's spirit fled out of his sickened body. Already, the enemy's priests in thrall to Rome had spread whisperings—Gaiseric had heard them soon after they overran the town—that God had punished the Vandal's desecration of the church building, causing devils to bore into their king's body. Gaiseric scoffed at such blather. More likely the doomed defenders had coated their arrows in shit and pus that crept into his fated brother's heart and stopped it. It was an unkind and bitter deed that his own earls must give back, blow for wicked blow, and groan for hurtful groan.

Gaiseric told the *alþingi*, the gathered earls, all that. His thanes had buried Gundaric's body under earth with sword and shield as their ancestors had taught them, leaving his spirit to fly to the skies. Too, his Arian priest read Gothic words from Wulfila's Bible over the body and hoped Gundaric's soul would find the Father in heaven. Now in the *alþingi*, the *scope*, the shaper-of-stories, spoke with drum and song in praise of good King Gundaric and his forebearers.

Gaiseric looked around the ring of twenty sorrowful, waiting faces. What thoughts flickered there? What dreads and wants hid in the shadowy eyes of a few? No matter. He, Gaiseric, would steady both thoughts and fears of these marked by battle or by age and care. He would bestir others whose fierceness and hope shone outwardly. Those last swept their eyes, as did Gaiseric around the ember-wreathed fire while waiting for the songs. At the right time, the *scope*, the word-worker, touched his drum and sang the worship song of the long-gone, the newly dead, great God, and things which were to come. The *scope* began slowly, "Hear o Hasdings, hear," he sang, growing louder over the murmurs of men, crooning his split-line[1] rhythm above the roar of the fire.

When their ship-prow	Cut the freezing fog
The Hasding kings	Raus and Raptus
Led their men	Over ice-cold seas, to islands
Through empty lands	River riven,
Followed in faith	To fulsome summer
By Silings, wandered	To far-off lands
Warm in winter	Away from wicked winds
Found full game	Fish-filled flows.
That beginning was	A good sea-seek.

Gaiseric leaned in, listening, though he had heard the history of his people many times around the fire. He could tell it himself and had written some of it in Latin and Greek under the schooling of his friend, Innomenatus. Still, he listened with both ears as the shaper-of-stories sang the Hasdings.

Again Godigisel	Good to his gomes
Wisely chose	A welcome way
Brought highest hills	Between Huns and Hasdings,
The frozen waters	Crossed. Fought the Franks.
King so wise paid	Retainers rich rewards
And brought all over	Toft t' tor, safe, to greater gain.

---

1 Called *caesura* in Latin. Sometimes indicated in writen forms by || or as here by spacing. Ed.

That was a good king.
To sunny lands
Did wondrous work

And his son Gundaric
He brought men fine
Worthy his weird.

The *scope* had made and now sang this new part in praise of Gaiseric's brother, poisoned in war, who left his earls forlorn but in victory, proud. And Gaiseric then heard his own name, following his brother's—his nephew being just a babe—to lead his folk to prosper and live.

He is gone to God
Spent his soul
Great his ghost
To guide us straight

Swa all gomes go
Swa men could live.
Gave brother Gaiseric
To God and goods.

Alþingi, the gathered thanes, took up his name, and sang in time to the waxing drum his praises as their leader and king. Still young enough to cudgel and stab his foes, but wise enough to turn the heads of allies, friends, and foes alike, Gaiseric had distinguished himself in war and in council more than any. His stout standing—not as tall as many—was sturdy and sound, despite his shorter leg given him in battle by a stricken, falling horse. He was known, though, to be sly and quick, so all, not many but all, clapped-up his name:

Gaiseric is bold
Gaiseric is wise
King of Hasding

Gaiseric is stout
Gaiseric is king.
Of all Vandals hearty.

Rising to power, Gaiseric knew, was easy. The rest of his plans would be harder.

The new king rose before his council, the *alþingi*; he stood to speak. Always, he had much to say but spoke few words, keeping his own thoughts inside and clear, and even now uttered only what the time beneeded, nothing more.

"Hasding kinsmen, Alans, and Silings"—he named but the three largest of the many clans there allied—"though sad for the loss of a king but not bereft of friends I will lead you. Under Gundaric for the first time we have overcome Rome and beaten their allies. For the first time we have taken islands, have sailed the seas. Now, we must decide, seek in mind, the counsel of each for what we must do. Where we must go. I say only, 'Think.' We have Sueves to our north. Visigoths to our east. And Rome seldom gives in, even now with a child on the throne. We have work to do. Search your minds. We shall hear your counsel ahead."

With those few words, Gaiseric left them, his mind full of plans but careful in his will. He left the hall, allowing his earls their talk.

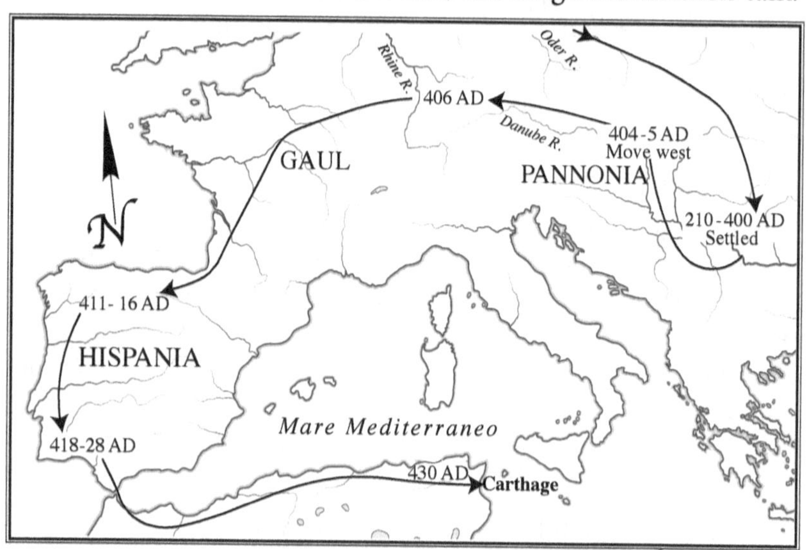

The Migration and Settlement of the Vandal Tribes 200-430 A.D.

He was not worried, but watchful. They had beaten the Sueves once, but war was wearing. His men had little left here to plunder. All the provinces, even were they to be forsaken, had waned to poverty over twenty years of fighting. Cousin Silings had nothing left but their lives. The Alans had kept their wives and horses, not much more. Gaiseric, himself, had little treasure to spread around. And Rome? Rome even though sacked when he had been a youth was still intent to hold Gaul and Hispania.

Gaiseric thought: Now the child-emperor enjoys the backing of Theodosius in the far-off East. I see, already, an army forming, Rome being scared of Vandals taking to the sea. And south? There across the straits, Vandal folk already in Mauretania peacefully traded, built, and made friends. But Bonifacius, the *Comes Africae*, the Count of Africa, was cunning. He knew when to fight. He knew when to bide his time, how to win. It was the Count he feared most. Should that Roman send his army, although small yet, west from Numidia, the Hasdings, Gaiseric's people, would be penned-up on all sides.

The king stood, his short-legged foot up on a rock. He looked to the stars. These are the same stars I have slept under in Pannonia, Germania, and Gaul. I will lie under them tonight in Baetica, Hispania, and where after that we shall see. War-weary, I must sleep.

He entered his tent. He removed his buckler and long sword. Put them near. His spear he'd left before at bedside. The new king removed his silvered helm and gray cape, his glistening boots, and hard leggings. He lay on his cot under one horse blanket—the weather had not yet turned—and let his mind go slack. Sleep now. Dawn comes soon enough for every man.

Gaiseric, the new Vandal king, dreamt of war beneath the walls of *Hispalis*. He and his brother had learned much from the Romans, from the Visigoths, how best to lay siege, how best to be patient at the gates of a town.

He saw Hasdings trotting beneath a thick roof of wet mud and reeds. They held it overhead on poles, moving toward *Hispalis's* gates. Gundaric was leading them, making the already bold-hearted fearless. "*Anananþan gomes, afgaggan gatas,*" he said, "Be bright, men, storm the gates." Above cowered the caged crowd, raining poison arrows around, pouring boiling water and hot oil down. But the Hasding roof held, and now Gaiseric's band ran forward with fire brands, shouting, "*Afarlaistjan king,* follow the king."

They stoked a fire against the metal and hardwood gates, thick and strong. Still evil rained from above, but the Vandal fires roared on sending black smoke above, choking their foes. "Do not think on death," Gundaric shouted, "only fate knows your time. Consider war-glory and treasure, honor and love." His men cheered at his words fought all the harder through smoke and raining hate until their fire outshone the sun as that day ended. The first gate gave way in the night. It was then, in the dark, that three arrows pierced his King.

In his dream Gaiseric again saw Gundaric stagger. His brother stumbled on. He helped him walk away out from smoke and fire back to his tent. Little did he know the king carried poison in his wounds. In two days more—he saw it again in this dream—the king cried out his last but he, Gaiseric, said, "Your thanes have spoiled the city where blood yet flows in the ruined streets. Cheer to you the mighty who has won."

Black smoke filled his dream, choking the old king and himself alike. Then out of the dream-smoke strode a man, dressed all in white. His robes in ample folds flowed free and full, were not unsmote by soot or grime.

"Who comes now? Coming for his soul?" He asked but then saw it was Innomenatus. "*Namlaus*, my friend. Are you returned?"

This man said nothing, but stood before Gaiseric and his dead king, taking out of the folds of his toga a papyrus scroll.

"Is this Gundaric's lay, his sentence, his passage to God?" Gaiseric wanted to know.

Innomenatus said nothing but forced the scroll into his hands and pointed his finger at Gaiseric himself, not at the king.

"I must read this?" Gaiseric asked. Innomenatus spoke with his eyes, and his learner from years before bent to the Latin script:

> *Noli timere Augustinus*
> *sed respice ad Carthaginem.*
> Do not fear Augustine,
> but look to Carthage.

"I do not fear that man, but his protector, Bonifacius," he said. And raising his eyes from his reading saw only smoke. Innomenatus was gone.

Gaiseric, Vandal-king, awoke then, hearing as clearly as if his *scope* were singing a forthright truth, "*Weird biþ ful arade*, fate is final."

5

Innomenatus Translates

How much one should trust a scribe or translator is a matter of judgment. Bonifacius in that regard remained vigilant and utterly suspicious. As a result, most often, perhaps because few in Africa knew the language, I noted his words in Greek tachygraphs though scribal notations are unreadable to most anyway, even in Latin.

Besides being more private here in the west, I find Greek more expressive, and, because I wrote and spoke it for so many years in Alexandria, Antioch, and beyond, I may know it better than my native tongue. Of course, I love not just the language but what has been handed down to us in the idiom's dialogue, story, and song. Latin is certainly its strong rival but, despite the empire, a lesser one, and I had always thought that Augustine would have blossomed as a philosopher had he been able to read the actual words of Plato in the man's language. As it was, like many who know through translation or commentary, he simply came to accept a shadow of what was said and meant. Despite this, the bishop anyway prospered intellectually if only within the Latin world. Perhaps it was that third man's dreams and understanding (the translator's, that is), that at this time proved quieter but of much greater importance. So be it. My only objective at the time was to survive.

Augustine could have done better had he been more than half-educated, going so far, I remember, as to demean the study of Greek. I understand his trepidation of outsiders. Having traveled the empire's vast reaches, I know there *is* reason to fear. But having studied some of the empire's languages and writings, I stand among its many, walk more easily in the people's shoes than does my bishop. I have been honored to write and translate for the notables around Mar Mediterraneo: Peter, the successor of Athanasius in Alexandria where I studied, Jerome in the holy lands, Wulfilas the Gothic Bible-maker, two emperors in the east, and that wonder of a barbarian, lately king of the Vandals, Gaiseric[1]. The latest two, Augustine and now Bonifacius, provided fascinating work at the end of my fifty-year return journey home. It is not the subtleties of the tongues, nor the greatness of the speakers themselves, but the shades of what is believed within the shelter of a home-language—what need not be said, true or not, for it is commonly known—that leads to understanding.

My experience in the scriptoriums of the world impressed on me the delicate nature of my present task, which, to save my sorry soul, needed thoughtfulness and care. If I were to avoid being hanged by one faction or another, Vandals, Romans, or churchmen, I had to deftly play, like the generals serving the child-emperor and the regent herself, one party off the others.

Bonifacius was watching carefully. So, when he dictated, I noted his words in Greek. This allowed me to jot down my own ideas before translating anything—always at the very last minute to ward off any wandering, curious eyes—into Gaiseric's language, a tongue much like Gothic which could be read by the count's wife, a Visigoth princess who had been schooled. So, it became much safer to hide behind my shorthand.

Not to be known by any in Africa, I say, I had tutored Gaiseric, the Vandal leader, in Latin and Greek in the years before he became king[2]. He'd held his own in both even after just two years when renewed war took him in its arms and away from schooling. Because Gaiseric was as bright as any of my students, perhaps the quickest

---

1 My unexpected encounter was made possible through recommendations—certainly unsolicited as at the time I was quite content to stay put, but such is *weird*, as Gaiseric called fate—yes, through endorsements of fellow translators I had worked with on Wulfila's Gothic bible so many years before and through the interference, as such is an emperor's right, of Theodosius II who sent me as a trusted servant and spy to the great-at-the-time general Castinus whose mission was to defeat the Vandals in Hispania. So, to Gaiseric, indirectly, I went, an erstwhile foe, becoming an understanding friend and tutor.

2 Yes, I had been conscripted to keep an eye on the Roman Castinus but was left behind when the same fled Tarrasco following his defeat by Gaiseric's brother. Stranded alone in enemy territory, it was not simply my facility with Gothic (hence with the Vandal tongue) that saved my life, but Gaiseric's recognition of my usefulness and his own hunger for the knowledge that seemed to buoy-up the flagging Roman state. I was treated well but held for several years during which I taught the king-to-be. Let it be noted that I also learned much through that barbarian tongue.

man I'd ever known, I could in my present circumstances wrap hellos and hints, revealed in cryptic ways only in Vandalic and, then only just before sending the missives, all the while I kept in Greek a few things Bonifacius need not know. I told neither the count nor his wife anything of this pupil of mine. If I was to be trusted, I could not know or have known a Vandal, especially that one.

The count was not the only one who wondered. I became concerned with what appeared to be a stroke of too-good fortune. Not that I did not trust *Comes Africae*, who was, in his open, soldierly way, much a Republican of the old stripe[3] but that I was certain my recommendation came from the bishop. That concerned me not a little.

Augustine had, I knew, recognized my younger face behind my gray beard that night. They say the eyes are the windows to the soul, and so did my eyes, even in moonlight, give me away as did the light of recognition in *his* reveal the bishop's feelings to me—especially in untranslatable moonlight. After laboring for two years in the service of the bishop without being seen for who I was, it had all happened so suddenly. Augustine, always a quick study, must have devised his plan for me even while he later dictated his diatribes to his early-morning scribes, for Bonifacius was knocking on my door before not even half a day's hours had followed my encounter with the friend-of-my-youth.

Taken by surprise, set back on my heels, I had to survive by relying on my long experience. I have served many masters. It is part of the trade. I've stayed in various houses of the learned and the well to do, translating or writing their missives and contracts. I have found out a single truth—this may have been so in all time since creation—that if you want to keep your fingers on the pulse of a household to know the news that might undo you, it is to the kitchen you should go. Not only did this practice kept me abreast of important news of those who employed me, but it also put me on the near side of a fleshy rotundity.

---

3 By this I meant he felt worthy of a crown but had the integrity not to seize it simply because it was there.

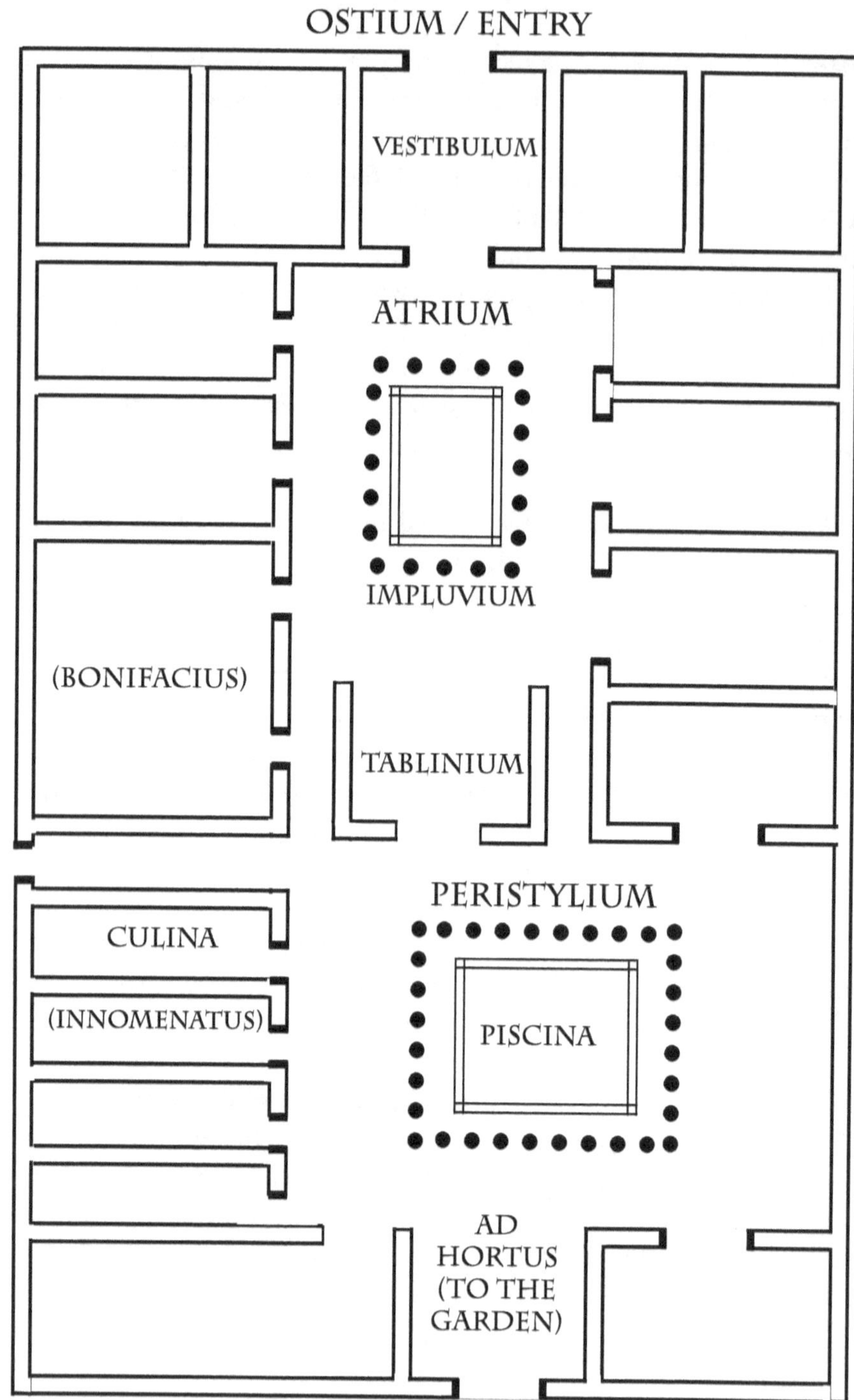

A Roman House - Plan View

The house of *Comes Africae* rivaled those of patricians in Constantinople, not in size so much, but certainly in opulence though that was of a military stripe, not overly, shall we say, purple. Even though it sprawled largely across terraces cut into the hills west of Hippo Regius, the family area was modest. The house, containing many rooms both public and private, also provided for those who worked to support the household: millers, cobblers, cooks, stable hands, arborists, farm workers, soldiers, and olive growers alike, taking up a great deal of the space. Often in the morning one could smell the crushed grapes bubbling in their vats below the first terrace. Of all these rooms there was but one available for my work and sleep at that time, and that was, fortuitously, right across a passage from the main kitchen, and not too far from the baths, a luxury for any scribe or bishop, for that matter. My cubicle stood immediately off the oversized *peristylium* which gave me good light for my work, a good view of the kitchen activity and the comings and goings of the visitors. Bonifacius liked to conduct business in the open, either on the portico overlooking the garden, or more rarely in the shade of the colonnade surrounding the *peristylium.*

As I became acquainted with the house, I made it my priority to ingratiate myself with the kitchen help as a way to keep careful watch and note of the business the count tended to, as well as to keep my traveler's ear to the ground for safety's sake. When I couldn't hear the count's conversations—when my host gathered his tribunes and friends in his study off the atrium, he was out of range—I eventually (not right away) asked about it in the kitchen, for not only did the women there serve the gatherings whether they were of two, eight, or more, but they also later on discussed what they gleaned while carrying in food and drink or waiting for the plates to empty. I smelled the sweet ripening fruits as well as the sting of vinegars when the servers felt ready to share news.

"Maria, have you a morsel of bread and cheese for a hungry scholar?"

"My dear Nomen"—for that's what the cooks called me—"can't you wait for the midday meal? Didn't you just eat two hours past?"

Maria played her game with me, making me beg. "I am starving in this house." Of course, neither of us believed that, and I was not truly hungry for anything but the news. "Just a smidgen? And a cup of that cool well water to wash it down."

"As you wish, Nomen, but you'll grow truly fat if you keep on this way."

"A small price to pay for the most wonderful bread in the empire!"

Not unlike the whole of humanity, Maria thrived on flattery. And as I munched, I deftly withdrew the news from her mind, sometimes without having to work hard.

"I see a visitor from Carthage has come."

"Yes, he is a bishop in command under Sigisvultus. They discuss the coming of a Roman envoy, a great negotiator they say."

I took a drink of the water, which was truly wonderful coming from deep within the well just outside, still cold and refreshing. "Oh, that can't be good news."

Maria cocked an eye at me. Though a Christian, she was superstitious and didn't like me leading her to think ill of anything. "I suppose that is for the count to decide," she said. She then went on with her work, and, maybe feeling too much curiosity on my part, refused to say any more.

"Thank you, Maria. I can now work on an eased stomach."

She looked over her shoulder at me and shook her head. "*Vale,* Nomen."

I returned her farewell and saved my prying for my next snack.

After my translation of the count's dictation, I read my summary for Bonifacius in Latin, sometimes taking the care to explain the parallels in the two idioms and pointing out the verity of his words changed into Vandalic. I had studied enough, though, to know how to shade meanings to get the Vandal king's attention without drawing Bonifacius to unduly suspect me. As a translator, I could not use my own name, of course. I wrote for the Count of Africa, so it was his name and seal that appeared on the missive. But I knew if I wrote somewhere in the script, *namlaus,* nameless, Gaiseric's name for me—I dared only to use it once—he would, knowing my story, at least suspect I was the one writing. He knew I'd crossed to Mauretania when I was released from his employ and soon after that moved on. Certainly, he would remember and believe that I would have traveled closer to my old home, Carthage, finishing as an unintended consequence the entire circumambulation of Mare Mediterraneo in fifty years.

And not that I was a military man at all, but in Rome, the empire East or West, and in the hire of those who need scribes, one becomes quite literate in the martial and political strategies the men around you employ. It may not have been clear to Bonifacius, or perhaps it was so clear that he overlooked its importance, that should Gaiseric commit four or five thousand men and five hundred to one thousand horse to assist the count in his fight against Sigisvultus, that the Vandal holdings in Hispania would easily become vulnerable to Sueves, Visigoths, or the Romans themselves. Perhaps *Comes Africae* did not care what happened in Vandal-held Baetica or, most likely, to the Vandals themselves.

I knew Gaiseric better. He was fearless, but he informed his bravery by clear vision and precise thinking. I suspected that this exploit, which would pay so handsomely, win or lose, was worth more than what was left in Vandalusia, as some called southern Hispania then, but more so, I knew he would not leave kinsmen behind to defend something they would inevitably lose their lives trying to save. That loyalty to his folk alone being well known among the barbarians accounted for his election as king. His character was bold. Once right action was determined, he proceeded without haste or fear. No, if Gaiseric came at all, his allies, kinsmen, and the many who hoped to escape the cruelty of Rome, slaves, the indentured, and the over-taxed would move along with him, helping in all ways to ensure his success. Baetica was indefensible in any case, walls or no walls. There were just too many enemies nearby. So, though we, I should say the count, asked only for a force of five thousand, enough to tip the balance in Carthage, I believed more would come. If that posed a problem, it would be for Bonifacius to solve. I? I was simply the scribe.

Still, I have not grown old (much older than I claimed at meeting Augustine—I am seventy-two at least) nor have I aged so gracefully by being careless. The power of writing, of letters, and of books, too, was well known to this Roman count. We both could swear that sometimes what is left out is more important than what the letter or book contains. Lacunae are just harder to see.

Such was the case for Bonifacius. True, he himself commandeered the provinces of Africa after, in a martial-pride huff, abandoning the self-styled generalissimo, Castinus,[4] "to his own arrogance," as he had said. Bonifacius had seen that in a fight with the Vandals Castinus was fated to lose.[5] So, the count increased his wealth by going to Africa—what general would not stuff his own pockets first—but held the provinces *for*, not against, the empire. True, he had supported his regent, Galla Placidia, in good times and bad sending ships full of grain and even African-minted money when she needed it. Nevertheless, his previous great deeds and golden reputation were sheared by a letter. Again, the power of words! A simple missive threatened to undo a man who was undoubtedly the finest soldier in the Roman army of the time.

His enemies in the capital, Ravenna, won the ear of Galla Placidia. Bonifacius, they said, was plotting to use Africa to starve Italy and would then invade to put himself on the throne in place of her son. Perhaps it was said:

"*Comes Africae* plots against you."

"That I cannot believe," Galla Placidia may have said. "Just now he sent grain and oil to us here. Why would he do that?"

"Bonifacius is a devilish fiend, my Lady. And I'll answer that: He does so to appear innocent and supportive. Until he strikes. He plays the Greek."

---

4 I note it here, since it is of no real importance, that I once more saw Castinus, then a refugee from war and a person of imperial interest, as they say, having supported the wrong emporetic candidate, in Hippo Regius. He thought me dead at the hands of the Vandals, and I, keeping my distance, took no pains to correct his opinion. He was mixing at that time on the edges of the swelling crowds of those fleeing the Vandal advance on Augustine's city.

5 It is odd that Bonifacius failed to recognize the same barbarian intrigue in Africa that had defeated Castinus in Hispania? He saw Castinus's fate from a different point of view.

"And what would you have me do, Flavius Felix?"

"Perhaps recall him to Ravenna. If he comes, you can question him. If he refuses to come, that is your answer."

It would be then that this chief rival, Felix, would send his own letter to Bonifacius, a warning. "Should you, *Comes Africae*, be recalled to Italy, beware. Forces here conspire against your life. Come at your own risk."

True, forces were conspiring. The letter, which I read to Placidia's envoy later on, says that much, but did it say who conspired? Or did it say, "Stay away at your own risk?" Exactly. That which is not said is more important than that which is. His refusal to appear in Ravenna launched not one or two armies, but three against Bonifacius. The current one well-led by Sigisvultus now held Carthage.

The warning had arrived. The summons had followed, and Bonifacius did not go. The empire called this a revolt. Soon those two armies from Rome appeared, and *Comes Africae* defeated both, more due to the treachery of others than to his own skill.[6] A more competent and greater force arrived, took Carthage and began negotiations with *Comes Africae*. A fourth invasion was now rumored—perhaps to be confirmed by our visitor from Carthage today, the very day that I began writing letters to Gaiseric on behalf of the count. A revolt, Bonifacius did not intend. Neither did he wish to be brought to Ravenna in chains. The invitation had sounded harmless but not in the face of the warning.

Such intrigues! Now, for myself, I wanted nothing more than to signal to my pupil that it was I, Innomenatus, who was the chosen scribe writing to him. My intent was as innocent as my own name. In part, I wrote for the count:

Ego vos invitem coniungere se copias, sed non dicere quod pretio,
I invite you to join us, but we shall discuss the rewards,
Which I translated for Gaiseric as follows:
At-haitan alls anaqiman, ak weihans-gild biþ namlausan.
Which Gaiseric would read:

---

6 This time the treachery came from the Huns in hire to the invading Romans. The pattern should be clear. *Caveat mercinarium*, watch your hirelings.

I call one and all to come, but the reward will be (the) unnamed (one).

So, I took a few liberties, but, again, language is not exact, as our good bishop would tell you. This would look and sound a bit foreign to Gaiseric, but I was sure the message would be clear: that an old friend awaited his arrival in Hippo Regius.

Working on this, Bonifacius and I sat under the portico, lined with slender columns, the floor being a wonderful mosaic in the center of which was depicted Bonifacius himself, throwing a spear into Authaulf, the king of the Visigoths, slaying the man and winning the battle. I could see why the count liked to conduct business overlooking the garden.

"What is this *alls* here?"

It was certain that Gaiseric would recognize my intent here. I spoke it only to honor what I already knew to be his response, that is to bring his people along, not to leave the weak behind. "It translates as 'you,' in this situation. I put it to mean 'you and your soldiers.'"

"And this queer-looking word, *anaqiman*, what is it?"

"It means more or less 'to come.'"

His curiosity ended there, I was glad, for he never mentioned *namlausan*, the nameless one which, I'm sure, looked to him much like all the other words in the text.

"Well, finish this now. I have a ship heading for Carthago Spartaria with the morning tide. If the winds are good, the Vandal king should have our summons in a few days. None too soon for the coming of the envoy."

I aim to please and finishing quickly, made a copy for myself and one in Latin for Bonifacius. It had only just sailed away to Gaiseric, it seemed, when Bonifacius would want it back.

6

Sabina in Thagaste

The journey to Thagaste proved more difficult than Sabina had remembered it.

"Isn't it always so with memory?" She asked Ia. "Like a pain you had yesterday becomes the feeling you cannot recall."

Ia squinted her eyes and pursed her thin lips. "Perhaps, but it is not so with words. The pain sharp words inflict can hurt for years."

Sabina loved her disputations with Ia. Her friend and sister was too open and honest to see the form and flow of the dispute and, so, was always at the disadvantage, something Sabina herself understood, having sat beside Augustine day in and day out while he argued with friends and foes alike. With Ia her companion though, the polemic stayed kindly. "It is so, Ia. I agree fully; however, I ask 'Is it the pain at first hearing, or at the recalling of the words themselves which have power over you because you remember them in the first place?'"

"I am sure you know the answer." Ia smiled widely, even showing her teeth. "Of course, I do not."

"Yes, my sister, you have but to realize that the discomfort of travel, like that of an ache in your side, cannot really be put into words. You might say, 'It hurts' or 'This cut throbs,' but you simply name the feeling without a description, so if you utter the word 'throb' after the pain subsides, it does not carry the feeling you named."

"Ah, my wise Mother. If you told me, 'Ia, you stink,' the hurt those words carry is recalled when I remember them. But why?"

Sabina grasped her friend's hand as they walked beside the lead oxcart they'd brought from Hippo. "Why, indeed? Because of your love for me. Because you want to be pleasing. Because you worry about bathing. And because the words brought forth shame like that Adam and Eve felt after the encounter with the asp."

Ia brightened. "So is shame not then the pain of original sin?"

"In a way, because embarrassment is a condition, part of the makeup of all who are human, just as our bishop says, but I believe for each of us shame becomes active only through the contempt of others. Augustine himself was filled with that at his mother's breast."

Ia nodded sadly, "Ah, I thought this sounded like an argument from our presbyter."

"Of course, Ia. How could I make such an argument by myself? Am I not simply a woman?"

The two smiled on each other over the wry question and swung their clasped hands as they walked along.

The trip from Hippo Regius to Thagaste during good weather—not so hot as it was that September—took nearly four days. This year, having to stop to let the animals rest and water frequently, it would take six. They traveled in the morning and toward dusk when the blaze of the sun was less fearsome. Then, still a day away from the cooling air of the mountains, Sabina fell ill from the heat. They had to stop and found a riverbank shaded by a high outcrop below a hill yellow with dust. There, sheltered from sight below the adjoining sheer knolls, they made camp and corralled their stock.

Ia cared for Sabina, watching closely every breath she took, keeping her cool with damp rags and making her drink water from the stream that flowed beneath the hill, sip after sip after sip. Her fever lasted nearly two days, and had she told Ia the truth, she had felt it a day even before those.

On the last night, when her fever broke, Sabina thought she awakened from a dream. She lay still on her bed, waiting for Ia to tend to her, tip a cup to her lips, but Ia did not seem to be in the tent. Sabina felt sure of this, although she sensed someone's presence. "Ia, is that you?" She raised herself on an elbow to see, and yes there was a figure, certainly not Ia who always wrapped herself in robes, crouched in the far corner of the tent, sitting on a wide, large, low jar of lentils, in a posture that told Sabina this man was thinking. "Where is Ia?"

The man, who seemed ancient, even in comparison with herself, turned only his head held on a scrawny, corded neck, and focused deeply-set eyes, nearly lost in the caverns of his skull, on Sabina. He smiled showing not a tooth, only a slim but open-mouth smile, and nodded his hairless head at the flap of the tent.

Sabina struggled up further and looked.

"She sleeps at the doorway," this wizened man whispered in a way that commanded her not to wake her friend.

Sabina then turned to her visitor. "Yes, she needs her rest. I have been a burden. Have you come for me?" Still, in her fever, she said it without fear, assuming this was her end.

The figure shifted his bare shoulders and chest away from Ia and crooked his hooked nose directly at Sabina. "I have not come for you, no."

She was neither relieved nor sorry.

"Why come then, and who might you be?"

The ancient one still crouched on the jar, turned fully toward her now. "You might say, I was in the neighborhood." He let loose a surprisingly melodious laugh and shook his head. "I sensed you might need some advice." His head bobbed in a nod of assurance. "It is not your time, Sister. I'm afraid your many troubles are hardly begun."

"Are you a warning angel, then?"

Again, the laughter. "No, no seraph at all. I simply know the truth."

Sabina wondered at this. "That is a rare gift, my man."

"Listen," he said. "Your grain harvest will be good. For that you can be grateful. Your soul-harvest might even be better."

"I am unsure of what you mean."

"Are you and your daughter not of the covenant of Christ? Yes, you are, but are you aware that not all who claim to believe are *Christicolae*?"

Sabina felt puzzled and uneasy. "I am pleased to be of Jesus. Why should I fear?"

"Even Our Lord met in secret until his time. Be as watchful as he."

Sabina let herself leave the elbow and fall to her bed again. This vision tired and perplexed her. "Do you refer to my ministry?"

At this she felt, not saw, the man beam warmly, not just in smiles but from his shaded eyes as well. "Yours and your daughter's. You prepare a way, but beware the serpent."

Sabina rested a moment, filled a minute full of breaths. When feeling restored, she rose up, sitting. She wanted to continue the conversation, but the old man was gone.

The morning dawned cooler, and Sabina's fever had broken and gone. "Finally, your nursing and cajoling have brought me back to health," she told Ia who was at her bedside when she woke.

Ia looked at her closely. "Actually, I ordered you to recover!" They both laughed heartily.

"I think I can travel today," she'd said.

"Yes," Ia agreed, "but you shall ride in the cart. No more walking until you are stronger."

So, there she was, perched like a queen on the low middle seat of the cart, being carried along with pomp and the graciousness of Ia, who walked beside her, chattering away about the harvest and reunion to come.

Sabina gave no thought to her dream which with the fever had disappeared into the night. Although not one word spoken had stayed in her mind, she felt a vague sense of unrest, but her daylight thoughts were now of her daughter, Sequia, whom she hoped would be waiting. They would work together with the sisters in the harvest. After more than two years, it would be a joyous reunion filled with laughter and fun, and perhaps, a few tears. And when the harvest was done, as Sequia would want her to do, Sabina would deliver her sermon of thanks and hope. Still, the prospect of speaking even of joyous things brought an echo of distress to her ear, saying, "beware."

On the eighth afternoon of the journey, a time of day not so warm as that they had suffered, since they'd climbed quite high in the mountains over Thagaste, they caught sight of the river and the fields that flanked it just below.

"Look, Ia, the fields are golden and glorious in the late sunlight."

"It will be a good harvest, a perfect year. See how the river sparkles and looks so full. It has fed the crop well. I can smell the faro brushes from way up here!"

Both women inhaled deeply, delighted at the scent of the ripe grain filling the little valley they approached. "Will Sequia be in the fields yet?"

"Not likely. She is busy and expected us days ago." Sabina strained her eyes to see the figures in the fields wielding scythes and rakes. Some were loading sheaves in carts, hauling them to the threshing room along a path that wound beside the stream. "There, Ia, they are already winnowing the early dried seeds. They are nearly half done already." Sabina clasped her hands and watched.

When sounding like a far-off whisper to Sabina, Ia said, "This weather has been good for the harvest," the *materfamilias* felt a queasiness well up in her bowels.

Their little band wound its way down the hill, traversing the narrow road that zigzagged across the steeps.

"It will feel better to walk now," Sabina said, and Ia helped her to the ground without argument.

At a wide turn, Sabina paused, looking across the valley to the rise of high hills beyond which lay Thagaste. She looked this way and that along the terraced steeps, searching for Sequia's farm, its house tucked into the hillside.

"I see the farm, Ia," she said, "Look just east of that orchard. Is that a red roof?"

Ia raised a flat hand shading her brow. "Yes, just below the olive trees."

"That's it. Built facing the morning sun and sheltered from the midday heat by trees and that huge outcropping."

"It hides from the westward blaze of sundown behind the towering rock."

Above the roof, several terraces up was the open space of Sequia's garden. Further above were grapevines and at the top her olive orchard. The goats were not penned but kept out of the garden and trees by fences atop berms.

"The hillside looks lovely and still green so late in summer," Sabina said. "Let us move on to the shade of Sequia's olives."

Ia prodded the oxen back into motion, and they continued down the slope.

On the other side of the rise of mountains, beyond a bend in the river flowing down toward Carthage, Thagaste sat above the fields and farms along the lower flow of the river. Thagaste was a town Sabina had thought, perhaps hoped, she might never see again. And she did not look forward to that part of this visit, though it could not be avoided.

The narrow paths leading toward that stretch of the river were paved with obdurate memories. Her early visits with Augustine to the farm of his father and mother, Patricius and Monnika, were checkered by shame. She was an unwelcome guest. Other than by Augustine and secretly by his father, one to be ignored by Monnika or ordered to work like a servant.

Patricius was kind but did not rule the household, only the fields, orchards, and his brazen lusts. The household was Monnika's place and everything about it she knew and protected as if when Sabina touched something there was sacrilege. That included her brilliant son, Augustine. Sabina was comely but landless and poor. Furthermore, the Augustinian matriarch suspected Sabina even then to be a Donatist—her parents had a local bishop baptize her in a Donatist church, the only Christian place nearby at that time—and, to a deep-believing Catholic like Monnika, Sabina was not only a concubine but was a troubling heretic as well.

Augustine himself had been a member of a sect, the Manichees—one he would later persecute as heretical—during the years of their visits. That was different, it seemed to Monnika. "Let the boy experiment and find out for himself of what the world is made and what place faith and religion really play in it." Augustine, in the eyes of his mother, could do no wrong.

Patricius, always pagan while he thrived despite the efforts of his wife to bring him into the modern life of the Christian empire, proved more civil. He kept his kindnesses to Sabina away from the ever-alert eyes of his wife, but let it be known to Sabina that he approved of her as the consort of his son. "Your beauty will hold him in good stead," he told her.

On this harvest trip, Sabina would pass many of the places that would remind her of the Augustine of those times—impetuous, argumentative, wildly inspired, and uncontrollably amorous. Her thoughts would light on the school he'd founded on his return to Thagaste after their escape to Rome and away from Monnika. His school was still in session after all these years, perhaps with some support from the bishop of the place, Alypius, and by the wealthy of Thagaste. It was a relic saved—like a memory of the generous spirit of Patricius—in celebration of the town's favorite son, now the most famous man in Africa. And that fame, Sabina thought now, had changed everything. The Augustine of these times was carefully vicious, ruled by doctrine, and, if rumors were true, cold of touch. Of course, the son would not offer accolades to his father. Augustine had chosen another Father over the one given him by birth.

When Patricius had been living, Monnika complained about Sabina only in private. That changed after Augustine's father was buried. One early conversation, though, Sabina remembered well. It was just after her paramour had announced his intentions regarding the two of them, and her first invitation by him to his home. Sabina had never been certain if she was meant to overhear the conversation. It burned in her mind nevertheless:

"That woman, that beast, that thing," Monnika told Patricius, "is not to be at my table." She said her words in an audible but soft voice, the kind of voice of reason she was famous for while commanding either her late husband or her son. Patricius argued little. He had his own problems with his wife. He did not need troubles over his son's concubine. "She can eat with the servants or with the dogs."

Simply, he said, "She will be eating from his table in Carthage."

"Oh, yes, and you will become as poor as she and her family for supporting the both of them there."

Patricius shook his head, "It is expected. It's necessary. The boy is no longer a boy. He needs a woman."

"Well, he has a mother," Monnika replied.

Truth be told, Sabina thought, Augustine had more than a mother's love. Her devotion to him was as unshakable as her faith in the Church, but it had always intruded in a way that was not becoming to a Christian.

Ia, knowing her *materfamilias* well, placed her hand on Sabina's arm. "You need not think of those long gone now. You've come to see your daughter, her faithful congregants, and the harvest."

"Yes, I need not think about the past, but something I dreamed last night brought those thoughts to mind." Sabina shivered.

"You are chilled. What was it?"

"I cannot for trying remember it at all, but like a portent, a cry far off, I can feel its return." Sabina drew up her courage, patted Ia's hand, and said, "We'll go and find my daughter."

For all the travel to meet her, Sequia was not in the fields. She had gone that day to tend the goats at her farm, the very place passed on to her through Sabina, ultimately from Augustine, the only token of his affections, or perhaps his contrition, that he was willing to show Sabina at the time of Monnika's death back in Italy. Sabina had lived there for years and was on the farm when Augustine started teaching again in Thagaste upon his return from Mediolanum. Sabina had not expected him and was, too, surprised to hear of Monnika's death. In any case, he shunned the farm and her, perhaps out of regret at sending her away from Italy. Years later, Sabina gave the little farm to her daughter when Sequia was fifteen and even so early in life had taken vows of chastity.

So swirled 'round by ghosts, Sabina with her oxen train from Hippo Regius wound its way along the river some miles more to stay with her daughter. And through the open gate to her land, Sequia rushed forward shouting. "*Salve, salve, salve!*" She ran to her mother waving her arms. "I wanted to run to you a mile up the road."

Sabina swept forward to embrace her child. "I let my world keep me away too long."

Sequia bent to her mother and held her fully against her body. "Nonsense, mother, you are here now, and I hold you close always."

"It is wonderful to be with you."

Sequia then embraced Ia as well, then both of them at once.

Sequia stood taller than her mother. Her dark brown hair was tucked behind a scarf, but her heavy brows accented her brilliant dark eyes below. Her nose, like that of Adeodatus, the brother she never knew, was straight and narrow, and she had his mouth, too, slim and bent toward smiling and wonder. Sequia's skin was a camel-brown like her parents' but had turned darker by farm work than Sabina's convent-sheltered complexion. Sequia's was an unmistakable Berber complexion. Even with her work in the country though, at thirty-eight her face was hardly lined at all. She'd grown strong through work, wise through study, and in many ways much like her father, one way of which was that she had many friends. Although Sequia accepted both Catholics and Donatists as companions, she went to great lengths to avoid the controversy between the groups. Some called her "peacemaker."

Looking at her tall and confident daughter, Sabina thought, oh, that Augustine were as wise.

"Come, mother. Sit in the shade of the olive trees. I have laid a table with bread, cheese, and wine. While the sun sets, you shall recover from a very long trip. Then we will meet the others at our prayer meeting. They are anxious to see you. Come. Eat, rest, and talk."

As the sun stretched the shadow of the rock outcropping that marked her property across their table and onto the house to the east, the women talked of the bounty of the harvest, of conditions at the convent and in Hippo Regius. Sequia told of the increase in her congregants.

"There are many coming in from the desert. And lately men and women living in Thagaste have sought us our. Interest in our ecumenical ties grows. We even have a pagan or two attending regularly. As Christ bid us we are carrying his message to all regions, except those far lands are coming to us rather than us traveling to them!"

Soon after the meal, Ia excused herself. "I cannot keep my eyes open. Please, you two, enjoy your visit."

They protested, but Ia resisted, settling into a bed she made in the cart for that night. Mother and daughter talked in the waning light of the day.

"I have heard worrisome talk of you in Hippo," Sabina said.

Sequia flashed a glance at her mother. "What do they say?"

"Only that new ideas are forming in Thagaste. Some say it is the work of Julian. Your name is not spoken yet. But the talk feels dangerous."

"And from whose tongue does the name Julian slip? From those near the bishop?"

"Thagaste is not so far away as Julian's Eclanum. And your father concerns himself with all 'threats' to his church. So, yes, I believe the talk comes from those at Augustine's side."

Sequia considered her mother's suppositions. "I admit, Julian has written me. Perhaps he would enlist me to his cause, but though he is married himself, he does not approve of women priests."

Sabina nodded.

"Those new ecumens I mentioned from Thagaste may well be sent by Bishop Alypius, who knows of my birthright. It is possible they come only to report. Tonight, when you meet them, I shall like to know what you see, though suspicion of others cannot be depended on. Mistrust is itself dangerous and can devour. It was even so that Christ opened himself to Judas. Still, his Word was not destroyed."

Sabina reached for Sequia's hand, taking it between hers. "Of course, you will be protected, but I worry, having seen the ferocity with which the crowds of African bishops ferret out heretics. Don't place yourself too easily among them."

"Dear Mother, though I am the daughter of a once self-proclaimed disbeliever, I will keep good company with Jesus and his teachings. Quell your unease." Sequia gave her mother a warmly stern look, "Come. We'll go lead prayers, and you shall see for yourself."

Leaving Ia to sleep on her cart pallet, the mother and daughter wound their way down the hill toward the plain below. Just above the first field, Sequia led Sabina around a sharp turn and to a grotto at the end of which two men stood waiting before a sheltered entry to a large cave.

"*Quem quaeritis[1], O Christicolae?*" They asked.

Sequia responded precisely, "*Jesum Nazarenum crucifixum.*"

Hearing the correct response, one said, "*Omnes intrare*, enter."

Inside they found several dozen people sitting on the cave floor below talking quietly, their voices filtering past them and high up into the dome of the cave. Sabina followed her daughter down crude steps to join the gathering.

Enclosed by the earth, surrounded by strangers, Sabina's forgotten dream of two nights before flooded into her mind, trumpeted by the warning, "Beware the serpent." She glanced around her, searching for the red eye of evil and found none. Instead, she felt the warm wave of welcoming words dancing around her, sighs and relief for her health and long-awaited coming. Sequia led them in prayer as Christ had taught. Before sharing the eucharist, Sequia introduced Sabina by her Berber name, *Tizem*. None had met her before though they had heard of her coming.

After Sequia led prayers, held communion—the sharing of consecrated bread and wine—and gave her benediction, small groups broke away here and there in the cave to share news and talk.

One such group gathered around their new friend, *Tizem*. Excited at a new and important member, they spoke all at once, incomprehensible in the echo-laden cave, until Sabina raised a silencing hand.

"Please, fellow Christians, I am happy to meet you, but speak one at a time, my dear ones."

A tiny, old woman reached out to touch Sabina'a sleeve. "*Tizem*, are you to tell us of the 'miracle in the desert?' Is that your story?"

"Yes, we want to hear it from you directly," said a young girl, perhaps the old lady's granddaughter. "It is the birth story of our leader."

"She who was born without a father," a farmer with a lame leg said.

---

1 A medieval trope, likely anachronistic here, meaning "Whom do you seek?" Ed.

Sabina looked at their expectant faces one after another. She said, "All in due time, I will say more of that and also tell what happened to me afterwards."

The young girl, undeterred, again spoke up, "Can we know now?"

Sequia broke in, "You know that *Tizem* has traveled days to reach us. Perhaps she will agree to speak, to tell her 'desert story' at our larger meeting within the week."

A large man carrying a baby boy on an arm said, "Many of us, but not all, know about the miracle in the desert, but from the lips of a witness who saw, it would be wonderful to hear."

Reluctant but persuaded, Sabina assented to relate the marvel of her story, in the next few days, and later as the members of the group passed up the stair on their way out, each touched her hand.

The mother and daughter took the path toward the farm in the late twilight of the harvest day. They trudged upward in silence.

"You are very quiet, Mother. What are your thoughts?"

Sabina stopped. She took her daughter's hand. "Let us take the higher path."

"You want to see the desert."

"Yes, even in this light. If I am to tell my story, I would look out upon that land once again."

Having worked their way to the top of a steep path, the two women took seats on a rocky toft looking out over the far-off Numidian desert. Sequia remained silent, leaving her mother to her reverie.

Sabina spent a long time watching the waning light, playing over the land and shimmering along the wavering ridges of sand far to the southeast toward Cydamus. She finally spoke as if from a lifetime ago:

"When Augustine left me in Carthage for the last time and I soon discovered I was with his child, I first went to my brother's in Madaurus over there," Sabina said pointing, though Sequidei knew the area well. "He kept me safe, but I was restive and felt called, drawn to the desert. After winning the argument with him after days of disputing, my brother sent me to my three cousins who lived in a village north of Cydamus, at an oasis where water pressed up by the weight of the mountains to the east welled into the desert.

"To cool after the heat of the day, all slept on my cousins' roof at the edge of the oasis, and there, from a little cabana I made for privacy, the shooting stars alerted me to your movements in my belly. It was as if each sparkling shot across the sky bid you turn over or kick! Then, wrapped in my blanket, the desert whispered to me, night after night, saying to me 'your child will arrive and spread open arms to welcome all the world.'"

Sequidei watched her mother as she told this familiar story. Sabina paused to gaze softly at her child.

"That special child was born, then, at the rising of a full moon—a sign among those in the desert both of brilliance and quietude, of wholeness and encirclement, of belonging and love. It was then I left off being a concubine and bit by bit started to become a priestess in the following of Jesus."

Sabina grew quiet again, then finally said, "I hope to find words to describe to our followers that intimate and marked time. The stars and moon have brought us here to be among friends to sustain the message of wholeness and togetherness in Christ."

Sabina, now fully leaving her trance brought on by the sight of the desert, turned to her daughter and said, "Your parishioners asked me so sweetly. They want to know, I suppose more about you, but I will tell them more about themselves." She paused, thinking perhaps of Sequia's caution over new parishoners coming in. "Those new Thagastans you told me of were not in the cave tonight, were they?"

"No, though once they hear that *Tizem* will speak, they will come to hear you, I'm sure. Even known as *Tizem*, you take a risk perhaps of being hounded and, certainly, misunderstood. "

"That will be as it may. You are, too, surrounded by friends. All I met this evening are truly followers. I saw it in their eyes," Sabina said.

"As ever, my mother, you see the love in people. Were it in us all."

They began walking again then, but the daughter stopped to

faced her mother. "So far no serpent has been sent to mislead us, no summons or notice has come to me from the Bishop of Thagaste, Alypius. Perhaps he hesitates because of my father, but neither may stay his hand when your words reach their ears."

Again remembering her feverish dream on the road to Thagaste, Sabina said, "We will be unafraid but as watchful as our Lord."

Augustine and Alypius

Outside the cathedral of Hippo Regius, a small band of monks, well-wrapped against the weather in gray homespun cotton, waited for the two bishops in the plaza at the foot of the church. When their bishops, who wore whiter canonical robes over their habits, each covering his head with signs of his office, stepped out of the church, the gray-robes grouped tightly around them, Augustine and the visiting Alypius, Bishop of Thagaste, awaiting their direction.

"Should we not wait for our arriving delegation to disembark and have them come up to the church?" Alypius tugged at the bishop's sleeve with words alone, careful not to actually touch his superior.

Augustine gave answer as always with a question: "How long have we known each other? How long needs one to observe, in friendship or in enmity, the thoughts of another through his actions or his words before that man knows what answer shall be given in any one circumstance surrounding his colleague?"

Since Alypius, as well he knew to do from experience, remained silent and attentive, Augustine, pausing only to be sure of his audience, continued, "It is necessary for us to greet our guests at the port as they come off their long voyage on that terrible sea the Lord has deemed to create, for two reasons, my friend and fellow bishop: One reason for this short journey from the monastery is that as I have heard from several directions over the past months that many of my parishioners believe I have fallen into ill health since they have not seen me publicly for the longest time. It is my duty to stumble down these Roman stones here to the place I would not otherwise go—oh, how even thoughts of the sea brings turbulence to my stomach and pain to my chest, neither of which I will ever speak—to be seen in my canonical robes and to give hope and strength even to those who seldom attend my sermons. Secondly, it is my duty to my guests who after a dangerous and no doubt an unpleasant journey on the

December sea—oh, how very disagreeable were my crossing to Italy and that lonely voyage back to Carthage without Mother Monnika, although Adeodatus, dear son, soon then to come of age, and Alypius himself, who is still here now quizzing me, were with me at the time on that horrid ocean where I thought at each hour that my life would come to an end either in God's raging air or in God's endlessly deep sea—they, our convénants, being battered in this blustery weather this time of year during which, if I were summoned by my Lord to sail, I would pray incessantly that his mercy would alter his will—how many overland trips to Carthage have I made in forty years, just to avoid that abominable sea? Maybe thirty three-day trips—these men deserve a warm welcome. So, after their tiring and certainly irksome voyage, my dear Alypius, I wish to personally welcome my African bishops to Hippo."

"Very well," Alypius, his friend of more than four decades, replied, "but please allow me to walk beside you or just behind, in case the devil rakes up a stone to trip you."

It was true. Augustine had grown old and was frail. He had made no secret of it in the diocese and had, even some years before, named his successor and then shunted to him the disagreeable work Augustine had wanted to avoid except for its necessity. Still, he could not be let to fall and hasten the preordained end of his life. Even he knew that truth. Alypius knew better than to argue further with the master of polemics. Though he called this very convention of bishops likely because, here in his, no in their old age, Augustine had met his match in disputation, it was a supposition they, neither Augustine or Alypius, would ever utter. But, yes, that was why the senior bishop had called this small conclave: to enlist the understanding and support of his African bishops—to teach them, he would say—to put an end to the Pelagian of Eclanum, the young Julian. Seventeen bishops from the larger dioceses were here already and twelve more from the direction of Lybia and Carthage were to arrive today. Bishop of Thagaste, Alypius, had been the first to arrive, having come the farthest, from Ravenna itself, in order to assist his friend and patron in the coming battle with the heretic.

"Let us swing through the neighborhood," Augustine suggested, "to avoid the forum." He knew even at this late date the public space was festooned with pagan images and shrines to Saint Stephen, whose remains had arrived from the Holy Land, not too many years before. Pagans like his own father and relic worshipers clung to their desperate faith, despite the teaching and consternation of the bishop. So would it be now. But did he have to see it?

They left the steps of the church, taking the harder way through the hilly and narrow streets of the old Christian quarter where, hearing the canonical bell and drum advancing, many of the parishioners, those not working the fields or shopping the market already that day, lined the streets to greet their famous bishop. Augustine blessed each person along the way, though some were pagan and others likely Donatists in their heart, yet many were faithful members of his bishopric.

"*Et erit fides in Deum, habeat vitam aeternam.* Believe in God that you may live forever," he encanted. Some who heard his words did not understand, but the bishop did not repeat his blessing in their Berber language, even though he knew it well.

The entourage turned south along the *cardo maximus* toward the river road that would lead them toward the harbor. All along the way, Augustine gave blessing to the people gathered to venerate their old bishop.

"Some of these, many I suspect, have never entered my church," he told Alypius.

His colleague said, "In their hearts they have. Give them time."

"Even the Father could not create enough time for some poor souls," Augustine said.

When they left the city walls behind, the crowds had grown thinner, and, once below the hills along the river bank, they disappeared entirely. The entourage rested; the two bishops sat beneath a fig tree waiting to drop its final fruits. Augustine, out of breath and already aching with the trek, drew Alypius aside. "This Julian is more than a pest. I fear his youthful energy."

"You were at his age a bishop already eight years. It was the year

Ambrose died."

Augustine found his friend's eyes upon him. "Yes, and we had begun the fight with the Donatists to save our African church."

"You will prevail over the young Pelagian as you have over so many. Wisdom shall prevail over youth."

"If God wills it. If no other challenges the church here."

Alypius stared at Augustine. "You cannot mean Bonifacius."

"Yes, him and any barbarian in the desert. He has fallen away since his wife died and after his voyage to Ravenna several years ago. He returned with that Arian wife! He keeps concubines as well!"

"But you said you would baptize his child."

"That remains to be seen. I trust it is the will of God." But relying on the will of God did not mean Augustine would do nothing. Bonifacius must come fully into the church. He was much too important, and wayward in his own praetorian way, to be let loose as he was in Numidia. Augustine hoped his scribe, Innomenatus, would be of some use in that regard. He now had someone inside the household of the *Comes Africae* who just might be useful. That also meant, Augustine felt, that the man was less of a temptation for him. Usefulness or enticement, either remained to be seen.

But this Julian—even though the bishop was a friend of the young man's family—so full of himself that he had called Augustine *patronis asinorum*, the lord of all donkeys, referring to his African heritage and the backwaters of Thagaste, accused the older man of being a misbelieving Manichee even now, and labeled him Punic, drawing attention to his birth as if his Berber blood had been disreputable as was his family's relative poverty.

So, what must he do but assemble his "donkeys" to assist in stabling this upstart? You, Julian, so finely born, so well connected as you think you are in Italy, Augustine thought, will feel the whip of Thagaste on your high-born flesh. This thought brought to Augustine's mind the letter he'd received from Sabina—this one begging his forbearance in the case of Julian—another letter he had sworn not to open or read, but which had called to him in the very late evening. "Yes, open and read, but you may not reply." It contained more prayers and advice about the kindness and gentleness of the Son.

Sabina had never again asked to see him or touch, not since they parted three days after burying Adeodatus so many years ago. But after she took vows and entered his sister's convent in town, he occasionally received letters from her, conducting a discussion with him—surprisingly like Monnika had done but in writing—sometimes regarding her own troubles in faith, but mostly in reply to writings of his that had come to her—and they were many—that he supposed the convent carried a small library of his writings. He had no desire to receive her thoughts and resisted the temptation to respond, but over time had found them useful, even if they ran against his own ideas. She had been a good learner of deliberation even though she had not been *his* student but for sixteen years only at his side.

Her latest missive, like many over the last few years, worried about his pursuit of heretical sects and persons, as being a weight to his soul. Sabina had always been gentle, but with age she had apparently perfected that manner and outlook. The nuns saw that and elevated her after his sister died, but to everyone's surprise and gratification, she remained, he'd heard, soft spoken, loving, and true. So, when Sabina wrote, taking him to task, really worrying about him, for hot pursuit of Donatists or for condemning his ex-friends still enthralled by the Manichees, he grated under her gentleness.

Her kindness suited her well, but driven, he had to continue his work, despite her mitigation. Chief donkey, indeed. It must be countered. Arrogance begot ignorance, that was clear.

"Are you ready to continue?" Alypius asked, standing.

"My thoughts ran deep just now."

"As always my bishop. As always." With that he offered a hand which, of course, Augustine refused.

"I'm rested but wait a while. I have a question of you."

Augustine's tone halted Alypius and he sat again. "A question?"

"I hear things."

Alypius shuttled just a bit away from his old friend, as if distance would protect him from interrogation. "Things?"

"Perhaps murmurs from the desert. Perhaps rumblings of heresies long past."

"My dearest Augustine, my friend and fellow bishop, ahead of me in faith, please be plain with an old man."

Augustine lunged into his diatribe. "Very well. There is talk of *women* preaching. Of secret meetings in *your* neighborhood. Of a rising of Donatists—even though Rome has ended their tyranny—and, more troubling still, of their *mixing* with other sects—Arians, Manichees, and even pagans—to swell their ranks and gain power."

"Not in my vicinity! No, your grace, the messages must be wrong."

Augustine turned a jaundiced, steady eye on his companion, a look Alypius had seen directed at others now disgraced.

"I ardently deny this suspicion," Alypius contested.

The bishop of Hippo smiled thinly on his friend. "I mention these whisperings only to draw your attention to them. You are often in Ravenna, at a distance even for more than a year, and cannot know everything that happens in your absence. There is some proof of the case. Letters from Julian are carried to Thagaste, I hear. I have not been able to ferret out this connection, but it exists!" Augustine slapped his raised hand down to his knee.

"I am in Ravenna no more," Alypius said. "As soon as I return to Thagaste, I shall look into the matter." Alypius, perhaps anxious to end this uncomfortable discussion, gestured to the path, "It is not far now." Apparently satisfied, Augustine rose and led their way to the harbor.

Indeed, the tiny port could be seen down the river bordered by the ancient Roman road. On the choppy bay, trimmed like the fringe of a robe in light aqua waves at the shore, a small ship bobbed and tossed across the darker waters of the open sea.

"There," Alypius pointed, "are your bishops. We will arrive just in time to refresh ourselves and greet them."

Down at the port, Augustine and Alypius rested on a shaded bench overlooking the rolling sea. The brothers busied themselves laying a large table in the port-home of one Valerius, a grandee in the diocese whose principal residence was very close to the monastery and church. There would be thirteen at the main board, and one of the brothers laid tablets inscribed with Augustine's etiquette at each table—swear and you forfeit your wine glass was one—in plain view of the seats of the arriving bishops. The tablets were necessary since Valerius would not allow the bishop to carve rules into his table. Still, the wishes of the bishop would prevail.

Outside, Augustine forced his eyes to the beach not far from the landing site. He was seldom away from the monastery, almost never by sea, as it sickened him, but he sat with Alypius for a long time watching the waves come in. The day was now fine, but the weather had been blustery and rain had fallen two days before.

"Look, Alypius, how each wave follows the other, each being different than its predecessor in complexion and complexity."

"Yes, it is a common sight," Alypius replied. And he knew immediately he had transgressed in the realm of ideas.

"Well, then, my friend, if you can see two that are common or the same, then you have entered the mind and design of God. Show me, Alypius, which two are twins?"

It was best to back down and agree. That, the bishop of Thagaste well knew. "No, of course, you know I cannot." Then trying to save face—a completely unnecessary and vain enterprise—he said, "If they could be made to stand still, we could examine them closely, find cousins, brothers, perhaps, or twins."

Augustine watched the waves. "Then you would have stopped time, my friend. Can you do that?"

Getting in deeper by the minute, Alypius took his favorite route out of difficulty. "Tell me then, my bishop, what do you see?"

"Look, this one rises tall and green, then curls and crashes on the pebbles. This next lays low and scoops up gravel. Look, this one simply flows low and drains. Some bubble and froth. Some swirl in eddies and recede. Some throw themselves on the backs of their fellows, either suppressing them or being carried forward. Others throw themselves at us, engendering the instinct to flee. And each one following is created out of a wide sea, living a short but eventful life!"

"Ah," said Alypius, "I see." He hoped, perhaps, that his friend would explain, and he was not wrong.

"This shows us two things: one, briefly, is that God's creation and miracles continue, ongoing in this and all time. He, the three-personed-God, is here, making the moon change, the sun to follow a daily and monthly course, the earth to push out grasses and fruit, the olive tree, here, to leaf, to flower, and to bear. Two, the waves show us that the differences of each person, his unique birth and upbringing, his education, his aspect of hair, eyes, mouth, and stature are all within the bounds of God's creation, as is his death, being, as we all are, dashed upon the rocks and sand of God's beach, but not unkindly, for we possess a beauty, like the waves, and olive blossoms, like the rolling landscape, but some will bubble away, some seep, and some come vaulting and falling to their ends."

"Yes," came Alypius's reply, "we *are* very much like the waves."

"Not so much, but some," Augustine said. "Look to the breakwater, there. Here come our friends. But wait. Observe there the action of the waves. See?" Augustine did not wait for a reply, "Within the shelter of the port, the waves no longer crash, roll, or heave so. They are calmed and follow each other in a more uniform way. Of course, still they dissipate and die, but are brought to an orderly and meaningful end."

"Of course."

"*Ergo?*"

"I suppose it is the arms of the Church that tame us as the jetty does the waves."

"Exactly! And that, my friend, is the proof of Julian's folly. He would have us run over the earth, each individual making his way alone with his own movement as his guide, without rule, without mercy, without direction, to die a solitary death without a savior. Is this the life we wish to lead? Is this the road to our salvation? No, only in the loving arms of the Church will we find calm birth and eternal rest. That is why this upstart, this serpent in fine Italian linens, this arrogance of arrogance must be defeated. The future of our Church depends upon this."

"I do not wish to interrupt, but here our fellows have landed. Do you wish to go down to meet them?"

"I am ready."

8

King Gaiseric

The Atlantic wind whipped Gaiseric's face. January's cold pierced his breastplate and woven leggings, but the Vandal king faced the raging fish-road, watching the white-headed waves being driven into the cove. His men around him wrapped themselves in their horse blankets, but the Atlantic gale, anyway, made them grumble. Still, not a one would break ranks and run to the fire. They were called there by their new king to watch the straits.

Gaiseric looked south toward Africa, Mauretania Tingitana, across the narrows from Baetica, the homeland the Vandals had fought so hard to get. In winter, the shores hidden across the straits by a harsh and forbidding sea, held little welcome. But the choppy waves also seemed to Gaiseric like slate steppingstones washed over in a rain of whitecaps leading, if one were careful, to a greater freedom, away from untrustworthy Goths and Sueves, and, better yet, far from the great hosts of Romans in Gaul and Hispania both, struggling to win the favor of their regent, Galla Placidia, at a cost, most surely, to his own Vandal and Alan bands.

The new king faced the sea, thinking. He considered the party of Ulfa, off to one side, all bunched together casting wary eyes at the churning waters. Better for my thanes to see it in wrath, than among calm whispers on a sunny day. Best to know the dangers ahead of us even while we leave behind the mantrap of enemies here.

He slipped a hand inside his pouch and withdrew the letter once more. The offer was good. The call for help was understandable, but who could trust yet another ambitious Roman general. Still, the terms were generous. The third of Libya offered were not the best lands on the southern shores of Mare Mediterraneo but served as a safer place than their Baetica where enemies hemmed him in on all sides. He turned from the wind—his men, he knew, hoped to go, but he would not give that order, not yet—and he read the words he now carried in his mind:

"*Fairraþro Tacapae faur Leptis Magna schold biþ þeins.* From far off Tacapae to Leptis Magna shall be yours." Gaiseric thought it odd they wrote in his language, not badly, but not right in all ways either. And "*ak weihans-gild biþ namlausan,* other spoils of war are yet unknown," that strange sentence brought Namlaus, Innomenatus, his tutor, to mind. Who else could write even this well in the Vandal tongue? There might be two in the whole of Africa, and this was no Goth. The word *namlaus* was unusual, especially in the way the writer had used it, since the idea was absent in the Latin text.

Gaiseric looked again at the sea where two years before, he'd seen his friend off. As Innomenatus had boarded the cargo vessel then bound for Africa Proconsularis from the port of Carthago Spartaria, Gaiseric removed the silver Arian cross from his neck, saying, "Keep this as my pledge of friendship. It shall help you in need." The nameless one donned the cross but first removed a finer one, a golden Catholic one, from his neck. Offering it to his pupil and friend, Innomenatus said, "Carry this *crux Romana* for protection. Let no one know from whom it came." His tutor boarded the ship that was carrying silver for Bonifacius and would then take on grain and oil bound for Rome.

Back then, he had wondered, "Does this friendship matter?" Now, especially after the dream of Inno in white, he believed it did. It is always good to have someone inside the enemy camp, he thought. Gaiseric saw that Namlaus might become even more useful a friend than he was before. Innomenatus bore little liking for Roman generals or for bishops like Augustine, and maybe less for the *Comes Africae*, Bonifacius. Let the exchanged crosses seal their parting as a new kinship. Their fates had become bound.

A shout went up! *Diups wegs!* The tide welled and splayed out a huge wave whose froth drenched their stand. Gaiseric laughed. "Now that we have tasted the sea, we should go back to our *alþingi*, my earls."

Only since September had Gaiseric been king. This was his first real test. The council had heard his mind about crossing with all his people, moving on to Mauretania. They had agreed that with so many Vandals already prospering in trade in Africa a move could save much war effort. Others—mainly Ulfa-kin, few but loud—said it was foolish, that they would drown, making fish fat on human flesh.

"First, let us look at the sea. Then tell us what it is in your mind." That had brought them to the shore. Now on the way back to the council grounds, all were soaked to the waist in sea water, and the nay-sayers were boasting and grumbling both, the loudest, Ulfa stirring his fearful pot. Gaiseric, though, was not king for nothing. Those who stood against him had grown fat on pilfer and pillage. Warlike, they were not. Too, he had revealed only to a few close kinsmen Bonifacius's cry for help. Gaiseric knew how to deal. He could bend his mind. It was never fixed but flowed like an underground stream. His purpose was hard, his timing was not. One more man might help but only if needed: Namlaus. The scribe would be useful to Gaiseric to quell the bickering of his men if needed. Most here knew Inno and although he was an African and a quiet yet professed Catholic, many liked him well.

All this was in Gaiseric's mind as they, cold and drenched, trudged up beyond the sea wall, passing Gaiseric's two lookouts who guarded the coast. Then they moved back downhill toward the welcome warmth of the council fire beyond.

The women there had warm grog and hot food for the earls. The wives served the meal to the men. The *scope* blew on his pipe and by the beat of his drum reminded all, in song, of standing over the Sueves and Romans at war. His song rose with his *waurds*, words:

Good Gaiseric	the Suevish cudgel grabbed.
At their king he threw,	In head, hit him hard
And down to death	that Sueve king drove.
Gaiseric gave good	to Guntharic his *gome*
Winning at war	with worthy weapons.

Gaiseric ate and drank his fill but watched carefully the men gathered around the table, men who would steer the course the Vandal people chose to go. He trusted they'd follow him with good hearts.

Gelimmer, his cousin, rose first to speak. "Well, we've had our sea-play, and have eaten well at our king's table, both meat and fish, our gentle women serving us wine. Bounty of the land we've won. Our *scope* has sung us of the battles for Baetica. Happy be our hearts."

"Now to our council. Tell us, thanes, of your will for the people."

Up shot Ulfa, gray headed now and long-toothed in old age, but always one fast in mind to anger. He loosed his words without first thinking. "Our good King Gaiseric has in mind that we all will cross the water to Africa, but we have seen the sea today. Even as it leaped up from its bed, it warned us that foolish ideas can lead to death. How many Vandal lives, and Vandal gold-hordes should sink to the bottom of the angry straits to quench our king's search for glory?" Some rapped their cups on the table in answer to his words.

"I remember, better than many here who are too young to know, crossing the frozen Rhine, leaving our homes behind to Huns. Even then we were landsmen, stepping only on the earth, and how we trembled even over the thick-frozen rivers. We walked to open Gaul's lands. No one then thought the Hasdings were fish. The mountains we crossed all on foot." Here Ulfa stamped his foot on the bench. "And in Hispania, we marched on solid ground. We are not seafarers, nor have ever been. This crossing would be wrong. I will stay and fight the Sueves. Fight the Romans. Fight the Visigoths or Huns if need be, but swimming the waves of winter is not what we must do."

A great cheer went up from the earls. Whether it was for Ulfa's speech or for the long history of the life of a Vandal, no one could know. Several drunken friends of Ulfa raised their cups and drained them. Now, asking for the bowl to be passed yet again.

Then Huneric the Elder stood—a hoary head all white with age had often worn his helm over longish locks in battle—he rose, not to toast the rabble fired by Ulfa's words, but to reach even further back in the mists of time to tell a tale:

"Godegisel, father of Gunderic, was a good king, strong and brave. He was first to hear of the Huns, fierce in hard battle, great in numbers. The Goths, Godegisel's neighbors, themselves were troubled and afraid. The good king held council, listened to his thanes. I was unbearded at that time, had just learned to throw the spear, but remember the fight to stay or leave. One earl—his name I know but will not tell here for he has grandsons among us—spoke up: 'I will not leave, but with sharp blows will fight the Huns, keep our land, our homes.' Brave words from a hearty earl. And many sided with him, but also listened with care to all the others before making up their minds. Godegisel finally counseled, 'It has been long since we first traveled here to Pannonia. We had wandered far before. It has been good to stay, but we now have to take up again our long-forgotten ways, fare far where riches lie, and learn again how we must live.' Such were his words. In the end, we left our homes to Goths then Huns, fled far and farther and made good on Godegisel's knowing ways. Though we have learned how to stand hard, look to your Siling friends here, now so few, who fought bravely but were ground beneath the sandals of Rome, all for spite. Are we to stand, now on that very same ground of Baetica, and ask Rome for war? War is the Roman's only love."

Gelimmer rose again. "And Ulfa, where were you when the Sueves swept down the mountains at our Vandal homes? I remember you riding, but I saw naught but your horse's tail. Is that how you will stand against Rome?"

Angry talk then flared and long swords drawn. All was quelled when their king, Gaiseric, rose to speak. "Save yourselves from each other. Sheathe your swords."

Huneric the Elder spoke, "Hear. Hear our king. Don't shame yourselves at council, drunken as you are. Let us listen to our king." At that the wives gathered the empty bowls and left their lords.

Gaiseric stood on the dais, held up his hand. All were quiet, waited for his words.

"You are all fearless and hearty. You can fight, that we know. Save that for later. We have a gift and a message." At his king's sign,

Gelimmer held up a small chest, "Golden rings and amulets galore, bracelets of silver and gold, *fibulae* of ships and goats and *trinacria* with silvered feet. To you I give these gifts. Now hear the message that is sweet to the ear. We have been named *foederati* by the Roman *Comes Africae*, Bonifacius who in return asks us to protect him, from whom? From the empire itself! This comes with offers of land, free passage along the coast, and freedom from Sueves and Goths on whom, should they attack us, the rage of African Rome will come down." Little grumbling was heard as Gelimmer laid out to each his treasure from the chest and the terms were heard.

"Since when shall a Roman, a renegade at that, be trusted?" Ulfa asked, still not done with his foolish speech.

"A friend of ours, you know him well, now in their camp has written the terms in his own hand." All waited. "Namlaus, you know him as, is on our side, is watching out for us."

"Ah, he, the Catholic priest?" Ulfa who with two earls turned to leave then said, "This winter sea will be our death."

Gaiseric had waited for this. "Ulfa, stay, brother. I agree with you. We have looked out between the pillars at the whale-road's worst today, but only water not blood soaked our clothes. We will cross soon but with only a few at a time during the winter blows. The winds will be our friends. Who would think we could slip past them in a gale? We must fool our watchful neighbors with hidden, stealthy movement until at the very tipping point with March storms near an end, all at once we will make our final crossings, leaving cities, ports, and fields stripped for a fool's taking."

Gaiseric stood tall with his shorter leg on a step and swept his gaze over his men. "I want no one left behind. We are a people. We must leave no kin to our enemies."

In the hall of the *alþingi*, Gaiseric looked over the gathering. Out of the silence following his words, he heard the beginning of the swell of widely spread handclaps, beckoning all to "yes." The cheers, too, grew. No one left the hall. Soon all joined, hailing their leader, feasting, and drinking again.

Gaiseric had won. The king prevailed.

9

Innomenatus and Bonifacius

It is not for nothing that I have circumambulated the Mare Mediterraneo—my journey formed a lifetime of labor—living in rich households, monasteries, hovels, and, when called for, caves of various descriptions. My travels have taught me much more than Greek, Hebrew, and Gothic. I've obtained a good feel for the philosophy that comes with each of those languages, perhaps more important than the words themselves. Latin is a stately language, terse, seldom elegiac or languid, forceful at most times. Greek feels inward-looking on the tongue, complex as the ancient minds of Athens and just as refined. I have always found Hebrew argumentative and somewhat mythic. Gothic, contrary to the descriptions of many Roman writers, describing the utterance of the tongue as "pig farting," comes with an active and colorful way of saying even the most mundane things and reveals shades of mystery when least expected. It has a music of its own, albeit sounding flatulent to some.

What was I saying? Oh, yes, what I have learned in this around-the-world lifetime, besides the philosophy. Philosophy: to the Greek mind is discovery and right living, to the Latin mind a social investment best dispensed with in favor of action. To Hebrews that I've known well, philosophy is simply something to be discussed. To the Gothic mind it means a journey over a misty sea in search of something to celebrate besides work. But here I am again, lost in my own philosophy, simply professing my ignorance.

That which I had hoped to say was this: I have learned to survive, becoming like water. Confronted by fear, I learned to slip away. Invited to the homes of the amorous, I spread out on the pavement, unable to be grasped. Tricked into binding ties, I evaporated. In short, I existed like water does, flowing continuously, growing deep when halted, plunging harmlessly on itself from on high, and, most importantly, seeping into crevices and unexpected crannies. This last ability grew to be essential in the household of Bonifacius, *Comes Africae.*

The "two-month" stay in the household of Bonifacius had already stretched to nearly double that. The count liked my rapid and accurate work and, himself lacking a good scribe at the time, commandeered my services much like he had assumed governance over the whole of Africa. Who was I to argue?

I had circled the great Mare Mediterraneo in my lifetime serving patiently and productively, entering the lives around me without leaving a mark, a stain, or a footprint. I have to say that this demonstrates that I am a man of much the opposite character than that of the friend-of-my-youth, Aurelius Augustinus, Bishop of Hippo Regius, who wandered little and mostly in the mind, a seeker of a truth beyond the plate on his table, who was a chisel unto the marble blocks of others, shaping in the world an indisputable form, but who in the short of it really was a hometown boy, a mother's companion, who wouldn't leave his appointed flock for anything. Most anything. Well.

Part of my lengthened stay with Bonifacius was spent waiting for a reply from the Vandal king. Our October envoy had trouble finding his way and was delayed waiting in Carthago Spartaria, for Gaiseric never appeared there. Our messenger finally took an overland route to Hispalis, a three-week journey, and presented his letter and the treasure chest, hidden amongst the load of figs he was, supposedly, bringing to the king. That was in December. The poor man, who had successfully delivered his charge, was then blown off course on his return. We did not learn until January that the Vandal council must take up the question before Gaiseric could answer.

"*Quidam Rex,*" said Bonifacius. He snorted, "Some poor king." To me, perhaps more of a historian than my employer, it seemed a throwback before emperors, to the age of the Republican Senate. I said nothing. *Comes Africae* stood little correction.

In the meantime, I took military dictation, wrote letters for my employer, took charge of recording visits to the count, and found time enough to chat with Maria and even to speak with Pelagia, the count's Gothic wife who almost immediately found my conversation quaint but comforting in that I spoke her language. There were plenty of Goths around, but, being lowly soldiers, they were not conversationalists.

In our talks, the pall of religion fell ever so lightly over everything, though she was certainly fair minded in her own way. I at first thought Pelagia had reached a comfortable compromise with her husband's religion, but several things taught me differently. The Church of Rome was not a welcome host in her house.

One such indication I observed was the inscription to be found on the wide edges of the marble altar in the household chapel, originally a Pagan shrine. I knew it to have read: "*Credo in Spiritum Sanctum, sanctam Ecclesiam catholicam, sanctorum communionem, remissionem peccatorum, carnis resurrectionem, vitam aeternam*, I believe in the Holy Spirit" and so on, like many another altar I'd seen. But those words,"*sanctam Ecclesiam catholicam*, the Holy Catholic Church," had been chiseled out, skillfully I might add, and I later noticed a new piece had been fitted in—and it was a very good match indeed both in color and in the working of the letters which had to be ever so slightly narrowed—which said, instead, "*ad perpetuam Patre qui est in caelis*, the eternal Father who rules in heaven. The original, of course, would have been offensive, perhaps heretical, in Pelagia's Arian eyes.

Another occurrence was the baptism of Pelagiana, Bonifacius's daughter, who he'd promised to bring to Augustine for that holy ablution. Not only had the bishop of Hippo Regius been misled by his protector and friend, but it was the Arian bishop of Sigisvultus, Maximus, who had come out none the better in a debate with Augustine just the previous month, who was the prelate bestowing the sacrament.[1] And how do I know all this? Water at the bottom of

---

1 It was not just the baptism or the count's deception, bad enough for Augustine to consider evil, but Maximus's involvement that stoked the fire of my bishop's distaste of Bonifacius after that point. Augustine thought he had dispatched the Arian Maximus in debate only to find him as it were sneaking in the back door with a knife. The whole event convinced me less of Pelagia's religious ardor than of her penchant for political meddling (she was a king's daughter, after all) and of the count's practicality or his quick grasp of opportunity, whichever you'd prefer. To say it gently, Augustine rent his robes and burned in resentment at the injury. I became even more careful as a result of it all.

the well is dark until drawn up, but water which seeps into everything is party to all. Without asking, that is what happened.

My short greetings and conversations with Pelagia expanded and began eventually to include news. To her, I suppose, it seemed confidential, being conveyed in what was a language incomprehensible to all in the household but her personal servants. The information gave me something to offer Maria in my frequent forays into the kitchen. A good gossip gives nearly as much as he is given. Each of us, over special little dishes she prepared just for me, became notable chatterboxes. Then, suddenly, Bonifacius himself began to confide in me.

It started much like my encounter with Augustine, in the middle of the night, deprived of the will to sleep, in my case, and plagued by the demons of sleep in his, we found ourselves in the portico overlooking the garden, sitting exactly before the mosaic of his notable deeds. He came up behind me.

"Sleep eludes you."

I stood and turned. "I beg your leave, Count. I thought the garden might engender dreams. I will return to my cot."

"No, no, Innomenatus. I am glad of the company. It is dreams that send me here. Dreams and worries."

"The Vandal reply?"

Bonifacius laughed, the sole time up until then I had heard him do so. "No, the displeasure of my wife."

Though I knew of her consternation, there was nothing here for me to say but, "I am only a scribe here. I've heard nothing."

He came close and did not laugh though his voice sounded merry, "Oh you fox, I've seen you with your ear dragging along the ground here and there!" I did not take it as an accusation but dared not say another word.

"My dame has pitted me against my bishop. Were she not a princess, selected for me by Rome, it would not matter. The good that Augustine could do for me is greater than any marriage. And now this baptism makes his help harder to get."

"It is a blessing. The child is shielded from Satan."

"It was a dangerous move," he said. "She is pleased, of course, but Augustine is furious. Not so much with Maximus, Sigisvultus's bishop, for he is a presbyter, or with Pelagia who is by her own birth an Arian believer, but with me.

"Augustine railed at me: 'You have risked the very soul you brought into this world. She is now unclean. She cannot enjoy a second baptism. Have we not made that clear?'"

I felt it prudent and truthful to agree. "Augustine is an unrelenting soul."

"What is worse is that I need his support more than he needs mine. Then again, I am still Catholic and do attend his mass. That stays his hand."

"He could not very likely go to Sigisvultus for help," I said.

"No. Maximus would be there. That would be unthinkable to Augustine. But even though he is an old man, perhaps needing protection more now than ever, he still has a fiery pen and enjoys influence in Ravenna, and there the clergy has become powerful."

"Yes, the bishop has his own army, his *bucellarii* of African bishops who travel back and forth with his letters."

So it was that I seeped into the private thoughts of the general.

Now, for the second time, Bonifacius laughed.

"Strength in numbers works for churches as well as armies," he said.

After that, since my chamber was on anyone's path to the portico, I started to listen for his step during the night. That was not the last time he took me into his confidence.

Maria was all ears.

"No, I wouldn't say the count is in trouble, heaven forbid, just that he ruffled the old bishop's feathers a bit."

She was stirring up some spicy lentils for me. "I know nothing, of course, but from what I have heard, our bishop Augustine is not one to fight with." She looked my way, hoping I would have something more to say.

"I know the man little. I simply work there. But I have seen things that might bode ill for anyone out of step with Augustine or crossing on the wrong side of the Church."

That got her going, and she was full of stories of the trials and tribulations of friends who had grown up as Donatists and who now had to hide from the authorities or convert to save the lives of their children. She looked at me carefully, drew near, and whispered, "There are a few here, under this roof, who still hold to that sect." It sounded somewhat embellished and fanciful, but Maria's words had a certain ring of truth about them, too.

"I remember some from my early days in Carthage," I said without thinking. And now I was in trouble.

"You are from Carthage, then? Did you know the bishop there?"

"I was sheltered and believe that he had already gone to Rome when I studied there." I do not know if she believed me, but since I said no more, that was all she had. "I'm really from Madaurus." Again, I asked for the heavens to fall on me.

"I knew some people there," she said yet again bedeviling me. Then, much to my relief, she added, "But they are all dead." She named them and mumbled a prayer for their souls. As it was, I had known their parents well, but this time I held my tongue.[2]

Perhaps not the most useful but certainly the most interesting information that was coming to my ears was that which Pelagia told me both about her father, part of the Gothic *foederati*, allies of Rome, and of her life growing up on the fringes of the Roman empire. Some of the household gossip I passed to Maria but kept confidence on the subjects Pelagia broached—gossiping knows its limits. Like most important people, the wife of Bonifacius asked me little about *my* life. Had she, though, I had a battery of varied stories to tell from around the empire. She became particularly interested in my poor efforts working for Wulfilas in Trajan's town, Nicopolis ad Istrum (in the middle of the Dacian nowhere) on his translation of the Scriptures.

---

2 You might well ask, "Why all this secrecy?" I say, "habit," but self-preservation plays an important part, as well. I've worked in the interest of the powerful, both political and religious, surviving through circumspection. It does not mean I've shied away from influence when I could bring about change, but it has meant I've lived to work another day. I prefer, as my nameless name assures you, my life's work to be anonymous.

I had my hand in the translating of *Luke*. Pelagia told me, "*Fadar, galaubida auk Wulfilas,*" that her father had been converted from the old religion to Arian Christianity by Wulfilas himself. It was, of course, possible, maybe even likely. Certainly, I was interested though the knowledge proved to be of little use.

"*Gahausja ata Vandals atbairun izo bokos du drauhtinon*, I've heard that the Vandals carry his bible into battle," Pelagia said.

I was more careful with this conversation than with my last chat with Maria. "I had not heard that." And I went further to cover my tracks through the desert. "*Ik fratha none faura Vandala*, I know nothing of Vandals."

"Were you not in Hispania?"

"Oh yes, but among the Goths there." She apparently did not know anyone who had led or served there. Quite a relief.

All this kept me busy. And there was the work too. And, finally in February, Gaiseric's reply arrived.

"It is all in that odd script of theirs. Go ahead, read it to me."

I skipped the first line: "*Namlaus aflifnai namlaus*, Innomenatus shall remain nameless," or the nameless one shall be left alone, and went right to the meat of the missive. "Gaiseric and his council of earls accept the gifts of Count Bonifacius and swear by the name of *foederati Romani* to defend the count from all foes, foreign and domestic."

"Excellent," Bonifacius said. "Now draft this agreement in the correct terms. It must be in Latin, but certainly you can provide a copy in their language so they can understand what they are signing."

I did as instructed and dispatched the decree, the translation, and, since I did not believe Bonifacius would bother to notice, a very short letter to my former pupil acknowledging his reply.

It was two weeks after that work had been finished and dispatched, that in the kitchen I encountered Maria surrounded with a great hubbub of activity.

"I cannot take time for you right now," Maria said. "We are receiving guests from Rome very soon, and the feasting shall be endless. No more little tidbits for you until the Italians are gone."

"I am content," I said. "Roman guests." I mused a bit waiting for Maria to spill her word-hoard. I speared a fig and munched on it delicately. Maria huffed a bit and shook her head. She needed prodding.

"These visitors, then, are not of the rumored envoy to come with soldiers."

She continued giving her help commands and slicing a mountain of onions. "No, no." She wiped her eyes. "These are old friends of the count. They live at the court in Ravenna."

"Ah," I said, and reached for another fig which movement Maria warded off with her knife. "I suppose I shall find out exactly who they are after they arrive."

"Yes. Now, out. Out!"

Of all the places I had visited and lived, Ravenna was not one. So, even after the two men arrived, they were nothing but names to me, though they apparently had the ear of Galla Placidia. The upshot of the visit I learned directly from the count, near dawn the following day. I heard him pass my quarters swinging by in his singular martial gait, and after waiting to see if he was followed or would return, dressed and joined him.

"It is a curse, but I cannot sleep. I heard you pass. Should I sit with you?"

He indicated the nearby bench. He remained silent, and I simply waited, watching the rosy fingers of dawn advance across the sky. Sometimes, silence is the best oil of conversation.

He sprang up from his chair and paced the portico. "I think sometimes that I should have taken to the monastery. It was my bent at the death of my first wife."

"It is not a bad life," I tried to sound disinterested.

He came back to his seat. "Less complicated, to be sure. But Augustine needed a soldier, not another monk. So, it was not to be."

"I trust that decision is not the thief of your sleep."

"No, it's hardly worth it." Again, he rose and paced. "I am released from one quandary only to find myself in another.

I spoke truly and coaxed him, "I do not understand."

"No, you wouldn't. I'm unsure of it all myself. I've been the victim of deceit."

Now *I* wanted to pace. Surely, the count hadn't discovered my slight deceptions.

"You shall find out tomorrow in any case since you will pen a retraction to the Vandal king, but it is entirely likely that I shall be reconciled to Galla Placidia and that Felix will be unmasked as the schemer he has always been." I had nothing to reply.

Bonifacius continued. "His letter to me avowed friendship and gave me warning of the regent's plot against me. Plot indeed! There was a plot, but it was his own! It was he, my rival, all the time. He invented the story and made it true by lying!" I didn't quite understand yet that Bonifacius had been tricked into defying the emperor's mother which device had brought on the wars from Rome, but neither did I ask the count to clarify. I am not one who cannot wait.

"Now, I must put a halt to the Vandal movements, which I know have already begun." He put his head in his hands and swayed slightly. What was a poor scribe to do but take note and quietly await the rising sun.

10

Augustine Dreams

Augustine awoke, surprised, as soon as he could brush the dust of sleep from his mind, to find himself not in the classroom in long-ago Carthage, surrounded by many friends all attending to his arguments on good and evil in the world, but in his own monastic bed adjacent to his library at Hippo Regius more than fifty years later. In the dream-throng of admirers, he had recognized Innomenatus. That had awakened him.

My Lord, to whom I give my life and labor, you know that one can in the business of the day shut out such longing sins as may come to mind only to be silently dismissed after which they pass on. But at night, My Lord, you know that man is defenseless, unable to will the body or the mind only toward Your praises and Your practices.

Is the worry of the night, then, a penance? Or is it yet another sin? Something that takes away from the work for and the praises of God. Does it depend upon what time of day? Absurd, of course. You my God are eternal in all three persons, fixed, if it is Your will, and unchangeable, so it must be sin to worry, even at night, since those thoughts, visions, and feelings are rooted in a falsehood: that the Will of God, like night and day, varies and changes. That cannot be since how can sinful men, all humans, follow a path of righteousness if the path changes from day to day, from hour to hour?

Augustine argued with himself, but he became acutely aware of another presence in his dream. Let me speak out to it. Let me ask if it be evil or good. No, no, that is ridiculous for if evil, it would still reply affirming its goodness. That is all a Manichean idea in any case, an alluring one, but certainly heretical. Are you afraid the presence is evil? Has Satan sent one here near my end to bait me, just as he had tempted the Son?

That worry crept in. Not that his own end was nearer, for he was old and ready to die, but that he wrestled with his plans for his library, his life's work, which he knew to be in disarray, fragmented, and ill-cataloged. He was not yet ready to leave though his body led him toward death.

Maybe I can put this question out to that presence I felt there in the dream with me, which might lead me to determine its origin. "Let me, Oh Lord, not doubt You but allow me to be ever alert."

At once, unsure that he had awakened at all, Augustine rose erect in his bed. He peered into the darkest corner of his tiny chamber. Is that a man hunched on my night jar? Like a sack of old bones. Does he rest his eyes upon me? The bishop leaned further forward, as much as his own aching bones allowed. I see a thin neck and a hooked beak, don't I? Does he smile? Or do I see a dark cavern set in a large stony ball?

Without provocation, suddenly again, Augustine thought of Innomenatus, and his night vision disappeared in the light at the first cockcrow of the coming dawn. "My dearest Lord, let me not be awake, let that phantom be a dream, choke off this longing which brings thoughts from long past to haunt and pester my addled mind."

He should have, he knew, resorted immediately to prayer, to singing a psalm, to further address his God, but instead he further spoke to a now disappeared Innomenatus. I am ashamed, like Adam, and cower behind a leaf. Oh, friend-of-my-youth, now come to me without a name, resurrected from the coffin I placed you in, how can I beg forgiveness? What have I done, my Amicus? Amicus, what have I done?

With those cries, if they had been uttered, the presbyter flopped back on his cot and covered his eyes with his hands. Almost immediately, Alypius, who had extended his stay in Hippo after the conclave, was there.

"Did you call me?"

"No," Augustine startled at his presence. "No, it was but a dream."

"I shall sit with you. Shall we pray?"

Infernal friend, always wanting to pray, to pry into my thoughts. Augustine considered springing onto that investigation his fellow bishop had promised in Thagaste. The bishop of Hippo Regius, though, was not yet ready for all that. He said, "Good Alypius. I shall rest, thank you. It is not dawn yet."

"No, just before. I will be in the *scriptorium* later."

Augustine watched his fellow bishop as he turned to go, the man who had followed him over half the course of their lives faithfully, admiring always, and always, Augustine reminded himself, without imagination. "Yes, then, I will meet you later in the *scriptorium*." Outside, within the monastery walls, the morning-bird sounded again.

More mundane thoughts now occupied Augustine. He had, he knew dreamed also of these, and one particularly speared him with the pain of shame, but not as sharply as thoughts of Innomenatus had done—yes, he would from now on call him Amicus. Well, I shall think no more of him this morning. The day is breaking.

The bishop's mind drifted to an issue more of the present world, the all too welcomed flattery of Darius, the count who had come from Ravenna to negotiate with *Comes Africae*. The man wagged a fluid tongue, his civility and education shone brightly but without the usual glitter of Latin rhetoric. I cannot say that I didn't welcome his good faith and well wishes. I certainly enjoyed his praise. I cannot, like Ambrose or Jerome, rise above that certain vanity of mine—I once wrote to them both, denying their wishes that I be a man higher up in the church. I truly, in the humility of our Lord, wished to be lowly. High office would be unseemly. Did I not say that? It would be again the love of knowledge rather than the love of God, but here I am, sought out by loquacious Romans like Darius who had won over Bonifacius and that one's Roman rival in Carthage as well. The man had a gracious way about him although, had I been but a monk, he would not have spoken to me at all.

The flattery rubbed the same bone Amicus had struck, the very temptation he had felt in the presence of *Comes Africae*. Yes, and now that Darius has said there would be peace with Rome, I shall be stuck with Bonifacius, a protector, but a dissembler, too, ruled by greed and vanity. I should have brought him into the order years ago when he begged us to accept him. But no, instead I traipsed a hundred miles past Thagaste to intercept him, to prevail upon him to keep his soldierly mantel for our protection. And now what? Even admonished for his concupiscence and lack of charity, he argues as he cavorts with his concubines. "I attend mass. I support the church. What I do is needful," he says. All true, but not enough. Not enough, as You know, my Lord, even though you made the man handsome to think on. Once again that morning, his loins itched and quivered, but, now fully awake, he directed his thoughts to waking concerns.

So, there shall be peace with Rome. The deceiver Felix's beguilement had come into the open. Bonifacius had been fooled into revolt, but, now that Galla Placidia had come to know of that plot, *Comes Africae* is once again folded in her politic embrace. "And Augustine?" The bishop, dangling his legs over the bedside, said aloud, "Ah, well. He shall live until he dies."

The count would be strutting once again when Sigisvultus sailed for Italy. Ha! And take that Arian Bishop with you, that Maximus of the stolen baptism. What a sly serpent he proved to be. He argued well, though it amounted to the same old chipping at the marble block that had been cracked and discarded years ago. If his Arian numbers were not so large here, we African bishops would have stamped the serpent where it lay.

It was Bonifacius, Augustine knew, who had finally granted permission for his own daughter's baptism. It was his doing, not his wife's or Maximus, bishop of Sigisvultus.

I am condemned to live among vipers. No wonder I lose my sleep. Again, then, the rooster crowed. The sun had risen. So shall I, my Lord, to work once more in Your vineyards, but not just yet, please a moment more rest in this bedding-tossed morning.

He thought once more of his "meeting" with Amicus, how he had sent him away to the count, to save himself his unforgivable, waking lust and sorrow: lust for the youth inside the fat, bald old man and sorrow for the lost name of him who was now without one.

He would, immediately, that very day write to the count demanding his scribe's return. He would claim, and rightly so, to have urgent matters in Greek to manage and must have him back, for that

Italian snake, Julian, had slithered into Thagaste, whispering in the ear of his own flesh and blood, working his own daughter to rebel and disobey all that he had worked to establish. Would that get the count's attention?

No, but there was something else.

Yes, I will tell Bonifacius what I learned from my bishop of Ad Fratres, in the east of Tingitana. The count's "guests," the vile Vandals, are marauding and pillaging already. I shall ask him: "Now what shall I counsel my bishops after the barbarians have killed at least one of their number? That *Comes Africae* shall protect them?"

11

Sabina Writes

Sabina sat in the convent courtyard under the blossoms of the olive trees feeling the April sun, finally after many days of rain. Spring had come to Hippo Regius, the rains would now pass and the sweet spring air would yet be cool in the evening and warm only during the day. The summer heat was yet to climb into the sky.

Even the advent of spring, though, could not warm her, nor could it sweeten her thoughts. The sisters saw only the side of her on which little had the look of change, but much that was hidden had altered Sabina.

She had been sitting there nearly an hour—all winter, in fact, she had continually failed to decide how much to say—thinking on what to write, how to say that which, she felt, needed to be said. But she was no closer to scratching into the wax tablet than on the first day's return from Thagaste. "I change like the seasons but am slow to turn." Sabina twirled the stylus between her fingers and pondered. The light filtered through the pointed leaves of the olive, making patterns on her hands.

"Oh, Sequia," she said, the dappling recalling for her the meal her daughter had laid upon their arrival in Thagaste. Then, too, the breeze, an evening breath, had stirred the trees, first shadowing and then lighting Sequidei's face. "Is it a sin to miss you so? I do not pine for you, but I miss your strength, your quick mind"—how like your father, how like your poor brother you are—"and your sweet wisdom, too."

That evening in late September had settled her mind. When they had returned from their desert viewing after first meeting of *Christicolae*, Sequia and she had sat up talking by lamplight until the moon rose, spilling light over the arbor where they still sat. In the half-light of that night, Sabina had recalled the fever-dream visitor of three nights before and felt an urge to share with her daughter the vision, which she now remembered with utmost clarity. Sequia would know what it meant. Something in the cave they visited that night had brought back her memories.

Sequia leaned forward on her bench, listening with the intensity of a polemicist, with the openness of a confessor, and with the softness of a counselor. She kept her attention rapt on her mother's words until Sabina uttered the last syllable of her story. Then, she spoke. "And you would like to know what?"

Sabina realized that she had posed a question, not just reported what had happened, or what she had dreamed. "I wonder does the visitor mean well?"

Sequia had learned, her mother did not know how, that the best way of sharing a conversation is to ask questions. She answered Sabina's question with another. "Did he demand something of you?" Sabina shook her head. "Did he promise something?"

"Yes, that I would yet have troubles but that the harvest would be good."

"Well, is there any evil in that?" Sabina thought not. "So, what would you like to know?" There they were again, back at the beginning.

Sabina puzzled for a moment and then knew. "Nothing I don't already see. I feel drawn to report this vision, this dream, these fevered thoughts to my bishop. Though I am not sure why."

"Perhaps he needs to know, though, perhaps, you need be wary of his interpretations since you'll not receive a reply." Sequia knew that much about Augustine. They would talk of him again that night, but not just yet.

Sabina understood that no answer would come from Augustine, but she was attempting that which her heart told her to do, sitting under the olives once again, trying to put into words something she was not quite convinced of, perhaps, did not exactly believe that she had even seen or experienced. Still, a quality of kindness and gentle sweetness, since she had recalled the dream while sitting with Sequia, had since surrounded the memory, something like the lilting breeze she now felt warming her cheek, assuring her that the visitor existed and was good, telling her that she must let someone higher that she or Sequia know.

Since her return to the convent in October, transporting freshly milled flour that filled the wagons, she had off and on again struggled to put into *sermo humilis*, plain Latin, what she felt and what she'd seen. "April is nearly over, a half year spent, and now, I must write," she thought. But words would not come. It was like trying to recall a pain once it had passed, she thought. Instead, she mulled over her long ago talk with Sequia about her secret and silent father:

Sabina had asked her daughter, "I feel it, but why would Augustine need to know about my poor vision? He has more important business than my dreams."

"Do you think knowing would help him in his struggles?" Sequia was well aware of the troubles of the African church. She had friends enough of all persuasions—even some quiet pagan believers—who felt free to discuss the issues, without, of course, offending those of a different creed.

"I don't know what to think, but I feel it."

"Is he doing the good he at first set out to accomplish?"

Sabina remained quiet. She knew the answer but hesitated to say. Then a rush of feeling welled up, and she did not stop herself. "When we first met, he was fearless and excitable. He wanted to find truth and to share it with everyone. He loved the world, all creation, and all those who people it. His presence felt sometimes like a lightning storm, sometimes like a warm-flowing river."

"And what is he like now?"

"I hardly know." She thought of the decades of his silence. "How old are you, thirty-eight?" It had been nearly forty years since they had parted. "I listen. I read. I talk to others." She fell silent, but Sequia, perhaps knowing she would continue, simply watched her mother search for words.

"No, he no longer loves the world, nor very many in it. I believe that he now fears it. In his mind, the world is evil, a devil's playground."

Sabina could see his early, hopeful words. It was true, the bishop's gaze was on heaven and his duty to the church, but he kept glancing warily at the earth. "Now he finds snakes enough to wrestle with." What had changed? Was it simply the passage of time, she wondered? No. Something else.

"When your brother died, so suddenly, so young, your father despaired. Before we laid Adeodatus to rest, I had never seen him so unsure, so beaten down, so guilt-ridden in all the twenty years since he chose me for his own. Your brother's death changed the man I had known." Sabina reached back to the funeral of her son, the first time in nearly three years she had seen her mate, her only man. "I was drawn to him, not for myself but because he needed comfort.

"Monnika had died not long after she had sent me away from him. Now, Adeodatus was snatched early from life.

"I went to him to soothe his wounds, to show that all was not lost."

Sequia knew, had heard the story before. "And he, this still young scholar, lately turned Catholic accepted your embrace and lay in your arms."

"For three days."

"Yes, then he rose and left."

"Left you inside me."

They clasped each other's hands.

Sabina continued. "He did not look back ever again. He had been transformed by death, was riddled with guilt, both for stumbling over his vows and for, through his doubt, blaspheming God who had taken his son.

"Yes," Sabina added, "he left in shame."

"But you felt no shame."

"No. He has been my only man. Even though I had vowed to remain celibate, lying with him was no sin for me."

"He had been with others."

"Yes. And I have you, my darling girl. A comfort in this life."

Her affirmation had faded in the moonlight that night. Sequia had risen and lifted her into an embrace. "The world is too beautiful to hate. When you have the strength, write your letter."

Still, she had not. Whispered danger forbade it.

The week in Thagaste after her arrival, with the harvest going very well, the three women, including Ia this time, joined a large crowd in the cave where they shared the communion with all those assembled. Sequia presided over the assembly. And when all were ready to listen to her brief sermon, Sabina spoke as *Tizem*, the lioness:

We are blessed in this company. From one, the living Christ, come many, and our many truly are, here, one. To this gathering all are welcome and blessed, bringing what they have, leaving with something new which Jesus Christ has bid us share:

"sic enim dilexit Deus mundum ut Filium suum unigenitum daret ut omnis ui credit in eum non pereat sed habeat vitam aeternam.

For God so loved the world, as to give his only begotten Son: that whosoever believeth in him may not perish, but may have life everlasting."

The words are handed down, yes, through the fathers, but also through the many of the desert, through the church, yes, but also through the worshipers, down from the thrones of bishops, yes, but also from the women of faith. Let all honor Him who would speak through us. And so, too, must you speak for yourselves, not only in response, but in harmony with your spirit.

You ask, "What of the miracle in the desert of which we have heard? Tell us." So, yes, let us speak of it.

"I tell you this that you may know yourself." [1]

Young and bereft, I found myself with child, that from a holy man. Separate, I was called, carrying that child, to the desert, to an oasis, in the early summer when the nights on the house roof are yet passing cool for sleeping. In those months late at night appeared a great sending of stars, shooting across the desert sky. Night after night for the longest time they flew fast over the horizon. Of course, as I did, you wonder that this could be sustained and what it might mean.

---

1 How Sabina came to know the gnostic texts and the canonical texts so well, I could not discover. I was not allowed to peruse the con vent library.

What came to my mind was as a gospel says, "When a blind man and one who sees are both together in darkness, they are no different from one another. When the light comes, then he who sees will see the light, and he who is blind will remain in darkness."

And still, I wondered.

Then, near the end of my labors, when my child came forth, as she made her first cry, that night the full harvest moon rose large over the desert. Luna in her fullness at that moment spoke to me as clearly as I now speak to you, "Of all gifts love is the greatest. Adore this child who will in greatness carry that love."

To those who dwell in the desert birth at the rising of a full moon is brilliance and quietude, wholeness and encirclement, belonging and love.

It is said, "Unto you is given the mystery of the kingdom of God: but unto them that are without, all things are done in parables. That they may see, and not perceive."

At that birth on a desert rooftop, light became manifest in sound, and two were born. One turned fully to the living Christ, albeit, like the bits of stars, little by little. The other was born in sound and light, the follower of God, even fatherless, given her purpose at birth. And that, as you can see here and now, is the miracle in the desert.

When I am gone, think on this and live accordingly, remembering what Thomas has told us, "Seek and do not stop seeking until you find."

Live, believers, side by side. Open your door to light. Listen in expectation and stay your ireful hand that every one may enter.

Now, go you all in peace.

Tizem disappeared then from the meeting, leaving Sabina once again herself.

Afterwards, at Sequia's house, mother, daughter, and Ia met and talked of the evening.

"You were radiant, *Tizem*," Ia said.

Sequia nodded. "Each ear listened intently, rapt."

"There were a great many," Sabina said.

"You met some of the Thagastans. Did any remember you?" Sequia asked.

Her mother thought a moment, then answered, "I met a good number, but most who knew me years ago are dead. A few were curious, perhaps too inquisitive. I did not see the light of Christ in their eyes."

Ia stirred and shuffled her feet.

"What did you hear, my sister?" Sabina asked.

"I was questioned," Ia offered.

Sabina took her hand. "Tell us. Please."

"One of the Thagastans wondered how we could practice open communion. 'Is it not mixing water and wine? Especially, inviting Arians?' He asked."

Sabina frowned. "And your reply?"

"I told him I was a simple Christian, not a theologian. I said, 'We bring all to the portals of Christ's words.'"

"A wise answer," Sequia said. She smiled on Ia, but said to her mother, "I see the hand of Alypius in this."

"And likely that of the bishop of Hippo Regius behind him," Sabina said. "It is to be expected."

That had been the first sign. Back at the convent, all the wheat flour having been stored and Advent nearly over, Ia in her timid fashion, again, tinkled an alarm bell once more.

"*Tizem*, I am troubled."

Sabina listened hard, for Ia used her familiar name.

"I have seen that same Thagastan who questioned me at the communion. He is here amongst the refugees."

Ia's *materfamilias* and friend smiled kindly. "Even those who pose questions can flee to us."

Ia was troubled. "Yes, *Tizem*, but the man suddenly turned away when he saw me and tried to hide his face. I thought it strange."

Sabina nodded. "We must leave room for the doubts of others," she said, but she felt suddenly awash in the words of her dream: "Be wary of the serpent."

So, she did not find strength to write even after Christmas.

Not long after, in January, the Bishop of Thagaste, Alypius, the closest bishop to Augustine called upon Sabina at the convent. It was unusual to see him although they had known each other in Cassiciacum before her return to Africa when Augustine and his academic circle lived as philosophers at that villa. Still, Sabina was startled that he had come. But since Alypius had always been kind and because he was more worldly than Augustine, many times traveling between Africa and Ravenna in the last forty years, he was pleasant and diplomatic. He had come to the convent before, likely at Augustine's request, once when the bishop's sister had died and a new *materfamilias* was to be chosen. Since then, he irregularly came to see how all went, but this visit was different.

"I come, I'm afraid, out of concern. These are troubling times," Alypius said.

Sabina was not clear on his meaning but replied in her encouraging way, "We have celebrated a great harvest, both at our granaries and our chapel. Is it not good that many now enter the services of Christ?"

"I am happy for the harvest. In Thagaste, too, the great bounty is welcomed," he said, "but I wonder if all who now crowd your gates and yards should be so welcomed."

The *materfamilias* thought on this ominous claim. Not just at the convent, but in the whole of Hippo Regius, large numbers had fled to safety in advance of the Vandal movements. Among them, Sabina knew, was at least one Thagastan, one who had not earned her trust, but she would say nothing about that man to this bishop. "We are careful, but still welcome as many as we can afford to feed and shelter," she told Alypius.

The bishop of Thagaste considered this, then went further. "Even in Thagaste, we have a dangerous mixing of people from far-off parts, some not of the Church—I suspect some Donatists and even pagans from the desert try to blend in with our parishioners."

Was Alypius trying to unsettle her? His word "dangerous" seemed out of place to Sabina. "I'm sure they look for safe haven in these troubles."

"As they may, but still we cannot enjoin all to our worship unless they are baptized in the Church."

Sabina would not argue that point with a bishop. "I see your concern." She stopped there waiting for Alypius to lead.

Alypius became plainer. "Especially in open communion sharing the Eucharist with these strangers is not allowed. Arians in particular look to enter in as their practices are similar. That is certainly not to be done."

Sabina wondered if he meant worship at the convent or among the *Christicolae* in his own Thagaste. She would test her acquaintance. "Must each, then, be questioned? We have hundreds."

This most diplomatic of bishops softened immediately. "No, no. That would interfere with your work. I speak only out of concern for you." The bishop paused as if thinking, then said, "So far, I have not discussed my fears with your bishop. He has been very busy. We only ask that you be vigilant."

Why Alypius used "we" Sabina did not ask. In any understanding of his statement, though, the bishop had included Augustine and perhaps the entirety of African bishops, perhaps the general Church. His mention of Thagaste could have been meant to soften the message by spreading out the worry or might be intended to signify his knowledge of the *Christicolae* outside of his city. It was certainly possible that Alypius knew about her own speech and her attendance at the open communion Sequia held.

Having delivered his cautions, Alypius appeared ready to leave, but he stood for a moment at the doorway, as if he had more. "There is one other concern."

Sabina waited. The bishop of Thagaste spoke uncertainly. "There has been talk, loose rumors, regarding the appearance of a 'miracle child,' one born fatherless in the desert, one, some say, destined to lead our African church." There, Alypius halted and set his gaze directly on Sabina. "It is said to be a woman."

"Not a child?" Sabina said.

Alypius corrected himself. "No, they say she is now grown and leads worship in the countryside. Have you not heard?"

"Yes, something, but I pay little attention, being occupied with my work here at the convent."

"Beware. Report anything you hear immediately."

The warning, if that was what it was, halted any willingness to speak with Alypius and further dampened any enthusiasm she had to write Augustine. By the time the bishop of Thagaste was gone, Sabina had already decided to wait to write her letter.

And perhaps that was not bad, for long about the end of February came a letter from Sequia in which she included a letter from Julian of Eclanum who was now finding favor in Constantinople under the protection of Nestorius. His letter to Sequia encouraged her in the ministry she had chosen, asked for prayers for his restoration to his bishopric, and hinted at a favorable intercession with Augustine whom he said he had gravely injured.

Sequia had corresponded much with Julian since she had met and been influenced by Caelestius in her youth, just as had Julian, and thought to ask her mother to write to Augustine, saying that Julian had admitted wronging him.

Instead, Sabina wrote back cautioning her daughter that the African bishops were alerted to rumors of heresy there and were looking to make an example of someone. Who better than a confederate of Julian who, until recently, had been condemned and was without support?

"Our work here is enough. Please avoid entangling yourself in far-off political fights. Remain at peace, my daughter."

Soon, yet a fourth concern arose, but this one encouraged Sabina to write to Bishop Augustine. The horror of what had happened so near to their lives in Hippo finally gave Sabina reason, even after so long a time, six months, to send Augustine a plea and also to reveal her Thagastan dream. After half a year, she would finally write.

Sabina began her letter in a roundabout way. With the news that would get the bishop's attention. "I have received a worrisome report. It comes from the sisters who had sought refuge from the Vandals in

Portus Magnus and then had to flee once more."

It had been Ia's youngest sister who in the middle of the night clanged the convent bell as if there were a fire. The sisters who answered the call had to carry her to Ia's cell where she babbled incessantly and wept uncontrollably. "They came at night." She wailed again. "Horrible men. Threw women out of the house. Before our very eyes, they cudgeled the good bishop Regianus. They threatened to slay him with a long sword. And then they took him away." The woman shook. She shivered.

"Bring blankets. Stir the fire," Sabina had said, taking charge. It was late March then but cold at night. "You poor woman. The things you've seen. Who were these? Barbarians?"

"Strangers. Not from the desert," she sobbed. "Our fishmonger led us to his boat. We set out in the dark of night. Days ago. We wanted to come here, for safety, with Ia." Again, she broke down.

So, Sabina wrote: "Their community had been harried by a group of barbarians—not those of the desert, but newcomers, marching tall and fair, or on horse, small and dark, marauding and demanding treasure. The community first escaped Ad Fratres by sea at night, a terror in itself—she knew the bishop would agree as he hated the sea even during the day. They landed after two nights at sea at Portus Magnus, where soon they were again attacked. Others have carried the word here that even more pillagers are afoot, heading east. I write out of concern for my sisters in Christ who are asking me what they should do, where they should go, or if they should stay and pray the Lord will either keep them safe or open wide the doors to martyrdom.

"I shared my feeling," she continued, "that no ill should come to them. That *Comes Africae* will protect us all, or failing that, that God will make his will known.

"You may say, 'You write in a calming voice.' And I respond that my sense of peace even amongst news of murder and invasion emanates from a dream in which a very old man appeared, promising a good harvest. The harvest was good, better than any other year I've known, and leads me to believe that the Lord will provide." Sabina continued, telling each detail, her sickness, Ia's nursing, her fever and wakefulness, the old man, his words, and the feeling of calm that pervaded his visit.

She again wrote, "I should soon again write to the sisters who fled Portus Magnus but wanted to wait to hear from a higher authority what I might say."

She felt, then, the beneficence of the strange visitation, how it had gained her a new courage and faith in the fairness and tranquility of Christian life. Am I deceived? I know the bishop warns us of the evil that roams the earth—he has grown afraid as well as old—of innocents suffering in a hell horrible beyond imagination. Oh, Augustine, where did your learning and love lead you?

Sabina knew of the bishop's fight with Julian of Eclanum. What was well known, and worried over by all from Thagaste, to Hippo, to Carthage, was that the Italian bishop had accused Augustine of a long-standing Manichean bent, accusing him of the very heresy he'd spent years hounding down for believing that evil owned the earth sowing disease, pain, war, want, and early death.

She wrote: "I see now that the evil of war and destruction have beset our land. But, please, tell us that it is not God-sent punishment for our sins. Tell us of the comfort our Lord will provide. He bade us love one another. Even if these marauders are not Christian, perhaps we can turn them to the good."

She stopped. It was the bishop himself she wanted to turn to good. The fear that Ia's sister cried was only terror. That, like the moon, changes if love still grows in a heart.

She wrote more, "Perhaps it is not our sin but our fear of a difficult path that brings on these dark times." That was enough for one who could not expect a reply.

"You are very far away," Ia said. "I've been sitting here shelling peas, and you never noticed. Look! My bowl is full."

Sabina smiled a bit confused. "Yes, I've been following my thoughts along many shores. I'd forgotten myself. How does Una, your sister?"

"In the day, she is fine, but nights are fearful for her now. They were at sea in utter darkness, and, of course, had to run for their lives."

"Thank providence that she came this far unharmed. Her poor bishop—oh, I must add that news to my letter." Sabina turned once more to her message. Then she stopped herself. "I am afraid that this terror that seizes Una has unsettled me as well."

"Did you tell me that your night visitor promised a good harvest, but also that your troubles are not ended?"

"Yes, perhaps this is what he meant."

12

Gaiseric Out-foxes Darius

The Vandal column stretched for miles, and the dust it raised billowed into its own yellowish, stretched cloud that drifted out toward Mare Mediterraneo, then blew in behind them and west like a loose sail ruffling in the air. The campaign was moving along. The day before, the main group, including provisions, livestock, women, artisans, fighters, and children covered nearly six miles toward Portus Magnus. The pace through these lean districts had to be brisk. Later, when there was more to glean along the way and more business to conduct with the populace, they would not move even half that fast.

Gaiseric rode tall and stately as he imagined a Roman count might sit. He was flanked on his left by his *magistrum equitum*, master of horse, the highest-ranking Alan, an excellent rider himself, and on his right by his cousin, Gelimmer, his *magister militum*, his general, who was nearly always by his side. Following these three were fifty mounted Vandals and Alans and after, a thousand foot soldiers carrying their rations and equipment, followed by a multitude of ox carts and more of smaller push carts, pairs of stevedores carrying covered sides of meat or baskets of bread or fish on pikes, then by another thousand infantry bringing up the rear. Stretched along the wide Roman road leading from Ad Fratres to Portus Magnus, were more of the same: his captains leading cavalry to keep the pace brisk, then foot soldiers, carrying their own corn and hardtack as well as weapons and tools were followed by heavier provisions in carts, and more on foot, again and again and again, as many as twenty-five of the same formation. In the middle of each four-file ensemble, the women and children drove the livestock and carried skins of water and wine, leading oxcarts filled with all sorts of cooking jars and portable hearths from which jangling and clacking cooking utensils dangled. Other carts were loaded with sides of ox and cow and horse for roasting that evening. Many carried baskets of fish netted off the shore from Vandal boats. There were thousands of mouths to feed. The land and sea could provide some things, but the people of the Roman province of Mauretania Caesariensis would have to provide the rest.

All along the route, sometimes a mile or sometimes as much as four away from the columns, scroungers worked in groups of twenty, loading wood from nearby hillsides and pillage if they found anything in villages or villas they came across. Each group included four mounted soldiers and a number of ox carts. These parties followed the main group, catching up toward evening when what they'd gathered was needed.

In the distance ahead Gaiseric could see the dust raised by some of the vanguards of his army, two groups of a hundred horsemen, one north, one south, sent to commandeer provisions, to scout the very few Roman protectors, who were usually hiding within the villages themselves, and to make their presence felt. Gaiseric instructed his calvary captains directly: If you sow fright and terror, most will flee for their lives, leaving all goods behind. Those with carts and animals you'll have to ride down. Kill but few, but do so publicly that all will be afraid and do your will. Enslave no one unless you find value in their person. Slaves are unruly and are difficult to feed. Those you capture sell to the Moors, but bring the leaders and clergy to me.

Gaiseric had already lost some good men. Ulfa, who had spoken against this crossing and journey, had not been wrong, especially about his own fate. Of the many trips back and forth over March and April, Ulfa's ship was one of the last to leave and in good weather, too. But when it cleared to the open sea of the strait, a huge black squall flew in from the Atlantic and Ulfa's ship foundered and capsized. Only Ulfa's cousin Ulman and a grandson, Ulfasson, survived, one hanging on to a partly emptied wineskin, the other to a capsized dinghy. It was Gaiseric's own ship, following closely behind, that picked the boy and Ulman out of the sea. Immediately Gaiseric named the youth to be of his household. He carried no hard feelings for Ulfa. Ulfa's ship was not the only one lost. A few lives and

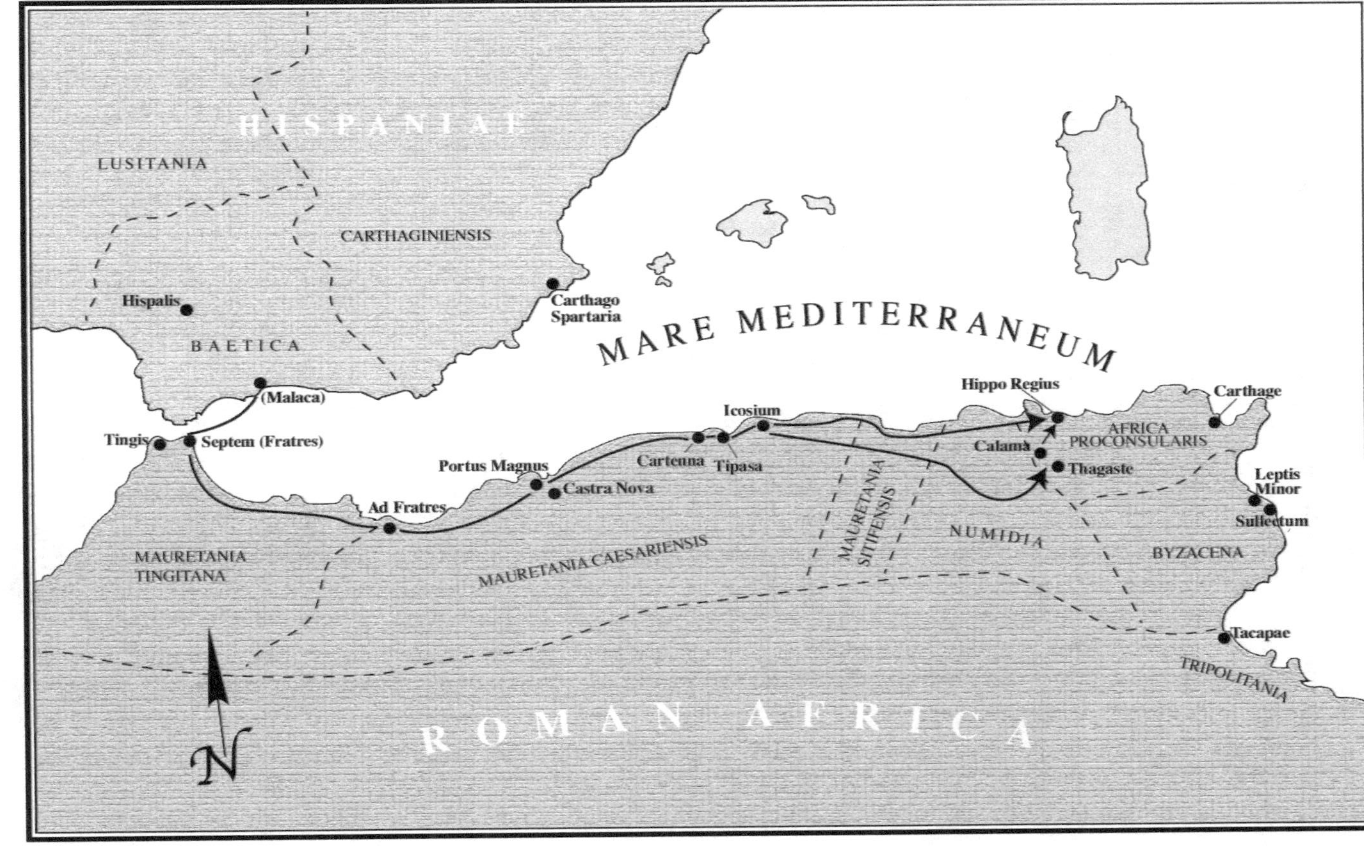

The Path of the Vandals, 429 -430 A.D.

livestock went to the bottom of the sea. Most, though, had landed safely near Septem Fratres and further east.

The land had not lain empty, and many whom Gaiseric joined there were Vandals and Alans who had settled in Africa in past years to trade with their kinsmen at Hispalis in Baetica. Those Moors and Berbers who had lived across the strait from ancient days, even before the Punic peoples, knew the Vandals already and, if they were alarmed at the increase of numbers—more than ten times their former population—they were either soothed by the promise of a soon-to-come eastward movement, or other than those who joined the horde, took to the mountains to watch what would happen. The few Roman soldiers stationed in the province of Mauretania Tingitana, who were responsible for keeping the peace, fled, many to Ad Fratres or farther east to Icosium.

Gaiseric had said in council: "Do not judge by what you see here. The riches of Africa lie to the east and shall increase with each day's march." He spread around more of the gold Bonifacius had sent, part of the second chest, placing items in his earls' hands to soothe their tired complaints that he'd overheard at table after they drank the African wine that had come into their grasp. He would not join in loose talk to the greater council, but his plans were fixed, albeit changeable, as the need arose. The king would share those ideas only with his closest kin, with the Alan *magistrum equitum*, and a chosen few of Siling Vandals who had followed him.

At night he roamed the encampments beside the Roman road, visiting the fires, making sure provisions were available and not misused. Gaiseric was not himself a road builder or a maker of anything but boats and tents, but he often told those gathered around a fire in the summer night that they should give praise and thanks to whatever god they chose for the labors of Roman slaves paving the Vandal way to better lands ahead. On these evening visits, cantering along the road, he brought, among his bodyguard and retinue of kinsmen, his *scope* who offered at least one song to every camp. One he sang in praise of Gaiseric but also telling of the crossing and recent victories over Sueves and Romans alike. At each of these camps, the king, standing amongst his powerful men, simply watched. He looked out for allies, friends, and most importantly, strength which he would need when he met Bonifacius in battle. For Gaiseric knew that it would come to that and beating *Comes Africae* would leave but two battles to wage: the war of minds with Augustine and the fight for Carthage. It was the first that he had to plan, for once Augustine fell Africa entirely including its capital would follow. And the capture of Bishop Regianus from Ad Fratres proved most helpful to his plot.

His men had first seen the bishop while he was trying to bury the chalices and crosses of his church. The vanguard brought that small treasure with the bishop and threw both at Gaiseric's feet. "*Bisainan alhs awistir*, Behold the church's sheepfold," meaning the bishop's treasure. They then pushed the prelate down into his silver. Gunter struck the man.

"Leave off," the king said. He strode forward and looked down on the prelate.

"You were found burying this silver, is that not so?" Gaiseric demanded.

The priest, guarding his head with up raised arms, trembled, shaking amongst his holy vessels and implements. "Only as I was instructed to do," he said, adding, "my lord." Gaiseric kicked the man savagely in the stomach, following him as the presbyter crawled through his silver, trying to roll away.

"Your cudgel, Gunter," and now in a rage, Gaiseric swung the heavy club striking the man over and over. Finally, his anger subsided. Regianus, now bleeding and broken, begged for mercy and promised a greater treasure.

"Something better than silver, more valuable than gold."

"Tell me what you mean."

"I will, I will. But please don't beat me more."

"Drag him to my tent," Gaiseric said. "I will hear of this treasure myself."

Gelimmer and Gunter dragged the presbyter, howling in pain, along by his arms and, when they arrived at Gaiseric's quarters, dropped him to the ground. They stood, waiting to hear, but the king said, "Leave us now. I shall be in no danger." The two eyed each other but did as they were asked.

"Come in. Sit," he told his prisoner. The man did so, groaning as he moved forward and lifted himself up. "Your pain shall soon enough leave you," Gaiseric promised. "Drink." He offered the bishop the African wine. "It is quite good, from Tingitana."

Regianus reached cautiously for the cup his captor offered as if he expected to be pummeled again. Gaiseric sat and stared at the man. "So, what is this you have to say?"

The man wiped his mouth on his sleeve and caught his breath. "You march to Carthage."

"Who says?" Gaiseric roared.

Regianus covered his head with his arms. He cowered, saying, "I assume, of course. But where else would one go? Perhaps to Hippo, but not to dwell very long."

Gaiseric as was his wont said nothing. He waited.

"Well, whether it is to Carthage or not, you will likely encounter the Bishop of Hippo Regius, my overseer. He is a worthy opponent, perhaps greater than *Comes Africae* himself."

"We will defeat both."

"With one, I can be of help."

Gaiseric watched, saying nothing.

"The bishop fears three things: an Arian conversion, the destruction of his Church, and a simple truth about his life. It is with the last that I can help."

"Say," the king commanded.

"In his famous *Testamentum*, CONFESSIONS, he does not tell us all. Some things are glossed over, many not revealed, and others still ignored."

"I have read the book. So?"

"He fears this truth."

"What truth?"

"At the time of the death of his son, Augustine conceived with his sometime concubine another child, a girl, whom he has never acknowledged. The threat to this wheedling truth of his might be useful in mastering the man."

Gaiseric considered the case. His thoughts ran along this line: It is not the foe with the strongest arm who is to be feared, but the foe with the strongest mind. An opponent's lies, especially those exposed, weaken his *möd-ge-ðaenk*, thinking and plans.

"And where might one find this girl?"

"She is a woman now—her mother still lives in the cloister of Hippo Regius—but the girl herself abides in Thagaste on her dead grandfather's farm."

"And her name?"

"She goes by *Sequidei*, follower of God. Everyone knows her as Sequia. She is well-liked and chaste, but bishop Augustine thinks her a heretic. She shelters Donatists, pagans, and," looking carefully at the king now, "Arians, too." As if to add fuel to his weakling fire Regianus whispered, "It is said she preaches from the gospels."

Gaiseric watched the man. Some of what he told might be true. He would find out. This man, though, if he so easily would betray his famous superior, could not be trusted nor kept close, and he could not be let go.

"Is it your will to change to our faith?" Gaiseric put it bluntly.

The Catholic bishop did not hesitate. "Why yes, we are much the same. I have Arians among my flock. Would I then lead my little church again, in Ad Fratres?" Gaiseric found Regianus shameless.

"We shall see."

The Vandal king said nothing of this betrayal of Augustine but later sent an eastern Berber who had joined his army to spy out the bishop's daughter, Sequia. He would learn what he needed to know.

When he called in Gunter and Gelimmer who had waited close by, outside the tent, he told them, "Find this man some help. And arrange with our own bishop for this one's baptism in Portus Magnus. When we arrive there, Regianus wishes to publicly renounce his Catholic faith."

And that is what they did in the presence of a crowd of the bishop's former parishioners. Regianus was not, however, named bishop of anything. Within a week, he was discovered, they told Gaiseric afterward, stealing a chalice from the altar of the new Arian church set up in the old Catholic space. Then, Regianus suffered a public beheading following his shaming in the local arena.

Gaiseric had much to think on and did not give thought to the fate of Regianus-the-foreswearer. For his treachery, his dishonesty, theft, and weakness, Gaiseric told his kinsmen, there is no place for such a man.

The Vandal army crept forward. It was more than an army. Composed of clans that for years had moved together by mutual assent, it moved as a nation, sometimes three, four, or more miles a day. Then some days less than two. At Castra Nova, an emissary from Bonifacius, Darius was his name, sent word that he would like to meet Gaiseric outside the town at a villa of one Honoratus.

"One would expect this. He sends a silver-tongued serpent in place of an army." All this told Gaiseric that Bonifacius was weak. Then he told his cousin, Gelimmer, "Take but few men, find this place, and watch for three days. If it is safe, send for me. I will meet this Roman."

And they did meet.

Following a small vanguard of Roman soldiers in full regalia, Gaiseric rode through the Roman town of Castra Nova with his retinue of earls and one hundred of his best fighters, a force much larger than the *bucellarii* Bonifacius has sent to escort Darius. The king of the Vandals feared only the perfidy of his own kind but knew a show of force would speak loudly to the Roman, Darius.

Though the town was not large, it impressed Gaiseric with its trim, straight streets, some quiet residential ways, others broad thoroughfares lined with shops and artisans' workspaces. Gaiseric dismounted to walk these roads paved in the Roman way with wide flat stones and lined by raised pedestrian walks, one on either side.

Along one spacious road, the Vandal king halted his march to watch Roman athletes wrestling on a huge colonnaded yard. His earls, still mounted, spoke quietly both in admiration and derision of the fighters' grips and skillful moves. The wrestlers largely ignored the sight of foreigners in their town but stole a timid look or two at those whom they called barbarians, moving through in formation.

Not far from this square, the Vandal file passed the baths and further on an odeon, its red exterior painted with scenes from plays and entertainments produced in the theater. At the corner where they would turn to mount the hill to the villa of Honoratus, Gaiseric came off his horse and entered a shop where he paid from his own purse for sausages fresh-made and for cured olives, both gifts for his Roman host. The king remounted, secured his purchases in saddle bags, and led his men out of the town on the *Decumanus Maximus*, the great highway.

His men had acquitted themselves well, keeping a stern and fierce decorum as they filed through Castra Nova, but now on the open road, they joked and laughed about the fear they saw in the peoples' eyes, as well as about the goods they saw and desired. Gaiseric, too, saw much that he wanted, but less of merchandise and riches than of the way of life and accomplishments of a race. He admired the efficiency and elegance of the town's design. He had seen many a town, mostly sacked and ruined by his own armies, but this one, though timorous and subdued by the Vandal presence, was alive and working. Trade and creation of goods were flourishing everywhere. To the long-wandering king, the playthings the townspeople enjoyed so casually—stately streets and roads, tall houses and public squares, athletic games, theater, music, well-cooked foods including pastries he had never seen before—told him of a civilization that had not only conquered but had also built in the wake of its wars.

As the column rode into the hills, Gaiseric ruminated on the accomplishments of the Roman mind. For it is not the weapons or force, the king thought, that create what I've just seen, even in this small town, but the unity of a people and the power of the will. The conception of this city formed its stones. The town did not grow of itself but was planned. I am weary, he thought, of simple pillaging and constant travel. We are no better than the desert nomads, forced to move in order to live and to maraud in order to prosper, never still enough to construct, create, and build. We have destroyed towns and cities but have not planned and built them. It is *that* I long for.

Gaiseric thought in much detail of the civilization his people could build now in comparison with that the Romans had accomplished. He desired to rule a society, a culture more permanent than that he knew and shared with his earls. The Roman town became in Gaiseric's mind a model for a Vandal city, the *alþingi*, the beginning of a senate, and the men following him to the villa one of many legions of a Vandal empire.

Once at the house of Honoratus, it was not the villa in itself but the graciousness and intelligence of Darius, his host, that lifted Gaiseric's hopes, not for a settlement even though the place was sumptuous, promising of more wealth beyond, but for the order and civility that could be learned from Romans like this one. For in the king's mind was much more than pillaging, battle, and booty. Gaiseric now harbored thoughts of a lasting kingdom spread across Africa.

The house was open and light, appointed with the Corinthian columns favored by the Romans of those days, decorated with hunting mosaics that spread fowl, rabbit, deer and their hunters across the floors like the life of the forests themselves, and filled with sounds of water, which ran everywhere, tinkling, gushing, bubbling and flowing while keeping its presence lightly in the back of the mind. In a dry land, Gaiseric thought, water truly was life itself. Looking at the house, Gaiseric immediately understood two things: first, this villa had been selected from a list of many other but lesser houses and second, that stories of the wealth of Africa that he had heard much of his life were not exaggerated. The king of the Vandals also knew from his experience that any house, no matter its size or beauty could easily be pulled down.

"*Salve amici Bonifatius.*" Gaiseric's host greeted him as a friend of Bonifacius. "*Salutatio, mea te Comes Africae et a Valentinian, suam de manu regis Roma,* the count sends his greetings under the welcome from Valentinian, emperor of all of Rome." Gaiseric understood that the emperor was just ten years old, that he did not yet know the name Gaiseric, and that his mother had not been told of the presence of his people in Africa. That last revelation would have been unwise.

He replied in good Latin, "*Salutatio consilio rex Vandalorum. Placeo mihi in occursum adventus sui,*" and translated his greeting immediately for his men, "The Vandal *alþingi* and king salute you. I am pleased to meet you." His facility with the language set Darius on his heels, but the Roman was quick to recover with an invitation to the meal that the cooks of Honoratus had prepared.

The feast, for that was the only word by which it could be described, was elaborate, set out beautifully, and to the Vandal men with him, Gaiseric knew, was an invitation to staunch the hunger earned by long and dreary travel. Despite the sumptuousness of the board, Gaiseric wasted no shame but proudly presented his purchases to Darius who, of course, graciously accepted them and had them placed among the varied dishes served.

Even Gaiseric had never seen white bread, accompanying several wines and set with olives, grapes, and black currants. More familiar brown and black loaves stood cut on the table. There were cooked eggs, goodly cheeses, pots of honey sweet and fragrant. The table was set with milk, figs, and pears. He saw purple carrots lying beside sausages, roasted duck and goose; there were oysters and snails laid among the other foods everywhere. Darius swept his arm toward the long board, "Eat your fill. Drink. Then we shall talk." He guided their gaze to apples, quinces, pears, strawberries, plums, melons, cherries, which Gaiseric had never seen, and apricots, an exotic delicacy. Some fruits were dried, others fresh.

Gaiseric warned his men in Vandalic: "Partake sparingly. We have riding to do."

Darius floated along the table pointing and saying, "Try this mullet. Have you eaten dormice? They are an outlawed delicacy in Ravenna. Here we have veal slaughtered and roasted just today, and these oysters are good both for digestion and virility."

Gaiseric took the lead: a cup of wine, and small portions of the eight or ten dishes Darius had mentioned. It was obvious this was very much a trial of wit and culture, and the Vandal king wanted to learn as much as possible about this Roman and the lordly place from which he came. His Vandal men followed suit, sampling everything but not gorging as they would have wished.

They ate eggs, cheeses, honey and milk, ricotta buns, poppy seed bread, sweet cakes with honey, sausages, goose flesh, sweet buns with black currants, snails, and a host of fruits, fresh and dried.

Darius and several of his party ate huge quantities of everything. "My favorite is the duck with a little, very-hard-to-get lemon sauce, deep, rich, and sudden on the palate. A real surprise." Gaiseric added a slice to his plate and daubed on the sauce.

He tasted some. "It recalls red currants on black bread, but less sweet and sharper on the tongue," the king rejoined. Gaiseric better enjoyed the earthy vegetables, all fresh: radishes, asparagus, cooked parsnips roasted and dipped in honey (his favorite), green peas, fava beans, and chickpeas.

The two leaders talked, over their sampling and chewing. Each was sizing up the other as they spoke of the far-off lands they had traveled. Darius said nothing about business. "And now with *passum*, or with beer if you prefer," said Darius, "my personal cook's famous fruit tarts and sweet wine cakes. Food of the gods." He raised an eyebrow at the utterance of the pagan slogan. "The cakes are cinnamon, red wine, and honey, baked in a tender crust." Some of Gaiseric's kin asked for the beer, while their king sampled the sweet raisin wine. Every man ate cake and tarts.

The Roman emissary was not one to be rushed. The meal spent the greater part of the afternoon, and Darius recommended a nap before revealing his news. Gaiseric closed his eyes but stayed awake as a sentinel to any trouble that might arise. Snoring, some soft, some uproarious, was the only interruption that he perceived.

When it was time for business, Darius was direct.

"Time alters all," he opened.

"Yes, I have seen many changes even in my short life," Gaiseric said.

"Bonifacius values your service and your loyalty."

"We too, Vandals all, prize our friendship with Rome." He referred to the recent *foederati* arrangement.

"Yes," Darius said, "yet *Comes Africae* will not be attacked. He has restored the trust of Rome."

"Ah, then, no fleet from Italy shall come?"

"No, unless to carry home Sigisvultus and his men."

Gaiseric would not ask more. Let the Roman lay out his words as he had his victuals.

Darius did not wait longer. "We realize, with such a company as you have brought, somewhat larger than agreed upon, turning back is impossible. The original lands assigned you are east of Hippo and Carthage, too, neither of which you must pass."

The Vandal king watched his host and Imperial negotiator carefully. He would be wrong to attack the man or argue these sudden strictures set by the Roman general, Bonifacius. What would Darius now offer in compensation? Twenty shiploads of gold and silver could not buy the Vandals' way back to Hispania. Perhaps all of Numidia would not be enough if Gaiseric were so inclined. "So?" He asked.

"The count welcomes you and your peoples as neighbors and *foederati Romani*. For your intended service, he offers all the lands west of Mauritania Sitifensis as far east as Icosium. It is the count's wish that you use the lands well, stand to defend Bonifacius against aggressors, Moors and Berbers alike, and retain, if you so desire, your Arian faith although the count does not wish you to harm or convert the Catholics in your lands."

This last demand was obviously from the bishops of Hippo Regius and Carthage. We shall see was Gaiseric's thought. Since he was sure he had the upper hand, Gaiseric could too be gracious. "You, count Darius, have hosted us well. We thank you for the repast and rest. Tell the count of Africa that his offer is kind. We have no desire but to live in peace among friends. We, then, expect no forces to attack our advance to Icosium. We can defend Bonifacius against the desert peoples of our provinces as would any ally of Rome. Tell the count, please, that I and my council value our Arian faith and find it generous that we may keep it, and also say to him that the Catholics in our lands shall be free to worship as they wish without fear of violence or harm."

What Darius thought of his rather long speech, Gaiseric did not know. And as he told his council later, "I do not care. Our advance has so far been unopposed. Why should we expect anything else even up to the walls of Hippo Regius, far beyond these cities the Roman has now given us?"

Gelimmer spoke. "This province is large but will starve us into submission for its lack."

"True, my cousin, but Gaiseric has eyes for more. I would rather have Numidia by force than the status of hungry foederati."

A cheer went up from the earls, except, Gaiseric noted, from Ulman, who sought the ground with his eyes. But immediately the man felt his king's gaze upon him and spoke boldly, "Yes, to be allied to Rome right now is weak and senseless." The earls again hurrahed.

"I did not argue with Darius," Gaiseric announced. "I went there to understand."

He now knew. "The count of Africa has thrown a tasteless bone and expects the Vandal dog not to bite." The council erupted, but Gaiseric continued. "Darius will return to Carthage with his agreement, then he will sail to Ravenna with Sigisvultus leaving Africa to us. Bonifacius will once more turn to his concubines." All laughed.

"The Vandals will halt," the king of the Vandals said, "but it will not be for long."

13

Innomenatus, Called "Amicus"

Ignorance is a man's happiness, unless war rages around him. Then, he best have his bags packed and be ready to flee.[1]

I had been happy, well fed, and blissfully occupied at the count's villa, but I could not ignore the sounds of battle around the house, especially when *Comes Africae* himself involved me in the skirmish. The Ides of May arrived as did then a letter from our bishop, Augustine. Since Bonifacius had appointed me his personal secretary, I, of course, prepared the missive to read to the count, even though the message concerned my own stay with him. The bishop wanted me back. He cited his truly important work against the Pelagians, particularly Julian of Eclanum, the son of a former friend and prelate.

"It is of the utmost importance that bishops of the east, particularly Macedonia and Greece itself, stay informed on our efforts to contain and purge this most dangerous heresy which has now sprouted evil seed even in our own backyard. To do so, we must translate my letters and studies regarding these fallacious ideas into their language, Greek. Therefore, you must send my scribe back to the monastery at Hippo as soon as he can come. Send him with this letter, today if possible."

The count frowned at this request. "He well knows what we are up against. This Vandal presence must now be contained. The bishop's battle with heretics is of no importance in comparison." He strode around the room muttering. "I know what it is. Julian has called our friend Augustinus a donkey, actually, the head mule amongst asses." He laughed but then paced up and down in silence. "What could he

---

1 Despite having quoted this many a time, or because I have so often, I have not been able to recall for years where I first heard it. Perhaps it is age that hides the name of the man. I do know I said it in Dacia, in Gothic, while I was doing my translations of Luke amongst those new Arian Christians. This tells me I learned it there or perhaps in Alexandria shortly after the death of the patriarch Athanasius who had many occasions to keep his bags packed for the cyclical banishments and returns he made. In any case, the saying has served me well and has often led me ahead of impending storms that began sweeping through the empire even before my birth and will likely continue long past my death.

mean by this taking root in Africa?"[2]

Now, Bonifacius is a sturdily built, soldierly man, and carries himself in tight formation, but in his pacing, with each step, he became even more rigid. His shoulders tightened beneath his tunic, stretching the fabric across his back, and the heels of his sandals scraped the floor with each successive step. Finally, he came to a stop and having thought of an effective reply to the bishop's command said, "Reply to our bishop. Say this: 'The needs of the church will be best served with the protection of the military authority here, as you yourself, my Bishop, have often pointed out to me. Since in this case, he is performing work in the interest and benefit of all Africans, I cannot yet honor your request for the return of your scribe.' I will tell him no more, for he will twist whatever I say to his purpose."

Bonifacius was not wrong, for he had just then said enough to fan a lick of flame into a conflagration. In two days, a rather short time for all that was said, the presbyter shot back, "The needs and the authority of the Church outstrip all armies, all war, and all that you might call protection. Am I to enlist both the authority of God the Father and of those who will only too willingly listen at the court of Valentinian and his mother? I cannot think that it would be good for you to receive orders from Ravenna which you in your newfound accord with the Emperor would most truly have to obey. Therefore, send my scribe to me or provide actual and true reasons for your dalliance." Well, no need to go on though the bishop did, *ad infinitum*, and had said plenty as a preamble as well.

"Read the excerpts only," the count said. "I do not want to hear it all."

Truthfully, I had not read it all myself. The intent was clear, threatening.

"I will not be accosted by a holy man, especially in military matters. Tell him this: 'In the very near future, we will send Count Darius, whom you know and who brokered peace with Sigisvultus

---

2 I had no idea that Sequia of whose existence I was ignorant at the time had carried on correspondence with the upstart Julian. She was, I came to know, very much sprouting and, perhaps, spouting dissension in Thagaste although she could hardly call her father, even in secret, an ass. That Augustine knew of the connection is less surprising than that he stayed his hand in swatting this heretical fly. Perhaps his heart *was* tender after all he had inflicted on Sequia's mother already.

and Rome on my behalf, to negotiate a halt of the Vandal advance.'"

Bonifacius detailed his plan, including some of the incentives he planned to give the barbarian king and closed, "Until the mission of Darius is complete, I will need the services of your scribe."

The friend-of-my-youth who had always recognized opportunity, whether it was presented or was hidden from view, took little time in his reply. Give nothing and take as much as possible seemed always to have been his motto.

"You may keep my man for the short time Darius is away. When he returns with the truce, you must send my translator back immediately. Another condition I require is that Darius, to whom I have written separately[3], shall conclude as part of the agreement that all Catholic presbyters and ecumens alike shall be left free to practice their faith and be immune to persecution or acts of violence and savagery." He went on to say he had heard from several sources of the capture, forced-conversion, and martyrdom of Bishop Regianus of Ad Fratres.

"So be it," the count said, "let that be part of the agreement. I hardly think the barbarian will care one way or another."

I added Augustine's demand to the decree of truce.

"Oh, Maria, I shall miss you greatly," I was telling the cook.

She removed two loaves from the oven, shutting its hatch with the handle of her peel and sliding the hot bread along its shaft onto the table. "You will miss my cooking, I think."

It was more out of kindness than truth I replied but have found it always a good practice to leave the door open behind me. "I believe it has been our conversation that has nourished me more. I have enjoyed your stories."

She shoved one of the loaves into my sack along with a bit of cheese and a few olives. "That should keep you for a day." I hugged her.

"*Vale*, Maria."

Count Darius had returned shortly after mid-June, having been quite successful in his dealings with Gaiseric. So, Bonifacius had no

---

3 Augustine had always built a hedge around his vineyard in addition to posting dogs at the perimeter. Had he been a general, he would have been famous for using this two- or three-pronged pincer in his fights. As a polemicist, the bishop knew how to approach frontally while tiptoeing up from behind!

choice but to release me. All well and good, but I tried to visualize the exchange between Darius and Gaiseric and who, really, had the upper hand. I imagined that the count put on the sumptuous Roman display of goods and generosity, and that the king kept his short sword sheathed and watched carefully. In my view, Gaiseric came out ahead. What could the Roman do? Yes, I thought, Gaiseric will halt his advance. Likely everyone with him needed a good rest anyway, but what I had seen in his camp some years back told me that the Vandal could not stay put for very long, especially if there were riches beyond measure on the road just ahead. It was that very road on which I would travel, though not very far, to return to my cell and my work in the monastery, and—how could I suspect it?—to fall directly into the hands if not the arms[4] of Augustine, friend-of-my-youth.

The day of my return, the bishop sent for me, I thought to begin the translations of his latest improvement on his little book, the crushing of the bishop of Eclanum, Julian, which he called *Contra Segundam Juliani*, "More Against Julian." I was wrong. Oh yes, that assignment would come soon enough, but I found that the bishop had other things on his mind besides rooting out heretics.

"*Receperint, amicus et salve*, Welcome and good health, friend." Augustine proffered his hand to be kissed. I complied.

"*Sum lateus esse hic*, I am happy to be here," I fibbed, once again hoisting my weight and straightening to stand before him, but the bishop floated a hand out pointing to a chair set to his right.

"Sit, please."

I wouldn't say I warmed to his friendly gesture, but I did as he bid me. I took the chair and waited, ready for anything to come. And I had to wait some time, particularly in the eerie silence of one so usually full of words. Eventually, Augustine spoke.

"*Meus amicus*, my friend, *ut non dicum Amicum*? May I not call

---

4 Did I desire this? Despite the cooling of the aged furnace, perhaps. I would rather be accused of lust than of morbid curiosity. That man had been not only the friend-of-my-youth but also the best-friend-of-my-youth, but despite all our learning and experience since, the imprint in our youthful cheese-husk only grew deeper and harder in its aging.

you Amicus? I do not much care for that other name."

"Innomenatus?" I said.

"Yes, that." It was as if he refused to say it.

"Of course, you may give me any name you wish."

"Then, Amicus, I must admit that I've both looked forward to and feared your return."

"Feared, my Bishop?"

He looked into a distance. Gazing to the same place I too could not help but to see fifty and more years back. In a minute, he spoke slowly, nearly halting after each word.

"I know you, Amicus."

"Yes. You do. I am your scribe, your Greek translator."[5]

"Of course, that is plain. I mean I know you from long ago from schools in Madaurus and Carthage, in the salons of the Manichees, and on wild excursions we made to the Colosseum in Carthage, and during late night walks and talks on all sorts of what we thought to be serious subjects."

It was all true, but I said nothing.[6] He continued.

"The friendship-of-our-youth presents me an opportunity," he said now looking directly at me, piercingly though I could not guess what he meant. "All people here, except Alypius, know me and have known me only as their bishop, their spiritual leader." I nodded, and he continued. "That fact makes it difficult to discuss certain, let me say non-bishoplike ideas."

Finally, I spoke, defending him to himself. "I understand you to be quite open about everything. Even farting." He giggled. I kept my presence.

"Ah yes, my now famous discussion of flatulence." He drummed the arm of his chair and, I thought, sighed. "In each man, no matter his position in this world, no matter what he has or has not done, in each, I say, there is a dusty corner into which he sweeps thoughts and ideas that may conflict with his presence, with his demeanor, with

---

5 I risked trying the bishop's patience but staunchly refused to refer, just yet, to our youthful dalliances.

6 I did not then wish Augustine to define our interactions, but I did not want him to think I had come to Hippo for anything but work. Silence was my way to draw out his intentions without defining my own desires. In any case, I knew he would have the last word no matter what I said.

his known history, with what those who depend upon him expect. Do you not think so, Amicus?"

"It sounds true, but Lord God sees into all corners. Does He not?"

"My Lord God is not of this world, and I speak only of this, our human world, evil as it is."

"Then it must be so."

He shifted in his seat and cleared his throat, with a sound like that of a singer rising to a higher or more sustained note. "I have had a peculiar dream, a vision perhaps, that I would tell you of, if you consent to keep it to yourself."

I had lied at least once to him already, and since that moment, I'd found it easier to dissemble again. "I can do that, yes."

"Then listen without judgment, if that is possible, but only hear what I say. I will brook no interruptions during this, this story, or questions about it afterward." I nodded and he began:

"I do not sleep much. I do not sleep well. I am used to having my thoughts and my conversations with God the Father as my company. We alone converse much of the time, though I must admit His messages and His answers to my questions do not come quickly in words but often later, during the day, during my work, as inspirations and directions already taken. That has always, since my baptism, been the case. Until recently, you see."

I acknowledged with a nod.

"A little over a month ago, I woke to a feeling, and it was an unusual, foreboding feeling. Perhaps I had been worried, and it seems for good reason, by these barbarians Bonifacius has let loose in the land, or by this pesky, invasive heretic Julian and his idiotic name calling. Perhaps I am simply getting old. In any case, this felt different.

"I sensed a presence in the room, off in the furthest and darkest corner of my chamber. I rose in my bed. What I saw, though indistinct was a man, thin in some parts and plump in others. His belly seemed to protrude, his head was round and large, but arms, if he had any were thin and his neck like a narrow, twisted branch. He crouched over my jar as if using the thing. I wonder even now if I saw a hooked nose or a beak. His eyes were deep set, profoundly recessed each into a hole. But why, you wonder, do I tell you of this?"

He stopped there. I said nothing.

"You may answer my questions."

"No, I do less than wonder, but why?"

"I tell you this because this presence reminded me of you when you were sick so many years ago."

This was no time for me to say anything.

"It was the eyes," he said.

I couldn't help myself. "Did you not say the eyes were hidden?"

"If not the eyes alone, then the speech as well." Augustine ignored my breach of promise. "All the better. Yours have been hidden from me for over fifty years, yet I have not forgotten their singular aspect. Even I, the master of one million words, cannot describe them accurately, but I know your voice and eyes, heard and seen or not. I recognized your look and sound immediately the night we collided. Call it a mystery, very much like the mystery of love."

"Love?"[7] The word seemed foreign coming from Augustine.

"Yes, I confess it, for I loved you back then, and knew at once that night, months ago, that I love you still. And over that lonely span, I have wrestled over the probity and comeliness of the feeling. In your absence I held it close until when in a dream or waking vision I recognized you. Despite my clever but almost naked disguise, I knew, just as I know that God the Father heads the Holy Trinity, that love is not sin but salvation. I know it without words. And thanks be that it is in old age when the fires of lust have burned to ashes and cooled to nothing, that the Divine Father has brought you back to me. It is a sign, as surely as the powers housed in the holy relics we now enjoy here in Hippo Regius."[8]

I felt invited to ask, so I did. "A sign of what?"

The bishop peered at me in a not unfriendly way then spoke, "We shall see, Amicus, friend-of-my-youth. Together we will see."

---

7 Yes, I interrupt yet again, but only to say that but for the exaggerated sense of his description, the man he described could really have been me, scrawny in parts, bulbous in others, and blessed with a noble Roman nose of ample proportions.

8 In his later years, Augustine's skepticism regarding holy relics was overcome by a fascination for those that had been fetched to Hippo Regius.

With that, he gave me a document, assigning me to his sole service, as his *scriba supra omnibus*, a personal and private attendant. "I want you near, even when you are not in my presence," he said. Later he assigned me new, obscure, and I have to say not very comfortable quarters, which turned out to be temporary, a place as far from his chamber in this small monastery as could be.

The work, though, would be close.

There was no need to say it, but I knew right away that my elevation would lead to trouble, mostly for me, for there were many others who considered themselves tightly tied to the bishop and wanted to be closer to Augustine than the stranger they knew as Innomenatus. However, the Bishop of Hippo Regius was not a man to deny.

14

Augustine Confesses

Augustine awoke, slowly shedding a troubled, restless sleep, to the profound silence of the monastery.

"The dead of the night, again," the bishop muttered.

The dying odor of incense from the evening mass led the presbyter to lift his slight torso off the bed. Elevated on his elbows, he peered into each inky corner of his room as if trying to discover the location of the censer.

What are you looking for? He wondered, and before he came fully awake—always a time at which he realized he was not alone, that God the Father was with him—was startled to see the wavering figure of Amicus, as he called the man, hovering before him at the foot of the bed. The bishop shot up erect, became fully conscious, and began immediately to pray away his vision, reciting his most precious psalm:

> *"Domine ne in furore tuo arguas me neque in ira tua corripias me, . . .*
> Lord, rebuke me not in thine anger, neither chasten me in Thy hot displeasure, . . .
> *revertere Domine erue animam meam salva me propter misericordiam tuam*
> O Lord, deliver my soul: oh save me for Thy mercy's sake"

Augustine sang the song twice, but on the third repetition stopped short at the seventh verse:

> ". . . I have grown old amongst all my enemies."

Ah, it is no good, he decided.

Worries over the recent persecution of Catholics by those Arian devils, the Vandals, haunted his recitation.

True, he decided, but more so it was thoughts of Amicus that had danced around the words as he uttered them and fluttered around his mind like moths around an oil lamp. He rose fully, slipped his feet in the sandals at his bedside and donned a robe against the coolness of the summer night. I will fret over the Vandals later. Now, I will go to the-friend-of-my-youth, Augustine ruminated, and will confess the sins of my mind, to purge these ridiculous flights of an old man's dreams and imagination.

The bishop slipped from the cell and through his library where one of the scribes slept over a copy of *Contra Segundam Juliani*, "More Against Julian," and stirred at Augustine's passing.

"Sleep, my son. I am but taking the night air," and the man dozed off once more.

Now, Augustine entered the ambulatory—it is small but wonderful in its colonnaded symmetry, as neat and steady as a good argument, he thought—and there the scent of the pomegranate and olive leaves from the *palestrian* garden struck his nostrils with an alluring and spicy fragrance. The brume of the trees flooded his senses and swept him forward along the columns toward the cell of Innomenatus, the bishop's Amicus and friend-of-his-youth, but as he turned the corner of the passage which way would lead him to Amicus, the presbyter drew himself to a halt.

No, no, no, he thought, whatever are you doing?

He wiped sweat from his brow. Are you to be carried away by the smell of a flower? By the flame of a long-gone youth? By the craven lusts of the night? The bishop stood stock still. Why have you left your bed to wander even this far, wrestling conscience against body? The bishop's keen mind replied. There can be but two reasons: either for the satisfaction of the flesh or for the fulfillment of pride have you risen. Augustine judged his conscience and prayed: Dear Lord, my Father in heaven, save me from both body and hubris—neither points me toward you, my God. And with a rustle of his robes, the bishop turned about and rushed back toward his cell.

He passed the library door but not wanting to yet again disturb his sleeping scribe moved around the corner to his proper cell door. It was locked from inside. Nothing to do, Augustine thought, but return the other way. This time it was empty. The scribe had gone to bed. "Good, good," the bishop said to the empty study and moved on into his room. Immediately, he enjoined the psalm he had earlier left off, and this time through felt no flirt, no tremble around the words that had many times before and did now comfort and soothe him:

revertere Domine erue animam meam salva me propter misericordiam tuam
O Lord deliver my soul: oh save me for Thy mercy's sake.

He repeated the full chapter and verse three times—once for each person of the Trinity—then climbed back into bed.

Leave both Vandals and scribes behind, Augustine thought. For now, he felt drained, weak, and in need of sleep.

And as the bishop of Hippo Regius slept, the moist, balmy, and redolent earth floated in the sea of God's universe carrying along the garden, the monastery, the walled city of Hippo, the entirety of Africa peopled by Romans, Berbers, and, now, Vandals, and all that had moved *per omnia saecula saeculorum,* forever under the sky, according to its own stamp, of which the nature of mankind was not only the essence informed by love, by error, and by anguish and hunger, but also shared with all creation that which Augustine had felt in the garden surrounded by his monastic hall. In slumber, he grew sensible of the ancient aspect of this buoyant motion that rocked him there at the center of his city on the north coast of Africa, and that soon increased to a pitch and a roll, bringing him dreams of the Mediterranean waves he had twice ridden, that had two times sickened him, and that now with a sudden suction dropped from out beneath him. The bishop woke.

Let it be dawn, he hoped, but when his eyes opened there was darkness only, but not emptiness. He inhaled the residue of the fust of the putrid sea, the ghosts of the night-effusing trees, and the piquant sting of a swinging censer—and with the twining of each of these three in his nose, Augustine, still fully asleep, sat up in bed.

"Who's there?" he asked.

"You have returned so quickly. All of a sudden," the voice said.

"What is a scribe doing in my chamber at this time of night?" But this, he knew, was not his scribe, who was likely fast asleep on his own cot.

"Did you not go out with confession on your mind?"

And with that question, a faint golden glow in the far corner of the room revealed the figure that had months back reminded Augustine of his Amicus, but that now seemed smaller and carried a voice not at all like his friend and translator. The query itself throbbed in the bishop's skull and flushed him with a chill up his spine and down his arms. He shook.

"Was that not your thought?" the dream prodded.

"And who under God's creation asks the Presbyter of Hippo Regius such things in the middle of the night when all should be sleeping? There are but two reasons. . ."

The voice interrupted, "It is but a single and simple question. Do not disparage yourself with argument nor with highness."

Augustine, as if he were again in the ambulatory, was stopped.

"Was it not your thought?"

"Yes, yes, it was. That is true."

"And why did you stop and turn back at the corner? Was it the fragrance and softness of the gardens that frightened you?"

"The earth is impure, it leads to desire, to lust."

"Who says? And were you not afraid?"

Again he was stopped. It had not been the Vandal invasion and persecution that had instilled fear in him. The reason he had wanted to confess to Amicus was that he had held on to and cherished his sin. That made him afraid and worried for the present time and too, for the eternity to come.

"Yes, I was, I am, afraid," he said.

"Why not, then, go? Face your fear? There is yet time before the cock crows."

It was at that moment that the bishop awoke, realizing he was speaking to himself. No one else was in the room. "I need no pushing to do right," he said. "I will up again and go straight to Amicus, wake him if necessary, and tell him all."

This time Augustine locked the passage door to the library and left directly through his cell door. He strode the hallway, went around the corner that had stopped him before, passing by columns towards a close and crooked passage that sprouted off the ambulatory and ended, he knew, at Amicus's chamber. Soon he saw that the door stood ajar and lamp light shone into the corridor. The bishop slowed still in the shadows and halted his march. He felt his heart pounding hard from his quick steps, and again he mopped the perspiration on his forehead. I'll just rest a minute here, a short time. And as the bishop of Hippo Regius pressed himself deeper into the darkness, he found himself listening to two distinct sounds: the scratching of a quill on parchment, short quick strokes, and a humming that rose to a faint and breathy singing. The song, he did not know. The language he heard was unknown to him. The flicker of the lamps, for there must be two at least, the rhythmic sound of the pen, and the strange-sounding melodic chant released in a smooth, airy voice drew him closer to the doorway like the ring of the silver bell inviting cleansed souls to communion. Then he stumbled, caught himself on the stones around the door, and emitted a short grunt. He heard the stirring of robes from inside.

Amicus came to the doorway. "My bishop. Are you sick?"

"No, no, Amicus, I am sleepless but quite well. I was pacing the garden walk and saw your light." Augustine knew that was impossible in such a bent and convoluted passage. He hoped Amicus would not note the inaccuracy.

"Ah, yes, I am translating for you. Will you come in? The lamps have warmed my room. You shall sit in my chair. I have a decanter of water here to refresh you if you'd like."

"No, no, well, thank you, Amicus, perhaps I will." And the bishop for the first time in over fifty years entered the bedroom of the friend-of-his-youth and whirled, it seemed to him, along hundreds of hallways, through thousands of nights and days, and following scores upon scores of arguments backward to the occasion of his horrible transgression and the burying of a love. Now, all the rest—forums, teaching, preferment, sermons, letters, accolades, and dozens of conclaves—collapsed, and in this tiny cell at the heart of his own monastery, he again found love rise. He moved inside and to make more room brushed the door closed. "Yes, I will sit awhile."

The bishop sat at the desk and gazed around as Amicus reached above him with his pudgy hands for his cup and then filled it with water from a pitcher near the bed.

"This room is very small."

"It is all I need, my Bishop." Amicus removed the parchment he had been working on to his pallet and set the cup before the bishop. "I am not often here but to sleep or to briefly finish the day's work."

Augustine let his eyes wander over the walls, the back of the door, and along a shelf above the desk. "You have no crucifix, Amicus." The discovery disturbed him.

Amicus sat on the bed and, too, looked around as if sensing the bishop's discomfort. "I believe someone scratched the sign of the fish over the lintel outside. This is a Christian house."

"I will send you one." Augustine looked again at the walls as if searching for a spot to display the cross. "And perhaps I should find a better place for you. Here it is too close, too stuffy. I would like you to have air."

"Shall I open the door again?" Amicus sounded solicitous.

"That was not what I meant, my friend. It is something else. It is the reason, the true reason I have come searching you out at night." What these three statements sounded like to Amicus, the bishop did not know, but he realized immediately that he must clarify his intent to erase the sense of innuendo that buoyed the words. "I have come to a conclusion." The bishop's voice crackled, perhaps in its own deception. "About housing you, Amicus." The prelate coughed and cleared his throat.

"More water, my Bishop?" The scribe drew Augustine another draft. "Drink, please."

Augustine sipped from the cup of Amicus and began again.

"As my chief scribe, I think you need to be closer to me. There is a cell that sometimes Alypius uses when he is in town. It is much larger and has a window looking into the garden."

"That one directly across the passage from your chamber?"

"Yes, that is the one."

"And Alypius?"

"Oh, he is in Thagaste much of this year and next Spring will take the river to Carthage on his way to Rome. No. You shall have the room. I owe you that much."

"Should these larger quarters be offered to our refugee prelates? Those who have escaped the Vandal advance?"

The bishop muttered, "They have abandoned their posts. I hesitate to house them so well."

"And so . . . ?"

"You shall have the room."

"And this is the 'true reason' you have sought me out tonight? To inspect and change my habitation?"

Augustine, for the second time this night, found himself concealing his reasons. "I often awake with ideas that need to be inscribed before they disappear. Tonight was one of those with no one near." The bishop thought of the scribe sleeping in the library, but he continued. "I have come to this conclusion. I want you nearer."

"You owe me that much? What of that? What of *owing*?" To Augustine his tone was like a prod.

Augustine began, "And who under God's creation asks the Presbyter of Hippo Regius such. . . ," then checked his words. Amicus sat on the bed in silence.

The small room grew closer. The lamps' flames burned erect in the still air. The two men there, facing each other, sitting very near, listed towards one another in a tense quiet that neither moved to disturb. Then, Augustine rose decidedly though slowly, turning towards the door. He fumbled with the latch. Amicus remained absolutely still. Then the bishop let his hand drop and turning from the door once again took the chair.

"What was that song I heard you singing as I stood outside your door?"

The unexpected query shook Amicus from his quietude. "Song?"

"Yes, you sang in a foreign tongue. What were those verses?"

"I was reciting the *Songs of David*. What one you heard I do not know."

"And the language?"

"Hebrew."

"One of those you studied in Alexandria."

"A little, but I truly learned all I know in the Holy Land."

Augustine sighed. "Yes, you have traveled wide and far."

Again a hush fell upon the room until the scribe cut into that lull once again, this time gently, softly repeating his question, "How is it that you *owe* me?"

The bishop eyed his host. "I took your name."

"Perhaps, but you've given me a new one."

"I erased your path, like sweeping a palm frond over your steps in the desert."

"I followed my own way. I have always been solitary. It is my nature."

"But we were together for years."

"I admit that but only know I'm forever one and never the other."

"I owe you for my sins."

Innomenatus, in an altered but familiar voice, that of a priest leading a convert to the light, asked, "You wish to confess?"

Still uncertain, perhaps fearful, the bishop rocked in the chair and finally wrested out the word, "Yes." Augustine clasped his hands on his lap, looking at them as if praying or struggling. After another minute of silence he said, "Out of anger at your leaving, I killed your memory. I murdered myself in spite. I would enslave not comfort you, for *I* was the one that needed salves. I hardened my heart and ceased to love. It is very late to say it, but it is so."

The-friend-of-his-youth contemplated his bishop a moment, then said, "It is never too soon to be kind. You must go in peace and be forgiven." And with that, Amicus—the man Innomenatus, friend-of-Augustine's-youth rose, went to the door, and opened it. "Rest now, my bishop. The day is nearly upon us."

And as Augustine, bishop of Hippo Regius, came to his feet, Amicus took him into his arms and held him as he shook.

15

Sabina at Work

The convent bell rang once again. That's four times this morning, Sabina thought. She worked over a little sketch she'd made of the convent and grounds surrounding it, looking for more space to shelter the refugees streaming in from Cartenna, Tipasa, and even Icosium, all fleeing east ahead of the Vandal horde to which the governor Count Bonifacius had given all of Mauretania Ceasariensis. Some who had come from as close as Numidia where Count Bonifacius himself still ruled were not immediately threatened but were very much afraid. Many of those were the wealthy who carted their valuables and households with them. But those whom Sabina and her sisters had taken in were the poor, smallholders, or craftspeople who had actually seen Vandals with their own eyes and were terrified. She did not ask any if they were baptized in the Church, and many she knew were Donatist. Some were pagans.

Yesterday, her closest friend and sister had come to her. "Tizem, how on earth could our governor just give up so many people and cities to these barbarians?" Ia wanted her *materfamilias* to tell her.

Sabina did not know the answer but had told Ia, "Some of these newcomers are Christians, themselves. We cannot truly call them barbarians even if they are Arian."

"They do not act Christian, Tizem. Haven't you heard the stories?"

Indeed, Sabina had heard more than she could bear but listened in her patient kindness, for she knew that the stories, true or exaggerated, must be told, that they should not be held within. Tragedy was common in these flights from invasion as was loss, mostly of property or of livelihood but sometimes of lives that succumbed to disease, hunger, or accident. Notably absent from the stories, Sabina had noticed, were murders or killings at the hands of the Vandals, though, perhaps, the dead told no tales.

"Yes, Ia, I have heard. And those stories are sorrowful, but we ought only to listen and not to judge unduly. All must be welcomed. It is our faith."

Agitated, Ia had grown frustrated by what she felt was her sister's complacency. "Not judge? These barbarians are worse than the desert tribes. So cruel. So base."

"My dearest sister and friend, you do yourself ill by speaking so."

"What if it were your daughter caught by these fiends who confiscate farms and mistreat women, even virgins."

In great patience, she overlooked Ia's rude stab, although Sabina had indeed thought much and often of her daughter at once fair game for heretic hunters like her own father and now in a precarious place facing an invasion. She had worried that Sequia might suffer persecution at the hands of the Vandal Arians, but she let those thoughts like other worries blow like tiny seeds through her mind without taking root to blossom.

"Please, my dear, do not speak so. Sequia is safe in Thagaste, and we shall not worry overly about her. Like her, we have work to do right here, sick to tend, multitudes to feed, and shelters to build. Let us give our attention to those and not to fears, rumors, and hatred. We are Christians whose purpose is to comfort and counsel those in need."

With that, she had sent Ia on her way, but Ia's upset caused worry about her daughter to swirl once again in her thoughts. The Vandals, it was said, had agreed to live within the boundaries of Mauretania, to move no further east than that. Even so they ranged freely, pillaging, testing defenses, stealing. Sabina had not been to the Vandal province, but sisters from that land had characterized it as one of hard-living, not as fertile nor as hospitable as Numidia or her own and Sequia's state of Africa Proconsularis. It seemed, then, that these Arians, the Vandals, might not be content with the gift of such a poor land with the wealth of Numidia just eight days march from Icosium in Mauretania.

Well before Ia worried her about Sequia's safety—forgive her for Ia herself was fearful and did not know the harm she had done—Sabina had written to her daughter:

Sabina, a follower of Christ by the will of God, to Sequidei, her beloved child,

Grace, mercy, and peace from Christ Jesus our Lord.

Our town is filling with those in flight. Running before the onslaught of the Vandal tribes, many are panicked, terrified for their lives. I think the fear is for little reason, although they could not very well stay at home and fight the invaders with hoes and rakes. They should be thankful they were allowed to escape though sadly forfeiting their property.

You are far from danger now, but I worry for you, and I hope that after this year's harvest is taken in and stored, you will come to Hippo for a time to join our work here, to visit me, and to minister to those here who thirst for Christ's truth. For your safety, please think on it.

In the fellowship of Christ and from the heart of a mother.

Sequia had returned the favor, telling Sabina not to be concerned, that all was peaceful as ever in Thagaste since it is even further from the new Vandal border than Hippo. Sequia's letter had calmed her mother's fears only a little, but Tizem found some comfort in a new acquaintance with a Berber merchant, a neighbor, one called The Cheetah of Chaouïa because of his ability to travel without detection. This man, Aksil, who had turned during troubled times for merchants from travel to running the Roman stables promised to be helpful since he knew the back ways to Thagaste. Sabina had been acquainted with his family years ago and would not hesitate, she told Aksil, to ask for his help.

So, the *materfamilias* of the convent of Hippo Regius felt more content with and full of hope for the safety of her daughter, for Numidia, and for all those in Africa Proconsularis. She turned her attention to the difficulties at hand, a stream of refugees at her door.

Yes, the bell rang again and again and was answered each time. The sisters turned away only the wealthy who could easily find other housing. The poor and those who had fled with nothing she welcomed and provided for. But now with the continual knocking at their door, Sabina found she had also to provide comfort for her fellow house-women.

"And where, my sister," asked Ia, "shall we find food to feed all these?"

"Ia, we own a great surplus from last year's bountiful harvest. Our granaries are still nearly full, and the gardens and orchards have grown profusely in good weather. No one shall go hungry."

"The numbers increase every day."

"Look here." Sabina proffered her drawing of the convent, placing her finger here and there as she explained. "Here we shall expand the garden. Our guests will help dig and till and tend as well as we. There, we will erect tents I have procured from friends in the desert south of Thagaste to shelter the most recent arrivals. It is outside our walls, but safe here within our protected city. That site is large enough for three score men and young boys. The families will camp among our orchard trees where shade and water will be near."

"But where shall they prepare meals and eat? They will burn our houses down with their cooking fires."

"Oh, Ia. You chafe so. Be at peace." Sabina set her steady hand on Ia's arm and looked into her eyes. "All shall go well. We shall prepare everything in our kitchen. Our friends will eat in our dining hall."

"Both are too small," Ia interrupted.

"All shall be done in shifts. Nine meals a day instead of three."

"But the work!"

Sabina clung to her patience but frowned Ia's objections down. "Our new residents have brought ready hands that know how to bake and stew, that can sweep and clean. The sick shall rest, the rest shall work. Don't worry, you'll see."

And the eternal optimism of the *materfamilias* quieted Ia's worry and prevailed over all the sisters' brooding. Once the house was full, Sabina reorganized the twenty sisters to watch and run the household in four groups with each assigned twenty-five refuge-seekers. She devised and announced to all schedules for eating, cleaning, gardening, and repairing to both workers and patients alike, so that when the ill recovered they could join in. Through it all, in the daylight, Sabina urged and encouraged her sisters and their charges with charm and steady grace. It was only in the dark of night that her fears gnawed at her sleep, keeping her awake far past bedtime.

As the household settled to its rest and even the men and boys outside the gates were quiet, Sabina's mind nagged and nettled her. The horror of the stories she'd been told rose to ever more grotesque form and size.

"Already we'd fled Ad Fratres and Portus Magnus," a grandmother some years younger than Sabina was telling her, "trying in vain to stay ahead of those horrid barbarians. They had stolen everything from the church and cut the head off poor Bishop Regianus. My two daughters were made to watch. We escaped and once in Cartenna, so far from home, we thought we'd be safe." The woman burst into wailing and could not go on. As Sabina tended the woman's wound, an infected gash oozing pus on her calf, her patient continued through her tears, "Yes, we thought we would be protected there. We were wrong."

"Were there no soldiers in the town? No Romans?"

"At first, yes. But then word came, from where I do not know, that the garrison was to leave. They did so, in the night! I only wish they had taken us with them."

Sabina smoothed a rosemary paste over the leg and wrapped it around with a loose cloth. "Keep this as clean as you can. Come see me in two days." She pressed the still crying woman to her chest. "Here you are safe now."

"I am. But my daughters are gone," she grasped Sabina's wrist as she spoke and now her words became the torrent that her weeping had been. "Gone. Killed or worse, enslaved."

"I have a daughter myself that I pray will be safe, but do not fear. They will be found."

"No, no, they are gone. A gang of Vandals, filthy animals, all with stringy pale hair and grimy clothing broke down our door when we refused to answer, six or eight of them. Immediately they laid their dirty hands on my daughters, rent their clothing, and pummeled them until they sank to the floor. All right in front of our eyes, my granddaughters' and mine."

"I am so sorry," Sabina crooned although the story made her want to scream. She heard her own voice soothing the woman and, maybe, herself at the same time. "Please stay calm, my dear."

"There was more. So horrible. My virgin daughter tried to flee but was tackled and dragged to the atrium of the house where other families camped. They held their long swords to her sister's neck until the younger submitted to their lust, one after another. Wild boars they were. I tried to save her but was cudgeled and cut—that is how my leg was slashed—and thrown into the stinking arms of one of their short, dark fellows. When they were done, they held my youngest at sword-point while they made her sister submit to their same debauchery." The woman wailed loudly again. "Right in front of her children, they worked their desecration on her body. Finished, they beat my sweethearts more and drove them along with them. They laughed as they pushed my naked babies forward with their ribbed shields."

"And you have not found them?"

"No. They must now be killed or enslaved. I have only my granddaughters with me."

"Cleave to them and care for their bodies and spirits."

The story left Sabina weak and distraught, but there was not time for either. There was too much to do. A fever had broken out among the men's and boys' encampment and half of those were sick, in need of nursing and unable to work.

All this burdened Sabina who was able to rest but little and to sleep hardly at all.

Ia lectured her, "You do too much. Leave off and let your sisters help. You must rest, or you'll become ill like the rest."

"Yes, I will, just give me some time. Someone must lead the evening prayers and services."

It was rare to conduct holy services so publicly—it had been years since any but the sisterhood attended readings and prayers in the convent chapel—but Sabina in her role of *materfamilias* to the convent was a spiritual leader as well and, so, assumed the canonical privilege and duty, something she had felt free to do only in Sequia's quiet chapel outside of Thagaste. Here, word of her pastoral care would find unfriendly ears. Still, Sabina felt compelled, driven to speak the words of Christ.

Her chapel was a barn renovated thirty years before. On its white plastered walls Sister Lydia had painted her frescoes, loaves and fishes, the good shepherd, and in a far corner a woman baptizing a new convert. The room was crowded this evening. The sisters sat with the infirm on the benches and many sat on the floor along the walls. In times of trouble and sickness, people tended toward the church for comfort. These were difficult times.

Sabina knew that many here had never sat in the presence of a woman prelate, unofficial as that concept was, much less had they heard of such a thing, not since a past now so distant as to have been forgotten. Despite her clear and welcomed leadership among the sisters and refugees, some would be confused by, perhaps angry at this unfamiliar sight. But in Sabina's own upbringing—her people had been Donatists, a sect founded through the patronage of Lydia, the martyr spiritualist (for whom their own Lydia was named)—women often led groups in readings and prayers, so Sabina felt less reticent to preside.

Sabina walked graciously to the little altar, stood tall there, and began, "Now let us pray," and led the gathering in the recitation of the Lord's Prayer. She followed with her favorite psalm of David, the sixth, and the doxology, her voice, low pitched and melodious, filling the small space with hope and sanctity,

Gloria Patri, et Filio, et Spiritui Sancto.
Sicut erat in principio, et nunc, et semper, et in sæcula sæculorum.
Glory be to the Father and to the Son and to the Holy Ghost
As it was in the beginning, and now, and ever shall be, world without end.

Sabina gave way to Ia who read from *Luke* and *John*. When she finished, Sabina preached on faith. She spoke slowly, as steadily as she could before such a large crowd. She spoke of the fear running in the streets of Hippo and throughout the provinces. She spoke of the large community of Christians of many sects and creeds who were there to help. And she finished by saying, "Remember that even in the grip of despair our Christ Jesus granted his peace to a fellow sufferer on the cross. In our troubles, do you likewise."

"Did I read well?" Ia asked Sabina after the evening prayers. "I was afraid of the murmuring I heard."

Sabina had heard but had ignored the voices. "Remember, Ia, our guests are weary and worried, too. They are not used to hearing women read scripture or lead prayers."

"And, Tizem, did I read well?"

Sabina embraced her sister. "Yes, my love, you read well. And now to bed."

Soon after the early August twilight, Sabina retired to her room. She forced herself to lie in bed, but she could not sleep. She mulled over the needs of her charges and the welfare of her house-women, her sisters in prayer.

"Lord," Sabina prayed, "grant that we shall pass this difficult time in harmony and with trust in your goodness. Watch over our house and all those here and in the city." She mused on the problems of the day and the great changes that swept all of Africa. Is this a punishment for our wrongdoing, our waywardness? She wondered. Is this persecution in return for persecution? She thought of her Donatist parents, themselves refugees, fleeing to the desert to avoid the laws prohibiting their worship, their faith. And now an unthinkable threat to the persecutors had come.

Was it you, my bishop, my Aurelius, my Augustine, that brought this Arian plague upon us through your incessant hunt for heretics, that now they come to you? The tide has turned, as it turned against Rome itself, years gone by, and perhaps we and the African church shall be destroyed and ground to dust. Truly, charity is the greatest of virtues. Would that you had practiced love in place of polemics. It was with these churning thoughts that Sabina somehow lulled herself to sleep. Soon, though, she awoke with a question?

"Is it the way of Christ to seek retribution?"

At first, she felt it was she asking herself. Perhaps she queried her own person in a dream. Then, in her mind she heard the voice from her delirious night on the road to Thagaste.

"Is that what you believe?"

She thought that when she looked into the darkness she saw him, the same except robed like a monk this time. Whether it was a dream, self-talk, or vision, Sabina joined the conversation.

"No," she said, "I believe He taught us to love one another. Not to seek revenge."

The monkish man smiled, a thin line spreading wide across his face. "You are wise, Sister, but would the Father be adverse to his Son?" He did not wait for Sabina to answer but said, "The stamp of the Father is upon His Child, the Son, and it is from that fountain also that love, not redress, flows. From your own works, you know this."

"Yes, but why does all this happen now? The invasion? The refugees? The continual wrangling? I worry."

The monk now seemed to rise slowly from his perch in the corner, revealing himself as a large man. "Did I not say, 'Your many troubles are hardly ended'? It is the way of this world, like a wind off the sea swirling dust into the air, one thing begets the next."

Sabina still had questions but the monk silenced her coming toward the bed. "Rest, now, Sister. Sleep."

"But why so much suffering?"

The man, who had turned to go, looked back and smiled at her over his shoulder. "Why so much love?"

And with that, Sabina was deeply asleep. In the morning she would write to the bishop.

16

Sabina's Letters

If it were not for that second world—Plato called it the world of forms, Christ's followers called it the kingdom of heaven—some events would be difficult to live through serenely, with or without philosophy's comfort.

Such a period of time I spent with the elder Augustine. That second, older, and perhaps eternal world invoked the joys through which he and I had already passed, our wild youth in Carthage, an era of perfect love.

I had been ensconced in my new chamber a little over two months—fine quarters, they were, fit for and had been adorned for a visiting bishop—large, airy, and full of natural light—and Augustine had not forgotten to proffer the necessities, including presenting me with a cross to hang over my bed. More importantly, it gave me full access to his library which adjoined his own rather tiny and dismal cell, one much smaller than that he had bestowed on me. One might imagine the arrangement came out of generosity, something that can easily be measured and controlled. On the contrary, I believed it derived from guilt, not so easily stanched or steered, for which it is impossible to compensate. In either instance, I was the grateful but not guileless beneficiary.

Certainly greater than the comfortable cot and, for a monastery, charming bedroom were the hours allowed me to peruse the library unhurried and unsupervised. I was given for my work a table in a tiny alcove adjacent to the main library, a place I could translate undisturbed the many projects that required my Greek language and over which Augustine had spread his seemingly boundless energies.

As for the bishop himself, he ranged widely with a youngster's energy in the monastery, busy at the chores of the church and governance of the monks and ecumens. Whatever the source of this new fervor—its sudden rise was speculated upon both by those close to him and by those who saw him only from a distance—it livened the entire monastic community. Occasionally, I overheard talk about my own influence on Augustine.[1] He did spend a great deal of time in the library with me—something duly noted by those who would nudge me to the side—working to arrange the body of his life's work, putting it in a semblance of order and correctness.

"I am old," he said to me, "and will not last many years longer. When I leave my writings behind, they must be found all in place."

So, for hours at a time, Augustine supervised the correction and copying of his long list of books, keeping him near me in the library nearly half the day. He spent a lesser amount of time in the scriptorium with a dozen or more scribes, dictating letters many of which I later set into Greek and sometimes into Hebrew. He devoted yet another segment of his waking time to service in the chapel and cathedral. Of the suddenly springy step of the bishop of Hippo Regius, living two days in the space of one, barely taking time to eat or sleep, people would, of course, gossip.

Had he required my company during *all* that time, I would have been forced to escape, to flee to Egypt or even further to the far West. Fortunately, I did not need to attend the scriptorium or chapel but, mainly, to labor over Augustine's letters and documents in his fight against Julian of Eclanum, his latest hapless heretic. Mainly, I was charged with informing the bishops of the east of Augustine's outrage at and bedevilment of the Pelagians, who were now led by Julian.[2] Having been a young philosopher once, I was no stranger to the splitting of hairs though I had adopted a laxer, more accepting attitude as a result of my extended travels to lands foreign even to the

---

1 The ultimate source of some these whisperings was Possidius who later, living in the ruins of this library, was to write the bishop's life, *Sancti Augsutini Vita*, a copy of which made its way to me during my last years in the far West at a time when I saved my weary sight for writing. I must confess, I did not pursue the book, looking instead out on the Atlantic, resting my eyes on the horizon between bouts of my labor on *this* very story.

2 It is seldom wise to admit knowing, or even to have known, a heretic. Certainly, I told no one under Augustine that I had encountered both Pelagius and Caelestius after they traveled east from Hippo. I also failed to mention that I had read letters arguing against original sin that Julian, whom I had not met, had sent to a woman-priest in Thagaste, someone I was soon to know. Now, I found myself, in the voice of my employer, arguing against those three and against the patriarch himself, Nestorius, who was trying to save Julian, a brilliant but wayward believer. I rued my station, but I fulfilled the charge anyway.

well-traveled of my day. This battle between Augustine and Julian appeared to me a bit puffed up. On both sides. I could not conceive of any reason Augustine would pick such a hot bone with such a minor and far-away character.[3] What difference, I wonder, did the source of a sin make? For grown men to castigate each other *ad nauseum* over that point seemed to me the hard labor of manufacturing dross. Still, I kept my peace. I translated as faithfully as my errant spirit allowed.

Occasionally, during the workday and more frequently at odd times during the night, the bishop requested my company to stroll the garden ambulatory while he held forth with complaints about Julian, Bonifacius, and the Vandals—"those cruel barbarians," he called them.

Still, not much was asked of me, especially in light of my considerable talents, and since there were few kitchen staff who contributed to or even tolerated my gossiping, I found myself with time on my hands with which to poke around the library and my little office.

It did not take me long to discover beneath my table in a cupboard behind a little door decorated with two scenes from the life of Christ (or death, since one was the rolling off of the stone sealing an empty sepulcher) a small cache of letters—small only in comparison to the voluminous collections of epistles in the library proper—which were organized, it seemed, chronologically, though many were undated and were paired, incoming with replies. These latter were written in the crabbed, unpracticed hand of the bishop himself (easy to see that he dictated most all but these private writings) which I easily recognized, yes, even after fifty years, from his papers, (much better scripted than these old-man letters) that I had read during our youth. I soon discovered by reading consecutive letters that the replies (not every letter had one) had not been sent, a fact that Sabina, the sender of these notes (for many were very short) often complained of and sometimes decried.

In my perusal of these documents, I was careful in two ways: one to see to it that the letters and replies were placed again exactly as I had found them when I finished reading and that I was not observed

---

3 I was to find out that reason in the not very distant future. I became, then, possessed of golden gossip with absolutely no one with whom I could share it.

actually handling them. To this end, I secreted one or two in my clothing and scanned each in my cell by candlelight at night.

A most recent letter asked a piercing question, referring to the Vandals' recent invasion of Mauretania Caesariensis:

> Was it you, my bishop, my Aurelius, my Augustine, that brought upon us all this warring plague through your incessant hunt for heretics, that now they come to you? I need not ask. I know already the answer you will not send.

And indeed not only was the answer not sent, it had not even been written, perhaps due to the especially strident tone of the piece, but possibly, too, because of a singular mention of one Sequia "our dear daughter" to whom no previous references had been made. I was not certain of the "our" in this letter, but among the many possibilities was only one that would preclude acknowledgment or reply. Sequia, her familiar name, seemed to be the natural-born daughter of Sabina, clearly indicated by the affection expressed, but beyond that, I could determine nothing, though I could certainly speculate.

Of course, I knew who Sabina was. I had known her well during my years in Carthage with Augustine. He loved to keep her near him—silent, sitting not beside him but close—under the trees near the school where we students met to discuss the thoughts and manners of the times, usually in Manichean terms and always with philosophical airs. Sabina, her large, dark eyes trained only on the profile of Augustine, attended to each turn of phrase, to each of his energetic and forceful arguments. Even when she could have had an opportunity to speak, she demurred. I thought, she formed a delightful presence in the group that surrounded our best polemicist, the future bishop of Hippo Regius. He claimed then to adore her.

Yes, I had known Sabina. We three traveled together to Madaurus and Thagaste, stayed under the same roof both there and in Carthage, so close, in fact, that I often heard their loving moans in the night. Still, I had never considered Sabina a threat to my love for or closeness to Augustine, although in private he often denigrated their arrangement before me and swore his affections were mine alone. He could, it seemed though, not get enough of either of us.

Now, during the ensuing weeks of labor in the library, while I watched for a reply to appear to what I named "the Vandal/Sequia" letter in the cabinet where the letters were kept, I took, not exactly out of idleness, to practicing the bishop's peculiar hand—it was no wonder he seldom wielded a pen himself, so unreadable was his script—and became over time proficient at faithfully producing it. Having satisfied myself with my accuracy, I waited yet another week for Augustine to write a reply. Perhaps because the bishop was preoccupied with more pressing matters, he did not. So, I penned a reply for him with the proviso to its recipient:

> This letter will not be mentioned nor referred to in any subsequent replies or epistles.

I did not want Augustine to discover and spoil my enterprise. And with that, I sent the letter by a young man I knew from outside the monastery.

Though I could not share the motherly concern which likely bred Sabina's impious accusation, I felt saddened and piteous for the worry of a mother over her child, perhaps more so because the activities of my erstwhile friend, Gaiseric, served as the author of her fear and disquiet. Therefore, in no uncertain terms and in the name of Aurelius Augustinius, I encouraged Sequia's relocation to the safety of Hippo Regius as soon as possible, for I knew just how rapidly what seemed to be could change into what was to be.

> Yes, danger now appears remote, but haste is not imprudent. The walls of Hippo Regius are strong, as invincible as the Father's love.

Perhaps I would not learn of my own influence—I had forbidden its mention after all—but more than anything I had experienced since returning to Africa, I enjoyed this newly established correspondence with its generosity of spirit, especially since it was not in my name but in that of the friend-of-my-youth. I had truly become a clandestine gossip if not a hidden bishop, as well. And I went further. Not only did I encourage Sequia's relocation but worked on a way to elicit more information about her from this letter-writing mother. I had first, as any kibitzer or philosopher must, to make some assumptions: one, that Augustine knew little or nothing about this child of Sabina's, and then, that she would be unashamed to reveal its history and, perhaps, parentage. I had Augustine write:

> I have wonder and admiration of this second child of yours. What is her age, how is she in the world. A follower of Christ? A wife and mother in her own right? And, asking without regret or rue, in what ways—having the same mother—and how like our own son Adeodatus might she be?

It had not been even three days when I feared my careful plan had been betrayed. Of a late evening, Augustine appeared at my door, looking disturbed and angry.

"What is it, my bishop? You seem distraught."

He replied with a gesture toward the corridor and said only, "Follow me."

I carefully tucked the letter, an early one from Sabina that I was perusing, beneath other, Greek, correspondence on my table and did as he commanded.

When I entered the hall, the bishop quickly set out toward the garden at a rapid pace. I gathered my garments around me and hurried after him.

Once I gained his side he roared, "How can such deception and cruelty be allowed or brooked with a calm spirit?"

I have learned through hard experience with the high and with the mighty that silence and patience are one's best companions when under attack. I said nothing.

"Oh, that I were a man of earthly power. One to command armies to crush the perfidious who pretend to be friends! An emperor who can detect and destroy duplicity. How does God the Father allow such behavior?" He stopped and looked directly at me.

"I am sickened by this letter writing."

Thoughts of flight (to the desert or further) scratched a fearful itch at my spine, but still, I waited.

"Yes, what else can I do? Only write feeble letters of complaint against heretics!"

That they were his letters he spoke of soothed my fears.

"This horrid Bonifacius who pretends to be a general, who feigns a Catholic faith, who utters the name of Christ but really whispers, 'Barabbas,' has doomed us all: the African church, our influence in Rome, and our standing in the empire."

I hid my relief behind consternation. It was my former employer, *Comes Africae*, not my humble self who had put the bishop in a rage. I hazarded but one short comment, "And what has the general done?"

"Done? Done? What hasn't he done?" Augustine said. "He has loosed barbarians in our land. He has compromised our territories and has opened the door to Arian subjugation of our Catholic faith. That is what he has accomplished, and more."

The bishop again lurched forward, agitated by his own words. "And now, after ceding the whole province of Mauretania Caesarensis to those devils (Augustine threw his arms to the vault of the ambulatory) he brooks savage invasions and forays into Numidia itself, and so, close into our own province without lifting a finger to oppose this Gomberic, this so-called Vandal king."

"Gaiseric?" I corrected him. "Is it he?"

I was not surprised. At the writing of the truce of Darius, which I had penned in Latin and Gothic, I had suspected we had not heard the last from Gaiseric. I understood him. I knew he would stir from Icosium though I believed at the time that it might be a year or more, definitely not as soon as this. "There have been incursions into Proconsularius?"

"Not yet, but the Arians have raided and pillaged all along the southern Numidian border."

I instantly thought of Sequia, Sabina's daughter. "Horrors. Why there?"

Augustine stopped mid-stride. He nearly shouted. "There is no explaining either barbarians or heretics. They both do the devil's work, and I know this Julian somehow had a hand in fomenting trouble, nipping at the skirts of my bishoprics in Africa, in my very home, Thagaste!"

"Could that be?" I could not concur. "What word is there? "

"They looted the churches. Exiled bishops to the desert. And destroyed schools."

"Certainly an assault on the Church," I said, "and, yes, perhaps an attack on you yourself."

Augustine wrung his old hands. "Yes, it seems so. I know of some Pelagian sympathizers in the affected area." He touched his eyes. A tear? "Of course, these barbarians, too, attacked the women, singled out the celibates and virgins for defilement."

Now, I truly feared for Sequia.

"And Bonifacius does nothing. He does not appear when called. He does not respond even to my messengers, but turns them away without answer." Augustine swung around, took my arm, and stood close in front of me. "And what can I do?" He actually spat on the pavement. "Write letters!"

I reached for his hand, wrapped his arm with mine, and said, "Let us walk here in the garden." I turned him—he was light even when so heavily burdened with woes—toward the arch leading into the fruit trees. I knew from his *Confessions* that in such a garden he had experienced conversion. "Let the arbors sooth our worries as we stroll here."

There is little, I have found, more terrifying than the fears of an old man who has not as yet accepted death, nor anything more filled with gratitude than a *senex* who is offered sympathy. And so, Augustine who trembled on my arm beamed as well with warmth, reaching across to pat my supporting arm with his free hand and inclining his head toward my shoulder. "Rest easy, my bishop."

The tremors settled, and I felt his arm relax on mine. He sighed and grew even lighter. Then as we took a turn in the garden he sighed again and said, "There is more."

I waited for him to elucidate. We stepped carefully over the stones.

"Yes, there is more. It is of a personal nature."

A peculiar concept indeed for such a public man to cite, I thought. "Yes?"

He looked toward the path we walked on. "I will not yet speak of it." He regarded my eyes. "I will tell it another time."

As the bishop now appeared calm, steadier, and in control, I offered to take him to his cell.

"Please, do that, Amicus. Thank you."

We entered from the ambulatory, and I saw to it that he rested on his cot, covering him with a blanket in as tender a way as I could. The worst had passed, and he fell asleep almost at once. I slipped out through the library which at that hour was devoid of company but lingered at my anteroom desk momentarily. Without knowing why,[4] I lit a taper and sat, not to write, but to consider what had just passed. I wondered at the bishop's anger and at his later serenity, parsing out their causes. Too, I was more than curious about his unspoken, personal news

I brought the candle to the little cabinet which held Sabina's letters and Augustine's unsent replies. Opening the door to this alcove, the candlelight revealed a new arrival. It had been unsealed and, I supposed, read. This was Sabina's response to my reply, the only reply she had ever seen in all those years.

---

4 I should add, looking back at this day over the several intervening years, that I was shaken and dislodged from my usual perch more than I admitted in this passage. Had I used my earlier reticence in Augustine's employment to protect him from his own past or to guard me against his honest powers to move souls? He had now sought me out and rattled the shield I had raised against an unbridled world that spanned decades and an empire, making me again his foil, his love, and his savior.

17

Gaiseric Thwarts a Plot

Gelimmer's coming home to Icosium from his inroads to Numidia was long and tiring. Had he brought no news for his king, Gaiseric, he would have stayed to pillage more, but his watching had been successful. His cousin, the king, would want to hear about what he'd seen. Though Gelimmer did not yet know, Gaiseric, too, had news. The king's tale would not be welcome to Gelimmer's ears.

They met at midday in the talking-circle, a flat, raised area far enough from any tents, natural cover, or sharp ears. Gaiseric dressed in a light, Roman-style tunic warm enough even on an October day. Gelimmer, still in his road armor, took to one knee to greet his king.

"Rise, my cousin, we are kinsmen, alone here. There is no need for show. Sit and tell me your news."

His kinsman settled on the large, flat stone to the king's right and removed his buckler and scabbard, placing them to his side, sitting erect. "I have the two things you wanted and more." He told Gaiseric of the Numidian harvest, of granaries filled to bursting. "Wheat is even spilled in the road. Grindstones are worked by day and by torchlight."

"So, the rumors are true. Even as we starve, the Roman citizenry grows fat on plenty."

Gelimmer grinned. "Not all are still so fat. We slit the life of some who wouldn't give up their goods." He laughed, shortly when Gaiseric frowned. "The celibate women we spared of life are virgins no more." His chuckle this time died at once.

Gaiseric watched Gelimmer steadily, saying nothing. "And the goods?"

"A well-guarded cart caravan follows me. They will arrive before nightfall tomorrow. See for yourself the quality of both the grain and the flour."

"I will test fresh morning bread but will say no word of the quality of the women," Gaiseric said flatly, allowing Gelimmer a thin smile.

The Vandal king reached down beside his flat, high stone and lifted up a large purse he had brought. Opening it and reaching inside, Gaiseric produced a finely wrought, wide golden ring. He presented the band to his cousin. "This runic ring was of the horde of Gunderic. I again seal our kinship with it. You have done well. You have come back safely."

Gelimmer received the ring, kissed it, and placed it on a finger. "This shall never be removed while I live."

"May that be long. Now, open your tale-horde, tell me more of your trip, of your news."

"The whole land is in flight. From afar in Numidia, we saw a hundred caravans moving east toward Hippo Regius. Each rolled cart after cart of goods and provisions. We seized two trains and allowed all but the headman to escape. He told us of widespread fear and flocking to safe nests."

Quiet settled over the two clansmen. Finally, the king spoke. "Know that while you traveled, falsehood and underhandedness crawled out of their holes here."

"Not amongst our men? Snakes and knaves?"

Gaiseric carefully looked at his cousin. "The power of Roman gold is strong." Again he looked hard at Gelimmer.

"What? Who?"

The king traced the features of his clansman slowly and carefully. Gelimmer did not blink. He held strong and steady. He said nothing.

Finally, the head Vandal spoke. "The Roman truce maker, Darius, twisted the kin of Ulfa to his will. Last week, when we took the estate of Honoratus at Castra Nova where we had met the Roman, a servant in the household, one seeking to save his life, came forth."

"They brewed up wickedness even during our peace talk!" Gelimmer growled.

The king scoffed, "Even while we slept our bondman quietly counted his thirty pieces of silver!" Drawing his short sword, Gaiseric stood and stabbed the earth between the stones on which they sat.

"So the Roman's word means nothing?" Gelimmer asked. "The

pact is broken!"

Gaiseric put a foot on stone. "Yes. This poor land can no longer hold us. First, we shall punish the evildoers. Afterward, no more will we nip at the Numidian's borders but will sweep full force into their yard. It is the best luck that Roman treason has ripped apart our treaty. We shall gain gold by this."

The plot, Gaiseric told Gelimmer, called for his own poisoning. At Castra Nova the emissary's man had given a vial to Ulman, kin of Ulfa. The little bottle was well described by the houseman of Honoratus and was easily found in their tent while Ulfasson and Ulman ranged afar. "We tested the potion on Honoratus himself. It worked quickly but painfully," Gaiseric said. "Our men replaced it with a vial of mead."

Now, the king smiled. "The snakes shall salt my food with grog. Not with the Roman's death-water! Further, four Goths had arrived from the east, forswearing their Roman allegiance, to join our cause."

"No doubt they were sent to enforce the treason of Ulfa's kin," Gelimmer said.

"That is certain. I accepted their good will, but tonight at board you will see how we settle their handiwork." Gaiseric flashed a ghastly grin.

"As for Bonifacius, the bishop in Hippo, and the *populi Romani* to the east," the king said, drawing up his short sword and brandishing it high, "In days to come, they shall do more than flee before fear!"

Gelimmer rose and unsheathed his own sword, raising it to the king's in a salute to vengeance. "My blade will carry the blood of those Goths and Ulfa's kin, too." Both then sheathed their swords.

"Sit now, Gelimmer. What news have you brought of the woman?"

"She is Sequia or Sequidei, God's follower. And lives outside Thagaste on her grandfather's land. It is close to the Numidian frontier. She is a celibate and a Christian oracle. She gathers Donatists, Catholics, and even Arians to her. Some say she accepts pagans' devotion as well."

"This oracle, this daughter of Augustine, Sequia, hasn't fled?"

"No. Though she raises emmer with others for her mother's convent in Hippo Regius, she lives alone. They say she is unafraid."

Gaiseric pondered this news. "Each of us fears something although I sense it may not be so useful this time. Though a monkish life comes at a price, it can strengthen the *in-wit*, the soul. She must be taken alive and unharmed."

Gelimmer fleered only a second, then grew stern when his cousin stood serious and determined.

"I shall meet this oracle so famous for her constancy," the king said. "She will be useful to the Vandals." Gaiseric hugged his kin hard and slapped his shoulder. "Come a little early to the banquet. We will speak again there."

Seven places at the high table were set on Roman purple cloth with the best of Honoratus's silver plates and Vandal flagons. The banner of kingship, the words, *Gaiseric Rex* surrounding the image of the leader in profile all wrought in golden thread hung below the ruler's place. The king was flanked by Gelimmer on his right and hoary Huneric the Elder on his left. Ulfasson, whom Gaiseric had so boldly named kin when the young man's father and grandfather, both Ulfas, had drowned on the crossing, sat close to the king in a place of honor next to Huneric. Some grumbled at the seating of Ulman, also Ulfa-kin, to Gelimmer's right. Many murmured that he did not belong there. The Alan *magistrum equitum*, master of cavalry, and his brother sat at either end. Strung behind were the seven best of the king's guard, armed with both spear and sword. Guests were forbidden weapons at table. Horns, pipes, and drums wove tunes about the feast.

Into the center space below the high table, onto a wide place made for dancing, strode the *scope*. The storyteller bowed first to the king and then to the row of low tables to the right and to the left filled with thanes and kinsmen of both the king and the Alans. The poet then bowed graciously to each of the four Goths, the newest fighters for the Vandals, each pair next to a captain of the guard at the central stools of each long table. The king's guard stood behind these. To each side along the walls the rest of the Vandal *alpingi*, the council, sat on benches.

Then sweeping his arm around to all, the *scope* plucked his harp and sang, "Hear now retainers, kin, and thanes of the Alan-Vandal clans. Listen to my song." And strolling along the tables, he snapped his fingers and intoned these words:

An age ago	the honored Wulfilas
Wrote words	of God's goodly spell
From Greeks to Goths	giving wondrous words.
The Lord of Life	love-leaving Goodman
Found flesh	fulsomely filled
Followed faith	no fate to fear.

The singer, now between the ends of the side tables, turned to the head table, to the seven who sat in state and continued his song, waltzing before Ulfasson and passing the king to whirl before Ullman. All the host followed the poet's wandering and his words. Every eye but especially Gaiseric's and Gelimmers watched the Ulfakin and their Gothic friends as the song unfolded.

His way was wise	but death comes down
On all alive.	Only on Goodman
Was it wrongly wrought	killed by kissing
Betrayed and bought by	green-eyed gelt
By wretched wight .	his faith forfent.

At these words Ulfasson stirred and sought the eyes of his uncle, Ullman, who sat stiff as if deaf to what he'd heard. Ulfasson began to rise, but hoary Huneric steadied his shoulder with his hand and said, "Stay cousin. Let us listen."

Ever-ware, evil	wrecks wrong
Hangs heavy alone	full foul to drench
Fatherless of faith	ungirt by ground.

Now, Ulfasson sprang up. "No," he said, "not that, not to drown."

Ullman spoke. "Be silent, fool. It is a song."

The *scope* continued, and now all watched the Ulfa-kin.

Un-buried, unbidden   unfriended, unbanned
Not kindly, nor kingly   an unfaithful man.

Below, at the side tables, the Gothic recruits felt for the weapons they'd left by the door. They jumped up.

"Sit! You all." Gaiseric roared. "No one stir." He himself stood. The royal guard stepped forward behind the Ulfa-kin and the Goths.

"Our poet will finish his song."

Wulfilas's words   welcome the work
Of lightness and life   Lord who is love.
Betimes betrayal   he born was, rebirthed
Has suffered for all   sons of this earth.

Horns sounded at Gelimmer's signal and the feast was brought in. The silver platters from the house of Honoratus were piled high with meats and fishes, fruits and cheeses, breads and poultry, roasted gourds and soups. These were whisked away to the low tables and benches where the council members and warrior chiefs sat. To the high table women carried specially dressed plates for the king and his guests, each large plate bearing a good selection of each dish. But the plates set before Ulfasson and Ullman at the head table were bare of any food at all.

Ulfasson looked blankly at his dish. Ullman turned to Gelimmer and said, "What is this farce? Do we deserve no feast?"

As prompted, Gelimmer, and on the other side hoary Huneric said as one, "You our guests of honor tonight will get all you deserve."

Gaiseric stood and spoke in a quiet, calm voice. "Tonight we toast our Gothic friends and new warriors whom Ulfa-kin has brought to us. In greater grace, we honor Ulfasson and Ullman as friends of our house."

The king looked, puzzled at his guest's empty plates. "Ullman, how the kitchen mistakes you. Please forgive the affront. Here, eat of my own food. You as well, Ulfasson."

Ulfasson pushed up from his place. "No. I cannot eat. I have been ill." From behind, two of the king's guard pushed him down to sit again. The assembly grew silent. A pall fell over the young man's face. He looked to his uncle Ullman whose stern forward stare bade the younger man be silent. Then the king rose, lifted an arm, at which the royal guard behind the Goths swung harness-leather garrotes over the Gothic newcomers' heads, twisting them at the neck, kneeing their backs while others held down their hands with spear points.

Gaiseric spoke. "Our *scope* sang of our Lord in heaven betrayed by his own follower. Perhaps, too, the Romans have sent betrayers among us. It is good, though, that we grant mercy and share our bounty with the wayward." At this the plates of Ulfa-kin and the Goths were brought. Gaiseric himself divided his own food among them, giving Ullman and Ulfasson the largest shares. "Now eat my friends. Let no morsel be left. In trust and good faith, enjoy."

The king's soft words fell on the hush. Not one word was spoken in the hall. All watched the six so suddenly accosted.

"I have been sick," Ulfasson said again. "I cannot eat a thing." The nearby guard prodded him with his spear shaft. The youngster began to cry. "I am ill." He vomited over the plate given him.

Huneric comforted the boy. "Even now honor demands you eat, both grub and gush." The boy sobbed.

At this shoddy scene Ullman, the boy's uncle, raised a spoonful to his mouth. He chewed deliberately and swallowed, then helped himself again. Eating two more, he turned to the king. "It is delicious, my lord. I thank you." Looking at his choking nephew, Ullman said, "Now, you too, my boy, must do."

The boy rose despite the spears and roared, "You'll kill me, Uncle, for your own crime." The guards again forced him down and gagging and coughing the boy ate and wept and howled. He vomited again.

Gelimmer rose, "Drag these two and their Gothic handlers and all disgusting plates to the coop while we banquet. Tomorrow we will see to them in the pen before we set out to wrest away Numidia."

18

Augustine Drafts Bonifacius

I had not forgotten my bishop's words. He'd said, "Yes, there is more." I suffered in the intervening month an affliction common to gossips: weariness of waiting but a hope that he would elucidate. I had not found it unusual for Augustine to raise an issue only to let it slide out of sight for a while and then to suddenly resurrect the idea, usually in exactly the same tone of voice, as if it had only half a minute ago been first uttered, as if he had been arguing the point within himself for months. That he'd said his news was in nature personal more impressed me, and had it not been for that, I would have not waited a minute but would have dismissed his observation as extraneous—not that anything he intoned could truly be discounted.

On that evening of "more"—it had been in late September and still torrid for the harvest that year, the-friend-of-my-youth said, "It is of a personal nature," in such a mischievous, somehow titillating way, that I noted his precise tone which again rang in my ears when his messenger came this morning to my library office saying, "The bishop wishes to see you in the reception hall. He said it was personal." Certainly, the words were not delivered by this man in the timbre Augustine used—the messenger was one of the corps of truly virulent detractors of mine (I had, they thought, usurped the rightful place of many a good monk at Augustine's side, which in fact was true, although I had not intended it to be so)—but the tickle of the bishop's phrase nearly made me laugh even after so long a time. He well knew[1] how to enliven my curiosity with mystery.

"Please tell *our* bishop—I was certain to irk this good man by my emphasis—that I will attend him the instant I finish his letter." His letter was the latest of a short series of letters I had been sending

---

1 I've said before that it was his talent to move people, and I wonder, now after it all, how much of this ability was meant, planned, or in mind used, and what portion of the same simply poured forth as one's voice comes forth from throat and mouth in a timbre singular to one's self alone. Asked, Augustine would likely credit God the Father for the gift.

to Sabina using the presbyter's own name and practiced script, and when the man went away, I finished my note, sealed it as was appropriate, and sent it on with my usual trusted scholar, a sometime student of Hebrew who studied with me in the library. Carrying the bishop's seal, it would be passed directly to Sabina and that quickly. In this missive, I set out in our calendar Friday, November fifteenth, the beginning of the preparations for Christmas as the advent of a little adventure I was planning, hoping for distraction during that busy time in which the absence of a single stable hand (formerly a caravan trader who my kin near Thagaste knew years ago) and a few horses would not be noticed.

This matter I had been discussing with Sabina was much too important to wait even when summoned by Augustine. I, in the persona of the bishop himself, was planning the transport of Sequia from Thagaste to Hippo Regius. Her daughter's safety was worrying Sabina incessantly, and she fervently desired to have Sequia within the sturdy walls of the city. This was something which I felt certain I could accomplish from my present seat near to the bishop. The plan was hatched over our mutual concern for Sequia's safety which over the harvest seemed assured but which toward the end of October, hearing of Vandal forays into Numidia and some very near Thagaste itself, grew tenuous although Sequia continued to insist on staying, claiming that her flock of *Christicolae* depended on her.

Sabina had responded to a letter—it was one of my first trials—in which "Augustine" inquired about Sequia:

> I have wonder and admiration of this second child of yours. What is her age, how is she in the world—a follower of Christ?—a wife and mother in her own right? And, asking without regret or rue, in what ways—having the same mother—how like our own son Adeodatus might she be?

Sabina replied:

> One might well muse about my second child who now approaches her fortieth year as an ardent follower of Christ's teachings and ways. She is a friend to all seekers. And like Adeodatus whose life ended just as hers began, Sequia has chosen chastity as a way of life. In bodily form, her eyes

and nose might be his, and in a particular lift of her lips when about to laugh, she is his twin. Too, they both show a familiar firmness of will.

And this told me—as soon as the bishop had read it on his own, leaving it available then to me—both that Sequia was the exact likeness of Augustine's and Sabina's son, Adeodatus, and by inference that Sabina had almost immediately caught on to my devious trickery. She was playing along. I would not have to shock her later by admitting my Augustinian persona. She already knew. Likely, she also knew that Augustine himself would now read her replies (as he always had but without her certainty knowing). It was exactly the kind of disingenuous business—involving Augustine and his concubine in a late-life encounter the outcome of which could only be fascinating if not profoundly amusing—that I had spent my entire diplomatic life perfecting. What could go wrong?[2]

The soon-to-be presence in Hippo of a Thagastan farmer—Sequia, among so many other refugees pushed to flight by the Vandals— would be no worry and hardly noticeable to anyone. And, certainly I would reunite this daughter with Sabina, but I also entertained the spectacle of a reunion with the man I believed—I had more than a strong suspicion of this, to be sure—would prove to be her father, the-friend-of-my-youth.

Our plan, like many of my activities, called for secrecy and for as few people involved as possible, and, too, required a tidbit of deception, something for which I had developed a not small talent over the years of my travels. To wit: Sequia, who had the reputation of being an excellent horsewoman, might learn from my well-mounted messenger that her mother had fallen suddenly ill, shall we say, (not exactly a truth but certainly news to compel action because of Sabina's advanced age) and had asked for her daughter to come (again not just believable but generally if not specifically true). I had selected this messenger and traveling companion from among the great crowd of refugees that Sabina's sisterhood had for months cared for, one, I

____

2 I took care with what I knew to be a serious business and not only because of likely repercussion upon my own head, but for the reason that Sequia, Sabina, and even Augustine himself relied on my fealty and truth. I say it without pride of experience, "I had served great men for long and for good in this very same way."

found by my well-placed questions and proverbial listening habits, who had learned the road between Thagaste and Hippo Regius in childhood and who could be trusted to protect his charge at the expense of his life, the life which Sequia's mother had recently nursed to health and saved. It was helpful to me and to him, too, that this Aksil's father had known and was known by my family years before. Also, I would, as a representative of the bishopric, supply Aksil with good, speedy mounts and would dispatch him with the news (the unfortunate "illness" of Sister Sabina) from Hippo with the means of a fast return to bring Sequia back there. The lengthening November nights were to lend cover. And since both Sabina and Sequia had many friends both among Berbers and Romans, and among as well those fervid Donatist believers and too the less plentiful Catholics of southern Proconsularis, shelter and rest during daylight would be simple to arrange as needed, all for the sake of secure passage of a woman of great spiritual regard. Sabina, too, could make suggestions of safe houses and Sequia and our courier would add to the list as they traveled. Sabina and Sequia it was known were nearly penniless, neither subject to ransom, one being an ancient nun and the other a helpful celibate.

In any case, this latest letter set the date of the encounter with Sequia, who was innocent of our plot, and named some additional shelters along the way that I felt to be friendly. The precise path and times of arrival we were leaving to Aksil, my chosen messenger. All this business done, now I could attend to our bishop's Orphic summons.

The bishop's *tablinum* was seldom used for Augustine's meetings since he preferred the library and more informal conversation in the garden or ambulatory, but when greeting Romans of ample importance, the bishop invariably received guests there. The room formed a part of what had been the *domus* of a wealthy pagan which had been annexed as part of the monastery during the construction of the cathedral. I felt that Augustine enjoyed this connection to ancient Roman wealth and belief which he used as a gateway to the spiritual riches promised beyond in the church and monastery. To this purpose the bishop had the episcopal throne moved to this reception room from which he could survey the house and, especially, the main entry.

I, however, came by the servant's entrance (forever my favored approach to any place not only because it befits the status of a scribe but also that it affords a preview of what one is getting into) and moved through the *peristylium*, pausing at the rear opening of the *tablinum* which had been, with the approach of November weather, curtained off from the open ambulatory. Happily I came quietly, for within, both voices which I knew well were raised in ire.

"These brigands may well ferry oxen and goats, but they have no navy!" The rounded low voice of Bonifacius shoveled out words like fiery coals. "They can never seize our port."

Augustine's sharper, thinner voice, like a stiletto, cut quickly, "Nor did they have a large army, you said!" The timbre rose to the pitch of a stylus dragged across bronze, "And look what they've taken, what they've done!" Now the words climbed a scale. "Carnage! Theft! Murder! Violence! Torture!"

The hot baritone replied, "Are they not called barbarians? What to expect!"

"Yes, what did you, my count and protector, expect?"

It was Bonifacius replying. "I expect? No, I demand. They must follow our truce. Our agreements were made directly with Rome."

Augustine's knife cut deeply, "These heretics care nothing for Rome. They would bring it down, would profane even *civitates Dei*! The very City of God!"

Though I knew both these men well, I had never been in the same room with them together. And that alone stayed my hand parting the arras. I'd learned too well at the seats of power never to enter in the midst of argument for the sake both of civility and of safety. So, I stood there, less to listen though it was impossible not to hear, but to deflect the arm of anger from my helpless pate.

"Hippo Regius will never fall. I will wager my entire army that it be so."

"I hear this: You guarantee our port from the sea. But will you march against and destroy these fools of Vandals in open combat?"

Bonifacius answered. "The port I give you. It will stand and supply the town. But, your Grace, I think it unwise to meet head on with such an unknown force whose king is wily. I have other plans."

"Plans!" Augustine shouted. "You are a coward, Bonifacius. Afraid of a lesser army made up of inferior men." There was silence then, and I nearly swept the curtain aside, but the bishop spoke before I moved. "Plans? What plans?"

Bonifacius was slow to respond. Then he led with this, "You remember Darius, I believe."

"I am old, *Comes*, not infirm of mind. What of Darius?"

"The foresightful Count of Rome perceived Vandal intransigence and made provision . . ."

"Get to the point!" Augustine shouted.

I could feel *Comes Africae* pacing, just as he had during our late night conversations. He suddenly stopped his gait and turned. "Poison is the point!"

"A weapon of war, this?"

"A weapon of the court," Bonifacius replied. "These barbarians are nothing without their king. It is from him that all their success derives. Kill Gaiseric, and you kill all Vandals."

If I had entered then, despite fifty years of training at courts and cathedrals, my face would have betrayed my feelings. Gaiseric may now be a king and an enemy (he had always been a warrior) but to me he had been a pupil, and an excellent one, too. I did not want any part of a devious and painful death for him. I stayed outside.

"And how will you penetrate his camp?"

"It is all set. His own relation will spike Gaiseric's food. I expect to hear at any moment that the deed is done."

"You trust one of his own?"

"Can one trust a Judas? No. To ensure success, I have sent hence four of my best fighters pretending to defect to the Vandal cause, and to certify that this Ullman of Ulfa-kin—Bonifacius stumbled over the name—follows through with our plan."

I scraped my sandals over the stones to make sounds of arriving, parted the curtain, and entered. "I am sorry to be late, your Grace. All the correspondence is done."

"Join us, Amicus. No need to apologize. We've used the time wisely, the count and I." Augustine swept an arm toward *Comes Africae* who had been pacing as I entered and, not expecting my presence stopped and simply stared. He thought I had been rude, no doubt. Augustine contrived to dangle my presence and affiliation before the count who had been loath to give up my services. Their relationship was never more strained than at that moment.

I bowed. "*Vale*, my Count." He repeated the greeting and resumed his pacing.

Augustine was cheery, almost playful. "We have been busy with grave matters of state, but now that you are here we can move on to more ecclesiastical issues and some personal business."

I noted his term "personal" but found it difficult to believe that the bishop would reveal a secret reserved for me to his Roman protector. "If you are pleased, then I must be, as well," I said.

"Excellent!" The bishop pronounced the word as if it were lascivious and delicious. "Please take notes."

Oh! For a scribe to be without his tablet and stylus. "I will fetch my implements."

Augustine gestured to a small table at one side of the *tablinum*. "Stay. I have here all you need." He glanced at Bonifacius then began his dictation. "Note first that *Comes Africae* guarantees the safety of our port from both land and sea. The count also agrees to move his army against these barbarian invaders who are tromping about Numidia in violation of our treaty with them."

The baritone rumbled. "I said no such thing."

Augustine countered: "This attack is pending the outcome of the assassination of Gaiseric, so-called king of the Vandals."

Bonifacius muttered something, but otherwise was silent and kept at his turns around the room. He barely looked at me, but when he did and saw me busily noting Augustine's words, I thought he flashed a grimace my way. As for me, having heard this news from the *peristylium*, I was able to maintain a placid countenance despite uneasy feelings.

"Now, Count, my protector, favor me with an ecclesiastical task."

The count threw himself into a chair on the other side of the bishop's throne. "What else would you have me do?"

"Outside Thagaste, my hometown, lives a certain woman—she lives as no matter of interest on land once owned by my father—and who there is a well known and celibate spiritualist called Sequidei, follower of God. It is said she even reads the gospels. In public gatherings!"

Immediately I was alert to this surprise. Augustine knew more about Sequia and her activities than did I. Most certainly, I had awakened some mischief.

The count smirked but moved to hide it. "No doubt you object to this practice."

"There are but two possibilities in this case. One is certain, that her activities—imagine a woman acting as a priest—are unregulated and are therefore unknown in nature and scope. That alone is totally unacceptable in the African church. The other, rather likely without the guidance of our clergy, is that her spiritual acts are apostate and heretical, something which can only be determined through questioning."

Too often had I transcribed and translated lists of Augustine's questions. His mind quick and razor-sharp in youth had sustained itself and had additionally become more powerful than a grindstone as it closed its way onto conclusions. To be the recipient of his questioning was not pleasant and more often was a very dangerous thing. It seemed that no number of heretics convicted was enough for him.

"You want me to question this woman? What of your friend the Bishop of Thagaste?" The general stood.

Augustine glowered at the soldier. "Of course, not! You are not canonically qualified to do so. No, since Alypius is for a time at

Rome, what I desire is for you to bring her safely here to Hippo Regius where I myself will put her to the test."

I shuddered inside my robes at this. Now, if I were to bring Sequia to Hippo Regius, I must do so suddenly and in utmost secrecy. My shaking spun off droplets of sweat that were washing away any sympathy I had felt for Augustine. He continued.

"The roads so close to Numidia are made unsafe by these barbarians, and a woman will need an escort to remain unmolested. Send a detachment substantial enough to deter interference. Find this so called priestess Sequidei and bring her to me."

I entered a question at this as if desiring to note the point, "And when should this occur?" I held the stylus poised over the tablet.

"Can you be there before mid-month?" Augustine asked.

I dropped my stylus. Both the bishop and count looked my way as I scrambled to retrieve it.

"It is three-days travel without trouble. My detachment can leave the morning after next."

"So be it, *Comes Africae*, I can expect to see this woman at the end of a week."

It was doubtful that the count was more uncomfortable than was I, but knowing his moods and habits—he held himself rigid, tall, and motionless—I believed he was displeased. Doing the bishop's bidding was seldom a rewarding task.

For my plans, this move forebode disaster. Bonifacius's men would be returning even before my plot had begun unless we could move immediately and stay ahead of the detachment of a Roman cohort. It seemed impossible. All my despair and surprise I hid behind my placid expression of the neutral scribe, simply recording in shorthand the words that were spoken. But then something else disturbed me.

Augustine rose from his throne with a shout unbelievably loud for a man so frail. "Who profanes the house of God?"

Bonifacius drew his sword and strode forward to one side of the narrow end of the *impluvium* making a formidable barrier of himself.

I followed their gazes to the *vestibulum* where a crowd, something of a rabble by the noise it made, had burst in and was already filling the atrium. Against students from the *gymnasium* across the road, market shoppers from the corner lot, and shopkeepers from the front of the house, soldiers of the count's retinue vainly pushed back on the crowd which was following two files of guards between which stumbled a huge Gothic soldier carrying a bulky bag in his crossed arms. The man had been chained.

Bonifacius yelled an order to his captain, who broke ranks and took up the other side of the *impluvium* protecting the *tablinum*, myself, and the bishop. The rest of the count's men were pushed back nearly into the waters of the *impluvium*. Then, in that rolling baritone voice of command, Bonifacius boomed out "*Caesaris Caesari et Comes Africae nomine mortis poena consistit!* In the name of great Caesar and the Count of Africa halt upon pain of death."

He raised and brandished his sword, his captain doing the same, and the crowd stilled and receded a few paces.

The file of guards moved to the center of the atrium and fanned out blocking the crowd and fully revealing the giant in their custody.

At that moment, the event, whatever it was, clearly needed the authority of the army rather than that of the church. Augustine slumped back on his throne, and I went there to stand beside him, the view being better from the platform.

"What means this?" The count commanded.

The captain of the guard holding the Goth in chains stepped forward. "This man was discovered outside Igligili just as you see him, bringing a letter on foot from our Vandal enemies in Icosium. He insisted that he present it to you, my Count."

"It looks unsealed. Did you not read it?"

"No, my Count. It is written in their strange language."

"What of his bundle he carries?"

"He is bidden that none but you unwrap the gift from the Vandal king. He guards it always, holding it close even in sleep."

Bonifacius looked back toward me. "Come look, Innomenatus." And to the guard, "Give this scribe your letter."

I came forward to the count, but at that moment the Goth fell to his knees and moaned, "Grant me the death I have earned. Let me die quickly. Let me die now."

"What did this Goth say?" Bonifacius asked.

I translated.

Augustine spoke from his throne, "Do not defile this place with your executions. Away with you all."

Bonifacius stood rigid. "First let us hear this Vandal message and see his gift."

I opened the letter to read. It was in Gaiseric's hand, written in his Vandalic script:

> In trade for the small gift from Count Darius, I send you greetings and valuables from my own kin, carried in the arms of your trusted soldier.

As I intoned the last words "trusted soldier" the man on his knees raised the bundle in his arms. Offering it to the Count, he let it unfurl. He had hugged it to himself all across Numidia to Hippo Regius, for, as we now saw, he had no hands with which to grasp it. His hands had been hacked off, their ends burned. And as his parcel came loose and landed on the atrium floor, the odor of contagion spilled into the room. "Ullman and Ulfasson," the huge Goth said, and then himself fell fully the floor, knocking away the two dessicated and rotting heads.

The crowd, all of us, covered our noses with our robes. I tried not to gasp. One head bounced once and rolled to Bonifacius, who kicked it sodden and putrid into the pool. The second head landed with eyes that had sunken into its skull, staring in the direction of the count. There was a rush of the crowd to the door which movement simply clogged the egress and fostered fisticuffs.

"Outrage and blasphemy," Augustine bellowed. "You bring horror and shame into the house of God. Away with you. Away with you all." And seeing no one move, "Get out. Get out now, all of you. And Bonifacius, take your mess and your great Roman plans out, too. Plans! Plans!"

Even having seen many times the carnage of war firsthand, Bonifacius looked fearful and sick, backing away from the heads and the handless, sobbing man he himself had sent to Icosium to bring Gaiseric to his fate worse than death. Suddenly, the count stepped forward and raised his sword over the Goth's lowered head. But he was stopped by Augustine's next words uttered in a firm, calm, authoritative voice, "*Virum sanguinum in infernis arderet.* Murderers shall labor in hell for eternity. *Cessate ab insania.* Dare not desecrate God's house."

With that, Augustine called me to his side, and we left the room by the way I had come. Behind the *tablinum*, the household were out of their rooms, hoping to witness the ruckus. The cooks who stood in the private passage I had followed, plugged it.

"Your Grace, let us sit here under the *peristylium* and drink water these lovely kitcheners will bring us. We have suffered a shock." And so we did. And the water was cool and pure.

Having drunk, Augustine turned to me and said, "I am sorry, Amicus, that you had to witness such brutality and perfidy."

"It is the way of the world, my bishop."

"That may be, but I feel somehow I brought this on us."

I did not follow his logic. "How might that be?"

"I confess, I wished to parade you before Bonifacius. It was his comeuppance. But it was wrong. Also it is not that for which I summoned you." He took another long draught of water.

Hoping to move his conversation on to assuage my curiosity, I said, "I was told it was a 'personal' matter."

"And so it is. But with all that has transpired today, I will not yet speak of it." He looked into my eyes. "I will tell it another time." He patted my hand as if to soothe my obvious curiosity. "Soon."

19

Innomenatus Seeks Sabina

What drives a man? Is it fear? Ambition? Hate? Certainly not love. Perhaps it is principle.

I contemplated this conundrum as I wound my way south through what should have been the quietest streets of the city, most of which were even in the dusk surprisingly peopled. Most there were refugees. The sun had set far below the shadowy mountain. I had left Augustine in his quarters and noted, as I later moved to exit the monastery, that he was at a library table in the company of several scribes. Likely he'd be there for hours.

Unnoticed in the streets, I was pushed onward to find Sabina and to reveal the truth to her. It could not be helped. I had brought with me her last letter, not without some trepidation lest Augustine look for it while I was gone, and not without some fear that my possessing it would offend the good sister even though I realized she likely suspected that another besides Augustine had written. I had slipped the letter out of the cubby and into my robes while the bishop rested. Why was I driven to act so? I wondered.

In the moment, I hoped to save Sequia. I had meddled in her life. I may have been instrumental in exposing her to the hawkish notice of Augustine. What had Sabina said? She'd written only, "my second child," skillfully dodging my implied question but fixing for both me and my bishop the time of Sequia's conception. I, adopting the persona of the bishop, encouraged her to proffer more detail even though I was uncertain what she meant or to what her information would lead. Now, I feared I had been too forward.

In Macedonia, they have a saying: "There is no fire so small but that with much stirring may puff up," which I repeated to myself as I moved toward the convent situated below the southern sandy brick wall of the city. The early November darkness had deepened sufficiently to shade my progress. It was not guilt that drove me. The woes of the world are deep enough without adding the overburden of remorse. As caring as I can be, neither was it love. Much less hate. I would do what I could to thwart Augustine's repugnant habits of persecution. Halfway through my circuitous route to Sabina, I decided it was principle that pushed me to action. Concern for Sabina's heart, yes. No mother, not even Augustine's Monnika, should witness the castigation of her child. I myself had withered before the consternation of the bishop, both as a youth and lately as he inquired into my identity. I was alert to his dealings: My apprehension extended to Julian, the bishop's latest heretical target, in Africa to the large body of Arians and Donatists, these last, already convicted heretics in Augustine's mind and in church annals, and I was fearful even for *Comes Africae* who roused Augustine's ire at the Arian baptism of his newborn—for any who would come under the scrutiny of the bishop of Hippo Regius were sure to be picked from mind's limb to mind's limb before being driven out to the desert of the damned, so much so that his terrible grinding away at heresy had horrified even himself. It was against those injustices I stood, albeit privately.

I also wondered. What drives a man such as the friend-of-my-youth to hunt and oppress his own child? That was a greater question to occupy me over the second half of my mission to Sabina. What sort of love under God is possible if there is no love for one's child, one's friends, one's spouse or lover? That may have been the central question Augustine should have settled. Perhaps he had in his way, but I did not need to *suspect* Augustine of cruelty. Despite his protests of rectitude to the Church and to the world in general, I knew his lifelong string of truly despicable acts, all of which pointed to truculence. In his early[1] argumentative wrestling, he was reputed to have clasped an opponent and to have bitten his ear as a reminder for him to listen. Augustine was ferocious, perhaps, unto bloodiness. Of all that, simply on principle, I would spare Sequia.

---

1 To be fair, I should indicate this is hearsay, perhaps just idle gossip. Of this incident that I had not witnessed I had heard several versions in far-flung corners of the world, some even positing that the ear was entirely gnawed off, others, on the nearer side of tale telling, that Augustine simply boxed the man's ear as would any sender do to a messenger. Some said the recipient was an opponent, others that he was a stubborn student.

Nor did I wish the bishop's implacable vengeance upon *Comes Africae*. They had not been friends since well before the Arian baptism, but it was clear to me that something still tied the count to the will and wiles of the bishop. Perhaps it had something to do with Alypius and Rome itself. I itched to find out.

I was, as were most throughout Africa and Numidia, happy of the count's presence and protection. For me the dangers were not great. I had friends on all sides, Roman, Vandal, and Berber, but the count even in his current inaction balanced power in favor of peace and prosperity on the promontories of Africa. Though there had been an increase in Vandal attacks, in Vandal advances, and consequent panic in western parts of Numidia and although Gaiseric's intention shone clearly—he would invade—just how rapidly and in what force that it was to be would be determined by the exercise of the power and the courage of *Comes Africae*.

As I neared the convent, more and more I had to press my way through crowded streets. I had not seen or smelled such herding since my years in Constantinople. Here the streets were straight but narrow. Raised sidewalks grew incommodiously jammed with pedestrians since shops yet stood open and because the carts running below in the darkness of the road presented such a hazard. I wove myself through to come behind a pair of soldiers going in my direction, and they helped clear a path, though I observed they did so kindly with respect to those walking the opposite way.

"What accounts for this mass of people so late?" I asked in my best Latin.

One turned his head to see me. "It's the devilment of the Vandals, *avus*, grandfather. All these people have fled to our safe city."

I accepted his moniker for me and asked, "Must I then be afraid of Vandals?"

The second soldier, less kind, scoffed. "*Manere senis fores*, stay within the walls, old man."

"More come each day," said the first. "Are you headed for the convent, *pater*? It is here."

I took one look at the people packed at the convent gate. "No, to the stables." I would enter Sabina's walls a different way.

"Go further then and to the right."

"Thank you kindly, *salve*," I said. The way they pointed led me along the convent's dark stone wall toward the city bastion, downward toward an equestrian gate near the barns that stood crooked between the towering city walls and those of the convent. The stalls were as full of horses as the streets were of people. No one dared leave animals outside the walls now. I inquired at the stable gate for Aksil of Chaouïa, my Berber guide and family friend, who being well known there by all could easily shepherd me in to see Sabina.

Aksil was a light and lean man whose rapid gait was in keeping with his name, meaning cheetah. He talked fast, too. "You've come seeking me, sir. I am honored. Come have dinner with us here. We have goat roasted with fig butter." He briskly swept his arm forward and stepped lithely between files of horses. "Come with me." And he was gone. I did my best to follow.

Over the simple and delicious family meal (my second that evening) eaten right by his cooking fire, Aksil and I spoke generally of the new dangers on the roads of Numidia. "I have heard," he said, "that Vandal patrols have entered even Proconsularis from Numidia." He shook his head. His people and mine had endured many invasions, but keeping close to the desert, had avoided most direct damages. "There are many stories, but most cannot be believed."

I enjoyed rolling out the words of our native tongue and listening to Aksil's fluid and fast elocution in Berber. He had for twenty years brought caravans through Thagaste on his way to Hippo Regius from his desert gardens and groves. He grew dates, mostly, and had many stories to tell. As a merchant he knew Latin well enough to do business, and I asked him, reluctantly, so we could speak more privately in front of his family, "*Quod et loquimur Romani*, shall we speak Latin?"

"*Si volueris*, as you wish."

I told Aksil that our little jaunt must come sooner than I had expected. Fortunately, he was free.

"I can leave this very night." He pointed to two young men at the fire. "I have sons to carry on here."

"Fine, but I must speak with Mother Sabina, first. Can you show me the way to her?"

"She may now be at vespers, but let us see."

I gave thanks to the family for sharing their meal, telling them that of all in a household I valued the cooks most highly. Then, we two departed. Aksil led me nimbly through several alleys and up several stairways, then, spoke softly at a small gate which was quickly opened. We entered the convent proper.

A barrel-shaped woman, bustling among the crowd at the entry, supervising her sisters in feeding the multitude gathered there, looked toward Aksil and smiled widely. "Our horseman is here. Come help us."

"I will," he said, "but I must first conduct this monk to *Materfamilias*. Where might we find her?"

The woman frisked me with her broad gaze. "And who may you be?"

"Innomenatus, a Madauran scribe in the service of the bishop. I have a letter for your sister." I wanted to seem both general and local to deflect suspicion and spoke gently to reassure this formidable woman.

"Do you come from the bishop, then?"

"That I cannot say, but this concerns Mother Sabina's daughter, Sequia."

Aksil said, "This man is good. You may trust him, Sister Ia."

Ia frowned at me still and said, "Let me announce you and see what she says."

After waiting a goodly time, we were brought to the garden and met the head of the convent, Sister Sabina.

The woman I met looked tall even seated. Her carriage was erect but not severe. Her hair, as white as wave-caps on a breezy beach, cast a contrast with her almond-husk-colored skin, quite smooth despite her age. She pierced me with green Berber eyes, oases in the indomitable landscape of her face, and so told me at once who was in control here. Still, she spoke softly, kindly.

"Please forgive us suspicion and worry," she said. "The times are difficult, and with so many strangers arriving, we are careful here." She looked steadily at me and added, "But then, I see you are not so strange as I at first feared."

I did not know exactly what she meant. "I am Augustine's scribe." And with that, I presented her with her own letter.

She only glanced at it and returned it to me. "You have changed your name since we sat together with my young paramour under the palms in Carthage, but your face is altered less than mine in age." Now she smiled. Her eyes glistened in the torchlight and held me in their gaze. "Your presence here in Hippo Regius with my letter in your hand answers the questions I have lately pondered." She grinned now, a bit crookedly, and her eyes narrowed and darkened. "What shall I call you now?"

"'Amicus,' after the bishop's name for me, or 'Innomenatus' if you prefer. I left my birth name years ago in the desert on my way to Alexandria, but I have followed Aurelius in many ways all during my life and do so closely again now."

"Welcome then, Amicus. If I know you from Carthage, slighter then and more hirsute now, I recognize you better another way: as a visitor in my dreams."

Sabina puzzled me. She had grown deep in wisdom as well as verbal sport.[2] "I hardly know what you mean," I said, "but am well flattered. Thank you."

"Neither our youth together nor my visions are why you have come this night. Whatever your errand, I am relieved." She let me struggle with this a moment before continuing, "When Ia announced your coming, I started at the mention of Thagaste, thinking that Alypius, the bishop there, was come again to investigate rumors of Pelagian heresy."

Aksil turned to go, but I stopped him. "With Sister Sabina's leave, please stay. What I bring concerns you as well."

So, we sat with her, and in a calculated way with only as much

---

2 I remembered Sabina as always serious but loathe to speak her mind. Still, I had in our youth sensed a profundity that she refused to reveal publicly. She was nearly the diametrical opposite of her lover, Augustine. She yet used few words but was now, I saw, unafraid to voice her thoughts.

candor as was called for (and *that* more than was necessary on my part, for Sabina *had* grown incisively wise), I began to explain:

"It may be my errand here touches on a heresy. You can best judge that." I drew on my recent history, leaving out mention of the shouting match between the bishop and Bonifacius. "Some time ago, I served in the household of *Comes Africae*. I have many friends there still. Thus, I learned of an army excursion to Thagaste to arrest a woman who farms near there, on suspicion of trading with our enemies, the Vandals. Thinking this was the same Sequia we hope to bring to Hippo Regius for safety through the plan we have been working on with Aksil, and as this Roman detachment is now due to leave in only two days, I took it upon myself to come here, to arrange a hastier mission than originally planned."

Sabina spoke. "I have worried less about the Vandals than I have over our bishop's heretic-hunting. I have felt sure it would be only a matter of time before Sequia's words and works within her holy community would draw his attention south to Thagaste. Bishop Alypius warned as much back in January." At this Sabina drew forth the very letter I had posted to her early that day. "I received this missive today. This tells me then that Augustine does not know you are here."

I could not bring myself to confess.

"Was it not from you?"

Was she sparring with me now? All I was willing to say was, "I know of it." And I added, now admitting to all but writing the letter, "The news from *casa bonifacii* must alter the timing set in that note."

Sabina was alert, listening. "I have thought all along that another voice was involved. So, it is you who seems to have broken the bishop's many years of silence."

She was spry and had caught me in a lie. And as it is often best to admit one's deeds in the forced light of day, I said, "Yes, I confess. It is I."

"But should my daughter not flee to the desert rather than into the arms of the very authority here that wishes to arrest her?"

Now it was my turn to skirmish. "Would she flee?" I asked? She gave no answer. "Would you not have her here?" Again, silence. Sabina crossed an arm under her breasts, crooked the other on it and rolled her fingers before her mouth, in thought.

"Aksil is prepared to leave tonight. Can your sisters provision him quickly?"

She did not move that hand. She raised an eyebrow and turned her gaze to the open sky above the olive arbor, looking long ago and far away. I sat. I waited.

My Berber friend stirred beside me. "I must go to ready everything," he whispered, bowed, and like the scent of jasmine on a dry breeze, disappeared.

Finally, Sabina looked back at me, frowning. "Look you, Amicus, something is amiss here."

I felt the midday desert heat beam from her hooded stare, but I kept quiet. "You say heresy with one voice and treason with another. Perhaps confusion over the source of danger will confound Sequia's escape from trouble. You indicate the bishop but say the count. Which is it?"

Sabina had wasted none of her young years at Augustine's side. Even through her quietude, she had obtained a fierce sense of argument. I was again trapped. "Yes, as strong as Bonifacius is, he is not the prime mover. You are correct. It is at the bishop's word that *Comes Africae* sends his men."

She did not appear satisfied but took her gaze from me, much to my relief, and looked upwards again. "That makes for more sense," she said. "Yet neither the count nor the bishop will prevail."

I took this to mean she approved my mission, Aksil's journey. "No. We shall succeed in this."

Materfamilias smiled thinly. She shook her head as if about to correct a child. "You are indeed a student of the world, but I'm afraid you do not look further than the stones of earth or the wetness of waves in your philosophy." Sabina held her next words for effect, then said, "I was warned of something of this in a dream, Amicus.

"From a hill I know well, overlooking Thagaste, horsemen dragged a woman toward a gorgon with white braided hair. I awoke at a

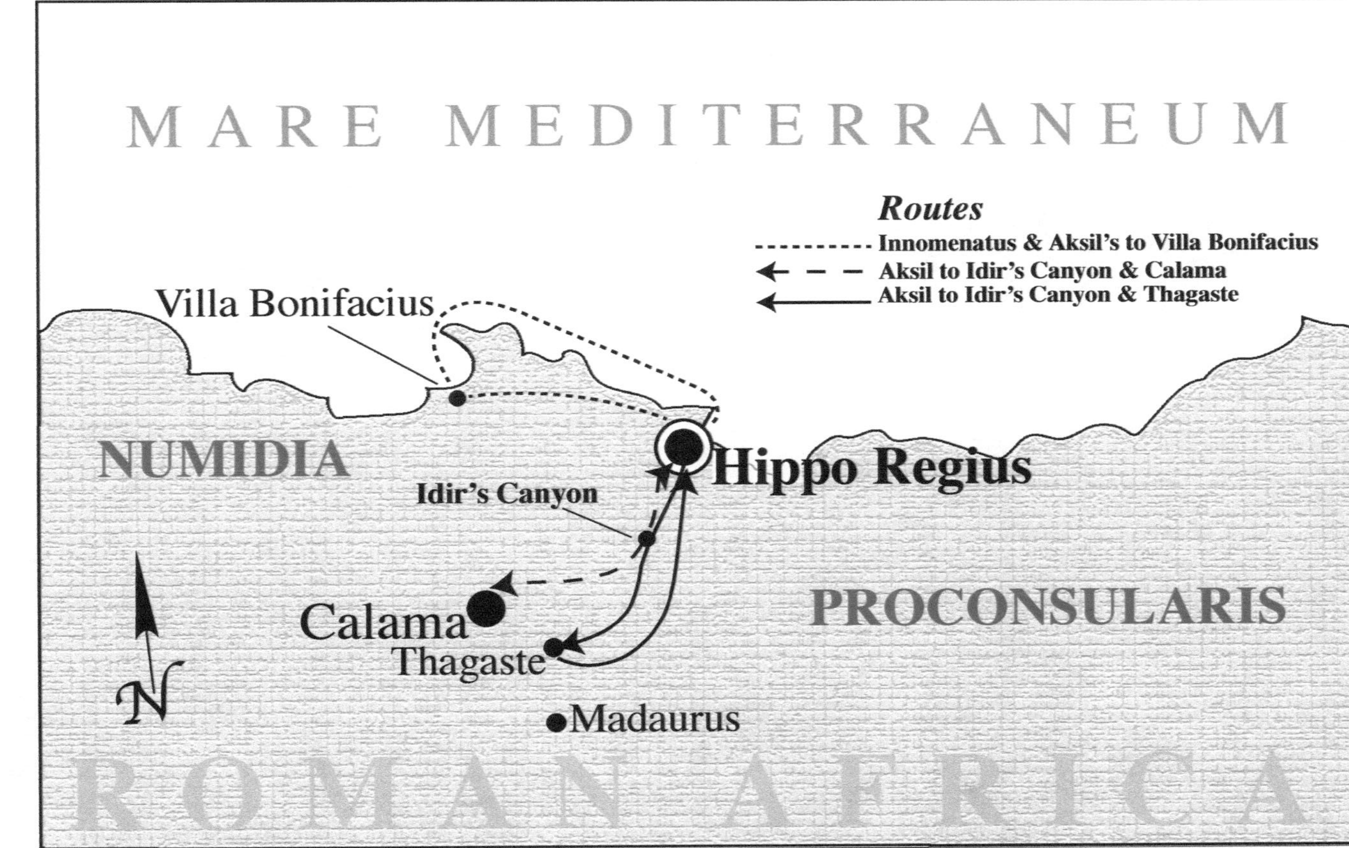

Aksil's and Innomenatus's Travels in Numidia and Proconsularis, 430 A.D.

scream, mine or the woman's I do not know."

I am no believer in dreams but harnessed this somnambulistic coincidence to press my case. "Then it is indeed best to send Aksil immediately to stay ahead of the Roman *maniple*."

Sabina stared into her hands as if looking there for something. When she met my gaze again—did I catch a glimmer of amusement in that glance?—she said, "These were not Romans.

"Nevertheless, we shall see. Whether it is Roman militia, Vandals, or Catholic bishops, I agree we must act." She shooed her hands out toward the trees as if sweeping her dream from the air, then, placed her palms decidedly together in her lap. "As a world observer, I should tell you this now: Years ago, I entertained guests here in Hippo Regius, men who had fled the invasion of Rome. Though they found little shelter here such were their ideas apostate to the bishop and his followers, their more inclusive leanings for the Catholic corporation were very attractive to Sequia, who was a young girl then, and she afterward developed a spiritual community incorporating some of these Pelagian thoughts—for the men whom we both met and studied with were Pelagius himself and his young adherent, Caelestius. She has in the past few years renewed her acquaintance with these principles in a form taught by Julian of Eclanum, a correspondent of hers. No doubt this knowledge has seeped over to Aurelius Augustinus."

Now all was in the open. I had no need to hold back.[3] "Julian is certainly on the bishop's mind these days," I confessed. "I have heard directly again just today of it. Still, I believe Sequia will be safer here at the convent than anywhere in all of Africa. The sooner the better. Danger is near, but with all the refugees flooding the city, she is unlikely to be sought here or found."

Sabina stood. "Yes, danger is near, and I have been warned of troubles. I had long thought they would grow dire."

I wanted to disabuse her of those fears, but she continued with words I had not wished to hear.

---

3 I did not, however, reveal my acquaintance with Pelagius and his followers during their residence in Antioch. Diplomacy, perhaps personal safety, outweighed principle and fulsome honesty at that instant.

"I know you, Amicus. You are here. I believe your good intentions, and I understand you better than you know."

I was to leave with a greater burden than the one I brought.

Sabina summoned Ia with a little bell and gave her directions to provision Aksil.

She stood to kiss my cheek, saying, "Thank you, my friend. Now return home by another way."

20

Fraudem, Latin: Treachery

The cheetah of Chaouïa had traveled two hard nights leading his spare mounts, picking his way carefully through shallow canyons and racing across stubbly open fields. Early in his journey Aksil was aware of unusual movement in the land.

On his second night out, he heard a number of restive horses in the distance and another time studied their sign on the valley floor at the river crossing. At least a hundred horse and thrice that on foot, he thought. Later, from the shoulder of a copsed hill close to dawn on the third day Innomenatus's messenger saw a much larger force far off, coming out of the west, moving into the north end of a long valley. Even from afar their height in the saddle and tall men's gait marching confirmed what he'd thought before: Vandals were loose in Numidia. They were moving toward the south of Africa Proconsularis toward his destination, Thagaste.

Two nights later, around midnight, traveling fast under a quarter moon, he approached a wide clearing, a small field lying fallow, its wildflowers gone to seed. He paused, listening not daring to move from his sheltering grove until he was sure. His nose caught the scent of horse dung wrapped by smoke. He waited a long time, listening over his heart-clamor for any sound to carry across the expanse. He heard nothing, only the odors of encampments: cooking, horses, and day-old waste that drifted now and again, reaching his nostrils. They were dung smells, old, perhaps a day or more. Finally, Aksil entered the meadow on foot, leading his mount, ready to jump into his saddle and race away to the other two he'd tethered on the edge of the clearing.

Within two hundred paces, Aksil came to a ditch that smelled of earth recently overturned. The trench wall was topped by sod and sharpened wooden rods sticking upward toward the stars. The quickly executed organization of the camp told him it was a Roman *castrum* thrown together for just one night. A Roman detachment was on the move. Aksil retied his spare horses to poles outside the enclosure, and mounting the third, rode around the encampment. The entry to the field had come from the north, from the direction of Hippo Regius and just west of his own incursion; the company left the camp, moving toward the south, his own course. About twenty horse and one hundred afoot, he thought, a small *cohort* sent by Bonifacius. He sped back to his horses and urged them on, traveling south along the path the Romans had made. If he hurried and rode long, he might find Sequia before the Romans arrived. He had only one more night. They were moving openly and were going fast.

That morning under cover of the rising sun to blind any curious eyes, Aksil led his three horses down the face of a yellow dirt rise to a farm tucked hard against the hill and sheltered from sight by the next steep knoll. He brought the mounts behind an outcropping and through a wide fissure in the crumbly rock into a natural corral that held two other animals, an ox and an ancient horse. A wiry, dark and bent-over figure emerged from the small hut that backed up to the far side of the outcropping.

"Idir, my friend," Aksil called out.

The man advanced as fast as his age allowed and came very close before speaking. He peered into his visitor's face. "So it is you, Aksil. Good health! Welcome." Idir placed his hands on the taller man's shoulders. "Let me see you." Aksil grasped Idir's shoulders and held him.

"There is not much to see but road dust and weariness."

"I'm nearly blind, but I know you look good, always the same. Come to the house. You can have cool water and a good rest."

"It is the horses that need to drink. I'll tend to them."

"No, no. You refresh yourself. Let me take their care. Two are not too many for me."

Aksil laughed and said, "I brought three."

The old man nodded. "One stood behind another! I'm no good at counting legs."

Aksil stayed throughout the day. His friend Idir, who had known

Aksil's father for many years from his caravan traveling through from Thagaste to Hippo, came in and out of the house quietly and cooked a dinner of stewed vegetables spiced with small bites of hare meat. "Quite flavorful, thank you."

"It is hard to see, but my snares can do my work." From the stories Idir told of barbarians in the area and from his knowledge of how fast Bonifacius's men traveled, Aksil decided he should proceed with only one mount, riding fast and then come back to Idir's farm, riding double with Sequia.

"You know you are close, so go south around Thagaste and down onto her farm from the hills. "If those pirates see a single horseman, they will chase. Alone, you are a target," Idir said.

"If I can leave two with you, I'll take the fastest." He did not mention the Roman *cohort*.

Idir finished his stew, wiping the bowl with the last bit of black bread. "I will care for them as if they were my own. Next time, I will set the table for three!"

Aksil rode out in early twilight. He had made good time the previous night, and he would reach Sequia's farm outside Thagaste before dawn. With luck they both would see Idir the following night. At first daylight, though, having approached from the far side of the farm, his hopes were dashed. Sequia was gone. The animals were gone. Her terraces had been ridden over and despoiled. The storehouses were empty, the doors wrecked. At the house, Aksil saw signs of struggle and more pillage. A broken pot littered the floor with flour. At the gate, leading down the hill, he read the marks of a dozen horses and the ruts made by several carts.

"Pillaging Vandals," he said.

Aksil thought of Sister Sabina. This would distress her greatly, but now there was little he could do about it except follow the trail they made in hopes somehow of finding Sequia, escaped and hiding, somewhere along the way. He swung up on his horse and started toward the gate. Suddenly, he swung around entirely and raced back the way he had come, up the terraced hill behind the farm. Horsemen! He thought. And infantry.

Though he had arrived before the Roman detachment which must have stayed within the walls of Thagaste while he rode at night, the soldiers must have made an early start. Now they'd arrived at the farm. Ten horsemen entered the gate, and four sentries, planting their pikes, stood at the entrance while other foot soldiers crowded into the small farm yard. The rest of the detachment took up positions along the road below.

Two of the foot soldiers, inspecting the pens and coops, quickly picked up his trail and began climbing the hill. Aksil unbridled his horse and sent him back along the path as he hid himself in the vineyard above, as best he could among the harvested vines. The soldiers encountered his horse four terraces below his hiding place and looked jubilant with discovery of a such a fine animal. They roped his mount to lead him down, and as they turned away, Aksil stole further up into the shelter of Sequia's olive grove. He'd lost a horse but was spared severe questioning and, perhaps, injury or worse.

"This is the work of barbarians," Aksil heard the captain of horse say. A shout went out then from the two who'd found the horse.

"Look below, Captain, Vandals in the valley."

All, including Aksil who parted some branches to see, turned to the narrow U-shaped valley below. A train of four ox carts guarded by horsemen and a small number of tenders moved out of the trees along the other side of the river below, setting out to the west across the fields. The tightly-tarped carts looked full and slowed the band's progress even on the dry November ground.

Aksil had glimpsed the trail the Vandals used, winding down the steep hill. This path, he knew, gave way to a plain shouldering the bend in the river below. Stuck at his vantage point high above Sequia's farm, hemmed in by Roman soldiers, Aksil watched Bonifacius's detachment leave in rapid strides now veering off to its left, following the Vandals' path leading to the river. The two with his horse were ordered to remain guarding the farm. Aksil turned his attention to the plain beyond the river to the Vandal party. Among the tall-riding horsemen, one flanked a figure walking tethered to a cart. To Aksil it appeared to be a woman. If that was Sequia, at least she was alive.

During the tense minutes following, Aksil divided his attention between following with his eyes the Vandal caravan and its captive crossing the plain below and the two soldiers who guarded the gate. It was not long before he saw the Roman detachment press at full battle speed onto the field hot on the trail of the Vandals. At such a pace, the *cohort* would overtake the barbarians quickly. Though it was certain that the Vandals had spied the advancing Roman fully-manned force at two hundred strong, the caravan continued to lumber along at a patient pace. In minutes, now entirely exposed on a slight rise, it stopped. The Vandal horsemen turned, spreading themselves in a line facing the oncoming Romans and a bevy of arrows flying toward them. The carts halted at the very crest of the hill, harried by a vanguard of Roman cavalry. The central figure in the Vandal line raised a horn to his lips, blowing loud enough for a faint note to reach even Aksil's ears high above the plain. From his post above it all, Aksil could see what the Roman pursuers could not.

As the clear ringing of the horn reached him, Aksil felt a chill that swept from behind and perceived a swelling shadow overtake the Romans and, in less than a minute, the Vandal train. Others had heard the call as well, for at a second horn blast, a Vandal force twice the size of the *cohort* stormed the hill crest revealing themselves to the charging Romans and scattering the vanguard. Behind Bonifacius's men and off to the west from the woods at the river's edge rode out more than a hundred Vandal horsemen who raged directly toward the *cohort* from behind. Now walled on two sides between not one but two superior forces—it seemed to Aksil that each Vandal company was twice the size of the *cohort*—to its west and north, the Romans could escape only to the south or the east. Both ways were bounded by the river, and over all now a sheath of night descended as if an arras had been pulled over the sun. At that instant dark shadows and swirling dust cascaded down on both Romans and Vandals.

Aksil turned to look behind and saw a towering storm rolling and raging like a dry ocean in the sky lifting and spewing waves of sand ahead of its course. He had little time to squat and pull his robes over his head to shelter, but all along he watched a battle unfold below him.

The Romans initially held their formation, but two of their calvary suddenly broke toward the east bend of the river, the one furthest away from the enemy. With that, two more broke south, and immediately the Roman phalanx dissolved into a mob without cover, without discipline, without order, fleeing the field, trying to reach the river yet with no sense of the oncoming desert rampage rushing down on them. Those riding toward the south (back toward Aksil) witnessed the peril of the squalling turmoil and swung to the east following the remainder of their retreating company. Stragglers were easily overrun by the Vandal cavalry that thundered across the plain, cutting down all in their path and pursuing the Roman horsemen in flight to the east.

Aksil, tightly robed now, moved toward the farmhouse still peeking at the two guards as they yelled at each other over the carnage below and danger at their back. They quarreled. One shoved the other down and swung up onto the horse. He rode off with his fellow running and shouting behind him. Aksil loped to shelter, putting the house between himself the horse thieves.

With one last look at the ox train that was indistinct now and about to disappear in a sea of sandy air, he saw one of the carts overturn as its lead animal bucked in terror at the black clouds and now howling winds. Aksil was forced off his vantage point and into the house. He saved himself witnessing slaughter.

What was it that Bonifacius had written? *Quid sperare barbaro fraudem*, what would one expect from a barbarian but treachery? Gaiseric, standing, waiting for the woman to be dragged up the hill, played the phrase over his mind.

The count's letter had been intercepted, oddly Gaiseric thought, near the city Castra Nova, at the time his vanguard came to seize the town and the house of Honoratus. Even now, after he'd broken Bonifacius's Roman treaty, the phrase amused him. For fraud and broken agreements, the Romans themselves were unparalleled. His former sponsor, *Comes Africae,* knew that better than any Vandal.

Bonifacius himself had both sown and reaped the grains of Roman disloyalty in Hispania years before and in much more recent times had pushed for Gaiseric's own poisoning at Ulfa-kin's hands.

Now, with the rout of his Roman detachment, the count would likely claim more of the same, *fraudis in Vandalorum*, Vandal deception, when truly the encounter was a mere accident, a freak of nature in some ways, one in which Gaiseric had taken clear advantage. He regretted only that the woman had been exposed to danger during the skirmish and had been lightly wounded. All in the little caravan were spared the worst of the sandstorm. The desert blow had saved her and many Vandal-Alan lives. Would this be another betrayal like that of Ullman and Ulfasson? No. Gaiseric had kept knowledge of this woman's relationship to the Bishop of Hippo Regius a closely guarded secret that only Gelimmer knew. No devilish plan. Only by accident. Pure chance. Gaiseric chuckled. Life was ruled by *weird*, fate, which no man—Arian, Christian or Pagan—could know or withstand.

Down the hill, his men struggled with the woman. Even wounded and beaten raw by sand, she fought each step upwards. Gaiseric liked her spirit already. She pushed her buttocks down, digging her bare heels into the yellow, infirm, sandy turf, and the Alan and Gaiseric's cousin, Gelimmer, were forced to pull her up by her arms and toss her forward, making little progress with great effort. It was no use to bellow orders from so far away. Gaiseric stood, his good leg down hill of his crippled shorter one—the most comfortable position he knew other than straddling his horse's saddle—looking down over that distance, trusting his earlier order would be obeyed: Do not harm her. They were right not to mount horses. The hillside they climbed was very steep.

Quid fraudem is what this woman thought awaited her. Of course, a Nicene Catholic would distrust any Arian: Goth, Vandal, or Roman. Gaiseric smiled to himself. She herself—Sequia they called her— would betray and unseat old Augustinus, all the while unawares of her own perfidy. The king again smiled, yes, *fides Punica* the Romans called it, Punic duplicity, *ufar-swaran* to a Goth. Now he laughed.

"I've been too long among both Romans and Goths."

Gaiseric, with his royal guard at leisure behind him on the farther, gradually-falling side of the hill, let the threesome struggle with the slope, and looked out over Thagaste, past the hills far off to the western sky above the Numidian desert. The sun had set only minutes before behind the still-rampaging dust cloud now far off to the west, but the horizon was dark already, reddening only at the fringes of the tempest there, a wall of sand pushed by whirlwinds. Sunlight quavered above the desert nimbus. The last sandstorm of the season? Yes, if it could rain in the desert, but it could not. Not even now entering winter. In any case, nothing that made up that waste would be likely to keep the Berbers living there from travel or from attack. They lived on sand, perhaps ate the stuff. He could not trust them as enemies, much less, like the Romans, as sometime-allies. Best to keep them to the south, away from his own path and destination. The coming taking of Thagaste would insure that.

With his men close enough to hear him, Gaiseric shouted, "*Atta þana himinan, quþa izwis, baira mid hondum*! Carry her for God's sake!" Gelimmer lifted the flailing wrangle to his shoulder and said something to the Alan, who then grabbed her wildly whirling legs. Gelimmer carried while his partner held off her kicking. Their progress quickened.

His men's behavior did not surprise him. Nothing surprised Gaiseric, now. He had seen too much. He had been all his life on the move and in a fight. Born between the wars of Theodosius, he had crossed the Danube as a young man to enter Gaul, further to the Rhine where the Franks fought the Vandals fiercely. Years later, after passing through the heart of Gaul eating off the land, taking advantage of yet another Roman civil war, his tribe crossed through the passes of the Pyrenees into Hispania. After fighting off the Sueves, Gunderic, his then king, moved the Hasding-vandals to the south toward Seville, where, when Gunderic died, Gaiseric became king. He was thirty-three years old then.

And now two years later, he fought for Numidia, to soon sweep, he hoped, further into Africa Proconsularis. First though, before the walls of Hippo Regius, he would face Bonifacius and his Roman legions, and he hoped, eventually Augustinus, the man who, Gaiseric well understood, blocked his way to Carthage and a true Vandal kingdom. If the walls of Hippo held, then with Augustinus it would be a battle of the mind, and to thwart the bishop's obvious advantage there, this woman, Sequidei, would be his best weapon, a cudgel to beat on a hypocrite. When Augustine fell, the rest of the Catholics would, too.

If the bishop knew, as he must, that Vandals as well as Romans and churchmen worked through fraud, it was fitting to upend him with one of the bishop's own: an upstart Catholic, possibly a Gnostic believer and heretic, a countrywoman, most potently, a secret, unaccepted daughter. Gaiseric would test if this piece of fate, one that could have only been ordained by God Himself, was deception or truth.

The scene of that discovery months before was vivid in his memory. His men had dragged the local presbyter out of his cathedral. Thrown before the Vandal king, he wailed and wept:

"Lord Jesus, help me." Gunter had struck the man. "Mercy. Mercy," he shrieked.

"Leave off," Gaiseric had said to his men. And to the priest, "*Quo appellaris nomine*?" What is your name?

Through tears he blubbered, "Regianus."

"Well, Regianus, where has your flock gone? Did you counsel them to leave?"

"No, I did not, but they were afraid and fled to Hippo."

"And why are you here? Stealing from your God?"

He wailed again and groveled in the dirt. "No, no. We have no treasures. Only those relics you've taken from me." He stopped his tears and craned his neck to look up. "The one valuable I have is a story, a legend. You will find it interesting and quite useful."

"You will give up your faith for a story?"

The presbyter pushed up his body, stretching his spindly arms like a waking dog. "I am not ready to die. It is Augustinus whom you want. Not a country preacher." He smiled. "Listen to the tale." His smile melted to a sneer.

"Well, tell me then, Bishop Regianus"

Yes, a true stroke of luck, this story of the bishop that had come to him through the weakness of Regianus of Catena. This legend the man told freely spoke of *filia Augustini*, the daughter of the Bishop of Hippo Regius. Though a child whom he had not acknowledged, she, if his flesh, could be most helpful.

Gaiseric rubbed his short leg gently. "Well, now we shall see."

The trio arrived, and his soldiers stood before him with their burden. He spoke in Gothic, "Gelimmer, let her down." His cousin treated the woman gently but stayed away from her legs. The Alan took a kick to his cheek, drew his short sword, but sheathed it with a look from Gelimmer. "*Knussjiþ foran kaisar Vandalis*, Kneel before the Vandal king," his cousin said with a push that sent her to her knees. Gaiseric stepped forward and spoke to comfort the woman: "Don't fear," he said in her language. "*Vale. Nolite timere.*" This had no effect on her, and she rose and darted away from the king. Gelimmer blocked her escape.

He stood, dignified. "Please. Sister in Christ, sit here." The king indicated his chair, a sometime throne his guard had carried up and set on a dais of thin-hewn stone. Again, in Latin he said, "You've had a difficult time with these ruffians." Gelimmer, reluctantly, at his gesture brought the woman to sit.

"Look here," Gaiseric swept the area of the barren hill with his hand, "there is nowhere to run." She stopped her struggle.

"Bring me that wine and some bread," he told the Alan in Vandalic, "*Brigga þatta.*" He asked Gelimmer for water and cloths. To Sequia he said, "You are injured. Let me clean and dress your wound. Please, eat something. Drink our wine. It will restore you." He himself sipped, then offered her the cup.

"Let me see your wound."

Sequia regarded the ground, saying only, "It is nothing."

"It is full of the desert and may fester. Please, let me help."

Reluctantly, Sequia exposed her dirt-caked calf which had been not too deeply cut. Gaiseric knelt and worked tenderly on her extended leg, now using water and the cloth to clean and press the cut. He then poured a draught of wine over the wound, flooded it with water, wrapped the other cloth around the leg, and tied it firmly in front.

"It will heal well. Avoid dust storms."

His humor seemed to cheer Sequia somewhat.

Gaiseric then stood before her, his long leg off the dais, the other bent above it. Her two captors stood away, behind her. "*Gratam tibi, filia Sabinas*, welcome, daughter of Sabina," he said, using her mother's name.

For the first time, now at the mention of her mother, Sequia looked at the king. Was it suspicion? Surprise? Relief? Gaiseric knew he first owed her some comfort, some reassurance. "Yes, I have heard of you both. Sequidei of Thagaste, the servant of the Lord. Was it here you were born?"

She spoke briefly. "*Carthago.*"

"In Carthage. And your mother?"

"Yes, here."

"Tell me about her."

Now, suspicion did rush to her cheeks. She sat in silence.

"There is no danger. I believe she is in seclusion, behind the walls of Hippo Regius. I will not harm her."

"*Non intrabit illuc.*" You won't enter there.

"*Aufto.* Perhaps. *Videbimus.* We'll see, but even when I take the city, she will be safe. It is my promise as a brother in Christ."

"*Vos ne fratrem.* You are not my brother although you are not godless."

"We Arians do believe in the same God. We serve the same Master."

The woman then recited her creed. When she arrived at the words, "*consubstantiálem Patri*," she stopped.

Gaiseric replied, "*Credo in Deo Patrem, in Jesus Christi, et in Spiritus Sanctem,* just as you do although we think fathers are older than sons." The woman folded her arms and said nothing. She looked past him toward Thagaste.

He'd admired her fighting spirit, but right now he had little time for her ecclesiastical spunk. *Videbimus*, we'll see, he thought. Gaiseric shifted his weight. His knee ached. He looked at Sequia and said, "Sad. I had hoped to make us friends. Your reputation for openness as well as spiritual purity had heartened me."

To Gelimmer he said, "Brigga *þatta min hors*, bring that one," pointing to his horse. The king rose to the dais. "Salve, Filia. Good-bye." And to the pair who'd brought her, "*Eam ad vobis relinquo*, I leave her to you." And in the language they understood, "Keep her safe." He mounted the horse, stretching out in the saddle, relieving his pain, and looked down on Sequia. The woman looked from Gaiseric to Gelimmer and from Gelimmer to the Alan. The king moved to descend the backside of the hill, but before he went very far off, the woman leapt from the dais and sprang after him, "*Ob amorem Jesu, exspecta me*. Wait for me."

Gaiseric reigned the horse. He hoisted Sequia and settled her behind him. "Hold on to me." He guided the horse zigzagging down the gradual back slope of the hill, relishing her defeat and thinking of his next step. Her captors followed with the others who had guarded the hilltop.

Twice a victor that day Gaiseric rode tall.

21

Second Confession

As I tread the *cardo maximus*, the main way and at this hour the quickest route back to the monastery after my visit with Sabina, a phrase from Cicero flowed like a ribbon in my mind. "*Rerum principia parva sunt*," he'd written, "the beginnings of things are small."

At first, I had simply wanted to know. I could not resist Sabina's letters, reading a few, later a few more, soon including Augustine's unsent replies, finally all, and then actually replying and encouraging additions. Now I was trudging home from meeting her, fuller of mischief than ever before. I had wantonly asked a man to imperil his life to repair my labyrinthine ideas hopelessly lost in their own complexity. Certainly, what started simply had grown intractably tangled.[1]

Alternately, I comforted myself with *nil desparandem*, never despair. The phrases in my mind were like two peeved cats chasing each others' tails, around and around again. Such are the dismal times of an errant gossip.

On returning, no sooner had I removed my wraps from my little jaunt than I answered a summons at my cell door. It was not the first time that the bishop had sought me out personally, but the timing of this visit unnerved me. Augustine asked no questions about where I had been or why but simply motioned me to follow. Then my apprehension grew as we cut through his chamber and went directly to my little office off the library.

"Please, help pull back this table," he said, and took up an end of my small desk.

We set the table aside and immediately, Augustine opened the

---

1 To my credit, I believe, I was ready to stand my ground and see my circumlocutions through even though I had enemies close by, watching and waiting, as well as friends who might turn against me as soon as I slipped. Less worthily, let me admit that this occasion was not the first nor would it be the last during those years in Hippo, that I thought to flee—exactly to the place I now sit writing this very phrase—not only to preserve my life but to save the story I had labored over and would work on diligently to bring to the world albeit what I did not witness turned on much guesswork.

cubbyhole beneath it, taking out the letters I had perused and had so carefully restowed. He piled Sabina's missives on my desk while I played my best at astonishment.

"What have we here, my bishop?"

"These are what I want to discuss."

"Of course. I am at your service." I did not commit to knowing about them.

"But not here. In your chamber. Come, take up a bundle or two. I'll carry the rest." He was, as always, intent on accomplishing his immediate task. Just what his business now was, I could only wonder about and fear. Still in the dark about what was to happen, I simply did as he said.

My bishop spilled from his shaking hands a part of his bundle, and as I knelt to recover them, I thought to slip Sabina's latest letter, which I still had tucked in my girdle, into one of the piles. I resisted the impulse. We gathered all and went directly to my room.

Once in my cell with all the notes and letters spread out on my olive-wood table, Augustine carefully reordered the mess, putting (as I well knew the chronology) the letters in their exact order as if he had memorized (as I had) their places. "So, I shall explain. Let us sit now."[2]

So we did. We sat facing each other with the letters we were both so familiar with between us on my table. The bishop hid his still-shaking hands in his lap and breathed heavily. I poured him a cup of water which he let stand on his side of the table. Finally, calmly, Augustine began.

"You recall, I'm sure, my mention of dreams some time ago. I reported to you then, in June, I believe, that my dream-visitor reminded me of you as a sick-unto-death youth. That was true then, but since, I have rethought my own recollection. Yes, I thought your image came to me then, but having had more such visits by a mysterious figure and, at nearly the same time, a shimmering image

---

2 I may not have realized I was safe just then, though looking back on it I must have been relieved that there was no indication on the bishop's part that he thought his letters had been discovered, much less that they had been thoroughly read, and even manipulated. Perhaps some of my relief derived from being just a bystander, becoming free of the need to actively lie.

of you at my bedside, I now see there is a difference in visage and in voice, and that my previous thoughts were simply wishes wildly exaggerated by cravings of the body, old as it may be."[3]

I waited. The bishop was laying out an argument and was not to be interrupted.

"Especially, the voice. For this figure's articulation over time and added night-visitations has become a tone of command." The bishop looked up from his hands to regard me. "Your voice is soft and inviting. You speak no decrement."

I felt almost as if he would reach across to pat and hold my hand. I did not move in the slightest.

"This is the 'personal matter' I mentioned before and again this morning. The struggles these dreams have engendered have finally led me to this."

He fell into silence again in a way that seemed to beg for a reply. So, I hazarded a question, "And what is the 'this' you speak of?"

"This is my confession." His hand glided above the letters he had lined up on the table. "I present these as evidence."

"And what of the voice in the night?"

Augustine straightened in his chair and regained his normal forcefulness. "I have concluded that the voice is mine. It bid me come here. It bid me trust my confession to you. Those night-utterances told me to confess again, my second confession."

If it were only the correspondence, I felt he had little to confess. But he continued, saying, "I confronted myself in a dream with these words: 'Was it you, O bishop, O Aurelius, O Augustine, that brought upon us all this Arian plague through your incessant hunt for heretics, that now they come to you? Need I ask? I know already the answer.'"

As uncomfortable as I was with the friend-of-my-youth taking Sabina's words as his own, I said nothing, waiting, as a good listener must, for what else would come. And perhaps he remembered Sabina's letter—a letter I perceived and later confirmed was not

---

3 Augustine was famous for his explanation over lascivious thoughts and reactions during sleep, inferring, I think, that the soul was not in control during sleep and, therefore, could not be charged with, for example, the sin of masturbation while dreaming. So, his lust for love he at this time expressed was not wrong.

included in the bundles we brought to my room— during his dream and only thought he had spoken the words I was sure he quoted. After all one should, initially at least, overcome suspicions and give a penitent the benefit of belief. At the time I had no notion that the friend-of-my-youth was practicing deception. I felt that it was I who was doing just that.

Augustine again looked at me as before—did he discern doubt in my demeanor? Then, overcame any reticence and reached out his hand to lay on mine. "Be my confessor, Amicus. You are the only man I can entrust with the truth."

I doubted then as I doubt now the verity of his statement and, as Augustine would often say, in "exactly two ways." I asked myself precisely two interrogatives: Will he tell me that truth? And why choose me, a lesser person, and not an equal such as Alypius, Bishop of Thagaste? However, despite doubt and a foreboding sense of cataclysm, the gossip in me overcame questions and caution with hardly a pause. "As you wish, my bishop. It shall be so."

Augustine began. "These night visits, these arguments with myself, abated for a time but recently resumed. It seems the closer these Arians approach the more frequent my dreams become. Nevertheless, what I said to myself, whether in a dream or in a state just prior to waking, startled me. Could it be that I and not Bonifacius loosed these barbarians on my African church?" He looked at me.

I had no wish to comfort him, nor should a confessor (or gossip) do so in the initial heat of disclosure. Instead, I flushed with gratitude that Sabina's words, however recast or reported, had had an effect on the man. A sudden and perhaps vain hope came to me that the friend-of-my-youth could yet be saved from his own iron will.[4] And now, as he seemed to require of me some answer, I said, "Surely the burdens of protecting the church are grievously heavy."

"It is not that which I fear."

I waited, avoiding any repartee.

"I ask if these Vandals have come for me, to torture me, and to

____

4 It was a mettle that fostered his fixation to send me off to Alexandria without blessing and without a name, his gall which repatriated Sabina to Carthage bereft of her son and of her lover, or the cold resolve with which he hounded the Donatists, Pelagius, and Julian to figurative if not physical death.

convert me to their heresy. I could not stand such pain as they would inflict. I have to avoid them even if it might mean my death."

Certainly, the Vandals had not come solely for the friend-of-my-youth. Only Augustine would wonder if they had. I knew for certain that Gaiseric cared nothing for converting bishops, without, I admit, a political purpose. I asked the obvious. "Are you ready to die?"

"No," he said, pointing to the letters. "These and my writings prevent me. I cannot approach my end with these untold."

We both knew, though he did not suspect that I understood that he knew, that a confession without that important missing letter he had recited already, mentioning Sequia, would not wash all his sins away. Where was this leading? I was unsure, though I breathed so much more easily knowing that my prying into the cupboard-of-his-sins—I supposed he might call it that—was as yet undiscovered.

"I want you to read them and see to it they are destroyed."

I wasn't ready to agree but said, "What have you to say about them? Why not destroy them yourself?"

"I confess before God and you, Amicus, that these letters contain my sins."

I knew better. The letters contained only Sabina's ruminations. "And what might those be?"

"That I have read them. More so, that I have kept them. And even more greatly that I hold them vainly in my heart."

"My bishop," I said with utmost subtlety, "what could they contain so damning (I dared to say that word) that you must reveal? Are these your thoughts?"

He looked at me as wide-eyed as a tiger trapped for the kill. He frowned. "Amicus, these letters are from Sabina."

I played a boorish trick. As if I did not remember, I said. "Sabina?"

"Yes, Sabina of Carthage. The mother of my child, Adeodatus."

I just had to make him say it, and more, "Why would it be a sin that she had written?"

"Oh Amicus. It is no sin of mine that she had written, has written, and continues to write to me. That I secretly enjoy it, though, must be wrong. Even though I do not reply, it is depraved. As I've said, I have kept these, have cherished them, and have told no one."

My incredulity might have shone through in the smile I barely suppressed.

"I sent the woman away, but I never drove her from my soul. That is a burden more massive than the duties of the church."

I sorted through the letters listlessly and curiously—it was then that I confirmed the letter he had quoted, and which also contained the first mention of Sequia, was missing. Missing too were Augustine's unsent replies.[5] "If you hold these dear, would you not regret burning them?"

"It is an act of contrition, though I cannot bring myself to do it. I am strong enough only to confess my wrongs. I ask you to do my penance and destroy them."

Despite the irregularities in the collection of which I should have had no knowledge, and though I did not agree with his exact description of his wrongs, I gripped the bishop's hand and went further than he expected or approved of, saying, "*Ego te absolvo*, I absolve you of sins: of titillation, of perfidy, of hardheartedness, and of tyranny."

He rose from his chair. "*Absolvis me vexerunt*? You absolve me of persecuting?" Suddenly, he was the Bishop of Hippo Regius again, not my penitent.

"Yes. Did you not worry over 'your incessant hunt for heretics'?" I quoted his own words, and Sabina's passage.

He sat down hard. He was thinking. "But the letters. What of them?" He pleaded.

"Unread, what should I know of them?"[6] I gathered them up carefully and placed them in an empty cubbyhole over the table. "Should there be a penance, I will say so later. But for now will your absolution bring peace to your heretical wars?"

---

5 How many a time had I withheld information, detail, whole and shameful acts during conversation and even during confession? I could not confront his suppression of Sequia's birthright, nor, really, could I condemn him in mind. We are only human. So, I probed and hoped.

6 I marvel now at my audacity. Was it not enough to go along with my employer and friend-of-my-youth? Must I emblazon my falseness by waving it about like a banner? I pretended no charitable advantage over Augustine. We were provincials cut of the same cloth no matter the Roman dyes that colored our fabric.

"Wars? What wars?"

"The one you conduct with Julian. The vendetta against Arians."

Augustine grasped the table edge. He was sweating even in the evening cold of my cell. Slowly, he said, "With Julian I am done. I fear but do not persecute the Arians."

I was ready to strike a blow at his deception. "And this one mentioned today, against a Thagastan woman. Sequia?"

He wiped his brow and cupped his hands at his heart. "She was brought to my attention. I did not seek her out. And though it is nothing more than an investigation, it is also true that women are the vilest and most hardened heretics."

"Very well, my bishop. Think on it for now. Perhaps leaving off will settle your soul." Standing then, and sensing it was my place to end not with a penance but a benediction, I said using the familiar, "*Pax tibi*, Aurelius Augustinus, go in peace."

The bishop rose and, placing his hands together ever so slightly and just a bit awkwardly, bowed to me, then left.

22

Rumors and *Comes Africae*

Suddenly, time stretched and began moving at a worm's pace. I had my usual work, but translation, at least in the official sense, was on my mind only as a drudgery dragging me along. The minutes I spent writing Augustine's words in Greek spelled a tedious labor in the face of waiting. I was anticipating two things beside an end to the unusually torrid heat this close to winter: First, the return of Aksil and, more immediately, evenings to spend with Sabina's letters now in my possession.

The fifth day after my errand to Sabina and Augustine's *ex parte*, partial confession, I began looking for word of Aksil's arrival though it would be at least a week from the night of his departure before he could possibly return. In the late morning of that day, the city's walls were shaken by *posuerat auersas*; what the Greeks named σιρόκος, fierce winds, sweeping a gigantic wall of dust up from the south of Numidia and Proconsularis. Everyone who could scurried inside, closing all their doors and shutters and covering window openings with hides or heavy curtains to keep the dirt and sand out. It was hardly worth the trouble for the air itself seemed to be made of dust. Into my cell only a sliver of dark orange light from the reddened sun penetrated, looking like a solid golden bar roiling with swirls of motes. The storm lasted most of two days and made the sixth and seventh days of Aksil's absence even longer. Burning red, the late autumn sun edged a degree at a time across the sky toward its resting point behind the western ridge of the mountain of Hippo Regius.

I had planned to meet Aksil and Sequia at the convent as soon as possible after hearing of their arrival. With me now, I would bring Sabina her letters, not being mine except by remission of their recipient, Augustine, which like the bishop himself, I could not bear to destroy. Sabina would be the one to burn them if she felt that necessary. But my aim was to preserve them as part of the story.

I rued not having done the copy work before when I had every letter and all of the replies, but now I immediately set out for the sake of history, I suppose, to translate those the bishop had given me and made note of what I could remember of those letters missing. All had been written in the common idiom, Latin that anyone seeing them could read. And because too many Goths, although most could not read, were in the employ of Bonifacius, I could not trust the letters to that language. And even Hebrew was known and studied in Augustine's library. So, though my mastery of Aramaic was imperfect, I chose it to preserve the letters of Sabina for later reference and, most certainly, to wrap them in a foreign tongue away from prying eyes, including those of the bishop himself.

His confession had disappointed me. Augustine had turned the night visitor into a voice manufactured by his own mind. The letters—oh how well I knew them and the replies—piled high on my desk spoke of openness and repentance, but the missing pieces shut passageways and smelled to high heaven of further rot. Especially, the lost letter identifying Sequia as "our daughter" and the later ones detailing Sequia's life spelled a politic action especially in view of Augustine's planned interrogation of her. It was hardly believable that the friend-of-my-youth, owning his life-long affinity to women[1] would deliberately plan a persecution of his own daughter. Still, this was the same man who had sneaked away from his doting mother, Monnika, sailing unannounced at night away to Rome, and who had summarily dismissed and sent Sabina off after sixteen years by his side. Perhaps, after all, he could deal unfairly with Sequia. He had done so, by his own admission, to her mother. Even then, to me it was unthinkable.

My waiting and my preservation of letters was interrupted on the eighth day of Aksil's departure, not by his return, but by the appearance of a ragtag pair of Roman soldiers who had ridden double on an injured horse from Thagaste. These counted as the remnant,

---

1 Despite relishing the company of men, in particular my company at that time and when we were youths, Augustine appeared preoccupied by women all during his younger years, starting with his mother and then Sabina. It was only after his conversion and Monnika's death soon after that he eschewed the company of women, at least publicly. I had long thought he hid his vassalage to that sex behind a holy visage, and the letters regarding Sequia returned those thoughts to mind.

so they reported, of Bonifacius's expedition in search of Sequia. The news of their appearance spread throughout the town and raised the alarm everywhere including in Augustine's library.

"Whatever are you whispering about?" The bishop asked his scribes.

They all fell silent, but one brave soul—perhaps a gossip at heart—piped up, "The Roman legion, they say, has been defeated."

Another offered, "Yes, outside of Thagaste. Only a few escaped."

"It was during the sandstorm," said a third.

Then, all the scribes began talking at once.

Augustine turned to me—I must have been absolutely ashen I felt so faint—and instructed me, "We must summon *Comes Africae*, immediately." Then looking at me closely, he asked, "Are you well, Amicus?"

"Yes. The news has frightened me. But, yes, I will send a messenger to Bonifacius now."

The friend-of-my-youth caught my gaze, "You are not to fear. I take it all upon myself."

I welcomed reassurance, though I trembled more for Sequia and Aksil than for myself or for him. The other scribes, thinking the bishop's words were for them, began to murmur comfort and care to each other, "The bishop will see to our safety. Never fear. You heard him."

I left to find my faithful courier, both to notify Bonifacius that he was wanted and to pass a brief note to Sabina whom I would visit that evening if she could see me.

I reported to Augustine the first task was accomplished. "I do feel a little dizzy. With your leave I'll retire to my cell for a rest." I was nearing completion of my "Aramaic" project but needed at least two more hours to finish. If I were to visit the convent later that day, I would want to bring Sabina's letters with me.

Bonifacius sent word he would come in the late afternoon, still hours off, and my messenger reported that Sabina would see me. No doubt Bonifacius had his hands full with the loss of his detachment, a calamity to morale if ever there was one. No one could blame him for not appearing right away. Preparation for an interview with an angry and alarmed bishop must be taken seriously. That interval gave me a longer session translating, and after finishing, I wrapped all the Latin letters as one, and dropped the parcel into a sack to bring to Sabina. Good news or ill, at least, I was bringing her something she valued.

The interview with Bonifacius took place near sunset, the sky still rosy and orange from the storm, and since I was feeling better, I requested to be Augustine's scribe at the meeting with *Comes Africae*. We went together to the *tablinum* to meet the count. The bishop walked rapidly in a strict gait faster than his age should allow which told me he was still furious. "Not only has *Comes Africae* failed," he said, "but he has failed gloriously."

"They say," I ventured to mitigate his cynical quip on behalf of the count, "they were outnumbered five times over and were surprised as well, not to mention the effects of the dust storm."

Augustine was not having it. "It was not the dust storm that blinded the count. His arrogance and carelessness worked sufficiently to that end. No one with a steady, outward eye can be surprised."

We arrived to find Bonifacius dressed in his long robes striding in the *peristylium*, working his fists, alternately smashing one into the other open hand, then that recipient back into the first. He stopped both his pacing and his pugilistics when we appeared.

"*Vale*, my bishop." The count only nodded to me in greeting.

Augustine strode past the count into the *tablinum* saying, "*Valitus esse*, had you only been strong." He sat on his throne. "Let us hear your news, *Comes Africae*."

I retired to my little desk at one side of the bishop and began note taking, leaving out the insult, though, of course, I took mental note of it.

Before Bonifacius could begin, the bishop started. "There are but two possible interpretations to the rumors terrorizing our citizens, telling of an imminent Vandal attack in the aftermath of your resounding defeat. One is that these stories of your *maniple's* destruction is circulated by Vandal spies who have infiltrated our city like the dust of a storm. The other is that you have committed the most ignorant blunder of your career, a testament to your incompetence and timorous behavior."

The count had begun pacing once again. He came up short before the throne.

"I sent, at your behest, a force appropriate to the task, more than sufficient under normal circumstances." Augustine stirred on his seat and was about to speak, but *Comes Africae* sped on. "They were preceded by a Vandal raiding party which pillaged the granaries of the farm and carried its owner off with them. My men, naturally, gave chase."

"Naturally?"

"The raiders were but a ruse to entice my men into a trap. A huge force, several thousands on foot and hundreds of horse, flooded out of the woods along the river and fell upon my detachment from all directions. The two who survived had been posted to guard the farm."

Augustine now stood on the dais and looked down on the count. "You say, 'under normal circumstances.' Can you call a barbarian invasion normal? And what of reconnaissance? Should you not know of enemy movements in our direction? Are you not watching these most vile Vandals?"

The count retaliated. "I told you this Gaiseric is wily. I have too few men to spread out in every corner of our provinces. Besides, the dust storm raised havoc with our escape."

"Am I to think those barbarians are any less affected by ferocious weathers than you?"

The count struck for the heart. "Every thing points to treachery. There is a *volpe* somewhere in your monastery." And with that, Bonifacius turned directly to me. "Who else knew of our plan, Innomenatus?"

I had thought all along that my presence in Hippo Regius would come to a sorry pass such as this, a moment of accusation, but I had not believed it would come so soon nor from this particular direction. I was truly struck dumb. The bishop, however, jumped into the fray in my defense.

Augustine roared, "Don't speak to me of foxes. How dare you

inveigh against my scribe? You know him well. He is above suspicion."[2]

"Of course, of course. But someone in your household informed the enemy."

"Or a shifty sneak in your Gothic house did so."

Bonifacius did not respond.

Augustine sat again and crossed his arms. "Blame does not suffice as an answer. What of the woman? What of Sequia of Thagaste?"

"She was gone, taken with all her stores. My men saw her slain during the mayhem. I am afraid she is dead, a better fate than becoming a Vandal slave."

"Killed? Are they sure? How did she die?"

I wondered if I myself blurted those words or if Augustine uttered the questions.

Bonifacius replied to the bishop. "She was crushed beneath an overturned wagon. The ox was speared and went down, pulling the cart with it. My men saw it roll."

The bishop sat in silence for a long while. When he again spoke the anger that had edged his speech to this moment had settled into a flatter, directive tone. "Very well then, *Comes Africae*. I remind you of your duty to protect our city. Learn your enemy. Arm your men well. Prepare to combat this invasion." He stood, "*Abi ad Deum*, go with God."

We returned the way we had come, leaving the count standing in the *tablinum*. "That will be my last audience with *Comes Africae*," the bishop said. "I have no wish or use to see him again. May God guide him to our protection."

I said little, simply acknowledging his comments.

As we came to the garden ambulatory, he said, "Please retire to your cell. I will come to you directly."

---

2 His forcefulness in my defense was welcome but signaled, I thought, just the opposite. The Augustine I knew so well was not done with this accusation by any means.

23

Aksil Returns

Sabina thought she was awakened by stirring in the gloom of her nighttime room.

"The trials foretold are at hand," a kind voice reminded her.

She did not attempt to see in such a darkness. "Yes?" She asked, waiting for more.

The voice darkened in itself but remained sweet, "Those of great faith like yours are tried in the sorest ways. Cleave to the mercy and the openness in your heart."

Searching the ceiling beams she could not see, Sabina lay flat on her back alert but floating on a cloud of patience. No other word came through. Then, Ia was speaking.

"Good morning, sister." Ia swept around the room arranging the few things Sabina kept in her cell. "You have slept well and long. Good. Shall I bring you something to eat here?"

If this is the difficulty he spoke of I shan't worry, Sabina thought. "No, I shall join the sisters."

Ia laughed. "They finished their meal an hour ago." She swept the arras back to reveal bright sunshine falling from the high window, the only one in the room. "I will bring you the porridge we saved aside the fire." She went out.

In the silence Ia left behind, Sabina sank back down on her pallet searching for the words she had heard during the night, words spoken, she now thought, in a dream. "Cleave to the mercy and the openness in you." Why now? Have I not been tested enough already? Thoughts vaulted to her mind before she could restrain them. She saw herself with the youthful Augustine: fleeing the domineering mother in the African night, then two years later shamed and returning home alone, again, then after three years—they had just buried their only son—rejoining him in her bed at Carthage. She felt a flush of anger.

And now he would attack the daughter come of that Carthaginian union. He would attack the mother herself. He would brand them heretics to try to save his Church, his true and only child.

Sabina stopped her hot thoughts. Hold fast to love, she told herself.

Ia brought in a tray. Setting it before the *materfamilias*, she said, "You have a visitor, a quite insistent visitor who says he must see you immediately. That Aksil of Chaouïa is the man."

Sabina's heart leapt. "Bring him in."

"Eat first, sister. He is filthy, shedding sand and dust everywhere."

"No, I wish to see him now, thank you."

"Here?"

"Ia. Yes, here. Has he brought Sequia with him?"

Ia shook her head. "I do not know." She turned and left, returning quickly with Aksil. He, still wrapped in his traveling robes, fell to the floor, weeping as soon as he saw Sabina.

Sabina rose from her bed, cloaked herself and knelt beside the shaking, blubbering man. "Ia, please pour our guest some warm milk," she said and to Aksil, "Please, my good man, eat this cereal. You've been traveling and must be starved."

Little by little Aksil, famished, distraught, and coated in desert dust was coaxed into stilling his wailing, into rising from his knees, and into taking some porridge and warmed milk. Sabina spoke softly to him of his obvious trials. She refrained from pulling news of Sequia from the demoralized traveler. Sand and dust crusted Aksil's hair and clothing. His hands were dirt itself and his tears had cut channels through the layers smeared over his face.

"You came to me as soon as you arrived, I can see. Thank you for that, my friend."

Aksil again began to choke and moan, but Sabina's hand on his head staunched his cries. "Tell me. Tell me your story," the *materfamilias* said. She offered him a damp cloth to clean his face. "I want to hear the whole tale."

Once soothed and cleaner, Aksil told Sabina of his journey to Thagaste, of the Roman and Vandal forces in evidence along the way, of the horror at the farm, and of the battle on the plain below the farm. "And just as the armies clashed, the huge Vandal horde against the tiny Roman detachment, the wind rose and the sky to the south behind me darkened. In two minutes all was engulfed in a sea of dust and sand."

Sabina shook her head. "You say that you saw Sequia. Where was she in all this?"

"She, a Vandal prisoner, was tethered to one of the carts. Those wagons held her harvest and her goods all of which were gone from the farm." Aksil began to weep once more.

"She was spared death, then."

"The last I saw before all disappeared in the storm was the ox pulling the cart speared and falling to the ground. Then, I could see nothing else."

Sabina heard again her night visitor say, "Your trials are at hand." Sorely, resisting the quavering she felt in her throat she said as calmly as possible, taking him away from his failure back to his return, "You have suffered for my sake. Tell me how you found Hippo once more. Tell me of your homeward journey."

Comforted by Sabina's soft words and patient goodness, Aksil explained his return: "I'd lost my horse to Roman soldiers at the farm. Clouds of dust and howling winds surrounded me. Glad I was to be a man of the desert. No one could see or trace my movements. I took the shortest, surest way back to my friend, Idir, following the river. Even along the banks in Thagaste there was no one out, and I was not detected. Wrapped in these filthy robes, undone of my provisions tied to my horse's saddle, I was quick and moved north with the wind."

His telling of the trip back north soothed Aksil. "That afternoon, which could have been blackest midnight, I reached Idir's hidden mountain ranch. He'd moved my two horses into his little house with him to keep them healthy in the storm. We wrapped their ears, eyes and muzzles in loose garments to keep the sand out. They could not see anyway. I would be their guide. All along the way, I thanked my father at every step. Over thirty years, he had worn the paths, and for another twenty years in my own caravan trading days I had followed him. A half century later, I could keep to the trail, blinded and deafened. Even so, on the second day of the storm at the place they call Hell's Cascade, the following horse slipped at the edge, and even as I wrapped the tether around the horn of the other and spurred that mare forward, she faltered. The second could not be saved. I cut the rope to preserve my mount and myself. I will always hear her whinnying scream that ended at the bottom of the canyon." And Aksil began his weeping again.

Sabina, joining in his grief over his fallen horse, never afraid to be interested and kind, interrupted. "What were her markings? Her color?"

Aksil smiled at this chance to memorialize a favored animal. "All black with a heart-shaped flame below the eyes. A beauty to see."

"You did well. Though sorry for your suffering, I am happy you've returned."

Aksil heaved a sigh and clamped a hand to his mouth. "I failed. I should have traced Sequia's track, but without a horse . . ." his voice trailed off.

"Providence guided you and brought you to me," Sabina said. "That is a sign of success. Do not fear. Return to your wife and your son Ehgil. When your friend-without-a name-visits, I will have him learn of your difficulties and happy return."

Alone again, Sabina wept. She searched Aksil's news for any hope. Her dream had promised not just trial but implied a better resolution. That all should end in a dust storm in captivity to strangers was impossible for her to believe. But what more severe trial might there be? Whirlwinds such as had descended on Aksil and Sequia often kill travelers exposed in the open. Surviving that, would she perish at the hands of barbarians? Even escaping, Sequia would be pursued as a heretic by her own father. That itself was unthinkable. How could a mother cling to mercy? Her belief in clemency extended long but less so to herself than to others. She could hope that Sequia for her own sake and for the well-being of her followers would live and find pity even in the heart of a Vandal. After all, though enemies, they were still Christian. That thought settled her. She found comfort there.

Yes, mercy, but also openness. That was what she and Sequia had so long fought for in their own way. Where Augustine had cut off so many—he had called it unifying the Church—and sent them to figurative death in the desert, they, his womenfolk, had worked to include, to bring in and hold the faithful. That was the true farming Sequia had been pursuing in Thagaste, raising new crops under the Son in fields, ripening in the open. Should Sequia be lost, Sabina, as old as she was, resolved, right then, to act. Let Amicus invent ways and devise plans, as she knew he would, but she in her daughter's name would in right time move straight to the source.

24

Death and Despair

In the hours following our parting from Bonifacius, I felt more a slave curled up on the bishop's doorstep guarding him and waiting for his summons than a I felt scribe or a confessor. Perhaps it had seemed that way since our adolescence in school, but this night, with my fears for Sabina at a height, the uselessness of my service pained me sorely. The letters were finished, my transcriptions hidden, so I turned to my manuscript.[1]

Shortly after midnight, Augustine, well past anger, came to me, appearing much less strident than when he left me hours before, dressed now in the plain robes of a monk. His voice low and soft, he said, "I have been praying."

"All these hours?"

"Yes. Praying over two conundrums: one over your fealty, the other over my immortal soul."

"My loyalty to you, to the church, to our youth?"

Augustine looked at me sternly though in not an unkind way, furrowing his brows over softening eyes. "You stood accused today, and I defended you. I must, I find, grind to dust the seeds of my doubt that they might not sprout or take root. Can I in the name of the Father, of our brotherhood in Christ, content myself with your constancy? Do I not still know you from lying in your youthful embraces?"

"Without doubt, my bishop."[2]

Apparently satisfied with my quick and forceful assent to fidelity, Augustine sank to his knees, guiding himself down with the stiles of

---

1 Yes, the one you now read, the one I had compiled since arriving again at Hippo Regius, the same I planned to leave behind to explain the other side of Augustine's story.

2 I had feared the count's suspicion of me would arise once more, and I had prepared myself to answer just this question without the least of hesitation no matter what qualms I harbored inside. I was ready to swear to the Father, the Son, and to the spirit of our friendship-in-youth my faithfulness to the bishop. I still believe I did so out of consideration of Aurelius Augustinus rather than of my own wellbeing though ending my life in prison or worse was not what I sought.

the chair, bowing his head and saying, "I am chastened. I am now truly ready to confess."

With that he produced a pouch from beneath his robe. "These are the rest of Sabina's letters and the replies I wrote but did not send, neither of which I showed you before. Now that the woman, Sequia, is dead, I am compelled to tell the whole story."

Unwilling to agree, I thought *reported as dead*, but said only, "As you wish."

"No, as I must, for I have sinned and not being shriven have compounded sin on sin as is the nature of man."

"Please, my bishop, sit on the chair."

He did not move from his knees. "No, please." He raised a trembling hand and grasped my robe. "Join me here as my confessor."

I knelt, and in due time, the bishop began, at first in the tone and cadence of a historian.

"Toward the end of the reign of Theodosius the Great, I returned to Africa, bereft three years of my Sabina and for a full year, of my dear mother, Monnika, but happy in the brilliant company of my son, Adeodatus. Alypius followed me also."

Augustine wet his lips and sighed. He lowered his voice to an intimate softness. "We settled for a time in Carthage where, suddenly, Adeodatus fell ill and quickly died."[3] The bishop's voice fell to a whisper, "He was only nineteen." Again he ran his tongue over his lips, his beard I noticed was moist. "For the first time in my life, I was alone. Even the comfort of God the Father seemed remote from my heart. Alypius felt far away as well. I suffered doubt. The old heretical, Manichean idea of evil ruling the world swirled around me. I feared for my new faith."

The friend-of-my-youth shook in all his limbs now. His beard seeped. "At the funeral of my son, his mother, Sabina, appeared. The woman I had sent away at behest of my mother now came like a minister appearing in full sun, a dove winging above her and around.

---

3 It may be noted that Adeodatus, whom I knew well as a babe, died at the exact age I had fallen ill and, to Augustine, died, both his son and I in Carthage. How heavily this coincidence weighed on Augustine, I do not know, but the remarkable closeness Adeodatus and I each had to him could hardly have escaped his brilliant perception.

I felt as the Baptist must have felt. I took her presence as a sign, as a gift from The Almighty."

Augustine clutched my arm. "I was weak, Amicus. I had lost everyone I had loved on earth, and lonesomeness gnawed at my thoughts. I looked for comfort in faith, but it was not there. Death stood in its place. I looked for sustenance in The Father but felt denied; 'Oh, why hast Thou forsaken me?' So, sickened by grief, set upon by fears, and bedeviled by doubt, I fell into the arms of my concubine of old." Now, he full-out wept, quivering before me in a pitiful heap.

I waited a long while for the bishop to compose himself, to continue. When he again began to speak his directive, argumentative voice reasserted itself. "Of course, I knew it to be wrong, a sin, a diversion, a thing like sheltering under the rock away from the face of God. Oh, I hid in that woman, running from my fear and grief, from a wounded faith, and for a night and a day and another night, she comforted me, soothed my bereaved heart in the softness of her flesh. We stayed abed with each other for two days. By dusk of the second day, though, I began to ache with other pains, the stabbings of remorse and shame."

I asked him, "Must there be shame in comfort? Remorse for love?"

Now he became the high judge, glowering at us both. "I was sworn to celibacy. I broke my vow twice, this second time with Sabina. Once in Ostia with another concubine. I had publicly declared it. How could I teach, how could I preach while playing the hypocrite? I said nothing to her, but at dawn of our third morning together, I resolved to stop, to renew my vow, and to leave."

"And so you told her your misgivings."

"No, no. So alluring, so loving was her touch, so open to me that I was doubly shamed at my unfaithful thoughts about infidelity. I was tongue-tied."

I nearly laughed at the concept and thought, Oh, that I cannot believe.

"Yes, I was that sinful. I grabbed her goodness for myself. I took all I could stand, convinced at the same time that I would leave. In

Augustine of Thagaste dwelt an apostate thief of love!" His voice rose sounding like a self-condemning God pronouncing a sentence. "I sinned and stole and sinned even more, never telling a soul." He buried his face in his hands and rocked side to side emitting a stiffened, writhing moan. "Forgive me for I have sinned."

Augustine went on, describing the fragile state of his mind during those days and nights, unable to eat, impossible to attend to study, and even his writing had failed him. He worried about the strength of his new faith, about his mission to teach, about it all. Through that time, a trusting Sabina comforted him in the ways she knew, in the ways she had learned from Augustine himself. For three days and nearly three nights, they indulged in each other.

"Then," he said, "like Judas sneaking away from the apostles, I slipped from her arms, washed, and clothed myself in clean robes. I left her, hours before dawn, journeying toward Hippo Regius." He renewed his sorrowful sobs. "Again, I left her. I left her with money! For shame. For shame."

I rose, sensing he was at an end, though I was not through just yet. "Please, my bishop, take the chair." I sat opposite that seat and asked, "So, then, Sequia of Thagaste you believed to have been—my own voice caught on that necessary participle—your daughter, a posthumous sister to Adeodatus?"

Still kneeling on the floor, Augustine gazed up at me with horror painted across his face, his deep-sunken eyes, sodden beard, and wide open mouth all seemed to scream in terror. "You think that? How? No, you are wrong. An apostate Donatist-lover, Arian-apologist. No. Absolutely not." He lifted himself up.

I almost quoted a later letter from Sabina, one I was not supposed to be acquainted with, but held myself in check. "You don't suspect?"

His voice now rose with him and turned hard. He stood over me now. "Who here dares to contradict the Bishop of Hippo Regius?"

Now in such a mood, in such a frenzy, he was not able to reason or even to hear me fairly. "I am but a friend, a confessor, a simple scribe."

Augustine ran his hand over his nose and mouth then down his beard. "If you are a friend, then be not a scribe. Write nothing of this, of my words, of your thoughts, of my visit. Be a confessor only, an intermediary with The Father. Be as He is, silent."

With that, except for what seemed an involuntary but restrained lunge of his hand toward the letters he had brought, he turned and immediately left me alone.

Augustine, Bishop of Hippo Regius, the patriarch of the African church had once again gained the ascendancy, but I, friend, confessor, and scribe would be all I could to him but especially, and against his dictum, the recorder of his raucous, difficult, and hesitant confession.

The night was well past half and much too late to see Sabina. Sleep was impossible. So, I wrote. I noted all while it freshly rang in my ears.

I waited until early dawn to leave the monastery for Sabina's convent. As before, I took the long way and entered through the equestrian quarter where I might not chance to be seen. To my delight and great surprise, there I encountered Aksil.

"*Vale*, my friend. You have returned!"

The desert cheetah looked pained. "I have returned, unfulfilled in my mission."

"No. Your return is success itself. What news do you have of Sequia?"

Aksil shook his head sadly. "The Vandals had captured her before I arrived. Stole her and her goods."

"The Romans say she was killed."

He fell to his knees and hid his face in his hands. "I feared that truth, but the only Roman soldiers not killed were near to me when the storm hit. They saw less than I."

What had he seen? "You say she lives?"

"Sister Sabina will tell you. I spoke with her last night immediately on my return. She assured me that her daughter still lived. As for me, I saw nothing to naysay her, though what I did see did not look good."

"So, you saw her alive?"

Aksil continued, "They say that a mother knows in her heart the wellbeing of her child. The good sister senses her daughter on earth. So, hope remains alive."

I bid him rise and lead me to the gate we had entered before. It was attended even that early in the morning, but we were made to wait outside. Not too soon, Ia was brought to see us.

Through the grate she peered at us. "What news do you bring, Amicus?"

"Only news you have already heard."

She made no move to open the gate. "And that?"

"Roman tales from the desert which you already know are false. And these." I lifted the parcel containing Sabina's letters. "They are letters read and returned by the bishop."

Ia looked at me, a curious bewilderment pressing her eyes to slits. "And how do you come by those?"

Her demeanor pressed me to demand, "That is something the *materfamilias* and I will share. Please conduct us to her."

"Our mother cannot attend you."

Even to Sabina, maybe especially to her, I would not reveal the substance of the bishop's confession, but I most certainly would tell her how her letters came back to her. And perhaps should Ia know, that would soften her reluctance. "The bishop gave me them."

Now her eyes widened. She turned aside, her mouth firming to a line. "Gave them you? To return?"

"No, Sister. To read and destroy."

"And why bring them back?"

"They again belong to Sabina. She may do with them as she wishes, but when I see her I will counsel her to keep them for a time. Now, please let us in."

"Our mother cannot attend you." Ia eyed me carefully, gauging my expression. "Late last night, she was taken away."

"By whom? Whatever for?" How could I expect this? I was dumbfounded. "I do not understand."

"Nor do we. We were told nothing."

"Taken away? By Roman soldiers?"

Now, Ia revealed her suspicions, "No. By officials of Bishop

Augustine of Hippo Regius. She is arrested, taken to prison, they said. Surely, you were informed?"

"No. How early?"

"Many hours before first light," she said.

Though it may not have been exactly true I said, "I have nothing to do with this." The shock of this news loosened my grip on the pack of letters, and it fell to the ground. Whether I said it aloud or not I do not know but I seemed to hear, "She was to reread them with the unsent replies the bishop just last night bestowed on me."

Ia shook her head. "Are all men such mysteries?"

"Certainly you do not mean me," I said.

"If you wish to see our mother, inquire at your bishop's carcel. I cannot let you in."

I retrieved the letters. "I cannot bring these back." I held them out to Ia. "Keep my parcel for Mater's return."

"When will that be?"

"I will find her and work for her speedy release. I hope to obtain reliable news of this tragedy as well as of the whereabouts of her daughter."

"Pass the letters through the grate. I will keep them," Ia said.

I swept my arm back toward my Berber companion. "Our faithful Aksil, here, is ready to go forth to Sequia's rescue as soon as we find her."

"No. He will be killed, surely."

"I know some among the Vandals. Perhaps they can help."

Ia put her hands together as if in prayer, but said instead, "Yes, all men are mysteries."

25

Vandal Victories

In the nave of the former Saint Peter's church in Thagaste, at the early setting of the October sun, the victorious Vandals celebrated. Before what had been the altar and was now the throne of their king, Gelimmer and his Alan counterpart, *magistrum equitum*, master of horse, being the most prominent pair of the force capturing Thagaste, led the toasting and the boasting before their leader in the uproarious hall. All along the rounded vault, Vandal voices caromed and echoed to the far reaches, even to the immense, stoutly made doors. Wives and the young clad in reds and whites came round the tables that were spaced throughout the wide hall with platters of food and huge pots of wine, serving and singing in alto or soprano voices that wove their way through the din of the festivities. The tallest and fairest of those women approached the *magistrum equitum* to fill his cup before he spoke. The Alan stood forth, raising his ewer of good wine that had been recovered from a farm in the valley—so far Gaiseric forbade partitioning the goods of his captive, Sequia—bowed to the lady, and in halting Vandalic with the sound of the *scope*'s harp as accompaniment recited this short lay:

Fast as lightning	lining the skies
Our horsemen	hounded, hunting
Red clad Romans	Routing those *wegas*
Crushing under hoof	cowards, crawling away.

The verse was plain but brought the assembly to its feet, toasting the power and skill of the Asian horsemen, their welcomed allies. When the welling cheers melted, Gelimmer, whose woman it was who had served his Alan friend, stood tall, like a giant next to the small and quick *magistrum equitum*, extending his cup to be filled by his handsome wife. He drank and then spoke:

"I cannot intone verse as well as our master of horse"—raucous laughter ran the rounds of the curtain-draped hall—"but I was at the battle. I saw our small train of farm goods and hostages set upon by the huge force of Roman-paid fighters who in their *ofermod*, error and over confidence, swept down like desert jackals on a wounded lamb. But how their smug advance did reel when the bleating sheep turned to stand against them. And how like wounded leopards did they break and run when in turn they faced our sun-glittered swords"—cups and flagons banged approval on the tables—"and how fast did they flee before our gazelle-like horsemen"—there came more banging—"taking to the woods to hide from our fearsome force! That a worthy foe had braved our sharp swords and fleet ponies rather than frighted hares. Let us follow the deserter's tracks to the walls of Hippo Regius to call out the leader of these cowardly cattle, *Comes Africae*, the weakling Bonifacius."

The roar of voices and the sweet scraping of swords unsheathed mixed with the womens' song and cup-clatter brought all to their feet in a single shout: *fragistajan gadaursan Romani*, we vow to destroy Bonifacius. Gelimmer stood tall and proud before his kinsmen.

Now Gaiseric, the good king on his dais below the dangling Catholic cross in the former church apse, rose over the party. He held aloft burnished armor of a fallen Roman captain. "To Gelimmer I give this battle garb traced in silver and lesser but like to these his lieutenants. To his able men shields, knives, swords and axes of the Roman *maniple*. You deserve no less. You will in the days to come fight for more. To our *magistrum equitum*"—Gaiseric held up a finely-wrought saddle, worked with battle scenes of Hispanian campaigns and, separately, horse reins with silver medallioned bridle. "Such a saddle and harness is worthy of an earl leading such gallant men. More horse shield and worked brass trappings go to our Alans according to their rank and deeds." Gaiseric's own sisters went among all the soldiers and horsemen giving to each a golden brooch from this campaign and presenting jeweled rings of gold, taken from the clergy in the province of Mauritania, to the two generals serving their brother.

The king spoke. "Both horse and foot battled bravely and hard, struck with the force of the windstorm, biting like the sand blizzard that came upon us all. We have given worked gold and hammered silver gleaned from the field whose carrion was covered these two days in storm-dust. Now at the end of the wicked weather, we feast, recount the glory-deeds and, surely, voice our want of Roman wealth." Gaiseric stepped forward two paces.

Up went the call, "Listen to your king."

"Though the taste of winning is sweet and though we gained goods in the fight, leave haste and empty boasts to our enemies. Now is the time for rest and the feeding of our people. Yes, we will bring all of rich Numidia under our hand to rule, not destroy. Yes, nearly starved out on the thin harvests of our Roman-given provinces, now we will fill our granaries to the brim with the fat wheat of the plains we have taken by arms. But let our enemies stew on the fear of our feats for a time. At first, they will prepare busily for our onslaught. But we shall wait. We shall move carefully. Let Bonifacius begin to believe we will be satisfied with Numidian spoils. Let him hope we will stay away from his walled cities. Then, when their sharp knives of readiness have dulled with the grit of waiting, we shall come, well fed, all together, hungry for the fight. They, ill-warned. We, ready. They, soft with wasting. We, hard of mind. They, fretful with in-fighting. We, bound with our *weird* and will.

"In the meantime, we hector their minds, fire up their spats, and grow stronger. We will let loose a play to needle their thoughts with the doubt brought of their own deceit. Gaze at the growth of our plot as you would at the aging of your children, with wonder and joy. At the last, Hippo Regius will be ours and Carthage thereafter."

Shouts thundered within the walls of the former cathedral. Proud oaths and brotherly toasts flowed aloft. Gaiseric was their wise king, brave and true. Of all the Vandal kings past, Gaiseric was wisest. And so sang the *scope*, the Vandal poet, in praise of the king of the Vandals and Alans, and as that song continued in worship of their leader, Gaiseric brought Gelimmer, his cousin, and his Alan master of horse to his private rooms beyond the narthex, motioning his sisters to bring food and drink for them.

Gelimmer, full of wine and victory spoke first. "Should we not ride hard after those who escaped? We can meet head-on any force sent south to defeat us."

To his sisters Gaiseric said, "Food yes, but do not fill the cup of my *magister militium!*" Gelimmer started up, but sat quickly once more. The king, cousin or no, would not be wronged. And to his generals Gaiseric said, "My sisters are here to serve and to hear. I trust to their care this woman, Sequia of Thagaste, captured at some cost and kept with great effort." The master of horse rubbed his cheek and laughed. "Treat her well. Serve her as one of the royal house. Give her no cause to fear or flee."

The sisters bent their knees yielding to their brother's words. To his generals as well Gaiseric said, "Let it be known that Sequia of Thagaste is our friend. She and her goods will be safe. No man or wife will meddle with her. They say she is a priestess, a seer who preaches and reads the gospel. So be it. Let her join our liturgy if she will. Let her win friends and deal *godgang*, good will. You'll see how useful she'll be. Listen and heed. Now, my kinswomen, leave us." He also dismissed the Alan, saying, "Go pass round the war prizes and news I've dealt you."

He turned to his cousin. Gaiseric spoke: "Now is a good time, gentle Gelimmer, but now is not the best time to attack. Yes, we have won a battle. Surprise, bravery, skill, and fate have prevailed. But this horror for the Romans will only sharpen their guard, their training, their readiness. Let us give them time to build and, then, to doubt. Give them time to again grow lax. Let us not show our great strength which they have yet to know. Let us gather up all the stores we can find. Our granaries are low, starved by a stingy Mauritanian harvest. The fat of Numidia and the south of Proconsularis will restore our people, our troops, and strengthen our chances during what will be a long, tedious siege. Let us take time to sow dissension and fear within the walls of Hippo Regius. We will draw the enemy out when we are strongest and defeat him before the walls of his own capital, before the eyes of all. Keep your men trained and ready. I will tell you when the time approaches to teach Bonifacius that their *ufar-swaran* means empty boasting. Now leave me to think."

Gaiseric looked round the former Catholic rectory still hung with apostolic banners depicting Peter in Rome, one showing him on his upturned cross. He found it difficult not to admire the patriarch's courage, a plain man as Gaiseric understood, simple and true. How can one such as Augustine not find such a fisherman the one to follow, the king wondered? The bishop's complexities and arguments will twist themselves around his very neck. No great loss, but better that he take many followers with him, and best, show Bonifacius his way to defeat.

The Vandal thought about Sequia of Thagaste, the Bishop of Hippo's unacknowledged daughter. He would use her as a natural wedge driven deep into the stump of forces inside the walls of Hippo to split binding rings apart. Once the daughter grew talked-about, some faithful would retreat from Augustine. Others fearing treachery might revolt. *Comes Africae*, already no friend, would demand explanation and deny any ransom. The bishop, too, would refuse tribute to return one he never wanted close to him. Then even more hate would fall on Augustine's head. A military leader like *Comes Africae* without spiritual center could not endure. The Vandal king's plot, he knew, would weaken Bonifacius just when he needed the greatest and unified strength.

Gaiseric thought about the capture of Sequia, of the peculiar mission that sent an entire Roman *cohort* to escort or to seize just one woman. He pondered the reports and his own sighting of a lone horseman, a Berber, following either his own advance-men or the Romans, or both. Just who was clear: a skillful, caravan trader. But who had sent him? Not Augustine. The bishop had connived for the *maniple*, surely, but why? And Bonifacius? Gaiseric did not doubt *Africae* was but an instrument manipulated by the bishop. Yet someone else was there, acting behind the walls. One whose interest was wider than his resources. The mother? Perhaps. But method and timing spoke of someone knowing, caring but wily, one without power but owning influence and quiet daring. Gaiseric could count only one such person whom he knew lived behind the walls of Hippo

Regius. He was sure that if he waited, he would know for certain and would use that person for good, but for now he would follow his own mind-plans and work.[1]

Gaiseric moved down the rectory hall away from the din of the celebrations. He stopped at a door guarded by two of his kinsmen. "Join the feast now with my thanks. When you have eaten, send me two cousins to stand watch and yourselves return after midnight." He gave them each a silver coin that depicted the profile of Bonifacius. They grinned at the florins and pocketed them.

Gaiseric unlocked the door, nodded a goodnight to his men, and entered.

The room suffered some austerity but was solidly furnished for the comfort of a bishop, perhaps for Alypius himself. The windows were high and small. The stone walls, plaster-covered and were here and there covered with cloth hangings.

Sequia sat on a bed against the wall at the far corner of the room with her knees drawn up. Two tapers lit her suddenly anxious face. "Have no fear," Gaiseric said, "I come to talk."

Though far from fierce, she spoke unafraid, "I was only surprised. I am with God and do not fear."

"So they say. May I sit with you?" Gaiseric settled himself on a stool near the bed. "You preach the gospels, I am told."

Sequia raised an eyebrow. "Why do you ask?"

"Hear me, Sequia of Thagaste, daughter of Sabina of Carthage and Augustine of Hippo Regius, you are safe in my camp, safer than anywhere in Thagaste, more so even than in any other place in Africa. Yes, you have friends in many parishes but enemies too, as you have seen by the Roman force sent to find you. Here you have only those who serve me, and here you are my guest."

"A guest behind locked doors?"

"Only for your time in Thagaste. When we move on our way north, you shall have the run of the camp. By then all will know my will that

---

1 Lest I be thought more seer than scribbler, I say that these thoughts came to me later from the king himself. Let Gaiseric earn the credit. All was his plan. I only took pains afterwards to inscribe his thoughts.

you are to be free and protected. I ask of you only that you will not flee my keeping. You may join our worship and do your best to teach my poor Christian kinsmen."

"And the Alans, too?"

Gaiseric understood the evangelist in her who recognized the Alans from the far reaches of *Mare Major*, the Black Sea, as a fertile field for her faith. He took to heart her wants. "If they will listen, yes. They have their own strange ways."

"Nothing is strange to The Father."

"We have Donatist supporters with us as well. Are heretics welcome in your church?"

"Bless them and keep them," she said "All may come in."

"And Arians?"

"They already believe in the ways of Christ."

"Some, yes."

"They shall win greater faith."

Gaiseric smiled. "It is true, then."

"That every person shall come to Christ in his own way?"

"That, yes, and what is said that you are a sister to all."

Sequia did not reply, and Gaiseric leaned in toward her. "You are welcomed here as a friend, a believer, and a guest, but I must speak truly to you. Know that when the time comes, I will ransom you."

"You may do as you wish, but no one will pay."

"Not even your father, the bishop?"

"Especially, not him. He does not care that I exist."

"Why then send the *cohort* after you?"

Sequia look closely at Gaiseric while she mulled over his thought. She did not argue but simply said, "He will not pay."

"Even then I will be satisfied," the king said, "I will take what treasure is mine and restore you to your kin as well." He rose, bowed slightly to her, and went to the door. "Rest. We shall be moving at sunrise."

That night in his dreams Gaiseric saw the battle to come. The walls of Hippo loomed red above them. Out from the gates spilled the Gothic army of *Comes Africae* marching in phalanxes, spears glinting in the sun, pacing before red-clad horsemen. The numbers were great, but even in their pace, heavy and deliberate in the dream, Gaiseric read fear and uncertainty. Lifted on the wings of that timorous and wavering spirit, Gaiseric flew high as the walls and higher, looking down on the walls, the land below them, and the river beyond which (surely an error of Bonifacius) were sequestered perhaps five hundred horses waiting to be called into the battle at the opportune moment. The riverbanks had grown soft from mild spring rains two days before, making a barrier to fast attack. Gaiseric checked from his lofty dream-perch his own army and cavalry. The horsemen hidden from view below the hill on which the infantry took formation, not squares but chevrons and double columns. From on high the Vandal king saw how it would go, how the battle would be won without much loss, with little effort.

He saw on the battlement walls the bishop Augustine looking on knowing not what he saw but still lecturing Count Bonifacius on what he could have done. The stately general waved aside the would-be warrior-bishop who still continued his harangue. Further to the south of these two bickering headmen, he, the same nameless one he'd seen in dream-white before, his teacher Innomenatus again held a scroll, unfurling it across the air that separated him from Gaiseric. Even as it fluttered and twirled in the wind, twisting this way and that, Gaiseric read, could almost hear, the rhyme:

Þata king scolde	*gold-giffa be*
þis wifa scolde	*be free.*
When the king	given gold can be
This woman	shall be free.

Gaiseric—still in his dream—looked to the city wall, seeing Innomenatus pointing at the woman Sequia of Thagaste who was in the company of an older, smaller woman. As the Vandal king lunged out to catch the scroll, he turned, the wind halted, and Gaiseric fell out of bed instantly awake.

26

Fear and Joy in Hippo Regius

Perhaps it is because I died and came back to life sometime in Advent that of all times in our calendar, the weeks before Christmas are the most precious to me. That month is usually full of promise without need to pay, just as my resurrection and journey to Alexandria was filled with excitement, opening a broad horizon of unlimited learning.

In Augustine's monastery from mid-November to the Holy Mass of Christ, we are a bustle for the praise and cheerfulness in our breasts. How can one, neither Manichean nor pagan either, not be warm to the idea of a savior advancing upon us?

Well, this year proved to be different. Aksil, it is true, returned alive, but had I not risked his life with my interference? Sequia was killed, likely, though I held on to her mother's hope for a safe return. And what had become of Sabina herself? What part had I played? The burden I carried into Advent weighted me with guilt. Too, I had set Augustine off by touching on his fathering of Sequia, something he was not ready to admit and a thing he had, now with the incarceration of her mother, no reason to confess. Augustine had acted decisively immediately after my probing during his confession. Just what jail held the *materfamilias* I would discover, I had to discover. And worse than anything else, I would be forced to work alongside the bishop, without acknowledging or even hinting that I knew anything about his terrible actions. If all this was too much, there was war afoot.

Truly, both joy and fear—are they opposites?—were advancing. This year the birth of Christ had arrived in the company of the terrible force of the Vandal army, moving slowly but inexorably nearer our town. It must have been the storing up of Advent felicity that deflected the worry and anxiety that certainly had to rankle the mind of each person within our walls. The number of refugees grew as the Vandals marched forth capturing villages in both the south and the west of Numidia. Each time before a town fell to the Vandal sword a glut of farmers, merchants, townsmen, and clergy arrived at our gates, clamoring to get in.

To those knowledgeable of Roman civic governance, those like the friend-of-my-youth Augustine and my former employer Bonifacius especially, the times were worrisome, for the coming of the Vandals appeared less like the front line of an army sweeping across the land to pillage, more like a folk settling the territory into which they passed. Gaiseric, my pupil and the Vandal king, looked to have the genius of Caesar and Constantine combined. He seemed an avid and adept conqueror and a city-builder as well.

"There is much killing, to be sure," Bonifacius told me during a surprising summons to his villa—one Augustine allowed with provision that I return in five days—ostensibly to translate incoming and outgoing messages of importance, "but there is no indiscriminate slaughter. Just enough to terrorize, enough to remove previous leaders who could never be counted on, but fewer deaths than one would expect." The count was pacing up and down on his garden portico. "I hear that much is taken but bit by bit some lands confiscated are returned to their owners while others—formerly held by my allies— are kept to be worked by their new Vandal landlords. It is a sly and well planned strategy."

"How is that, my count?"

"This Gaiseric gains lands and the fealty of the populace, who are relieved to still live, and of the minor land owners gladdened to retain at least a share of what they had before. Also through their 'kindness' to the populace, the Vandal lords learn from their neighbors how to work the land rather than to despoil and leave it."

I watched him pace and puzzle this through. Finally, he said, "It is an old Roman method of conquest."

"The Vandal king, then, has been a student of our law and culture." This was a thing I not only knew but for which I was, though not solely, responsible. Gaiseric had been the best of my pupils.

Bonifacius stopped. "It might have been the devil himself who tutored this barbarian. How else could he perfect both language and political learning while fleeing at the same time Huns and Franks as well as the Roman legions themselves?" He then turned directly to me, saying, "Do you know this man?"

"Yes, by reputation, of course, *Comes*." I would volunteer something but as little as possible.

I thought that his hand wandered toward his belted dagger. "And what can you say?"

"Only what I repeat from others that the king of the Vandals is a wily opponent, somehow carrying deep and wide knowledge of the mind of the Roman world"

"Who says this?"

"I should not tell, my lord."

He let his hand fall. "It is most certainly Augustine. Never fear, I will report nothing to that man."

"I have heard Gaiseric the Vandal plots against the bishop in order that he might sow disunity in our city."

The count stood still. "That barbarian not only jars our trust in one another, he seems to have the knack of instilling trust in very many that he now over-lords. Contrary to the practices of our own Catholic bishops, this Arian allows all to attend his churches, even Donatists and pagans. Through some intervention I do not understand, he harnesses the heretics to pull trouble away from him and to push it toward our side. Then, he invites Catholics to join his fold."

Bonifacius began his pacing once more, back and forth over his own mosaic image at the center of the colonnaded entrance to the garden. "There is no love-loss between Bishop Augustine and my command. True. Still, I am sworn, and it is my duty to protect the city." He straighted to his full height. "And that duty I will perform when, no matter what magic the Vandal king works, that time shall come."

Bonifacius stopped and sat, apparently done with his fretting over the Vandals. The count struck a friendlier, informal pose, crossing one massive haunch over the other and setting his elbow on his knee, he crooked his huge hand beneath his chin. Casually, he said, "My wife asks about you, Innomenatus."

Never before had he mentioned her interest in me, and I heard a note of danger in the situation although Bonifacius, far from guileless, was no sly dissembler. "She misses your nimble conversation."

"She likes to hear and speak her own language. That is all," I said.

"Come, stay another day to chat. It would amuse her."

I used my most avid but guarded tone to reply. "Well, then I shall, of course, especially if Maria can fix me a lunch."

The count was well aware of my affection for the kitchen and gave out one of his rare laughs. "Scribbling stimulates the appetite, they say."

I gladly lunched with Pelagia—Maria's efforts in the kitchen never failed to amaze my monastic palate—getting what I could from the Gothic countess but staying continually aware that anything I said could come to the ears of Bonifacius. Therefore, I guarded my mouth while playing the loquacious chatterer. I wanted to find out as much as possible about the abduction of Sequia and what I had not heard: the unofficial story of the returned Roman mercenaries. Perhaps, even news of Sabina's whereabouts might surface.

"You have a very good appetite for a scribe, my man," Pelagia said, watching me gorge myself on Maria's roast lamb drizzled with pomegranate sauce.

"Contessa, I work in a monastery. We are free from want, but our provisions are meager."

She smiled slyly. "Then is this (indicating the tray of delicacies) a sin?"

"No, my lady, I have taken no vows but that of accurate translation."

"Strange for a monk to have no vows to keep him close to God," she said, "unless The Father commands the Greeks and Romans in the Hebrew language. Then, He would keep you close."

Her levity tickled me, so I gave her a genuine smile and a laugh. "The gnostics of Alexandria say we hear God's words in the language each one of us speaks."

"Truly, a Babylonian idea."

"Ah, I rue the loss of Babylon."

"And my whole household the loss of Thagaste."

She was leading me, I knew, but in the direction I wished to go. "An unexpected loss of life. I'm sure it has tested morale. The count appeared concerned, angry."

"Yes, angry with that bishop of yours."

"For wishing the *cohort* be sent?"

"Not only that, though it was surely an excess and a trap. Why though having got his way would Augustine send a Berber agent as well? In advance of our forces? And on one of our own horses!"

Here I warned myself to tread carefully. Aksil, living outside the monastery walls of Christendom in Hippo, was subject to Bonifacius's Roman law, although a rushed visit to Aksil calmed my worry:

As soon as I left Pelagia, I hurried again to Aksil's house outside the walls. I was too late.

"Oh, yes, the count's inquisitors have already been here," Aksil told me.

It frightened me. "What did you tell them?"

"Only the truth, that I had received a request from the monastery to release several mounts to a Berber tradesman. He was, I thought, traveling to Calama to bring urgent messages to Bishop Possidius."

Aksil's bending of the story accounted for Pelagia's commentary. Apparently, Bonifacius had determined that Augustine required the horses for his purposes. "And so nothing more has come of it?"

Aksil smiled. "It is commonplace to exercise our steeds in this way. Horses must be ridden. Was Bonifacius convinced? I suppose so. No one has again spoken of it until now."

I did not allude to my knowledge gained from Pelagia. "Rest assured, you are safe."

Aksil pursed his lips and shook his head. "The desert is my safety, as eternal as the god you call The Father himself."

The man was every bit a philosopher as Mani or Augustine.

Before my rush to Aksil, still in my interview with Pelagia, I told her truly, "I know nothing of the bishop's plots. This one is very much odd, isn't it?"

"Perhaps not so unusual for one used to spinning—spider-like I cannot but think—several threads of an argument at once. Yes, the man's horse was one of ours."

"Stolen?"

"Commandeered from the city's southern corral beneath walls of the convent."

In an effort to turn away from this disturbing news which was soon to send me to Aksil and to learn more of what I had hoped for, I said, "So these two soldiers who returned have stories to tell."

"The count believes more of what the horse that they claim they 'found' says than the blather of those two." She drew herself up to her full height, "My father did not brook sole survivors. He would say, 'They stink of cowardice.'"

Her father, Beremudus, had successfully fought war upon war both against and on the side of the empire. "You have been at war most of your life, my lady."

"Yes, and I am tired of it. Thagaste's fall is an old story of inaction and blissful ignorance followed by action too late such as this foolish but unavoidable training schedule that is now in full press. I came to Africa to be rid of conflict, but it has followed me like a pet goose, squawking with each new step."

"Still the honking of the two smelly geese who returned must give us something to know, knowledge of the Vandal strength, for instance," I said trying to guide her to my purpose.

"If I didn't know you as a simple gossip," she said looking strangely stern, "I'd think you a spy."

I laughed as easily as I could. "I suppose I ask too many questions."

She disarmed me with a warm smile. "You are right. They are fat, lazy birds. Those two will likely die in prison or at the head of a phalanx."

"Sad. And they reported this Thagastan woman's death?"

"Those who run from battle should not tell tales of bravery or pretend to knowledge they cannot hold."

"Their report was false?" I held hope for the verity of Sabina's faith.

"Sheep's gut." She said and rose to go. "It will do no good to beg for your silence, so I just will not tell you."

And with that flummoxing appraisal, Pelagia left me, a gossip as empty of news as his own plate was of food. I had discovered little about Sequia and nothing at all about her mother. Still, what Pelagia hinted at could not be far from the truth. I could guess the unfortunate survivors had fattened their observations in an effort to be important and less expendable. The death of their intended quarry, Sequia, they might have thought would exonerate them of duty.

I left the house of Bonifacius turning that over in my mind, telling myself to adhere to the truth or suffer the two soldiers' likely fate. Pelagia's and her husband's insinuations reminded me that eyes watched and ears listened all the more sharply close to a crisis. I scurried, in a wandering way to avoid detection, quite indirectly south to the horse barns of my man Aksil.

The vigilance I write of may have been true of the governing Romans and of those like the recently arrived Possidius, bishop of Calama who was close to Augustine, but could not it seemed be applied to the friend-of-my-youth who himself now seemed oblivious to most everything: to a steady stream of heresies from all directions, to quarters overflowing with refugees, to increasing costs of food and rents, unto the fearful rumblings from both the humble and the high. The bishop, after his late night confession, floated, it seemed to me, on a euphoric cloud of beneficence. I had not in youth or before his latest confession seen the like in him.

Did I trust this new lightness? Not after what he had done. One minute he'd wrapped himself in sincere avowal of wrong-doing, and the next minute, having left my chamber, had sent a militia to whisk Sabina off. How could I believe anything he said?

He moved through his duties and through the celebration of Advent, Christmas, and far into January seemingly without a care. He often ministered to the newest and the poorest refugees liberally giving blessings, housing when he could, and sometimes even small stipends.

His wondrous ebullience cheered the populace. The people were talking: "The bishop will save us from the Arians." "No harm can come to the seat of the African church while Augustine lives." "We count upon the bishop to show us our way." A great wave of relief and contentment emanated from the man in what had begun just two months prior as testy times now washing over the swelling numbers of residents of Hippo Regius.

I wondered about this new-found levity and energy. One possible source was the recently established residency of Bishop Possidius from the Calamic See that the Vandals had taken, which seemed to provide the bishop with an eager helpmate in his duties, freeing Augustine for new enterprises. Perhaps, too, had a weight of sin, one he had been carrying for forty years, lifted from Augustine. Was it his confession—that confession, like his previous one to me, had been partial, hardly a complete one which truth eventually would spell a heavier need to tell—did that confession buoy him, turn him to a new light? Did he feel closer to his dear Father? It could not be known by the many, perhaps any at all but me, that his new freedom of thought and energy resulted from the disappearance of two people who had worried him: his concubine Sabina and Sequia her daughter.

The bishop's about-face cautioned me. I became guarded when in Augustine's company. I had been reminded of his methods and knew that I could easily find myself on the wrong side of the bishop no matter what affections he swore, especially, since Possidius was now so close to him. Even so, when he had time to spend more idly, he spoke to me of the simpler days of our youth, of our schooling, and of our discussions of the philosophers Plotinus and Mani. Especially, this latter surprised me greatly since just recently his young nemesis, Julian, had begun to accuse the friend-of-my-youth of a clearly heretical position, Manichean leanings. But this new, carefree Augustine felt at liberty to revisit our old arguments. I listened with an ear attuned to my own fall which could come, I knew, with little warning.

Augustine talked of his long-ago meeting with Faustus, the prophet of Mani. "God forbid that I should have missed my epiphany, my conversion. Had I not met Faustus, the so-called prophet himself, I might have remained in that erroneous Manichean fold."

Since I, too, was more comfortable talking of the past than of the dismal present, I said, "I recall how disappointing his visit to Carthage was to you."

"The man could not explain even the simplest mysteries of his professed faith!"

"Your questioning of him was painful to watch," I admitted.

Augustine was indignant. "I became *his* tutor!"

These moments he allowed himself to recall, but in our few conversations between November and the middle of January he never again mentioned Sabina or Sequia as if those two had never existed in his world. For that reason I rued the outcome of his confession which seemed to have blocked any revelation of Sabina's whereabouts or any mention of Sequia's life or death.

And so I came to believe over those three months that it was indeed the confession after the reported death of Sequia that had transformed him into a lively, lithe figure and conversationalist. But the euphoria, if that is what it was, would not and did not last. And if the cause of its end was bad news to the bishop, it would the best of news to Sabina were she able to hear it wherever she was.

Though it was not revealed immediately, I had been right to think that Pelagia could lead me to Sabina. It was her curiosity—perhaps sensing from a woman's perspective the importance in worldly events of the existence of a still-living concubine—not my need to know that led me to Sabina. Perhaps emulating the emperor's regent-mother, Galla Placidia, the Contessa Bonifacia, had assumed an active role in the count's administration, persistently influencing the direction of their mutual fortunes. Bonifacius's *bucellarii*, her dowry from Beremudus, were still loyal to their princess, and insured not just her safety but her sway as well. She had clashed with Augustine over the baptism of her daughter and would not forgive his intransigence. This was all good fortune for me, for when Pelagia questioned me, I was able to pry out the information I desired.

"Tell me, translator, what you know of the bishop's concubine."

I played my tedious and artless role as ignoramus, saying, "I know only what I have read in the bishop's *Confessio*, that he had one for a long time. She bore him a son."

Pelagia was more direct then. "Everyone knows that. He never named her. Why?"

"Perhaps he sheltered her in that way." I persisted in cloddishness.

"And what came of this sheltering? He sent her home, he himself says."

"Yes, back here, to Africa."

"And not long after the death of his mother, Augustine also returned. Is that not so?"

"Yes, back to Africa," I said, still playing for position.

Pelagia regarded me firmly setting her eyes on mine, "So, did they never see each other again?"

Having no knowledge of this outside of the confessional, I felt it acceptable to plead blindness. "I have seen no evidence of that. Perhaps they wrote to each other."

I had no other way to interpret in her grin than something akin to cruelty. "I will give you something to gossip about, then. My husband, at the quiet behest of the bishop, holds a certain Sabina of Carthage, in his private prison. She has long been in the convent in the south of the city, lately its *materfamilias*."

"I see," I said, hoping for more.

"I suspect this woman is or was the bishop's concubine. The one he wrote about so unfaithfully in his famous book."

"Why do you suspect this?"

"Late affairs reek of suspiciousness. This Sabina of Carthage is of the right age. And despite actively preaching, more so she has sermonized on readmission of heretics to the Catholic church."

"It seems what the Lord Christ had asked. Many do so."

The cruel smirk again appeared. "Yes, but in the realm of Bishop Augustine here in Africa they do not for long, at least un-beset-upon by the terror of a heretic hunter. She, however, has persisted for years in her ecumenical efforts and without reproach! Explain that."

I did not want to answer. "I cannot."

Now she looked at me earnestly, knowingly, "Not yet, but you will."

Torture and mayhem trilled my sudden desire to flee. Still, I asked, "How so, my lady?"

"Though the count has little interest in the woman, I would have you interview her whom my husband holds and obtain her story, determine her identity. I will know the truth that I suspect lies with her."

Even though I was beholden already to two masters, Augustine and Bonifacius, and at least one other mistress, Sabina, I was in no position or mood to decline the offer or the order. "I am at your service, of course, but are not others better suited to extracting this woman's truth?"

"No. She must not—so my husband has promised—be harmed. This is more the mission of a silver-tongued gossip." At that a smile forced its way onto my face. Without acknowledging that felicity, she continued, "I will see you have access to her cell."

27

Sabina's 

I followed two of Pelagia's *bucellarii*, one of whom I recognized from the day Bonifacius had first summoned me eighteen months past, through the winding streets far south in the town toward the river, a very old part of the city, skirting the convent and stables and running nearly to the water. At an entry beneath a low, red stone arch almost too narrow to allow the two soldiers to pass in tandem, my escort spoke through a grate in that thick, ancient olive wood door. When it opened, the pair ushered me through to a chamber hardly large enough for our party, especially since it was occupied by a jailer even more rotund than myself. This man led me down a dim corridor that smelled of the dank river to the cell where I found the imprisoned Sabina. The keeper bid me squeeze past him into a high room lit only through a crack in the stonework at its ceiling. My guide left me there, locking the door and shuffling back down the hall.

My eyes strained against the darkness, but my ears led me toward Sabina following her quiet, expectant query, "Who has come to witness my glorious misery?"

"*Materfamilias*, it is Amicus, your sorry friend, Innomenatus." Guided by her voice I found her perched solidly atop a raised pallet in the dimmest quarter of the room. I extended my arm and she, more able to see than I yet, took my hand.

"Blessings. You are welcome in the name of Jesus and his followers." Her voice was changed, perhaps by the solidity of the walls and ceiling of the chamber, still firm but thinner, less commanding than at the convent, sounding more contemplative, though, as she had always, she spoke kindly saying, "Be not sorry, my friend. Come sit with me on my bed. It is the only comfort in this hole into which the bishop has cast me."

A new bitterness rose through her tone, and I nearly wept for her pains. I sat next to her there and confessed. "I am sorry and unworthy.

All this and more are my failures. I feel lost."

This brought a sigh, and, while denying my role in her jailing, she wept openly. I could do nothing but sit with her, staunching my own sorrow. After some time, she looked at me closely in the dun light, and spoke.

"If only your admission were instead spoken by Aurelius Augustinus rather than by his old friend. It is for his obdurate heart that I cry."

I waited for her to continue, which after a long pause, during which I surveyed the dismal place she was kept, she went on.

"I do not weep or worry for myself or for Sequia. Even here, maybe especially here held in silence, I feel assured of her life and wellness. You, Amicus, have less to do with all this than I have. Still, I cannot deny my part in stirring the bishop to his dire action against me. In my letters I surely roused his conscience and consternation."

I interrupted her. "No, no. It was I who pushed him to it. I confronted him during a confession. I thought admitting his fathering of Sequia would clear his troubled mind."

Sabina took the news in carefully and slowly. She reached for my hand and said, "You cannot own that, Amicus. The bishop himself would hide that sin even against his own God. Despite what he preaches, he chose this path of his own free will. He would silence the world to cover this over. That is why I weep. He may save his church and reputation but lose his soul."

What could I say? We were sure only that Augustine was, as he had been since we all were young, sovereign over our lives.

As if to better explain herself she said, "Listen, Amicus. While you studied in Alexandria and Jerusalem, we, Augustine, Adeodatus and I, lived at Cassiciacum in that most beautiful corner of Italy. Those were the happiest days of my life. He surrounded us with philosophers and sought truth and sound principles of living. I wish you could have seen Aurelius then, at the height of his secular intellect, admired, of course, and loved. Adeodatus attended each word that came from his father, often repeating to me the arguments he'd heard during my forced, frequent absences—I had the household to operate, an unkindness that Monnika bestowed on me, because I could not, nor did I, complain. It was her move to keep me away from the daily gatherings around her son. She, of course, stayed at his side."

I could sympathize, for I had known the woman. "Monnika ruled like an empress, even in our youthful days. She liked me a very little."

Sabina continued, "On a day I shall never forget, I was summoned to a room not unlike this one, at the base of the villa, next to the tannery. Monnika was there with a hostler. She commanded me to leave immediately—yes, I was told this not by my love and father of my child but by Aurelius's mother who could not conceal her relish in dispatching me—to return to Africa. And when I found then and there that I must leave behind Adeodatus, flesh of my flesh, I wept just as you have seen me do today and as I had not done since. I cried not for my loss but for the hardened heart of Augustine." She again wiped her eyes. I waited for the rest.

"Without a word allowed to my son, without a minute to see his father, I was whisked away by the waiting horseman, taking with me only my heartbreak and emptied love back to Africa." She rose and paced deliberately around the confines. "Now, this not unanticipated but sudden act by the bishop brings back all my past, especially, his cruelty, for though Monnika reveled in her duty, I knew then that he was behind it, the same way he now pushes Bonifacius to hold me here. For years he had tolerated my preaching and gnostic-like thinking, but I suspected it was only a matter of time and opportunity before the solipsist in him would act. Without Sequia available to defend me, he felt free to move."

She sat once more and looked—I could now see—at me curiously. "I am thankful for your presence, but how surprising that you have found me and have been able to enter my shameful palace. How did you do it?"

I surveyed the dank chilly place. "I am sent by Pelagia, the wife of Bonifacius."

"Yes, the Arian-Gothic princess. Some of her *bucellarii* hear our sermons at the convent and some attend me here, too. I have thought of her at times as a benefactress, working through her men in arms. Why has she sent you? Of what interest might I be to her?"

"She would have me extract that, though I have told her none of it, which I already know, that you are the same unnamed concubine of the young Augustine of whom the bishop has written. She wonders, too, if you still see him. Without knowing, of course, I thought her inclined to favor you and your cause as much as she knows of it. As for me, I took it as an opportunity to see you and, I hope, to hearten you."

"And what will you tell her?"

I smiled thinly and bobbed my head comically. "I shall little by little give her the gossip she desires to hear. Of course, I will tell her nothing you would keep between us, and I must discover first what her purposes will be."

"She can be of help to Sequia."

"Somehow I believe she can be. Her husband, I think, knows nothing of this."

"Very well, Amicus. You are capable and experienced in the empire's courts far and wide." Taking from beneath her garments a small silver χρ, chi-rho, canted aside ⳩ she said, "Do this: place this Catholic emblem in her hand as a gift from me. Reveal what is best to tell her, but make sure to hold back enough to insure yourself another visit here."

And so, by leave of my Gothic lady whom Sabina began to call *mia benefactra*, I was able to stay close to Sabina from the ides of January to late-February, visiting as often as I could hide it from Augustine, all the while feeding Pelagia the truth in a trickle.

In prison, Sabina struck me anew. In her solitary trials there, I saw that she had grown deeper, more compelling, and concentrated in her thoughts. There was nothing morose or dark in her ideas. Sabina's hopes were high, and in my earliest visits, I was able to bolster optimism by telling her of Pelagia's cryptic commentary when she first sent me to the cell. "It was her way of telling me that Sequia may be known to have survived the attack," I said of Pelagia's refusal to reveal anything.

Sabina thought for a while. "And why would the contessa say, or not say, this to you?"

"She may suspect my involvement though it is hardly possible that she or Bonifacius know the extent of it. There is a sense that they suspect the bishop of interference and wish me to determine his reasons."

"And will you?"

Ah, how much to tell, even to Sabina. Despite nearly seventy years of practice, I had no instinctive way to determine what to say. Because I trusted Sabina's good, strong spirit and great faith, I settled on telling her some but not all. "I will listen. I will tell Augustine little and Pelagia less. For all at this point is speculation. The bishop would only choose not to believe. And moreover," I paused, braving the truth against a softer dissembling, "any meddling from *domus Bonifati* would darken his lately enraptured mood."

"He could not be elated by the reported death of his daughter. As hard as he can be, that is not the man I have known."

Indeed, Augustine had changed over the years of struggle in the public eye. He was no longer the sensitive, retiring philosopher. So here I had to run against the grain of my knowledge of the bishop. "Hardly. He is cheered, I believe, by a late confession he's made. That is all I can say."

Sabina's mind worked quickly, "So he has admitted his paternity!"

When I said nothing to this, she added, "Good shall come of it, I'm sure."

I was doubtful of that prophesy, but I had no desire to nay say at Sabina's expense. "Good has already come."

I certainly believed it at the time.

28

Sequia's Ransom

Yes, I believed that good would come through Augustine, but one's plans, growing ever more complicated, dress themselves in a cloth of darkness, appearing in shadow more real than either the stones or sky of waking life. Events, always unforeseen, though, intrude devices like a bright dawn suddenly piercing night as if to reveal to the-maker-of-schemes his own errors. I was humoring Sabina, much to my shame. I was deceiving Pelagia while helping her to beguile Bonifacius. And to Augustine I showed the faces of confessor, friend, and servant, all the time inveigling outside of his sight. Now, the sunlight of truth late that winter threatened to flood the very midnight of my intrigues.

Once again in the *tablinum* we awaited Bonifacius who had, to the bishop's dismay, demanded an audience for the "highest reasons of state." On the way, the new and lithe Augustine had lingered outside the kitchen conversing with the matron in charge. "What do you lack, sister? How many do you feed each day now? Do all get their fill?" It was the bishop's new solicitousness that charmed not just the kitchen help but the populace at large. Not that Augustine rarely met the people, but even those seldom in the church had noticed a swift and far reaching change in his demeanor. All felt heartened by it.

Done in the kitchen, the bishop turned to a duty he could hardly have relished. His request that Bonifacius bring Sequia of Thagaste to trial had ended not just in failure but in a tragedy of the most portentous kind and at count's expense. The bishop had not faced the Roman since just after the debacle at Thagaste. Now, it seemed clear that *Comes Africae* was coming this time to bring the bishop to terms. Even so, Augustine was wrapped in his most glad aspect, not to be swayed toward conflict.

The bishop took his place on the throne of the See and even before he was settled there, the arrival of the count was announced by the notes of trumpets at the entry. The count entered marching between two files of six each of Pelagia's battle-clad *bucellarii*, their armor glistening in the peristylium sun. Each shouldered a spear and carried a short sword buckled at his waist. The count dressed in a fresh white tunic trimmed in gold thread beneath a gleaming silver, gold-traced breastplate, his blood-red *palundamentum*, commander's mantel, draped around it all and fixed at his right shoulder again with the gorgon pin that had once before offended Augustine and was sure to do so again. His massive form stood tall, tan, and bold before the bishop, at which point he removed his Gallic helmet that was crested by a stunning brush of auburn horse hair. The sturdy general made no greeting but indicated the file captain who stood forth, saying:

> Bonifacius, *Comes Domesticorum Imperiali, Tribuni Foederati, et Comes Africae*, commander of the imperial forces in Africa under Galla Placidia Regent of Rome brings news of war and of the greatest import to Aurelius Augustinus, Bishop of Hippo Regius.

The captain strode forward, offering Augustine a scroll, which the bishop demurred to take, instead indicating delivery to me, sitting at my desk at the side of the room.

I was reminded, as the captain strode my way, of my brief duties in the capital, Constantinople, in a much younger but no less militaristic age. I couldn't say then or this time that the service was pleasant. I unrolled the scroll and scanned the contents which were written in Vandalic script and in Latin as well. The hand, I was sure, was Gaiseric's.

My practiced decorum fitted the occasion well, as I would have liked to celebrate just reading the beginning of the message—Sequia was alive and well—but felt a creeping sense of dismay as I read on— she was being held for a very dear ransom (*drauht-gilstr* in Vandalic). The message identified her as Sequidei of Thagaste, daughter of Bishop Augustine of Hippo Regius, prisoner of Gaiseric, King of the Vandal and Alan peoples in Numidia.

I was expected to read the scroll to the assembly, something I dreaded doing. Thus, I took it to the bishop whispering that I felt he should read it for himself first. I could speak it afterward. He took the scroll and lowly sounded it to his own ear.

As if a storm grew swirling out of the desert, Augustine's countenance darkened, the blood rising and blackening his swarthy features like a dust cloud rising to cover the sun. His thunderous looks burst forth through a scathing voice that sounded like a wind ripping down a mountainside. "Outrage. Scandalous lies. Unthinkable barbarisms. What do you mean, *Africae*, bringing these fallacious felonies before me?" The bishop threw down the scroll, which I retrieved and with it returned to my table.

Bonifacius shook his fist aloft as if brandishing the scroll itself. "What means this? Who dares this? Exactly, Augustine. Those are my questions."

Without waiting for an answer, the count stood forth, then began pacing. "In November you insisted on sending my troops to their deaths at the hands of those treacherous Vandals in search of, you said, a heretic to whom you wished to put questions." He came to the center right before Augustine and stopped. "Now, now that you have irreparably damaged the reputation and morale of my army which must soon again face these barbarians, we discover that you had a hidden and much more personal stake in bringing Sequidei of Thagaste to our city. She is your bastard daughter. Did you wish to save her? Or did you seek to destroy her, burying the evidence of your deceitful sins? What of the sending ahead of your Berber agent, or was he an assassin, to outpace us. Ha! Your humbuggery and conniving manipulation border on treason."

At the same time Bonifacius spoke these words Augustine continued his outbursts, repeating louder and louder each time, "Outrage. Scandalous lies. Unthinkable barbarisms," until his face blackened with the effort of a shout at the top of his lungs.

"Listen to my decision on this matter," Bonifacius boomed out over Augustine's protests. He handed another scroll to his captain who brought it to me. Augustine bid me read it.

"The government of Rome in Africa Proconsularis decrees

the actions of Aurelius Augustinus, Bishop of Hippo Regius a transgression of the laws of the empire, and thus shall charge you with the costs of the loss of our *maniple* and further forbids any funds whatsoever of the civil or military treasury be put against this ransom demand. Funds meant to recover said Sequidei of Thagaste shall be those of the Church in Hippo Regius or of the treasury of private citizens here."

Augustine raged. "I have no knowledge of military affairs. Your losses, Count Bonifacius, are of your own doing and have nothing to do with the See or with me. Your 'peacemaking' concession of Icosium and now of Calama to the Vandals was an act of your own cowardice and treachery which have spoiled many faithful lives and more recently nearly cost Bishop Possidius his own. Instead of haranguing me you should be capturing Vandal captains and tribunes, if they have such stations, to negotiate the return of this innocent citizen. We on all accounts reproof your decree. It cannot be effected against the Church. As to these 'revelations' regarding Sequidei of Thagaste, they are unfounded, unsubstantiated, and cruelly unholy blasphemies against the Church in Africa and against me. Who says the Vandals hold her? Really?"

Bonifacius smirked. He was ready. "The mayor of Calama who knew her from nearby Thagaste has come along with the ransom demand to assure us of her presence and her health." The man who Augustine and many others in the room knew stood forward at the entry.

"It is she," the mayor said.

Bonifacius continued, "Also granted safe passage was our garrison chief there who had met her twice in her meetings with her Donatist friends." The count turned to point at the man, standing next to the mayor.

"Certainly! A Donatist heretic! Not a daughter! That is proof of false-saying." Augustine nearly screamed it.

Bonifacius continued insinuating, "Who then would grant this woman the gift of a parcel of your father's land my bishop? First given to a concubine, mother of your son,[1] and then in transference from her to this Sequidei who is not, you say, your daughter!"[2]

"Say nothing of my sainted son!" The bishop yelled. Augustine, sensing a weak direction in arguments, took another tack. "I will never place silver or gold in the hands of deceitful Vandals." The bishop stepped down from the dais, came over to my table, and spat upon Bonifacius's decree. "Your authority ends at that door," he indicated the entry, "so remove your armed vanguard from holy ground . . ."

Bonifacius cut in. "Holy ground of deception, you mean."

Augustine ignored him and continued. ". . . and prepare for your all-too-long-awaited attack on that rabble of barbarians they call an army standing on our doorstep. Had you tended to your own pretended calling, waging war, these Vandals would be starving or be still be fighting Roman legions in Hispania rather than sending demands in gibberish to your weak military servants. And for the love of God, stop that pacing."

Bonifacius, who had resumed his striding about during Augustine's speech, stopped, facing the bishop. "We shall act when we shall act. As for you Bishop Augustine, you would be an Arian already had it not been for our power and vigilance. Receive your daughter as you can and then set her to her apostate trials. But keep within the walls of your monastery, since to sally forth to the city will mean arrest or worse. Already word of your peccadillo spreads, and the name of Aurelius Augustinus is dragged over the stones of our streets to the sounds of uneasy laughter."

"Silence. *Exunt*! Out, out, out!"

The audience was over. Augustine rushed from the room, Bonifacius spun around, marching out again with his Gallic helm atop his head, between his files of *bucellarii*, all to the sounds of trumpets. I stepped over to gather up the scrolls, Gaiseric's and the count's, still on the table. Then I went the way Augustine fled, rather

---

1 Instantly this told me that Bonifacius though he held Sabina in jail knew nothing of her identity. This was clear to Augustine all along. I supposed he could only hope to keep this other deception from Bonifacius's grasp.

2 Despite his ignorance of whom he held in prison, the count had discovered a great deal. How he had failed to make a connection to the woman in his jail, I could not then understand.

slowly I have to say since I had no true wish to overtake the bishop just at that moment. I picked my way along. I was sure Augustine would send for me soon, but for the moment, I had important news to convey in the south of town.

I brought the news to Sabina. She immediately rose from her chair at a writing table that, along with six candles which illuminated the surface, had miraculously appeared since my last meeting with her.

I unrolled the scroll of Gaiseric and read the Latin to which Sabina responded with a prayer. "I knew she lived," the mother said. "And with time she shall prosper through the ways of Christ."

Even to the face of her restrained joy, I felt I had to temper it further. "I doubt the bishop will raise Sequia's ransom. He seems to remain as obdurate as you suspected him to be and has admitted nothing, yet."

"You are sure about the ransom? Oh, how could he refuse?" Sabina asked.

I was not certain. "I can work on the bishop. If he will not pay, I will find other resources. Somehow, the tribute will be paid."

It was my sense that Gaiseric was not after ransom, the *weirgild*. He had told me once that a small tribe such as his could not count on alliances, such as the Romans held, or outright force, such as the Huns brandished, but had to rely on *inwit*, thought of a particular kind of slyness and stealth. "One must look one way and move another," he had said. "One must seem to be something and then be another thing altogether different."

Gaiseric's *inwit* had already led him to divide the forces within Hippo Regius, bringing Bonifacius and Augustine to each other's throats even before his Vandals appeared before the walls. The Vandal king waged a war of the mind in advance of physical warfare, something neither the military nor holy-church leaders seemed to realize. Would any listen to a transient gossip even if he knew and would tell the truth?

"Sister Sabina, rest assured that Sequia shall come here unharmed. It may take some time, but I foresee it."

She placed her hand on mine. "*Amicus meum*, I know the truth of what you say. I have seen it in my latest dreams. 'Your trials will end with your daughter at your side in this world, not the next.' My dream-messenger has said it."

I smiled to myself and felt a heat flush my countenance. "I must go now. The bishop will be looking for me."

And so he was. I slipped back into the monastery easily, moving past the centurions of Bonifacius now set as guard at the gates. Perhaps they were meant to proscribe Augustine's movements—he hardly ventured outside the walls anyway—or were meant to keep an angry and newly frightened populace from overrunning the place. In any case, most of these soldiers knew me as the scribe of Bonifacius and would not ask too many questions about my comings and goings. Still, I kept to the shadows, unwilling to raise suspicions on either side of the monastery walls.

I entered my cell to find the bishop seated at my own desk looking over some of the Aramaic translations I had made of Sabina's letters.

"Thank the Father you have returned." He didn't even ask me where I had gone, but launched right into an explanation of why he was there waiting for me.

"The condemnation of Bonifacius left me shaking in anger, Amicus. Never in all my life have my mental faculties quit me in an onslaught of ire. This accusation drained me of sense."

I moved closer to Augustine and laid a hand meant to be comforting on his arm. He withdrew from my touch. "No, no. Do not soothe my hurt or anger. The worst has past, and I am able to reason once again even in the face of some frightening visions." He rose and stood at the table, seeming to be uncertain of how to proceed. "What are these?" He indicated the letter-translations.

"They are letters, my bishop. Copies of letters I have written and sent to the east, to an Assyrian friend I gained while living there." The exact truth could not be told, so I spun up half-truths where I could.

"It looks familiar in a way."

I diverted his attention from the present, alluding to our studies years before in Carthage. "Yes, you have seen it in the Manichean liturgy."

"Aramaic, then."

"Yes, a form of it."

"And to whom do you write?"

"He is the Bishop of Constantinople."

"Nestorius?"

"The same. I met him in Antioch where I studied Hebrew." Wishing to avoid further examination of Sabina's letters, I tidied up the sheaves. "May I?" Sure as I was of Augustine's ignorance of the language, I hoped to prevent an errant name or word to raise doubt.

"And why do you write in such an obscure tongue?"

"We are friends, my bishop, and his position is quite delicate. We converse on topics somewhat unrelated to the church."

"Not Pelagian ideas?"

My smile was not forced under the circumstances although I tightened my mouth to make it look that way. "Hardly, my bishop."

"Yes, then. Put them away. I do not wish to know more."

I offered Augustine the chair once more, and we sat together.

"It is best if I start with our parting from the *tablinum*," he said. "I rushed out so mad with anger I could have spit!"

"You did spit, my bishop, on the counts decree." I thought he was about to laugh, but he frowned instead.

"So I did. But I left to seek just then some lonely, winding ways I know unlikely to be populated in order to walk, to restore my senses, to think. And as I strode and turned here and there, I argued with myself—at least I thought I declaimed alone—about what I had heard and what it meant. I turned over and over the words I had spoken 'unfounded, unsubstantiated, and cruelly unholy,' which I found, then, to be an accurate description of that event."

I sensed his argument coming and, since there would be no curbing it, I signaled my attention to it by opening my hands to the advancing torrent of words.

"First, 'unfounded', which is to say baseless. Who would take the word of a barbarian? Who could accept the accusation of an enemy?

What fool would believe testimony of a heretic? All the Vandals say is without foundation, all lies, all deceit. Rather than ask, 'Augustine, is it true?' Instead ask, 'Have you divined the source? Is it reliable? Can it be trusted?' These are the proper interrogatories!"

"Of course, my bishop." I had seen it all before and knew the uselessness of standing up to Augustine's character assassinations.

He continued. "Secondly, no single testimony alone is sufficient to establish the truth. Imagine were there but one instead of four gospels? If only Mark's brief account were known for instance? Singular belief and not knowledge of the truth would be required. That is why the Father decreed there to be four accounts, not just one, to provide substantiation through reason. One gospel inspires the soul to believe. Four exercise the mind to know."[3]

Though I, of course, said nothing, I couldn't help thinking of the others I had read, in particular the *Gospel of Thomas* and that of *Mary*. Not all brought the mind to knowing and occasionally, the multiplicity challenged belief. As was his place in the world, Augustine took to the wide Roman way, its posts set deep and its pedestrian ways high to mark the street against straying. I had found a much more wandering way to the things I knew or thought I knew.

Augustine forged ahead with his argument. "As it is with the *Novum Testamentum*, the New Testament, so it is with these allegations. 'They come to us,' I was saying to myself as I walked, 'not only from a questionable source, but also from a single source. The very truth could be left out with no one the wiser! So how can they be believed?' I continued to go, climbing stairs to the very city walls I know to be threatened by these heresies of Bonifacius and Gaiseric, both Arians! 'What if the citizens are all a-gobble about this? Turning false words on a hundred tongues make them no more true,' I said. 'They remain unsubstantiated.'"

It occurred to me that I was the first of many audiences that would hear Augustine's arguments. I was but a practice case, and I had to admit though only to myself that the polemic sounded good and might play well to many hearers if it were kept from the strident

3 I had been acquainted with six other gospels as well in my time in Alexandria, especially, those well known to hermits in the desert beyond the city.

tone I was hearing, though perhaps Augustine, I thought, was demonstrating the sound of his original, solo exercise in reason declaimed from atop the walls of Hippo Regius.

The bishop continued. "The third point I practically shouted from the walls of the city where the monastery enclosure joins our outer protections, *'cruelly unholy* are his words!' Was I, the Bishop of Hippo Regius, brought before an ecclesiastical authority, the Holy See itself? No. Was there anything more cruel to say about me than I had broken a long held and public vow? What civil authority is holy? None. So at the top of the walls looking down over the fields and roads of Proconsularis, I shouted to the sky, 'Who here dares to accuse the Bishop of Hippo Regius? Who can read the soul of the bishop? Who would cruelly turn the knife in his heart?' Oh, Amicus, I nearly flung myself from the battlements.

"The fact of paternity of Sequidei of Thagaste rests with God and with my confessor, but does not belong in the public eye! How dare Bonifacius invade that sacrament?"

Is he splitting hairs to save face with me, I wondered? Does he wish to silence the already silent? I wanted to avoid those issues, so I asked, "What of these frightening visions of which you spoke?"

He drew a long breath and sighed. "I am getting old, Amicus. It is more and more difficult for me to do battle and move on with my important work. I came away from Bonifacius angry, but my walk and arguments only made me more confused and tired. All I could do was to take to bed to rest my senses. I did not think I could sleep, but perhaps I did. For waking I heard a voice somewhere in the room, 'What troubles you so, Aurelius?' The voice spoke my given name. It was the voice of the gnomish character I had seen many times before crouched over my night jar, my *visita nocte*, night visitor. But this time, during the day, I saw nothing, only heard that very same voice."

"Is that all it said?"

"No." Augustine slumped over the table as if admitting the defeat of reason by holy revelation. He breathed with difficulty. I waited fearful of breaking in. Finally, he continued. "The voice said, 'What about Sequia of Thagaste so troubles you, Aurelius?' And pretending to reason and think, I found myself saying, 'It can be only one of two things: That I fear being exposed to my flock through what I have nearly confessed, or that I fear for her wellbeing and safety in the hands of the Vandals.'"

The bishop rubbed his face and eyes with tremulous hands. "His tone became sharp, 'When were you concerned for Sequia's care? For her health or prosperity?'"

"I could only then say the truth, 'No, never before.'

"And as if I had lost an argument I myself had laid down, he summarily replied, 'So, then, you fear exposure.' It was not a question. I admitted it and knew immediately what I had done: twice denied the sister of Adeodatus, my daughter Sequia, first to you in timorous half-confession and then in public before Bonifacius, you again, and all of Hippo Regius."

I felt now was the time for a confessor worth salt rather than dust to speak. "Will you confess it now?"

Augustine laid his arms across the table and lowered his head over them. He then raised his chin over clasped hands and said, "Father, forgive me for I have sinned. I have denied knowledge of, care to, and compassion for my natural daughter, Sequia of Thagaste, have forsworn relation to her before my confessor, and have publicly renounced my integrity and again rejected my progeny to all." He looked up at me, as lowly and sincere as I had ever seen him. "And what shall be my penance?"

I have to say that this was a place to which I had neither desired nor expected to come, but as dangerous as it might be, I would not forestall the necessity further, especially for Sabina's and Sequia's sake. "You shall do penance by accepting as your own Sequia of Thagaste and do so before all the priests, bishops, and sisters now resident in Hippo. Allow them to spread the word to citizens."

"May one inquire before accepting this penitence?"

I sensed another argument coming but knew true contrition required a clear slate. "Of course. Ask."

"Must the women be involved? The Sisters?"

"Why not?"

"I fear . . . ,"

Having jumped into the sea, I now swam strongly. "Fear what, exactly?"

"I fear that my acceptance of a woman, my daughter, who has openly courted Donatists and Arians, who has preached the gospels will set the church back to earlier, heretical times when women wrongly accepted an ascendancy among the followers of Christ. Confessing before women may give them the wrong idea."

"Was it not true," I asked him, "that women served our early Christian communities as priests?"

Augustine mumbled something that sounded like "that's what he said" but did not utter it plainly.

"That's what he said? Who?" I asked. And then I guessed it. "Your *visita nocte* said that?"

"Yes. In his own voice. I did not argue with myself."

"You two argued!"

"I simply held to what is known today in the church, that women priests are a throwback to wayward, ancient ways that cannot be tolerated in the modern Catholic Church."

Intuition guided me. I had been correct. "And he?"

Augustine would not mince words with me anymore. I could see it in the slackness of his face. "He said as if he himself had witnessed it, 'Women earn places as leaders in the church as they always have had.' He mentioned several I knew and others from the east whom I did not."

The history lesson must have been convincing for the bishop did not now argue against it, but I felt there was more. "And what else?"

Augustine clenched his hands now. "He said, 'You must acknowledge your daughter. As God does not abandon His children, so Augustine must not do so either.'"

He repeated the phrase under his breath and then quietly said, "I firmly intend with God's help to do penance and to sin no more."

Before I spoke my part, I insisted on one added point. "And what of the mother?"

He openly admitted it. "I had her jailed. I must now release her."

With the confession complete, I intoned my part, "*In nomine Patris, Filius, et Spritus Sanctus, absolvote.* I absolve you of your sins in the name of the Father, the Son, and the Holy Spirit."

And at those words, Augustine rose and was gone.

29

Pelagia Befriends Sabina

A wise friend once instructed me that the rue of mankind comes in that as soon as he perfects an insight, he is driven to share and so to lose it. Accordingly, to meditate on the glow of hope more than to jump ahead possibly disappointing Sabina, I waited to see that Augustine kept his word. After three days of anticipation without fulfillment of Sabina's release—truly, his words were not a promise or part of his penance—I could wait no longer, stealing away before dawn to her carcel.

Even early as it was, I found the entry to her jail heavily guarded by six *bucellarii*, the captain of whom halted me.

"No person of the bishop's house may come here. Who wishes to pass?"

About to explain, I was interrupted by the soldier whom I had known and who had been attendant on Sabina's ministry. "This man is of the count's employ."

The captain raised a brow. "A monk working for *Comes Africae*?"

"I am his translator at times," I offered. "The countess herself enjoins me to visit here."

My man nodded and immediately the guard detail parted and allowed me to proceed. Once inside, I headed directly for Sabina's cell but my familiar guide took me by the elbow, "Now to the left. Things have changed." Then I realized it was only the *bucellarii*, not the jailer, who attended the place.

"Follow me," my soldier said and led me down a torch-lit passage to an open doorway from which light from the now rising sun strayed over the floor. "Here," he said and ushered me through.

The light, coming through an oculus and six small but ample windows around the circumference of the domed ceiling, illuminated the room itself, furnished albeit sparely, which had six white painted walls plastered from floor to dome, and the two persons there, who turned away from their work at a broad table to look my way startled me all at the same instant. Sabina now living in sunshine with comforts aplenty stood before me in the company of Pelagia, Countess of Africa, my employer. For one of the few times in my life, I was speechless.

In the little time it took Sabina to meet me at the doorway where I had stopped short, all my labyrinthine deceptions and simple half-truths fluttered around my mind like moths roused to circle a candle. I felt as if I would dash myself in any flame were one hot enough be present, but Sabina, sensing my hapless state, comforted me in my irresolve, "All is well, Amicus, you are amongst friends."

Still, I wavered and said, "What has happened? I do not understand."

Pelagia now stepped forward, "Yes, Innomenatus, what has happened? It is you who know the mind of the bishop better than we."

With no other way out and the clear assumption that the news of Sequia's ransom was known to both these women, I relied upon my happy truth, "I've come with hopeful news."

Both women stood attentive, waiting. "Yes?"

"Two nights past, Augustine told me he would release Sabina from this prison."

Sabina's hands went to her lips as she sighed and looked decisively at Pelagia as if they had been discussing just that point. The countess asked, "Why have you waited to make the announcement?"

"I wanted to see if the bishop would be good to his word." At that point when she dropped her hand from it, I saw that Pelagia wore the ☧ I had brought her from Sabina two weeks before. And in an instant, I realized that Sabina wore an Arian cross much like one, but daintier, that Gaiseric had given me. The women before me had consecrated a pact, that much was certain, set in faith and sisterhood. Sabina shook me from my study of the crosses, continuing for her companion, "And now you've concluded he isn't trustworthy?"

I began once more to spin a truth, "By what I see here, he might have acted already."

Both women laughed, Pelagia heartily, Sabina kindly. "No,

Amicus," Sabina said, "what you see here is the work of the countess, not of your bishop."

"It is the work of the *materfamilias*," Pelagia rejoined. "Let me explain for my modest companion:

"Through one of my faithful *bucellarii* who has followed Sabina in her ministry—one that honors the Arian believers as well as Catholics—a sentry here, I learned more than my gossipy Innomenatus would tell"—here Pelagia scrutinized me with a knowing gaze—then continued, "I took immediate pains to furnish Sabina not only with my Arian crucifix but also with writing materials and some comforts, and soon after, we agreed that this airier place where she has been busy writing to the faithful far and wide, not just those in Africa, would suit her pursuits the better.

"I do this Christian service more from faith than those political motives I discussed with you. The mischief abroad in our lands cannot be, we two agree, eased by war but only through a faithful unity."

The *contessa*'s words eased my worry. For this time and in this company, at least, all that required hiding seemed now to be acknowledged and accepted.

Sabina enlarged Pelagia's revelations. "We were just discussing our plans. We know from a messenger that the bishop tried but has been unable to contact *Comes Africae* who is at Carthage right now recruiting and deploying more Numidian troops. We divined two possibilities for the bishop's seeking out the count, both of which are accommodated by my relocation to this lighted cell out of the bishop's reach: one, that he seeks now to destroy me—this she said with obvious regret—the other, that he seeks to free me. I'm afraid your news, supports neither one over the other."

I bowed to her reproach. "*Mea culpa*, so it is," I agreed.

Sabina continued, "You do well in your way, Amicus, and what you've brought me, solves the riddle of our further actions. I will not stay here, over-waiting the bishop's plans no matter what they are. Sequia and the many faithful in Hippo and beyond, including our Aurelius, need the unity I think our many-faced fellowship can bring despite the differences that only seem to separate us. If we can bind Arians and openhearted Catholics, we may tame the furor of our Donatists and bring peace even to the pagans of our troubled land."

"The bishop will forbid those ecclesiastic reunions even if it portends war," I reminded her.

Sabina, it seemed, did not wish to speak against her former paramour, so handed the conversation again to her friend and accomplice who had been pacing behind the table: "Bishop Augustine must see the need to demur," Pelagia said. "All the more reason to act ahead of his next move, whatever it shall be. Without hesitation, we shall make our way to my villa." She turned to Sabina then, "It means a delay in your return to the convent."

"Unfortunate," Sabina said, "but we would best be outside the confines of the bishopric where Augustine holds absolute sway, at least until his notions are clear to us."

I helped Sabina gather her belongings, including a surprisingly large number of letters she had penned over the past two days. "Your imprisonment has made you more prolific than a scribe," I said.

"Yes. I have been troubling all whom I know, and some whom I haven't known, to support us in the demands Gaiseric has made. Sequia's correspondent, Julian of Eclanum, may pledge support. Her parishioners in Thagaste, and even some instructors at Augustine's school there may also offer what they can afford. Many families here in Hippo Regius and in Carthage will help, as well."

"I must send to my friends in the east," I said.

The *materfamilias* shook her head. "You do enough, Amicus. Work to turn the bishop's mind toward helping."

I replied that I felt very little influence over Augustine's ideas or actions. "I will do what I can."

"I will have Maria make a meal if your information is helpful," Pelagia said and smiled.

"Visit me *domui Bonifati* when you have news," Sabina said. "From there we can plan the deliverance of my dear Sequia."

I had now become a direct instrument of the *materfamilias* of Hippo's convent, a duty greater than a gossip might fulfill. I knew then that I required help.

30

Public Confession

The weeks following *Comes Africae*'s announcement of Sequia's parentage, even beyond Augustine's newest confession and Sabina's escape *domui Bonifati*, were times filled with added tumult. In the face of yet another Vandal movement to the east of Calama that had shocked the province in February, hundreds of new refugees now washed into a city already full to the extent that now people were encamped and sleeping in the streets as well as on the rooftops of every house one could see. Despite the efforts of the civil authority, prices had soared even though food was seldom scarce. Bonifacius, denied for the time in his appeal for assistance from Rome, had contracted with the Numidian fighters of the east and brought many of them into the city. These desert people, tall, dark, and fierce, required housing and supplies which strained the populace even more. The movement of troops rang out unremittingly at the port and within the city, reminding all that war was afoot. Atop the waves of this tidal flow of people, animals, and the goods of war, washed the news that Augustine, Bishop of Hippo Regius and bulwark of the African Church itself had stumbled and was tottering toward a fall. Those who had looked toward the bishop as a beacon of hope in this terrible time felt themselves adrift on angry seas. The count's guard around the monastery was busy dispersing crowds that gathered for news or in demand of explanation.

After he left my cell, Augustine had indeed decreed Sabina's release but to his own custody, something that did not happen but which seemed not to trouble the bishop. Then, over a month later, after Calama had fallen, Possidius—the bishop there but already in residence with Augustine—brought into our cathedral delegations of other Catholic leaders, their churches destroyed or closed by the Vandals, along with important priests of these parishes who were all fleeing to the refuge of Hippo Regius. Under Augustine's protection, they were called together by their host. The Bishop of Hippo summoned these and his local prelates and monks to the main chapel of the cathedral. I thought that the friend-of-my-youth looked, finally, to be making good on his penance, for among those representatives from far off parishes, the sisters of Sabina's household were, too, called. I, myself, notified Sabina, who was still lodging with Pelagia at *Villa Bonifati.*

Along with many of the monks in Augustine's service, I was to be present.

At the conclave, I kept away, as was my wont, from the brotherhood of Augustine's long-serving religious household who held me, as was plain to all but the bishop himself, if not in contempt then most certainly under suspicion of being an usurper of or pretender to the bishop's chair. Neither the bishop nor I had made them aware of our youthful friendship nor had either of us been open about our meetings, discussions, and most certainly not about my status as confessor to the bishop. It was only Augustine's presence and clear favoritism that kept me from these men's swift condemnation. I would survive hardly a day past the bishop himself were any of these brothers to take charge. Under these circumstances and because I was the bishop's confessor, I kept toward the rear of this somewhat large gathering. Only one close ally, Alypius, next to me Augustine's oldest friend, still being in Ravenna, was absent.

The assembly numbered nearly two hundred, and when all seated themselves, the sisters at the far left-rear, Augustine stood before them to lead them in prayer and to recite David's sixth psalm, his voice quavering over that well-known sixth verse:

> I am weary with my moaning;
> every night I flood my bed with tears;
> I drench my couch with my weeping.

Finishing then, Augustine stood silent for a long time, and then said, "Let all who hear tell three others that this, my penance assigned me by my confessor, shall reach every Christian in the city by nightfall."

At the mention of "confessor" without gazing around I noted if any sought me out. None in particular looked my way though there was a great deal of gawking around.

Then, without hesitation but softly and slowly the bishop intoned his penance. "I accept before you, my brother priests and bishops and our sisters in faith, the woman known to you as Sequidei of Thagaste as my natural-born daughter, flesh of my flesh, and a believer in Christ." The murmur caused by his acceptance ran around the room and echoed in the vault above before quietly settling again over the crowd seated below. I looked toward the members of Sabina's household and saw not only Sabina herself in a hooded robe but beside her Pelagia dressed in a like garment. I had looked to see what effect Augustine's words had on the sisters but nearly shouted in the chapel at seeing the *materfamilias* and her escort, *Contessa Africae*.

The sight of the person of the bishop whom she had not seen since their last night together in Carthage when Sequia was conceived must have moved Sabina, but she wore her habit closely and was veiled from my full sight. Her figure gave no outward sign of joy or triumph even as Ia on one side and Pelagia on the other turned toward their sister each placing a hand on her arm. If Augustine saw any of this, he gave no sign.

What came after could have been part of the penance as heard by others, but I knew it was alone of Augustine's invention. His tone quickened a little and hardened as well.

"Since that long ago sin, conceived in a weakened state of grief at the death of my son, I have kept my vow of celibacy that engulfs all my long time as a priest and bishop of the Church. Let all hear that, also." Again the soft buzz of voices ran round the room. Augustine let it die as he had more to say. Now speaking clearly in words loud enough to bound off the surrounding walls he said, "You know that Sequidei of Thagaste, my daughter, is the captive of the bestial king of the Vandal horde—save her from harm, O Lord—and that an exorbitant ransom is demanded for her safe return to us." Again the crowd whispered for moments then silenced itself. "This saddens me, but know in these most difficult times that even an ounce of gold or an ingot of silver that passes to our enemy strengthens him and weakens us, but more, that any measure shown of frailty emboldens that vile tribe and cows our very spirit of resistance. Therefore, out of love for my daughter and for all whom she loves here in Hippo Regius, in Calama where she is held, and in Thagaste from whence she came, we will stand against any demand of tribute." At this there was louder discussion amongst the crowd which took a much longer time to quell. Augustine waited, for he was not yet done. "And to this Christian woman now being held in the heretical Arian fold and who has been, besides, known to have associated with Donatists and has been reported to have transgressed on the provenance of our priesthood by preaching in public as a prelate, we offer our forgiveness and absolution during her painful incarceration and pray for her eventual release and her return back into our Catholic family."

Without his characteristic extensive explanations, Augustine ceased there and intoned his benediction:

Genitori, Genitoque	To begetter and begotten
Laus et iubilatio,	Praise and jubilation
Salus, honor, virtus quoque	Hail honor and virtue
Sit et benedictio:	Be and blessings, too:
Procedenti ab utroque	From One through Both
Compar sit laudatio.	Let there be equal praise.
Amen.	Amen.

With this pronouncement he stepped down and slowly made his way through the crowd, gesturing his blessings without saying anything more. Passing Possidius, he grasped that bishop's hand and took also the arm of his best chancellor, the one who intoned morning mass for him, and made his way further through the multitude, many of whom bowed, some kneeling. I watched carefully at this point. And when he passed the sisters and all but two geniculated, he let go his escorts with, I thought, a startled sign of recognition whether at the presence of Sabina or Pelagia, or both and, looking suddenly to the ceiling, folded his hands before him and walked ahead ever more rapidly.

Most gathered there were not to notice the evidence of the bishop seeing Sabina and Pelagia together, but each and every woman in the crowd, as did I, too, carefully attending the scene, could hardly have missed his slur of neglect of these two who stood even in the crowd of kneeling women there.

I followed the good sisters out a side entrance where I saw Aksil and three other of his livery escorting Ia and her sisters away in a cart headed toward the convent. I caught up with Sabina before she disappeared in a phalanx of Pelagia's *bucellarii*. She told me in just a few words to wait for contact from Aksil to whom she had given certain orders. I could not hazard more of a meeting there in public even if I could have penetrated the guard, though I had hoped to talk more with Sabina. She left me to follow her instructions and was gone. I was not to see her until well past Easter.

In the street, what the people were saying about their bishop took hold of my attention. Augustine's announcement raked up rancor and defense, too. Many I overheard and some I talked with expressed a sort of confused anger at the bishop's admission:

"How can he free us from the wages of sin if he himself is a slave to them?"

"The bishop is steeped in concupiscence."

"*Fraude Romanorum*, Roman fraud!" Referring to his time in Italy, no doubt.

But others took his side:

"We've long known of his *Confessions*. This is simply a revision."

Another threw back, "Simple? Then why did he wait so long to admit what we all had heard weeks ago?"

Still another said, "The bishop could have hidden this easily. You must credit his public confession."

"Admire his courage not condemn his weakness."

And once these sympathies and abrasions made the rounds, those assembled ex-cathedra moved toward discussion of the ransom that was not to be paid.

"It is cruelty to let her languish among barbarians," one said.

A tall Berberish-looking companion enjoined, "He will secretly raise and pay the ransom. It would not be right, though, to announce it publicly."

A vociferous soldier said, "Not a penny to the Vandals. The bishop is right."

The threads of sympathy and faith along with antipathy and ire wove themselves into a ragged fabric of judgment, not of innocence or condemnation but of tepid hope and cautious optimism, for the populace depended on the bishop to guide them through a difficult time and whatever he had done or now refused to do was but the fringe on the civic garment they wrapped about themselves. It was Augustine who, through his guiding of Bonifacius, would protect them and keep them safe and fed. Just as the bishop would rescue Sequia from the barbarians, so would Augustine spare the people from a like perdition. The friend-of-my-youth now formed the last common hope of Hippo Regius, and what I had not heard put out was that this newly admitted sin marred or falsified his *Confessions in Thirteen Books*.

In succeeding weeks, I could not share even the mild enthusiasm the people held for deliverance. Augustine held firm to his denial of ransom, citing his original, public dicture and reasons of need, poverty, and waste. I came to believe that his position was informed in part by the same mood that had taken hold of him upon passing the assembled nuns at his announcement.

He had honored his penance to the word but had not, as prescribed by his night visitor whom I thought spoke the bishop's natural conscience, opened his heart to embrace the spirit of his avowal. I thought that he truly suspected the Eves of the world to be *perfidem mundi*, scourge of the earth, something his own experience and weaknesses had taught him.

Too, then, I suspected the truth of his pardon of Sequia's supposed transgressions of the priesthood to be not much more than a public show of beneficence with which now to dilute the clear distillation of his own peccadilloes. So easily pardoning Sequia ran against the grain of hundreds of years of Church history and of forty years of his own teaching. It was clear to me that in the mind of the friend-of-my-youth if a couple was bad, it was the woman who was the worse. In a word, he succeeded in blaming Sabina for his sin. His own tracking of ineffable deception back to Eve, our common progenitrix, said as much. It was a stain no laundering of prayer could efface, and it seemed to me, further, that he intended to punish his daughter, the heretic, by leaving her to what he believed were the evils of the Vandal race.

Somewhat less than two months after the count's accusation, it was fast approaching Easter, in late March that year, my efforts to urge the bishop to do something to help his daughter—knowing all the while that her mother whom Augustine never mentioned to me again, worked incessantly to do what Sequia's father would not— came to a head.

"No, Amicus, we cannot buy back the soul of Sequia. That is final!"

I noted that he referred to her spirit and not her person. "Can we effect her escape?"

I thought he might rage, but the bishop instead spoke calmly. "Perhaps the coming battle the count prepares for will free her or provide opportunity for exchange," he said.

I hazarded a contrary position. "Isn't it more likely that attack might lead to her death?"

The bishop looked sadly at me, his old eyelids drooped beneath his brows. "So shall we all die, Amicus. Some sooner than others."

"You don't mean yourself, my bishop."

"I do not mean you, Amicus, though we are very near the same age. I believe you will outlast me in this life."

Though I did not feel what I was about to say, I wanted to see his reaction. "Shall I not be permitted to prepare your way?"

"In this case, my dear one, I will be the baptist. I feel it in my bones."

I did not want this self-indulgent worry about our deaths to dissuade us of a conversation about Sequia's ransom. "And may I attempt to save your daughter? You don't forbid it, do you?"

"I do not seek her demise, believe me," he said. "Nor do I foresee it. Perhaps, you will see to her safety." And with that, he turned to the manuscript he had been reading, one of his earlier books, and, thus, ended our talk.

I had always known that from a man of such acute mind innuendo never occurred by chance, and so I took his "perhaps" as a command—at least it was a very strong suggestion—to make an attempt to save Sequia even though the bishop did not fully wish it. Certain or not, I was now free, by sanction of both father and mother, to set out to do what I could, something I had not needed his permission to already have started. That Sabina and Pelagia had prepared for this moment neither did Augustine nor I know. And it was at that instant that I received word from Aksil. His orders from Sabina were complete, and it was time for us to meet.

So, I took my leave of the bishop, then after a needed delay I used for writing two letters, worked my way through the crowded city streets in search of Aksil, the only man I knew who could do or who dared accomplish what Sabina needed to be done.

I had first composed a note for Sabina telling her I had received approval of the bishop to seek Sequia's release. Secondly, I wrote in my best Vandalic the plea I hoped Gaiseric would honor if Sabina's and Pelagia's ransom plans failed. Both letters, I hoped, would be delivered by Aksil.

Twice on my way, I and the crowd around me, most of whom were shopping at the food stands, had to press against the buildings letting pass detachments of Bonifacius's lately-recruited Numidian troops who must have been coming through the equestrian gate below Aksil's quarters. As I trod the streets toward Sabina's convent, I counted three such *cohorts*, each about one hundred foot soldiers but unaccompanied by horse. Two of these carried spears and elongated shields, one was helmeted thus likely Roman-trained. The other was unhelmed, a mix of shepherds armed with slings, and javelineers armed as well with knives and small round shields. The shoppers commented on the great number of these tall, dark soldiers—some said these desert dwellers were the fiercest fighters in the empire—striding, eyes forward, through the city, a place likely more populous than any they had seen in their lives. Whether they were proud or awed, I couldn't tell.

One shopper, loaded down with sacks of dates and tree fruits said, "These form the ransom *Comes Africae* pays to the Vandals: death and destruction!" I passed him in silence but remembered Augustine's arguments on the just war, knowing that this one like all the thousands that had gone before it would solve nothing but would only bring more conflict.

The detachments of mercenaries on the move raised the spirits of the populace more than they struck the people with fear of war. Short of jubilation, the mood in the streets was festive and certainly hopeful. After nearly a year of the relentless Vandal advance all across north Africa, citizens now hoped the scourge of barbarians would be put to an end. Despite Bonifacius's failure to enlist greater Roman help in the cause—civil wars kept the regent's attention focused on Italy and Gaul—it was clear to all, now that fighters were arriving, that the count would mount an all-out attack on the Vandal strongholds in Calama to push them out of Numidia or to destroy them utterly. No one doubted the great general's abilities. Africa Proconsularis would be saved.

More unusual than the Numidians on the march was the condition in which I found the equestrian center where Aksil and his family stayed. The traveling merchant sat on a box near empty corrals where just months before he had overseen the tending of hundreds of horses and as many cart-pulling oxen. A pall of absence hung in the air around him.

"*Vale*, Amicus," he said as I approached.

I looked around at the deserted pens. "*Vale*. Where are your charges?" I approached him and sat on a stone next to his roost.

"*Comes Africae* is training in the field these days. Spring pastures are full of grasses and flowers already and the work of mounting his attack on Calama has begun in earnest. I will have little to do until they return, victorious or not."

"Do you doubt a Roman victory?"

The many-years-experienced caravaner smiled thinly. "These are odd times in Africa. Once the barbarians were the Berber tribes. Now we have new breeds, Alans and Vandals. One can climb a mountain only so long until he must descend on the other side." He reached a cup standing near his simmering tea pot. "But I forget my duties. Please rest a while and share my tea."

The cheetah of Chaouïa shared the same serenity in leisure as he owned while on the move. Years of travel had honed him a smooth blade. We sipped the hibiscus—I thought he'd added some sharp fragrant mint to his brew—and enjoyed the settling evening.

Since I was there at Sabina's bidding, I expected Aksil to speak first. "Tell me, my friend, what is the message from our lady?"

"Her plans for the ransom are complete, except for a detail."

He told me that through the good services of his Berber merchants, two troves of gold had slowly been built up and hidden. The first to be given was stowed in Calama itself, buried in the basement of the public plaza over which Gaiseric's troops marched. Aksil knew the precise location. The second was in like manner sequestered in Heliopolis, but only Sabina knew its exact placement which she would reveal only upon the arrival of Sequia in Hippo Regius.

"Should Bonifacius prevail in the coming battle, both treasures would fall to the Romans," Aksil said.

"Sabina has done well," I said. "She has no need of me, I think."

"Not true, my friend. As easily as I can come and go merchanting, I have no access to the Vandal king."

"I see," I said, "and I am well prepared to help."

"Yes, Sabina knew you would be."

"I already have a plan."

Aksil smiled, this time broadly. "Yes, Sister Sabina advised me of your cunning. I suspect this plan includes me."

I nodded, sipped once, and continued. "I hope to give you safe passage to Gaiseric and a way to ransom Sequia, should all else fail."

"In that plan I want a part." Aksil had not been happy at his failure to reach Sequia just one day earlier which would have brought her back. "Yes, I would gladly do more to amend my shortcoming to the one who provided for my family and me."

I handed Aksil a pendant I had wrapped in purple cloth.

"What is it?"

"First, deliver a letter I've written to Sabina at the villa of Bonifacius, then as soon as you can carry this to Gaiseric, king of the Vandals, who will know it and will value it above a purseful of gold." Aksil unfolded the cloth.

"This is a well-worked cross. Arian?" He ran his fingers outward from the slim center to the broad arms and head of the piece. Then he balanced the crucifix by its pointed foot on his extended finger. "It is well matched, skillfully made. Holding it in his palm now he pointed to the inscriptions. "And these?"

"Runes. An abbreviation of 'Jesus, King of the Jews.'"

Aksil had not seemed puzzled but obviously did not know.

"Words from the first Christian crucifixion."

He nodded and waited for more, asking only, "What else do you wish me to do?"

"Well, before I saw these stables, I was hoping you would ride to Calama to seek an audience with Gaiseric. I have written him a message, here," I said, handing him the letter. He looked at it suspiciously as if it would harm him. He was outside of the literate world and would rightly worry over what he did not know. "It says that I have sent you to ransom Sequia with this cross. And I have written so in his own language."

"Is the cross that valuable?"

"No, but that which it represents is worth more."

"Christ?"

"No, friendship. Now listen: If he is suspicious, from me you must tell him this: 'Keep the Roman cross Namlaus gave you in return.' Speak thus to him in Latin. You might not yet reveal the trove of ransom that lies buried."

"And when I am stopped on my way to the king?"

"Say this in the Vandal tongue: '*Ik im frijond at Namlausan galaisjor at Gaiseric.*'" I had him practice the phrase until it could be understood. "Say, 'I am the friend of the nameless one, the tutor of Gaiseric.' That and the silver coins I give you will get you through. But can you get there without a mount?"

Aksil shook his head and beamed. "When I want one, I am never without a mount."

I handed him a purse of silver coins, the letter informing Sabina, and wished him well. "When will you leave?"

Aksil smiled his trust at me. "I am already gone."

31

Aksil at Calama

The fastest way to Calama, Aksil thought, was the longest. And though going mounted would be more comfortable than on foot, traveling only in the day as camels do would complicate the journey and cause it to be much more dangerous. The disruption the Vandal invasion wrought meant that there were bands of pirates on the loose, Vandal, Numidian, or Berber Amazighs making daytime travel a certain peril and possession of a pack animal an opportunity for robbery.

Once he delivered Sabina's letter and returned to Hippo, the cheetah of Chaouïa would walk, which would allow him to travel either by day or by night as he chose and afforded, dressed as he was in the poorest rags he could find, better security from pillagers. "Eight days," he told himself, "nine with a rest at Idir's ranch." If his father's friend still fed that ancient horse of his, he could make a mounted entrance into Vandal-held Calama, something more acceptable than a pedestrian appearance. Idir could provide better clothes as well.

The man who was never without a mount took to his own legs at sunset carrying provisions of dried fruits, cheeses, and salted meats on his back along with seven small purses, holding and dividing the coins Innomenatus had given him. "To lose one is simple; to lose seven is impossible," he quoted his father. He hid his money here and there deep within his pack and in his clothing and sewed the ankh and letter inside his horsehide tunic. Anxious to reach Idir, he set out guided by stars and his years-long knowledge of the land. He avoided roads in favor of trails he had followed much of his life, moving carefully and rapidly south and west.

Away from seacoast this early April, late winter temperatures and the Vandal invasions held the countryside unpeopled and still bare. Little preparation for crops was being made and even fewer acres than those already plowed would be planted. Aksil cut through abandoned farms and lonely, nearly empty villages, feeling even more solitary than when he had set out. A visit with his friend Idir and the desire to finally bring Sequia to her mother kept him hiking when he most felt like rest or sleep. When he did sleep, he favored caves or cypress trees where he could be hidden. In five days, one more than his horseback trip to Idir's place had taken, he arrived at the old man's secret ranch set within that deep crevasse high in the hills.

At first Aksil thought Idir was gone. Fences were broken down, the house looked abandoned, and none of his animals were in sight. After a long time of calling out and poking around, announcing himself and making his presence known, the old man, peeking down from a large, flat rock jutting over the floor of his canyon farm, called to him softly.

"Is it Aksil? Truly?"

Looking up along the sunny wall, Aksil shaded his eyes and greeted his friend. "Yes, I have come again and on the same errand. Come down, will you?"

Idir told him no. "You must climb up. Bring me a skin of water." And so, though worn out from his night's journey, Aksil ascended the cliff, carrying the old man's drink up to the doorstep of what he found to be a cave.

He embraced the old man. "Is this any way to live at your age?"

"I grew tired of being robbed and threatened. Now, when they come, I am hidden here."

"Didn't you see me?"

"No. I see only shadows, but I heard you coming a long way off."

Aksil thought about his sightless friend living high up a rock wall. "I would not have found you had you not called to me."

Idir laughed, showing his few teeth. "That is the idea."

"Yes, but one fall and . . ."

Again Idir laughed, "And I shall die? That will come soon enough." He shot his arm out, pointing. "Follow." Feeling his way, the old man led Aksil up a path, skirting the rock, that led to a small, open meadow sheltered from sight below. "You see? My goats and my horse like this place."

The horse came to the old man. "He looks younger and stronger now," Aksil said.

"I knew you would come back needing a good mount. Come to my sleeping-cave and rest."

Aksil napped while Idir prepared a meal of stewed rabbit and cheese, and when Aksil awoke, they ate and argued.

"I will take you to Calama with me."

"No, What is an old man like me to do in a city?" Idir said, "I am fine here. But take the horse."

"I will, but you shall ride him."

"And what of my goats?"

"We will bring them, too." And Aksil, as he knew Idir was lonely and afraid although his friend would never admit it, prevailed. "I have friends there who will provide." It wasn't exactly true, but Aksil hoped it would become so. That evening, he led Idir's mount and the three goats over the other side of the meadow following a stream to the valley below.

Progress was slow, but the Chaouïan had expected that. They were now moving west toward Calama where Gaiseric held Sequia, and Aksil wanted to move carefully, avoiding Vandal detachments and any stray Roman patrols. He knew what to look for and soon found it. More correctly it found him when he wanted it to.

At dawn, with the old man still sleeping, Aksil, readying breakfast, heard them. Alert, he watched intently, continuing his work. He spotted three missiles, rocks large enough to injure but not kill, sailing over the near rise straight at him. He dodged and rolled beneath them, just as the short spear whistled by. Amazighs' weapons, he thought. Berbers. Four men. Aksil called out in their common language. "Come eat with us two. We have rabbit and cheese. Warm milk and salted meat."

Again, he waited. If they were truly Berbers, they would attack no more. "Peace to the traveler," he said and slowly rose to stand facing the little hill that hid his visitors. Two of them climbed down from the rise. "We are an old man and a trader, going to Calama. I am Aksil of Chaouïa, son of the merchant Baldath." The two vanguards parted each to a side and kept their distance from Aksil equal as they approached.

"Where is the old man?"

"Here," Idir now said rising from his place, "awakened from peaceful dreams."

Now, the other two appeared above them and laughed. "We are sorry old one for shaking you from sleep."

They were kinsmen of men Idir knew—had known, he found—a mercenary patrol for the Vandal king, helping to watch his eastern flank. The six men crouched over the small fire Idir built to heat his game and fry the cheese. The Amazighs added dried fruit to the breakfast.

"Gaiseric is the man I seek." Aksil said. "I carry a message, an offer to him from Hippo Regius. And Idir, here, I bring to Calama where he can be amongst friends."

The last two to join them talked. The elder then said, "We can bring you some of the way and find you escorts."

Aksil produced two of his purses. "I have been given these for friends. Please."

His desert cousins were good to their word and in a day found Vandal troops headed back to Calama from a fortification they had garrisoned. Even though the Berbers vouched for Aksil and Idir, the Vandal captain held suspicions. "Why do you come? There is danger here for you." He said in broken Latin.

Aksil was ready though his pronunciation was rough. "*Ego im frijond ad Namlaus galaisjor ad Gaiseric*, I am a friend to Innomenatus, tutor to the king."

The captain understood. "What do you bring?"

Aksil brought out another two purses. "Only a little silver, a message written to Gaiseric, and a token for the king." He gave the purses to the captain.

"We will take you to Huneric the Elder in Heliopolis. He will decide if you see the king in Calama."

In two days Aksil stood before Huneric, the king's uncle. The visitor's speech was the same but better practiced, "*Ik im frijond at Namlaus galaisjor at Gaiseric.*"

"*Describere ipsum Namlaus*, what does he look like?"

Aksil didn't hesitate, "*Crassus, calvitium, et garrula.* Fat, bald, and gossipy."

The old Vandal burst into laughter. "*Et adducere*, and you bring what?"

Aksil removed his tunic and carefully snipped open the pocket inside. He handed Huneric both the cross and the letter.

The king's kinsman carefully examined both sides of the crucifix. "I remember this. When he converted, I gave it to him. He wore it always. How did you get it?"

"On parting, the king and Namlaus traded gifts. Your king now wears a *crucifixum auream*, a gold one." That was enough for the old man. He returned the Gothic cross and, without looking at it, the letter.

Huneric brought Aksil to Calama where Gaiseric saw him that afternoon. To Aksil's surprise, the king first opened the message and studied it, smiling toward the end. He examined the Gorhic rood and fingered the gold one he was wearing. Then, he turned his attention to Aksil.

The merchant wondered at the king's Latin, spoken with a Carthaginian accent. "Are you the one they call the cheetah of Chaouïa?" His knowledge startled Aksil.

"Some say. Yes."

"This is not the first time you've sought Sequia of Thagaste." Again, the king was in command of every detail.

"No, your highness, it is not."

Gaiseric nodded, appreciating his visitor's candor. "I shall not release her now. The *Comes Africae* will very soon move south to attack us, and a journey to Hippo might not be safe. When we have dispatched the Roman general, I will bring you both to Hippo Regius myself, and you will then take Sequia inside to meet Innomenatus and her father, as well."

"We enter again? How?"

"Unless they throw open the main portal to the city, you'll go through the southern horse gate, as you usually do," the king said as if he had seen it all himself. "In the meantime, you and your ancient friend will serve at my ward's behest. She could use your help in her chapel where Huneric the Elder spends much of his time." The king paused, thinking. "Say nothing of the ransom money that is hidden here and in Heliopolis."

This king amazed Aksil thoroughly. He was a scholar and, Aksil thought, a sage, and, perhaps, a magician. Gaiseric further astounded the Amazigh trader as he was first taking his leave. "Keep your remaining purses of silver," Gaiseric said. "You have earned them." The man seemed to know everything.

Even so, something the Vandal king did not desire to discuss was the hiding place of the ransom. Perhaps he knew the details already. "There will be a time to release my hostage, and at that turn you shall reveal the ransom's hiding hole," Gaiseric told Aksil. "You will sleep more soundly for keeping it secret." The king eyed Aksil and chuckled.

At first, Aksil felt a prisoner in Calama, but as the days turned into weeks, as a sharp observer who was free to roam the city, he learned to appreciate just how much there was to witness and do. Watching the wondrous movements inspired by the king's ideas, Aksil found the military preparations fascinating. Too, the activities surrounding Sequia of Thagaste and her ministry there in Calama drew Aksil closer to the Christians than he had ever expected to be in his life.

During the first week, Idir, who worked by Sequia's side, began day by day to see more clearly. Each evening, Sequia swabbed Idir's eyes with a "blessed solution" of herbs and recited over him psalms spoken in the Berber language. The treatment, lasting just one week, restored his vision, and Idir became quite useful to the priestess in the small chapel to which Huneric the Elder had appointed her. When not serving Sequia's will the two old men, Idir and Huneric, talked in the best Latin they could muster, using gestures when they could not understand each other's words.

The king and his hostage often spoke in the confines of Sequia's chapel. Gaiseric appeared to admire Sequia's ability to bring disparate believers together. At one time while inspecting the battlements with Huneric, Idir, and Aksil, the Vandal king looked long to the North, toward Carthage and Hippo Regius, saying, "You see that our priestess holds a treasure of great worth in her heart. Were it not for her ministry, many of these parishioners would be at each other's throats." He extended an arm in a broad sweep as if taking in entire provinces. "Such a talent will be of much use governing a new kingdom."

As he sometimes offered obeisance to Tanit, Aksil kept his religious ideas to himself. He was unsure exactly what the king meant by "a new kingdom" but understood clearly that Sequia's "talent" would be wasted under her father's rule. Many of his Berber friends and cousins fled the bishop's dominance, always wary of the scythe of the heretic hunter. To his surprise though, here, under Vandal rule, discussions were open and wide ranging. In the chapel, Aksil had sometimes witnessed the king's talks with Sequia and found out that she was less a hostage than an active guest. Gaiseric admired more than Sequia's usefulness. Her message seemed to strike a tone in the king's heart. Her independence charmed the king. It was, Aksil discovered, not even certain that Sequia would allow herself to be ransomed.

"Why would I go to Hippo Regius? My work here and in Thagaste is enough for three."

The king, far from forcing the issue, reasoned, "Even a short stay would do your mother good. Of course, to turn the mind and ways of your father might take longer."

"He will not listen," Sequia said.

"Perhaps, not in debate, but together again the two of you might bring his soul the comfort you know he craves."

Sequia shook her head but paused in thought. Then she said, "Perhaps. The time approaches but has not arrived. I can decide later, can I not?"

"For the greater good, I trust you will go." Then he offered her the golden Roman cross he always wore. "Take this with you for my friend Innomenatus whose good efforts will help you home."

Sequia would not accept the gift, "This may serve a better purpose. I will, though, enter Hippo Regius to be of use there. Her promise to go to Hippo Regius, at least for a time, pleased Gaiseric. The warrior king prevailed in his show of gentle kindness.

Gaiseric, also, seemed to revel in what he termed "the heretical stuff," the strident beliefs that drove wedges between the peoples of Africa. He was quite aware that his Arianism inflicted wounds in his Catholic opponents even before Vandal swords were drawn. "I shall enjoy listening to my tutor's late stories of the bishop, and perhaps even some about Bonifacius." Though the king stayed active in his *aha-arbadjan*, mind-work, still he was preoccupied mostly with the *haifsts-ganugds*, war-thoughts he was putting in place.

They were all busy but also readily aware of the military bustle around them. The preparations for 'Bonifacius's visit,' as everyone called it, were intense and became to Aksil more of a curiosity than even his friend's restored sight. The Vandal defense, which depended little on the citadel of Calama, became clear as Huneric fondly explained the king's genius for strategy:

As the Roman army marched along the main road from Hippo, Vandal skirmishers and Alan archers would harry the columns as far away as twenty miles, not trying to engage or draw them off but to create as many casualties as possible, "nipping" as Huneric said, "at the monster's heels." Then in the place the road narrowed and rose toward Heliopolis the Vandal detachments were prepared with rock slides and boulder-showers designed first to block the road and then when the column halted to bounce downhill huge rocks to crush the unwary. All this was to occur before the Vandals engaged the

Romans, as Gaiseric seemed to think, face to face on the plains below the hills of Calama. Once lured by a feigned Vandal retreat across the river, with the water at their backs the Romans would be attacked at once from three sides by a force far more numerous than the legion itself. Retreat would be blocked by a train of flaming barges the Vandal woodsmen had hewn from the forest beyond Calama. Aksil had seen with his own eyes these barges being built, loaded, and transported up river. The intricacies of the planning and its likely effect amazed him. The Vandals and, according to Huneric, Gaiseric in particular, had learned much of warfare in their travels, taking plenty from the Romans themselves.

Between his forays of curiosity about the military, Aksil spent time serving Sequia as she drew together through her preaching the mixed religions of Calama into a new Christian community. She had gained some favor by working to lessen the persecutions the Catholics remaining in the conquered city had suffered when the Vandals prevailed and took the town. Their own new persecution, in turn, drew down their appetite for slandering and attacking their old nemeses, the Donatists, who still clung to a shattered, now-deemed-heretical faith. Some from both groups attended Sequia's services which were also peopled with many Arian Vandals Huneric brought in. None of these groups would have ordinarily mixed with the others, but the presence of the woman priest seemed to invite community and cooperation rather than dissension. Sequia's message of Christian love in a deeply troubled world was what each denomination wished to hear.

Huneric played a leading role, as he had become devout in his elder years. He brought in his Arian friends and even some of the inscrutable Alans who worshiped their own obscure gods.

Aksil, who was neither Catholic nor Donatist nor Arian—he sacrificed to Tanit as his forebearers had done for generations—found himself drawn now to the Christian story that Sequia related in her sermons. The vast improvement in Idir's sight bid him listen more sympathetically. His and Idir's work were to prepare and serve food to Sequia's parishioners. Idir had not only become more useful as his sight improved but had also grown more cheerful, tending less to his old sarcasm, though he still enjoyed jibing his friend. He considered Sequia a miracle and a healer.

"You can see now even at night?" Aksil asked Idir.

"Not well, but in the day I can now see how ugly you are."

Aksil was buoyed by his friend's spunkiness. "How did this happen?"

"Ask your mother!" Idir shrugged. "Perhaps Sequia washed my eyes with holy water. Perhaps I came to believe."

To Aksil, Sequia was equally elusive. "How can it be that Idir regained his sight?"

"He has simply opened himself again to life. I know that ranching is a separate and lonely existence." She smiled kindly at Aksil. "Did you not bring him here for just that reason?"

"For his well being, but I did not expect him to regain sight."

"Yes, my dear, but he now sees more than many others in the desert, and is, even more, a good friend to them."

Aksil could not fathom it, but many changes were afoot in Africa. He did not believe it was for the worse.

Word came that the Romans were on the march. Alan riders relayed reports on their strength and progress. Bonifacius's army moved slowly but could reach Heliopolis in three days and could be in battle position in another. Calama came alive beyond imagination and day by day emptied of soldiers and cavalry.

"Come, Aksil," said Huneric, "I know you want to see this."

The old man brought him to the top of the north wall where Aksil watched the tall, blond Vandal warriors march down toward the plain below. Huneric boasted of their deeds and bravery.

"You can see from here how they position themselves among the wooded hills on each side of the plain. And look further off to the town of Heliopolis atop its own hill. Gaiseric's surprise will meet them there."

Aksil squinted over the five miles to see the bastion outside Heliopolis which would tumble over the Roman vanguard. "Will

Bonifacius march into that trap?"

"It is just a little surprise to slow them," Huneric said. "They will retreat and be forced to split their army to go around the town one way and another. The fallen boulders will narrow the path on each side."

"So their forces will be weakened."

"Yes, but more important, they will be out of communication, unable to see each other." He traced the two paths, pointing to each side of the hill facing them. "From here, though, we will see everything. Come and watch the flagmen signal to our generals below. That is my station in the army, Colonel of Signs."

"Will it happen as you say?"

"As Gaiseric says," Huneric corrected. "Wait and see, tomorrow."

Between their vantage point and that of the neighboring town, Heliopolis, the river Seybouse, down which would appear Gaiseric's flaming flotilla, wound its crooked way over the fertile plain. By Huneric's permission, Aksil would be able to watch the coming fight unfold from the safety of the wall top. He was unsure what would be the outcome, a victory for Bonifacius or a Vandal win. After the hospitality he had enjoyed in the Vandal city of Calama, a Roman victory might spell trouble for him.

In either case, he readied himself for his and Sequia's return to Hippo.

32

The Battle for Calama

Well before dawn the next day, a great horn sounded in Calama. The trumpet blast repeated itself three times and from the plain below a great shout muffled by distance rolled up to Aksil's ears.

"It is the attack," he said to Idir. "Come to the battlement with me."

The old man demurred, saying, "I have more important work to do in the chapel. You go. War is a younger man's business. These new eyes would be spoiled to watch it."

Aksil stowed pieces of cheese and bread in his satchel and scurried through the town and up to his vantage point where Huneric and the king already peered at the neighboring hill through rising mist lit by the early morning light.

Huneric nodded at his presence, but kept his old eyes on the distance. Aksil followed his gaze. To the north, atop the hill of Heliopolis five miles distant, appeared two blazing fires, one at each corner of the walls visible from Calama. The flames curled around doubled trumpet notes in the air which relayed from one Vandal-held outpost to the next across the distance, sounding like faint bird calls at the start but increasing in volume as the nearer signalers picked up the sound, finally, becoming a boisterous cacophony of doubled notes.

"The Romans have split their army," Gaiseric said. "Sound the horn."

At Huneric's signal the great horn blared out twice just as the first rays of sun reached over the plain to the western hills beyond.

Aksil became aware of vague movement in the woods on the left flank. "Wulfson's fighters swing around to meet our forces on the west. They are to push the Roman wing away from the hidden barges until it crosses the Seybouse and rejoins the main Bonifacian army." Huneric indicated each movement, pointing and sweeping his arm

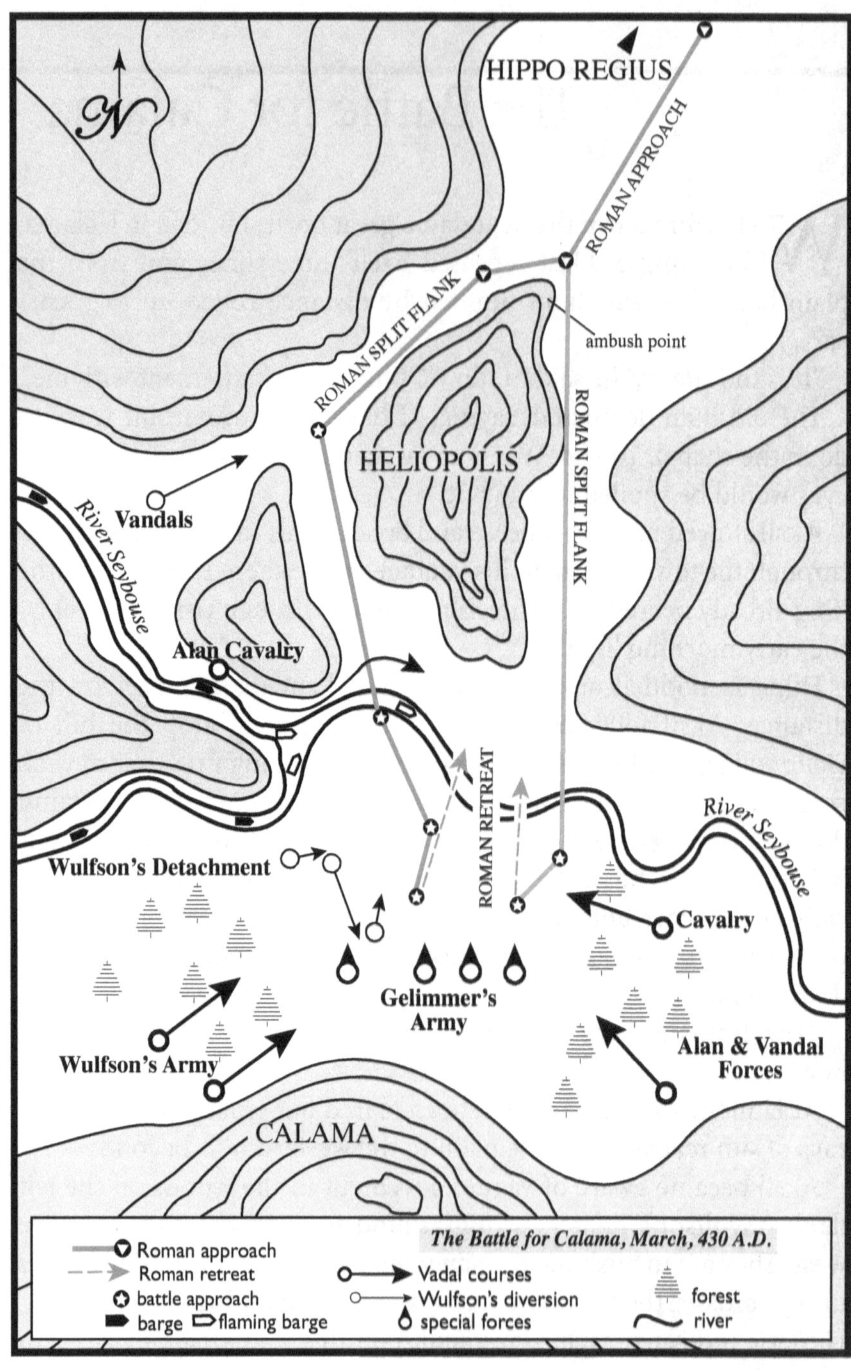
HIPPO REGIUS
ROMAN APPROACH
ROMAN SPLIT FLANK
ambush point
ROMAN SPLIT FLANK
HELIOPOLIS
Vandals
River Seybouse
Alan Cavalry
ROMAN RETREAT
River Seybouse
Wulfson's Detachment
Cavalry
Gelimmer's Army
Wulfson's Army
Alan & Vandal Forces
CALAMA
The Battle for Calama, March, 430 A.D.
Roman approach
Roman retreat
battle approach
barge
flaming barge
Vadal courses
Wulfson's diversion
special forces
forest
river

here and there. "With more light we will rely on the flags. Now that armies are in motion, trumpets will not be heard down there." And as if to punctuate the point a low roiling growl rose from the woods and the plain below.

"Gelimmer must march now," the king instructed.

At a signal from Huneric, six men spread along the wall's causeway loosed deep-red banners and swung them in unison left and right, right and left. Shouts rose from below the walls and Gelimmer's army was soon seen striding forward in formation. The flagmen furled their banners.

The plain just below the walls was now flooded with fighters in Vandal formation, trotting through the early morning sun. Gelimmer's phalanxes, six of them across the front and twelve more offset from the first in files behind that vanguard, moved quickly down the rises from Calama to the empty plain below. As the light brightened, it glinted off polished spears and helms in hundreds of points of light flowing rapidly, as a single constellation, to the middle of the plain, half the distance, two miles, from Calama's walls to the river Seybouse. At that first hour past sunrise no Roman forces had appeared.

Gaiseric sweeping his gaze constantly over the plain and the woods each side of it pointed his short sword to the west flank where some of Wulfson's men had begun to march north to divert the enemy. Now, though, a splinter of that force peeled off and looked to be fleeing toward the safety of Gelimmer's army which was advancing but slowly toward the river. Wulfson now commanded fewer men both in comparison to Gelimmer's force and to that number it had appeared to comprise when deployed by the double trumpet notes. Now those on Calama's walls saw that far before these running Wulfson-detachments stormed a much larger organized legion of Roman fighters, no doubt intent on gobbling up the smaller, receding force they now saw. This army formed the western split of Count Bonifacius's force, and they stayed well away from the forest behind which waited Wulfson's main army and his battalion that was to release the barges. The distance between the Vandal force retreating across the river and the advancing Roman army grew wider, as if the Vandals were making room for and inviting the Romans to the south-lying battlefield.

"See how they lure them in!" Huneric shouted. He raised a gloved hand holding a small yellow flag. "Golden time," he commanded. Again, the six flaggers went to work, this time waving large yellow banners stitched with golden threads that glittered in the sunshine. The signals were shortly answered by clouds of rising dust stirred up by Alan cavalry on the left. They swirled down the western rises, outflanking, herding in their advance the attacking Roman legions. At that same moment, the vanguard of the main Bonifacian arm to the east came into view, splashing across the far bend of the Seybouse to the eastern side of Heliopolis.

At a sign from Gaiseric, Huneric shouted, "Purple,"

The signalers went to work and were answered by a slow, awkward turn of Gelimmer's soldiers as if they were being pushed back toward the city's walls by the advancing arms of the Roman army, both of which had now forded the river, and by their own men, Wulfson's guard, running flat out homeward.

"They are retreating!" Aksil's panicky vision of a siege of Calama flashed in his mind.

"None such," said Gaiseric.

Huneric took Aksil forward to the battlement. "Watch the Romans learn their own lessons they have taught to us. This is no retreat." He swept his arm west where the Alan cavalry had lightly engaged the legions pursuing Wulfson's men. "They merely brush their hair with arrows," Huneric said. "They keep them in place, moving toward their doom."

Indeed, the horsemen were ever so carefully harrying the Roman west flank away from Wulfson's fighters in flight without inciting the Romans to turn and fight, instead pursuing the infantry further on to the plain while the Vandal horsemen swirled around and faded back into the forest only to yet again spill forth in another foray.

The ensuing maneuvers appeared from above to Aksil as would moving a herd of goats, skillfully run one way and another into a wider version of Idir's canyon hold. The Roman left flank turned now to join its main force that had crossed the river to march rapidly and directly toward what seemed to be a retreating line of Vandal fighters, Gelimmer's men. This movement allowed the Alan horsemen to circle away from the side now to the rear of the Roman left flank.

This was the time once again for red flags. "This signals the barges to begin to cinch the purse," Huneric said. "Red banners high!"

The move also called to the infantry hidden in the woods on the right and left to begin their advance, slowly at first, without showing their true strength. Within the time the Romans spent advancing within striking distance of Gelimmer's forces, the "purse" as Huneric called it began to clamp shut around Bonifacius.

First, joined by Wulfson's few, Gelimmer's men stopped and turned to face the coming onslaught. On the river behind, barges linked together appeared drawn by the Seybouse's current and Vandal oxen drays. Before the invaders realized the danger, the barges' oil-soaked freight of trunks, branches, and bramble ignited in flames twice the height of a sturdy Vandal, and Alan calvary on the right and left strafed the legions with spear and arrow felling a good many. Still the Romans marched on, facing Gelimmer's fighters ahead while new Vandal infantry now sped toward them right and left. They had yet to see the wall of fire behind them.

The clash of shields, swords, and helms in the collision of the Roman and Vandal armies deafened even those upon the wall. The uproar frightened the bravest among them. Seen from above it was as if precisely-lined walls of men bent and buckled, formed wedges that dissolved and winnowed and became a shindy moil of tumult and carnage.

Even a well-planned battle owns its failures. Gaiseric had conjured an old and wise strategy, but one defect saved the Romans and prevented an all-out slaughter. On the sharpest bend in the river, toward the right flank of the Bonifacian advance, the leading fire-barge caught a snag. Pulling harder, the ox handler upended the first barge which canted and capsized, blocking the channel and forming a bridge across the current. The barge's load spilled downstream, covering the surface in burning debris. The following boats collided with the overturned barge and stopped short. A wide swath of the river, shallow just beyond the curve, albeit aflame, lay open to retreat.

The Roman force was huge but soon the Vandal fighters entering the fray from their hiding places outnumbered the invaders and beset them on three sides. Gelimmer's front guard was decimated but the rear twelve detachments held fast until, at a signal from their general, they parted to admit the final Vandal and Alan forces meant to subdue Bonifacius.

Now, at the backs of Gelimmer's rear guard, came on the run seven new formations each led by three armored elephants bearing down on the already flagging Roman forces. It was at that sight, that mercenary Gothic infantry turned on their Roman companions who backed away as best they could from the deadly engagement. With those Goths now enemies, Bonifacius's troops, including his Numidian fighters, fled before the rampaging elephant-corps. Hundreds fell and were trampled. In disarray, all ran for that one opening in what was otherwise a wall of fire before them, leaving nearly a third of the Bonifacian force lying on the field.

Underneath a strong and faithful line of Roman archers thrown up on the far side of the river, what was left of Bonifacius's army was running for its life and for the walls of Hippo Regius.

33

The Siege of Hippo Regius

It was a week after the battle at Calama, early May, before the first detachments of the Vandal army appeared outside the walls of Hippo Regius, reinforced by the Bonifacian turncoat-Goths and a band or two of traitorous Numidians who saved their lives by switching sides on the plain of Calama. Bonifacius and his loyal guard took charge inside the walls of Hippo Regius. His army he stationed at the port. Both sides kept their distance and prepared for the coming siege, which had in reality already begun with the Roman defeat at Calama.

Augustine came to me at night. I first thought it was about the presence of the surrounding Vandal forces. I was working but not as he expected. I was writing this history of my years in Hippo Regius.[1]

We had talked little during the preparations for Easter at the end of March that year, or during the busy weeks of April, which marked the beginning of Augustine's reinvigorated push to write his *Retractationes*, his own cataloging of his life's work. He was up most nights reading his books, and often I found him still in the library at dawn working on his catalog. This night visit broke an absence of four weeks and established what was to become a close companionship, lasting for the short balance of his life.

I had certainly seen the bishop in the course of my days, for even though he had shunted off many of his duties to his named successor, Eraclius, he still wrote copiously of the events of the church and composed sermons in the library, but in the faint light of my cell that evening—it must have been past midnight—I was startled by his appearance. Augustine had grown thin, his hoary hair was full but white as the scud on the shores of the sea. He shuffled from the

---

1 It does no good to forbid a scribe from writing, or a historian from jotting down the details of his observations. Even though Augustine had enjoined me to abide without record, I thought what little harm would come of my scribbling would go unnoticed since the world as we had known it was clearly coming to an end. Better to keep one's truth entirely than one's peace.

door to my vacated chair at the desk, holding on to what he could with shaky hands, then plunked stiffly down all in one, emitting a sigh of relief.

"Welcome, my bishop. I am happy to see you."

He cocked his head at me, scrutinized my expression as well as my words, and corrected me. "You are shocked to see me. You see that I've aged lately."

It was useless to protest, but I did not want to comment on the obvious. "Let me pour you a cup of water."

He answered nothing but started right in on his mission. "I worry incessantly. I meet my *visita nocte* even in the day now. I'm fearful. I feel sick."

"Then I must help you, my Bishop."

He went right on as if he hadn't heard me. "Of course, I worry that I haven't the time to finish my *Retractationes*. The work is slow and arduous. What will happen to *mihi opus vitae*, my life's work?"[2]

I reassured him that it would live.

"Surely these vile barbarians will seize and burn my books. I cannot bear the thought."

Gaiseric, whose propensity to destroy was far outweighed by his curiosity and fervor to learn, came to mind. "Somehow, I think not. In any case your mind's children exist in copies flung across the empire."

"That's what he said," Augustine replied in a voice that betrayed disbelief.

"He who, my bishop?"

"My *visita nocte*. He comes to me constantly now, disembodied, and is everywhere. I think of Vandals stomping in my library, and he whispers in my ear, 'Somehow, I think not.' I feel fear of apostasy creeping up my spine, and I hear his voice say, 'Would you yield your faith for anything?' Oh, I rather long to hear, 'You will withstand their terror,' but I get only questions!"

---

2 Indeed, the bishop's fears were well-founded. His attention to the terrifying events of the past year and the continual pressure from heretical beliefs that must be countered had led Augustine away from his voluminous works. He would not live to finish putting them in order. That was left to Possidius who lived even amongst the ruins Augustine and his Vandal enemies left behind.

I was beginning to understand the sudden changes in the friend-of-my-youth's appearance. Not only was he working frantically and not sleeping much, but he was also fraught constantly with the voice of inquisition examining his own doubts.

I worked to quell his anxiety. "You will yield your faith for nothing."

He understood it wrongly. "For nothing? I will turn Arian to save myself from torture?" Suddenly, he bowed and held his head as if couching it against a battle going on inside. "For nothing. For ought. *Nihil.*" He seemed to be echoing voices from within.

"No, friend-of-my-youth—I had not before uttered that name out loud—you shall not yield for anything. Your faith will hold." He let go his hand and raised his eyes to me. "But you must rest. You must sleep and restore."

Fright widened his eyes. "I am afraid to sleep." He lanced out his hand and gripped my wrist tightly. "Stay by my side. With you there, I may rest."

I was nodding my assent but was occupied by his burning hand on my arm. "You have a fever, my bishop. You are ill."

And that night began the reversal of our roles as youths when I had fallen to the fever. I stood a nearly constant vigil at the bedside of Aurelius Augustinus, bishop of Hippo Regius, and friend-of-my-youth during the hours, which were not many, he was content to rest. Worried, fearful, and off and on, feverish, he continued his work in the library and, despite my every effort, retired to his cell only when exhausted. Then, once in bed, he would wax talkative and review his long-held opinions and arguments on celibacy, original sin, the apostolic tradition, and the Church. I took to napping in the afternoon that I might be able to remain attentive during these harangues. It was easier to listen to his occasional recounting of arguments against heresies—Pelagians, Donatists, Arians, Manicheans, and more—in which I found my mind stimulated in an effort to divine which strand of hair was split from its better half. What I took most interest in, though, were his sleeping conversations with his night-jar visitor, the gnome-of-Augustine's imagination. I eventually concluded that the bishop must be asleep though he took active roles in the discussion. During these spates of discourse of which I could hear only Augustine's part, the bishop rose up in bed seeming to peer—with eyes tightly shut—into the corner of his room and soon began to ask questions, make careful statements, and engage in respectful arguments, as if with God the Father, but since he never named his companion and because the talk grew quite familiar and sometimes raucous, he likely wrangled with that form of a man he'd described to me who, he said, hunched on his toilet and, I knew, could not be an actual person. I quietly heeded Augustine's part of the conversation and worked my mind quickly to supply the response or fabricate the material from the other side without knowing exactly what it had been. Sometimes I was forced to revise my sense of the repartee as more was revealed. Invariably, these sessions began with Augustine calling out:

"Who is there?"

There was no reply I could hear.

"Is it you? Ah, why are you come again?"

The response then set the direction.

"This siege does not worry me. We shall prevail," the bishop replied to the unheard.

A likely answer: "Yet, you fret about the Arians outside."

"Their faith is a poisonous heresy! It is like to sicken me."

My own assumption of the rebuttal was, "Why must you cast out so many believers on such scanty points, naysaying 'the Father is older than the Son'?" A bit of my own artifice, I must admit, but it fit.

"There is but one true way. We must carefully follow the steps of the Apostles," Augustine said.

And perhaps a retort such as, "There were twelve and Paul, too. Whose prints in the sand would guide you?" More of my fabrication.

Augustine spoke out, "Confusion reigns in the world, but God has given man the intellect to set and follow the right course."

And the argument went on. Finally, Augustine seemed forced to admit that it stood to reason that there were more ways than one into heaven and that schism was inevitable. But he still countered that silent contention: "That is why we must preserve the unity of the Church."

And the final rejoinder may have been, "Would it not be better to fling open the doors to all no matter what their path to the Truth?" That was Sabina's position, and I would have had the debate end so.

But Augustine fell back on his pillow muttering, I thought, "Gnostic."

During the months following the establishment of the Vandals before our walls, I was growing closer to Augustine—it was not something I desired though our relations provided me much to think on—but I was, too, striving to discover what had happened to Aksil and, consequently, to Sequia. With the Vandals turning up earthworks all around the walls of Hippo Regius and the city locked tight at its well-guarded gates, I was at wit's end to find a way to contact my man. Then, once the fortifications and emplacements were finished, a way found me in the person of Count Bonifacius. Apparently, he had thought better of his suspicions about my character—I had thought at the time that his wife's playful suspicions of me as a spy were only lightly entertained and confirmed it as she displayed more and more interest in Sabina. Now, as the Vandal earthworks progressed toward sealing off the city, delegations from each side began outreach toward negotiations. His concerns about me now allayed, Bonifacius appointed me, without the leave of the bishop, to attend the initial session that I might translate during the meeting.

I was loath to go without Augustine's assent, for he would, of course, know about it afterward. So, I approached him immediately.

"With the bishop's permission, I have been asked to assist the State in a parley with the Vandals."

Although he appeared deeply immersed in his cataloging, Augustine demonstrated once again that lightning apprehension of mind he had become so well known for. He asked, simply, "Why?"

"I believe I am called to translate."

He looked at me, I thought, strangely. "No, why should you seek permission?"

There seemed a hundred reasons, most of them obvious, such as "I work for the Church," or "I owe you allegiance," but the peculiar way he had phrased his query suggested he demanded a more personal answer, perhaps a profession of my regard for him.

The best I could do was answer with a question, "Am I not the friend-of-your-youth? Your confessor. Do I not sit up with you?"

Asking only set the stage for debate. "There are but two ways to answer my question," he said. "'Out of duty,' or 'Out of love,' don't you think so?" The bishop asked, grinning at me.

Still I resisted, thinking why the bishop should wrestle his preferred answer out of me as if I were a heretic? "I believe one may love duty and honor the duties of love, both."

Though I did not know why, he would not cease, and though I feared the result of the admission, I said it anyway. "It is you I love, my bishop, and have always."[3]

He seemed to gauge the heat of my admission. Apparently, it had been warm enough. He first said, "He told me so," then smiled vaguely and said, "You have my leave."

Who "he" was, I easily guessed. It appeared that Augustine's motives were now bound up in his visits with his gnome-of-dreams. I could not be one to complain of the tedium of the elderly, so I bowed somewhat and went my way to join the Bonifacian guard at the main gate of the city where a great number of officials, including the count himself, and a multitude of citizens gathered, abuzz with hope and well wishes for the incipient talks.

The call to "save our city" went up many times. Bullion and coinage were offered by the barrowful, which put me in mind of a kinsman's estimation of Rome: "*urbem venalem et mature perituram, si emptorem invenerit*,[4] a city for sale and doomed to quick destruction, if it should find a buyer." But Bonifacius, who would remain in the town, played down the enthusiasm. "Remember, tribute means defeat, yet we will meet these invaders in good faith."

---

3 Perhaps, I feared becoming more tightly bound, if that were possible, to the bishop's control, but there is forever a part of one's younger being that tends the fires of youthful love. The remembrance of the breath of a kiss is sufficient to move even an aged spirit. This was true of me at that instant. And, surprisingly, it did not hurt to say it.

4 Jugurtha. A distant relation through my mother, as reported by Sallust.

The two sides met days later under the sweltering August sun. A shelter was erected on a rise midway between the Vandal camp and the main gate of the city. Twelve men on each side attended. Six armed Vandals and a like number of the count's men stood at the perimeter of the open sided tent.

My private hope was that I could catch some hint at the wellbeing of Sequia, of Aksil, and of my offer as well. I was immediately gratified as Gaiseric himself attended incognito, as a translator not a king. Even in his plain livery, the man looked well, had filled out in his kingship and seemed taller than I remembered. I craved even a moment to speak privately with him, but it seemed impossible. I would have to wait nearly a month for that. For his part, the king had, I hoped, heard something of me from Aksil if he had become a captive during the weeks since his leaving.

The two ranking figures, Bonifacius's Captain of the Guard and Huneric the Elder of the Vandal faction faced each other flanked each by his translator—Gaiseric, unnamed as I was, took his place to Huneric's left—and an advisor, Gelimmer, and a Roman unknown to me on the right. The negotiation began with an exchange of tokens at each level.

I had brought a book, a hide-covered, copper-clasped psalter written in Gothic that I had kept from my time in Hispania. In return, from Gaiseric, my counterpart, came an olive wood box containing the same gold Roman cross I had given him on our parting four years ago, wrapped in two papyrus sheets. I saw then that the king wore the Gothic cross Aksil had borne him. On presenting me this gift, Gaiseric said in his Vandal tongue, *bisania haukuls, Namlaus,* regard the lining, Innomenatus.

I recall nothing of the meeting, being too fixed on my own mission, and excited to unravel Gaiseric's papyrus. I mindlessly spoke to our Captain the Latin words translating those spoken in Vandalic, although during the interchange, I did take note that Gaiseric's translations into the Vandal tongue were certain and clear. He had not lost his fluency in Latin. My task occupied me, but when Gaiseric spoke, I also felt elevated by the pride of a teacher.

Of course, as is usual with these mediations, little was agreed upon. The Vandals held the ground. The city, though, could be supplied by sea. Since much of the previous harvest had been brought behind the city walls, the invaders were to subsist on slim rations from their late conquests. The pariah of hunger and disease breathed heavily onto both sides. Neither made attractive offers. Each side probed the other. As for my personal task, I had seen with my own eyes that Aksil had succeeded. I expected, then, that Sequia had been saved. As the negotiation ended, and as I left the tent, a cloaked Alan soldier spoke to me in my native Berber tongue. "Show your cross to my son." With that, he bowed to me, looked at me once, and left with the Vandals. Aghast, I followed his retreat with my eyes. It was Aksil.

I burned to examine my gift, but waited until we returned to the city and I to my cell. I examined the cross carefully and found nothing worked upon it. Then I stripped out the papyrus lining from the box and found on it Vandalic script in Gaiseric's hand saying in part: "*at frums af nujian-monan af-gaggan bi Aina-daurabarn,* at the new moon go to the horse-postern gate." For that I would need Aksil's son.

The new moon would follow in three nights, so that morning, as I sat with Augustine in the garden, the moon was a waning sliver of gold rising in the east, waiting for its time to be swept away before the sun. That blessed hiatus gave me time to untie the knots I had bound around my feet in all my devilish dancing. I at least hoped so.

I could not tell Augustine what I was about. Despite his confession of fatherhood and his public declarations, I owed too much to Sabina and her daughter to risk an ecclesiastical arrest once Sequia entered Hippo Regius. And I well knew what Bonifacius would do were he to discover my dual role at his peace negotiation. The trick was to slip away as Gaiseric had bid me, to meet at the equestrian gate while still waiting on the bishop at the end of his work day and keeping mum on the entire subject. Intrigue is not for the faint-hearted.

That night before the new moon, Augustine's discussion with his gnome took a turn. Over the nearly two years I had resumed my place as the companion to the friend-of-my-youth, I had witnessed a plethora of moods in the bishop. He was often angry and scurrilous, but when unburdened, he turned gentle and kind. Augustine feared a great many things but had expressed great joy and gladness, too. The bishop strongly confronted people and issues, becoming stridently shaming, yet I had seen him supportive and helpful even when unsteadied and unsure. This night, these last two rose up in the bishop:

"Who is there?"

No reply came to my ear.

"Is it you? Ah, why are you come again?"

There came a very long silence during which Augustine assumed a listening posture. Then he became agitated.

"From whence do you get such words."

And quickly again, "From me? From that letter? From her!" And Augustine recited just as he had to me in his earlier confession: "'Was it you, O bishop, O Aurelius, O Augustine, that brought upon yourself this Arian plague through your incessant hunt for heretics, that now *they* come to *you*?'" This time he did not claim the words as his own.

With this utterance, the bishop, already sitting upright in bed, turned and dropped his feet to the floor as if to stand. "How could you know?" He asked. "You hardly move. You often have no body. You, you, you . . ."

As if he realized something, Augustine stopped. He slumped to the bed once more to lie down. "If you are not my own voice, and if you are largely disembodied, and if you, as you seem to claim, are watching over me, then, then, then . . ." With that the friend-of-my-youth fell asleep.

I sat with him until the morning crescent moon had risen. I never learned the conclusion he had drawn, but he awoke, after just four hours sleeping, cheerful and refreshed.

"I shall work long and hard today," he told me. "It is you who should get some rest. Away with you now."

34

Final Confession

At least in the daytime, the bishop's restored energy for and preoccupation with his *Retractationes* allowed me time to unlock the puzzles I faced. I shed the worry over losing him, especially at this difficult time. Were he to die, the city—not to mention my own precarious perch in the monastery—without its saintly leader would not fare well. Nevertheless his recovered ambition gave me time to arrange things according to Gaiseric's plan.

I went to Aksil's quarters and found his son Ehgil. I gave him the good news that his father was well, that I had seen him with my own eyes. When the jubilation of the rest of the family subsided and Ehgil and I were again alone, I posed my question. "Can you show me the horse-postern gate? I am due to meet guests, I believe, at the new moon." Such was my trust in Gaiseric and Aksil that the possibility of treachery barely passed through my mind. I did not think for a minute that we would be attacked to make way for the entry of a Vandal force.

Postern gates—narrow, single-entry portals throughout the walls of the city—were hidden from inside and from the exterior, of course, that they would be used only by officials to exit surreptitiously and not by traitors who might admit an enemy. Few knew their location, but, of course, being a keeper of the equestrian gate itself, Aksil and his son not only knew this narrow door, but were entrusted with a key as well.

"In two nights comes the new moon," Ehgil said, "so meet me then as twilight falls. I will bring you there."

I was glad of the hour since the newly-energized Augustine would be working well into the night. I hoped for continuing cloud cover and that Aksil would come in the early hours of night once complete darkness fell.

That appointed night, Eghil took me in hand—actually in hand since our way was dark and secret—and led me a circuitous route which behind a thick, locked door, gave way to a series of very narrow turns right and left, leading to a heavy iron and wood door. "This opens onto a copse of olive trees that shelter the opening. Please stay here and let me go out. If you do not hear three night birds sing, shut and lock the gate." He swung the heavy door inward, leaving the key in its way, and stepped beyond into absolute night. I saw nothing but, after a good while, heard the calls of Eghil's three night birds. After those ceased to echo, without a sound before his arrival, the familiar voice of Aksil spoke to me from outside the doorway.

"Innomenatus, stand aside and wait to follow me inside a way." Once in, he found my hand and led me, whispering to me as Eghil had which way to turn and when. When we stopped, he said, "Eghil is behind us. He brings Sequia." And soon there were three of us following Aksil back to the equestrian corrals where, by torchlight, I had my first sight of Sequia.

"You look very much as did your mother years ago," I said, after all this time not knowing how else to greet her.

"May mercy and goodness come to you, Sir. I have been told that you have conspired to bring me here. Although I have been treated kindly after my capture, I am grateful to be nearer my mother."

"I have done little, but I'm sure you would like to join Sabina now."

"Yes. Please bring me to her."

"That our friend Aksil must do. The bishop, your father, awaits me in the monastery above."

Augustine, as I myself had years before, seemed to rally time and again and to leave off his disputations in the night. So focused had he become on his work that he had no sense that Sabina had been freed. Through the turgid heat of June and July he had worked incessantly on his project and seemed to sleep deeply, though feverishly, in brief fits during short summer nights.

As a result, I had begun to spend more time with the Sisters, not simply because they kept a jolly and nutritious kitchen although it was a still wondrous place, but also to marvel at the work in the chapel where Sabina had taken up the ministry she and Sequia had begun in Thagaste, bringing together those of varying sects to worship, work, and live together in peace. There were a great many of varied faithful allegiances since all sorts sought refuge in Hippo Regius. Sabina worked with Ia and at times together with Pelagia who had also come into the city for safety the *Villa Bonifati* could not provide. It was this last disciple, *Contessa Africae* who likely stayed Augustine's hand from quashing the burgeoning community. Though he had not spoken to me of the goings-on, I was sure he knew or had at least heard about them. With Pelagia in Sabina's fold, though, Augustine could not act with impunity. *Comes Africae* stood watch.

In accord with instructions from Sabina, I was to look for an opportunity once she was released to bring Sequia to see Augustine. However, now that the friend-of-my-youth spent all his time with his works, breaking only a few times a week to attend his chapel to sermonize on leaving this world for the next, I had to wait, I thought, for the next round of illness before carrying through.

Then, in late August, just a few weeks after mother and daughter were reunited, the bishop, as I also had done years before, fell again into a fever and had to cease his work. I returned from Sabina's chapel well before midnight and good thing, too. Within a few minutes after I had taken my chair in Augustine's chamber, the bishop limped in and took to his bed.

"I am ill again, Amicus. I now fear this is my end."

His fever had returned, and he looked frightfully gray. As I ministered to him, as he had in youth once done for me, making him as comfortable as possible, cooling him with cloths dipped in mint-laced water, and rubbing small amounts of oil and eucalyptus on his extremities, I listened to the woes brought to his mind by fever.

"My reputation is failing, Amicus. I've taken unpopular positions lately."

Perhaps, he meant his refusal to ransom his daughter or his heightened Pelagian-heretic hunting of Julian. I didn't ask. Then, as I applied liniment to his legs, he told me something I might have guessed but was surprised to hear on his lips.

"Though I've carried the burden of my flesh so long, I still yearn after the clear, smooth muscles of a man's body and his hands upon me." He began to weep. "I thought my lust would cease, but that sin still wracks my ancient corpse. Especially at night."

"You, my bishop, have debated and settled that issue. Those moods while abed are forgivable."

He continued to snivel. "I do not feel the argument is valid now. Besides I said 'asleep,' not 'in bed.' Oh, why must I be so enslaved?"

"The Church and your faith have freed you."

"No. I've built a jail here to keep the world out. And now, I'm left alone to dream terrors."

I helped him drink from his cup. "You are not alone, but what horrors do you speak of?"

"I dreamed a Vandal horde had squeezed through the walls somehow, and these grimacing giants with stringy, yellow hair rushed through the streets. At their head was Julian hand-in-hand with Ari and Donatist apostates. Heretics all."

"We are securely locked within the walls. It was but a dream," I said, applying a fresh cloth. He pushed it off.

"I stood friendless and they stormed toward me yelling, 'Manichean, heretic!' I ran to the chapel to hide, but it had collapsed into a heap of rubble in the desert." Augustine began to shiver.

After covering him well, the spasms dissipated, and he slept. It was not for long, though, before once again he rose up and stared into the darkness at the other side of the room.

"You again. What do you want?" He spoke angrily but again began to weep.

"Why do you torment me with talk of this woman? I have no time for this. I must finish my work before I die." He fell back again, but continued to speak.

"No. I do not wish to see her again. I have already in the chapel. Nor do I want to meet the other. Leave me . . . ," he trailed off from saying "alone" but, then, continued, "No, no, don't leave me, but, please, let me rest." It became quite clear then that he had not been nor was speaking to me.

When the bishop remained in bed that following August morning, fraught with waves of fever, it was to the great and general alarm amongst his clergy and friends whom he summoned to his cell.

Surrounded by Possidius, Eraclius, and the faithful, I amongst them, he said, "Each man must die in his time. Would he be transformed and live again, he must do penance for his sins." According to the bishop, his redress was complete devotion to penitence throughout his final illness.

"Bring me those penitentials of David, his psalms, largely drawn, that I might read them from my bed continually through my tears. Let Amicus write them clearly and hang them near me."

The consternation of his stalwart supporters boiled over at this. "Allow, bishop, those longer serving to help. Innomenatus"—they refused to call me, as the bishop did, Amicus—"is yet a babe in our brotherhood."

Augustine roared out, "Who dares contradict the . . . ," when he began coughing. Having laid out his things in the room, I easily found the bishop a cloth and his cup of water. His anger passed as he drank, and he then smiled weakly. "Thank you, Amicus."

Then looking at his long-time supporters, he said, "Yes, Amicus, I call him because his is the prodigal friend-of-my-youth even from before many of you were born. Though he may be a stranger to you still, suffer me his friendship now." There was grumbling, as I had known before, and were Augustine not there, I knew there would have been threats. I retreated from the bed to stand behind the acting bishop, Eraclius, as Augustine dictated the conduct of his illness and his end. When he finished, he asked, "Where is Alypius? He should be here." I waited for Possidius to explain that Augustine's long-time companion, even since their days together in Rome, was yet in Ravenna.

The bishop shook his fevered head. "Oh, yes. I knew that." He asked to be left to rest and had me clear the room.

I was to attend the bishop day and night, from my post in the library, laying a bed before his doorway at night. He was to be left alone to pray and read his psalms.

"Which psalms might I copy?"

"You know these: '*domine ne in furore*,' '*in te Domine speravi*,' '*misericordiam et judicium*,' and '*de profundis clamai*,'" or as they were numbered six, thirty, one hundred, and one-hundred twenty-nine. "Draw them as large as possible, but only the first ten lines or so."

That night, while I watched Augustine, Gaiseric's army mounted a surprise attack at the port, entering, it seemed, through the artifice of treachery. The attack was repulsed with only two ships set afire and a handful of casualties on both sides. Later the very same night, at the equestrian gate, a party of Goths clamored in vain for entry, claiming persecution of the barbarians they had in fear joined at the battle of Calama. At the same time, a small force further to the south attempted to scale the walls amidst the hubbub at the gate but were repulsed. These and other incursions, whether actual or not, were on the lips of every person inside the walls, but I kept any from worrying my patient who had cares of his own. It was impossible for me to do anything but rue his pain and suffer with him.

In the next two days, Augustine's fever wracked his frame. He ate little, and the medicines brought by the physicians did no good. In his waking hours he recited the songs of David I had copied on to large sheets of sail cloth hung near his bedsides, reading each in its turn and by memory reciting the rest of "*in te Domine*," the thirtieth, often repeating its last lines over and over again,

> *confortamini et roboretur cor vestrum omnes qui expectatis Dominum!*
> Be strong, and let your heart take courage, all you who wait for the Lord!

He often raised his arm, preferring his right hand for me to hold, just as he had held mine in my "last" illness. "You have been a good friend to me, Amicus. Stay with me, even though I abandoned you that time."

"You must forgive yourself for your weakness, my bishop, my friend."

Augustine raised his hollow eyes to mine. "I shall not desert you again though I will leave you soon. You appear now as you have had from time to time as my *visita nocte*, night visitor."

"It was not I."

He answered kindly. "Don't contradict me, Amicus. There are but two types of visitor: *consolationibus et disputantionibus*, the consoler and disputant. You, my friend, are the first." He smiled such as he rarely did and said, "As the psalmist says, '*misericordiam et iudicium cantabo tibi*,' I tell you of the merciful and judging."

He grew tired and slept.

That night I saw or thought I saw the glow that had often awakened the bishop.

Wearily the bishop rose. As if dragged in chains from a dungeon of sleep, he pushed himself up on feeble arms, half-sitting, half-lying. "I see you've come again. I shall soon be done with you."

I now heard the voice, "I shall prepare the way, but better you sweep the stones before you step down that walk." The enigma of his speech did not seem to trouble the bishop who was in every way a master of metaphor.

"What am I missing here? Is there more to see than these old eyes can conjure?"

And what I thought the audible but invisible gnome intoned brought me back to Augustine's old argument that the voice was only his interior council. "There are but two visions of what is to come, either of which might pass into being alone. Though, the two depending on true penance, might both stand side by side as do the city of Rome and *civitates Dei*." The voice seemed to refer not to the bishop's book but the celestial city itself.

Augustine cocked an ear toward the corner and listened. "I do not see this. Show me."

As if a hundred lit candles flooded the room with light, a vision of the monastery fallen to ruin rose to our sight, Augustine's and mine, as if we stood before its gates. Blinded by the sudden light, I only heard the bishop cry out, "No. This cannot be." Then suddenly, as if we stepped inside the gates, we found what had been hidden beyond the pier supporting the half ruined arch, Augustine's library, standing yet and attended by two women kneeling in prayer before Possidius who was standing at its door.

"Let this be. Let it be," the bishop cried.

Sudden night returned through which I heard Augustine weeping between whispers of "Let it be." Then I grew intolerably exhausted and, before I could note more of this, fell asleep.

I was aroused by the slightest tapping on the door to the passageway. I opened it and found Sabina and Sequia had come unbidden.

"Come in. He sleeps now. How did you know?" Without answering, they approached the bed quietly and knelt at either side of him who for forty years had been as the Father himself, large in evidence and absent in form. To me, just waking, they sharply resembled the two women of the vision, and despite their quiet approach, Augustine stirred. He opened his eyes then and raised his head, turning first to one side then the other.

"Sabina," he murmured, "and Adeodatus?"

"Yes, Aurelius, it is I though not with our son but his sister, Sequidei."

Each took one of his hands, and the bishop began to weep.

I felt that my long and ungainly interference was now at its end, but Sequia, seeing me move toward the door, stopped me with a word. "Stay."

There was no choice left for me. I was to abide, not as a confessor, but, as if in unity with my previous witness of Augustine's life and confessions, as the chronicler of his final hour.

Neither of the women began the exchange. It was Augustine himself who spoke first, gently but with his usual authority. "I told him I would not see you, but you have come. Why?"

Sequia answered his question. "You suffer and know there is one salve to soothe your pangs. We come to hear your final confession."

Augustine gave Sequia an understanding look, as if he had known her words in advance. Then glowering looks clouded his face, but Sabina, rubbing the bishop's chest, said, "We come to console, not to dispute. We come to preserve, not to contend."

"What? What will you preserve?" Augustine voiced his skepticism.

"Your true work," Sequia said.

Sabina nodded and said, "We will save all the good you have done, letting all troubles fall away."

Augustine wept, hard tears and sobbing moans shook tremors in his chest.

Again Sabina soothed him, saying "It is not possible now to separate the good you have done from the harm that has attended you. Only you can affirm that which you already know as the only truth."

The old man looked from one to the other and did so again. The lisp of knowing trembled on his lips as if he understood that he but need say one word.

Again, each woman enfolded his two hands, this time kissing them, looking over their entwined fingers, waiting.

Again, Augustine looked to one then to the other now leaving off his tears. Finally, exhaling a long breath as if to concede to their presence and devotion he said, "*Mea culpa*, I have sinned. I have transgressed forgiveness itself and turned away from love."

Then, he turned to one, saying, "*te amo*," and looked to the other, firmly pronouncing the same words, "*te amo*, I love you." He assured his grasp of each of their hands and rose up a small bit to say, "*Vos amo. Semper amavi utrumque*, I love you both. I always have."

Now, inaudibly, he spoke again.

Both Sabina and Sequia bent closely to hear and then recited with him words I could barely parse and then only because I knew them, "*sed et si ambulaver in valle mortis not timebo malum*, for though I walk through the valley of death, I fear no evil," then with Augustine staring intently at them, "*quoniam vos mecum*, for you are with me."

With that, Aurelius Augustinus, friend-of-my-youth, bishop of Hippo Regius, and life-long lover was gone.

With that, without waiting, I, too, left but for another place.

35

Lighting-out West

It is unseemly at such a time to think of one's own mortality although that thought, like Augustine dwelling on lust, immediately and involuntarily presented itself. Having died once, I had little fear to do it again, but like Augustine, I was moved to preserve my most precious possession: my writings, as well as, again like Augustine, my brief time remaining in the world to set them in order.

Having preparations to make for an imminent departure, I left Augustine's chamber. In the ambulatory, I found Aksil who had accompanied the two priestesses.

"Come with me, Aksil. You can help me gather my belongings." I had little of value to bring away other than this book written on three scrolls that I bound together with strips of leather and the letters of Augustine and Sabina translated into Aramaic.

"I ask some last tasks from you, my friend."

"I serve you willingly," Aksil replied.

"I will go before you, but when the women return to the convent, meet me there to bring me to the postern gate. Can you guide me to Gaiseric's camp? Last, find me a dry hiding place for my scrolls."

"None of these are impossible though the last will be the most difficult."

We discussed caves and cubbyholes Aksil knew both inside and outside the walls which he had used for the keeping of trade items during his time at the convent gates. He would show me a cave he knew to contain several urns and which he could seal by dislodging boulders from above.

My part was now finished, my welcome worn, my friendship and curiosity fulfilled. I had begun my life at Augustine's side and had seen him through his final confession of love in this world and unto the doorstep of death. I took care to record, as a good scribe should, all I had seen and heard that was worth repeating, and on my way out of this world, forced by precaution to deceive Aksil, but as a friend, deposited only the letters in the cave. As I watched my Berber kinsman cover the entry, sealing with boulders the cave's mouth—its urns keeping the secrets of long loves—I loosed a small prayer to the world, "Remember us who have lived and left this earth."

At the Vandal camp, I was briefly reunited with Gaiseric who did not have to be told of the death of the bishop for he knew my presence there as proof of it. We spent parts of two days together, although he was busy with his siege plans. On the third day he said, "If you will travel again, I will send an escort."

And so I would. I would go beyond the very ends of the earth, as if I just happened to be in the neighborhood, to bring my old bones and my three scrolls, too, which I would there annotate, both to be buried at Canaria, the Isle of the Dogs, beyond the gates of Hercules where for a time I would work a little, rest a great deal, and every day watch the sea.

Appendicies

Manicheanism

When Augustine first arrived at Carthage at age seventeen, Manicheans were the main rival group to Christianity. They had been roundly condemned (as early as 305 by Diocletian and in 323 by the orthodox Eusubius[1]) and as such might have been attractive to a young upstart like Augustine, one with a pagan father and a devout Catholic mother to rebel against. Mani, the founder of the sect was eastern, exotic, and played into several of Augustine's interests at the time, astrology and the problem posed by an angry, loving god. If God was good, just, and adoring, after all, why did He allow such human suffering in the world? That was Augustine's question.

Manicheans were followers of the Persian founder of the sect, Mani (c. 216 – 274 AD). A helpful analogy might lead us to think of them along the lines of 19th century American Mormonism founded by Joseph Smith just before 1830.

Both are Christian sects with a founding prophet who deviated from the norm in several important and, in their time, disturbing ways: for Mormonism between 1830 and 1890 it was publication and promotion of *The Book of Mormon* and, particularly, the practice of polygamy; for Manicheans it was the preaching of dualism and belief in an elect: some few who would be "saved." The initial receptions of these theologies was a mixed popularity and, in opponents, a horrified, outright rejection. It is with this in mind we might ask why the promising young scholar, Aurelius Augustinius or Brigham Young for that matter, would cast his lot in with such an upstart group. I'll leave Young and the Mormons behind to look at Augustine alone.

The followers of Mani were on the surface accessible and perhaps more attractive—less sticks in the African mud than a more patrician, staid organizations like the church of Rome. The Manichees were themselves on the lookout for cultured, intelligent young scholars

____

1 Eusebius, p. 319

who could elevate their cause in the eyes of Roman aristocracy. In any case, Augustine associated with the group until 383 AD. Then two events changed his mind, which had always been bent on preferment and a profitable career.

First in 383, he met Faustus of Milevis, the top man in Manichean Africa. Augustine was disappointed in the man's intellect and knowledge. Second, a few years after Emperor Theodosius I decreed death for any Manichean monk found in the empire, Augusitne converted to Catholicism. For an ambitious man like Augustine on his way up and headed toward Rome, the Manichean sect was not suitable. He says of them " [they] were such frauds both to themselves and to others."[2] So, after a decade of adhering to Manicheanism, he jumped ship seeking, perhaps, a faster-track Roman preferment in Italy.

It is important to see Augustine in the light of hs abandonment of his Manichaean friends. The change mirrors his behavior in his separation from Innomenatus, in his sudden dissociation with Sabina, at his furtive escape from Monnika's oversight, stealing away in the night to Rome. His ability to cut off people resembles the facility with which he was able to sever ties within the Christian folds and become an opponent and, as he did with the Manichees, a tormentor of associated believers. His penchant for persecution encircled the Manichees, Pelagians, Arians, and a former family friend, Julian of Eclanum.

All Augustine's victories, he tells us, were in the name of God and betterment of the Church.

---

2 Pine-Coffin, p. 103.

The Donatist Controversy

In modern-day America, it is not too difficult to imagine two distinct but related religious bodies existing side by side; take a Presbyterian church on one corner and a Roman Catholic church across the same intersection, for example. Perhaps there might be a Jewish synagogue or a Muslim mosque just down the block. Each is cushioned, to great extent by a surround of pillows of political and religious tolerance. Acceptance might be the correct term.

In Augustine's day this was far from the case. On the northern coasts of Africa from 305 AD for over a hundred-twenty years thereafter, two solidly Christian (and listening to each, orthodox) churches coexisted, but the spirit of acrimony and even hatred between them filled the land with tension. The Donatist sect and Augustine's Catholic church fought each other in bitter struggles for primacy, even for their very existence.

The larger, Donatist side claimed the high moral ground. These Christians had persisted through twenty years of persecution under emperor Diocletian (284 – 305 AD) and, they said, never capitulated to or collaborated with the local persecuting imperial authorities. What became Augustine's side, the Donatists claimed, knuckled under to the persecutors, even handing-over their sacred scriptures and documents. One historian likens the feeling between the sects to the post World War II sentiment of the French underground toward Nazi collaborators under Hitler's heel.

The controversy intensified in 311 AD when a so-called *traditor* (one who "gives over" the holy scriptures to persecutors) was elected bishop in Carthage. The Donatists protested and elected their own bishop, openly splitting the African church in two. Over the next hundred years, a hot fight persisted between the two side-by-side sects despite interventions by Emperor Constantine and his successors and a long series of church synods condemning the disunity in the faith. It was not peaceful. Riots, church burnings, fist fights, and insurrections follow by banishment and exile, then resurgence, marred peace and unity of religious and civil life in north Africa.

In 409, at a *collatio* or comparison of the legal right to lead the African church, Augustine, the Bishop of Hippo Regius took center stage in Carthage. His arguments based in scripture and on the decrees of Emperor Constantine impressed the meeting conductor (a friend of Augustine) and thus confirmed the primacy of Augustine's church in Africa. The Donatist leaders proved inept at defending against Augustine, but they were clearly in command of their more numerous adherents and so persisted beyond the edicts of the *collatio*. It was decreed that all Donatist church property be forfeit and cleared the way for Augustine's persecution of them which lasted until his death.

With the *collatio* "feather in his cap" Augustine pursued Donatist Christians, pushing leaders into exile, commandeering Donatist property and cash, and forcing followers to convert to orthodox Roman Catholicism. The successful techniques he developed while suppressing the Donatists he used to hunt, hound, persecute and destroy other groups and individuals who offended him, even unto his own death in 430.

Finally, the Vandal invasion in 429 sidelined Augustine's efforts to repress the Donatists. The Vandals established for the next hundred years the primacy of another sect, Arian Christianity, in north Africa. Still, Donatist churches survived until the eighth century Moslem invasions.

The Pelagian Movement

Augustine's dogged pursuit of Pelagius, a man he'd not met, over thirty years reveals a bishop not only at the height of his theological powers but also one of what Pope Zosimus called "uncontrolled eloquence."[1] Augustine moved from one protected by the church to one whose mission is to protect the faith. He was also a man who had aged but had not mellowed, being fifty-seven during the Donatist trials and now sixty-four at the excommunication of Pelagius. We see him at age seventy-four facing Julian, a new youthful foe and heir to Pelagian ideas, and timorously watching the Arian Vandals approach to tighten a siege around him.

Augustine strenuously defended his ideas of original sin and the primacy of grace in Christian life against, at first, a young follower Caelestius, then in a long strident battle of words and politics against Pelagius himself. Both Augustine and Pelagius hailed from the provinces, rural Africa and Britain, respectively, and were both long time, respected churchmen and noted intellectuals.

Among other issues, the importance of the clergy to the Christian community was at stake. If humans could achieve perfection through exercise of free will and reason as the layman Pelagius said, there was less need for a Christian church led by priests. Theological issues played heavily, as did Pelagius's encouragement of asceticism. He bid wealthy Christians to abandon property to the poor (not to the Church). Augustine frowned upon that.

Pelagius taught that humans were born with a clean slate and were capable of leading sinless lives through the exercise of reason and free will. The grace of God through baptism, Pelagius agreed, was important in restoring those who wandered from the righteous path. Augustine taught that humans inherited Adam's and Eve's sins, that their free will allowed only to select sins, not to choose good over

---

1 Brown, pp. 356-364 for a complete discussion.

evil, and that God's grace was the only ingredient that could save their souls from hellfire.

The initial part of this controversy raged from 410 through 418, starting when Pelagius and Caelestius fled the Visigoth invasion and sack of Rome, going, along with a large number of well-to-do Romans, at first to Carthage. Incensed at their presence, Augustine and the African bishops drove these two eastward to Alexandria and, then, pursued them to Ephesus, Palestine, and back to Rome mainly through letters, pamphlets and declamatory documents written to a wide audience of politicians, thinkers, churchmen, popes, and emperors. The ferocity of Augustinian attacks were grounded in his victory over the hapless Donatists in the previous decade and continued twenty years beyond the death of Pelagius himself.

Caelestius was "tried" in Carthage in 411. Being condemned, he left Carthage to seek and receive ordination in Ephesus. Pelagius, meanwhile, went to Palestine where he "passed muster" in a 415 examination of his views. Augustine then enlisted African bishops to oppose Pelagius. In 416 the Augustinian faction of heretic hunters succeeded in convincing Pope Innocent I to condemn Pelagius. Soon after, Innocent died, and Pelagius plead his case back in Rome under Pope Zosimus who reopened the matter and commended both sides to peace calling the fight "hairsplitting . . . pointless debates."[2] Yet again, Augustine and the African bishops objected and in the Synod of 418, condemned both Caelestius and Pelagius. Zosimus was forced by the bishops through Emperor Honorius to excommunicate the pair. They were further posthumously condemned as heretics in Ephesus in 431.

---

2 Ibid.

The Arian Controversy

Come, sit with Augustine in his library in the early months of 429. He is intent on church business, some of which concerns heretics. The Donatists continue to plague his ecclesiastical rule. Pelagians still crop up here and there, and Julian of Eclanum writes high-style diatribe against Augustine himself. Rome fights civil wars. Everything's crumbling. Augustine might feel his life's work threatened.

That summer a new threat appeared: The Vandal army, heretics of the Arian kind, crossed at Gibraltar and were sweeping rapidly toward Hippo and Carthage. Even more disturbing was word of persecution of Augustine's outlying Catholic churches. The vandals had killed bishops, burned churches, and confiscated property. It looked like the end of the African church, perhaps the end of orthodox Christianity in the West.

By winter the Arian heretics had surrounded Augustine's bishopric, and he prayed for either deliverance of the city, for the strength to bear God's will for them, or for his own exit through death's door.[1] It was to be the third wish that was granted. The treatment Augustine dispensed to Christian heretics (exile, loss of property, even death) had now been turned upon his flock.

To the objective eye the Arian controversy boiled down to terminology, to the difference of a single letter, "i." The homoousian side, originated with the Alexandrian Athanasius, the homoiousian side with Arius, also of Alexandria. Athanasius claimed Jesus Christ to "be of the same substance" as God the Father; Arius claimed Jesus to "be of a similar substance." The controversy began in 321 with a condemnation of Arius. In 325 the Athanasian side put forth the Nicene Creed and again condemned Arius. In 335 Arius was readmitted to good standing and Athanasius exiled. This held until

---

1 Brown, pg. 424.

Theodosius condemned Arianism as heresy in 380.

By the time of Theodosius though—during the years Augustine became a Catholic and then a bishop—much of the eastern church, nearly all the Germanic tribes, and the majority of the Roman army were already in the Arian fold. The Goths, Visgoths, and Vandals carried their Arian faith with them as they moved west from the shores of the Black Sea, across the Rhine, into Gaul, Hispania, and Italy. Though Alaric who sacked Rome in 410 was thought to be Germanic pagan, it is likely that Christians among his army were baptized Arians. And not only were the Vandals Arian carriers of Wulfila's Gothic bible, but they were also willing to impose their brand of Christian belief on the Catholics of north Africa.

The difference between the creed of Wulfilas and the Nicene Creed show the divergence of opinion :

Wulfila: I believe in one God the Father, the only **unbegotten** and invisible, and in his **only-begotten** son, our Lord and God, the designer and maker of all creation, having none other like him.[2]

Nicene: We believe in one God, the Father Almighty, Maker of heaven and earth, and of all things visible and invisible. And in one Lord Jesus Christ, the only-begotten Son of God, begotten of the Father before all worlds.[3]

Even if Jesus was **begotten before all worlds**, that he was begotten implies he was not co-eternal, of the same substance as God. That God is **unbegotten** and Jesus **begotten** in Wulfila increases the contrast between the Nicene and Wulfilasic creeds.

---

2 Heather and Matthews, Chapter 5. [Emphasis mine, ed.]
3 Nicene Creed of 381 AD.

The New Pelagian, Julian of Eclanum

The final pursuit of Augustine's brings him from Milan in 487 at his wondrous conversion to Christ incited by an innocent child's song to a dark and dour last year of life in which he preached shame, predetermined sinfulness, and unremitting damnation for those dying without grace (unbaptized infants, for instance). He has gone from a softness of love to a hard-edged bulwark of rectitude.

The primary contestants and in very personal ways were Julian, bishop of Eclanum, northeast of Napoli, and Augustine bishop of Hippo Regius, but the confrontations were as much to do with backgrounds as they were to do with theology.

At the outbreak of their fight in 419 Julian was relatively young, just over thirty. Augustine was twice his rival's age. Julian was born to a married bishop and a Roman noblewoman, and he enjoyed a privileged education in both Latin and Greek. Augustine was of much lower and foreign, rural African birth to a pagan father and Catholic mother, and had resisted, even belittled the learning of Greek. So Augustine had less connection to eastern Christendom, centering himself in the Latin west and preferred the rural. Quite importantly, Julian was married and extolled the virtues of conjugal relations. Augustine professed to be celibate from midlife on. Julian was an insider vis a vis Rome with his Italian family connections to the likes of Paulinus of Nola and even to Augustine himself. Augustine was an influential bishop but always an African outsider from the Italian point of view.

Still, along with Agustine, a series of popes and patriarchs (Zosimus, Nestorius, Boniface I, and Leo), and the emperor Celestine enjoined serial condemnations of Julian.

Had Julian prevailed, the marriage of priests and bishops would likely have been more common. Marriage and sexual desire was a main topic of the dispute with Julian naming the "call to sex" a sixth sense. Julian's "Against those who condemn marriage and the profit is assigned to the devil" answered Augustine's "Of lust and marriage" with cosmopolitan expansiveness versus the African's insistence on shame and guilt.

Julian, a Pelagian supporter, disputed Augustine's concept of original sin as an affront to a loving and just God, contending that a predetermined life of sin could not be what God intended for his human creations. It would be un-Godly and unjust. In parallel fashion, Julian championed an open and fair discussion of issues while Augustine pushed for silence and condemnation, tactics he had perfected in dealing with the Donatists.

As a continuation of the Pelagian controversy, this fight began in 410 although Julian did not come into the open until after the 418 excommunication of Pelagius and Caelestius. Augustine directed his side of the battle from Africa. Julian was deposed of his bishopric in 418, exiled to Greece, then, going to Constantinople, was condemned in absentia in Greece in 421, in the Roman capital in 426 and 427, and twice more in 429 and 430.

Despite Julian's polemics, famously calling Augustine a Manichean and "the king of all donkeys," Augustine's tireless work against the younger opponent prevailed. It appears that wherever Julian went that Augustine, or his proxies, opposed him until 430 when Augustine died. Julian lived another twenty-five years still under the yoke of condemnation and derision as he became a teacher in classical learning of small children. He died in Sicily, 455, and was posthumously condemned again in 484 in Nola.

Fictional Figure

Aksil
"Cheetah of Chaouïa"

The history of the African provinces in the fourth and fifth centuries is written mostly from the Roman point of view. What shows through a thick carpeting of that Roman history of the Berbers, of the Numidians, and of the Vandals who throve in and survived the period is relatively little. One can read all about the African bishops, about Roman campaigns and trade, of theological and social debates without, perhaps, coming to realize the effects of desert peoples or of "barbarians" at all.

Be that as it may, of our principal characters only Bonifacius and Gaiseric are of non-African origin. It is entirely possible that Augustine himself was of Berber descent, and surely Sabina and Innomenatus shared some of that bloodline as well. And so it is entirely fitting that Aksil be included in the list of important characters and be cast as closely as possible in a Berberish profile, if only to inform or remind the reader that though this is a highly Romanized story—without Rome there would be no story at all—that non-Roman Africans lived and worked in the society that spawned the events and turns in this period.

So Aksil weaves his way within, through, and around the Roman, barbarian, and sacred worlds, serving and prospering in trade, in friendship, and usefulness. He can navigate in the outlying territories, be responsible in the city, and can carry his sensibilities and humanity on pagan or Christian ground. Aksil as a yeoman threads all parties together across racial and cultural lines, but he is, I hope, also the epitome of a natural, wider morality sometimes found missing in the supposedly more civilized reaches of commerce, politics, and religion. He is an Everyman, apart from the partisan divides of creed and rule.

Historical Figure

Aurelius Augustinus, "Saint Augustine"
November 13, 354 – August 28, 430 AD

Augustine, longtime bishop of Hippo Regius, modern-day Annaba, Algeria, was the quintessential provincial-African of his day. He died during the Vandal siege of his Catholic bishopric and was born only eighty miles south in Thagaste, now Souk Ahras. He had been schooled there, in nearby Madaurus, and in neighboring Carthage, a part of contemporary Tunis, Tunisia. All but five years of his long life were spent in Africa, mostly on on Mediterranean coast.

Very much of what is known of the man comes from his own writings. The preponderance of personal details are delivered in his autobiographical *Confessions* (397-400 AD), other observations through a posthumous biography by a contemporary follower, and by what has been said of him over the centuries by adherents to the Catholic faith and myriad biographers. Still, the primary source on Augustine remains his *Confessions*.

In *Confessions* Augustine characterizes himself as a wild youth, an aficionado of the Roman games, a profligate reveler, and a perpetual slave to sexual desire. All that youthful decadence is followed by spiritual searching well into and through adulthood.

At seventeen, he took a concubine, who is unnamed in *Confessions*, here called Sabina, with whom he lived for some sixteen years and by whom he sired his son, Adeodatus (372–390). Augustine ended the liaison (at the behest of his matriarch, Monnika, who had arranged what became an aborted marriage) sending her off alone from their home north of Milan back to Africa a few years before his own return. Most, though not all, historians and biographers of Augustine suppose that this couple never saw each other again. But at least one posits as inconceivable that they did not encounter one another at the funeral of Adeodatus who died after his and Augustine's return to Carthage. Here our plot depends on that likely meeting.

From *Confessions* comes another unnamed love of the young Augustine, a boyhood friend, here called Innomenatus, and as did Augustine's biographer, Gary Wills did, also called Amicus. The friend was a one-time Manichean fellow-traveler, without whom Augustine confesses "my soul could do nothing."[1] As with the loss of his concubine, Augustine makes much of the feelings dredged up by this tragic loss but fails to give either loved one the benefit of a name. Both lapses have licensed much speculation.

Augustine's great life's work in his ecclesiastical years was devoted to defining the boundaries of Catholic truth, touching on themes of original sin, predestination, and celibacy. Often his positions formed themselves through his fierce opposition to heretical movements: his own early devotion, Manichean thought, Arianism, Pelagians, and, very early in his career, the original African sect, the Donatists. The shock-force of these battles on a smaller scale resembled that likely felt so deeply by Augustine, indeed the entire Mediterranean world, at the cataclysm of 410, the sack of Rome, the Eternal City, by the Visigoths. That thunderous calamity fostered his extensive work *De civitate Dei*, *The City of God* (412-425 AD), a building of a theological wall he thought to be stronger than that of the fallen Rome.

Augustine died within the ramparts of Hippo Regius in the middle of the Vandal siege.

---

1 Pine-Coffin, IV, iv, 7.

Historical Figure

Bonifacius, "*Comes Africae*, Count of Africa"
383? – 432

A bare outline of Bonifacius's life leads from his success in Gaul, 413, to his leadership of a Gothic regiment in North Africa, a period in which he befriended Augustine. In 422 he was recalled to the court at Ravenna where he married Pelagia an Arian Goth king's daughter. He was then to campaign in Hispania against the Vandals, but infighting with Castinus, the other general involved, led Bonifacius to detour again to Africa where he installed himself as *Comes Africae*.

From Carthage in 424, Bonifacius cut off the important grain supply to Rome putting the squeeze on Castinus's rebellious intrigues. In 425, when Valentinian III (six years old) and his regent mother, Gala Placidia came to power, Bonifacius supported them against Castinus by resuming grain shipments.

Over the next five years, *Comes Africae* passed in and out of favor with Rome through intrigues and rebellious-looking actions. Eventually restored to favor, he fought and won for Gala Placidia's reign and died from battle wounds in her defense at Rimini, 432. Let us presume that Bonifacius was thirty years old at his first mention in Roman annals, as general under Constantius III, in 413. That puts him at forty-six during our story. As a military man in turbulent times, Bonifacius became one of the triad of generals competing, often in open civil warfare, to obtain or protect the western empire.

Only some of the foregoing is directly crucial to our story, but as background it helps to make sense of Bonifacius's part in *The Final Confession of Saint Augustine*

In these times it was de rigueur to hire, conscript, or otherwise find allies even among erstwhile enemies. So it is understandable that Bonifacius being somewhat an outlier could be thought to have invited the Vandals into Africa. That suspicion yet lives and finds a new home here. But maverick or not, *Comes Africae* being besieged by intrigue and armies from the empire had good reason to seek help where he could. The irony that he was defending against Rome only doubles when the tables turn, and, restored to Roman favor, he defends, unsuccessfully, the Roman province against Vandal invaders.

That Bonifacius operated much upon doubt and insecurity is clear in his doings with Augustine. They were initially friends and sympathetic, theological disputants. Bonifacius had at one time sought to join Augustine's Catholic monastery. The Bishop, in much need of a strong-armed supporter, rebuffed him. After Bonifacius married an Arian and, further, allowed his daughter to be baptized in that church, the relationship with Augustine grew contentious.

We are led to think of Bonifacius as a loyal supporter of the empire, despite the fact that he fought against Roman forces many times. He defended in Gaul, in Hispania against Castinus and his pretender, against the Vandals in Africa, and finally against Flavius Aetius, the most powerful general and threat to the throne whom he defeated. Bonifacius performed a balancing act all along, most famously when tricked by Flavius Felix into disfavor of Gala Placidia. Felix set rumors of a Bonifacian treason in holding Africa for himself. He advised the regent to send for *Comes Africae* saying if he didn't come that would be the proof. Separately, Bonifacius was urged to stay safely in Africa, which resulted in armies being sent to unseat him. The plot was eventually discovered, Bonifacius exonerated, and the Roman armies recalled, leaving him to face the Vandals himself.

He died in Italy two years after Augustine of injuries sustained defending the empire against insurrection.

Historical Figure

Gaiseric, "King of the Vandals and Alans"
c. 389 – January 25, 477

The king of the Vandals and Alans during the course outlined in this book left scant historical traces. What is certain is only that he led thousands of followers across the Straights of Magellan from Spain, moved rapidly across what is now Morocco and Algeria, laid siege to Augustine's Hippo Regius, and routed the Roman general Bonifacius at least twice.

Gaiseric had been king only three years when he turned forty at the walls of Hippo Regius. He was to live and prosper nearly fifty years more, but did nothing later that was not presaged by the genius that swept him and his peoples (including Alans and Goths) into northern Africa. Had he been born Roman rather than Germanic, he would likely have become emperor.

Despite establishing a stable and wealthy kingdom, lasting a hundred years, he has, until recently, either been ignored or treated unkindly through the literate, Roman view beginning early with Jordanes's sixth century description:

> He was a man of deep thought and few words, holding luxury in disdain, furious in his anger, greedy for gain, shrewd in winning over the barbarians and skilled in sowing the seeds of dissension to arouse enmity.[1]

Not unfair but hardly flattering. Judging from his success, Gaiseric won over Romans as well as barbarians, took advantage of endemic dissension within the Roman world, and shared, as many a ring-giver in Germanic cultures, his gain with his own people as well as with his allies. He operated a fittingly civil society peopled by those he brought to and found in Africa, a wide variety of races and creeds. And whether he was, as some suppose, invited into Africa by the

---

1 See Hughes, p. 64: quoting Jordanes's *Getica*, p. 168.

Roman general, Bonifacius, or took advantage of a dicey situation during Roman civil wars, it is known that he had been preparing for years, building ships at least three years before embarking on Mediterranean waters.

The Gaiseric found in *The Final Confession of St. Augustine* certainly acts cruelly but only with a reason. He understands human psychology, both strengths and weaknesses, and though steeped in his own traditions and culture shows interest in and became a student of the Roman ways. Whether he was a believer in his Arian faith is not clear, but evidence shows he did not persecute Catholics wantonly, though his Vandal successors did so.

Above all else, here and in the recent histories written of the Vandals, Gaiseric proves a military genius of the first rank. Even when out numbered and out-resourced he was able to prevail. Attacked twice by the full might of the empire, he repelled its forces. He won Carthage in a surprise invasion, capturing hundreds of Roman vessels in port, and famously took Sicily, landed on the Italian peninsula, and sacked Rome in 455. The Vandals controlled western Mediterranean shipping all during their reign. Gaiseric outlasted the terms of all Roman emperors in the west, the long reigning Theodosius II of the east included.

Here we see Gaiseric between September, 429 and late August, 430 in humble greatness: a student, a quiet thinker of few words, a strategist on small and grand scales practicing wisdom, patience, and fortitude. He is, not inconsequentially, a worthy friend, true to his man.

Historical / Fictional Figure

Innomenatus (Amicus), "the friend-of-Augustine's-youth"
c. 389 – c. 435

No story remains finished for long. Even an expansive writer like Augustine cannot lay down the final word of his own tale. There seems always more to say, another way to look at people, deeds, and landscapes. So, Innomenatus finishes the story for us.

We know almost nothing of the historical Innomenatus except as a latter-day example to Augustine of his own un-godly follies. What is given about Innomenatus in *Confessions* is so little as to leave room for summation here:

> Circa 375 back in Thagaste, "I had found a very dear friend." They had played, grown up, and schooled together as boys. Unsanctioned by God, he says, thus less true, the friendship was yet sweet within shared interests of Manichean belief. At the end of a year, 376, when the relationship was "sweeter to me than all the joys of life as I lived it then," the man died, "you [God] took him." The friend fell ill. His family, fearful of impending death, had him baptized Catholic while unconscious in a fever. He recovered from the fever and then warned Augustine, as if an enemy that "I must never speak to him again [derisively of the Catholic God and of his friend's baptism] if they were to remain close. Days later, the fever returned, and Augustine's friend died, "rescued from my folly," he says. Augustine left for Carthage again, distraught: "Tears alone were sweet to me, for in my heart's desire they had taken the place of my friend."[1]

Leaving his friend unnamed, however intended, invites questioning, speculation, and interpretation, even wild rendering. And so from this single source, in absence of corroboration, even the death can become metaphorical and the character able to spring alive to become a living lesson to an aging and suffering Augustine. But who is this man who died without a name?

---

1 Pine-Coffin, IV, iv, 75-76.

Here, he becomes an itinerant scholar, a professional scribe, polyglot and translator. He is a "world" traveler, circumambulating the entire Roman world inclusive of barbarian territory, excepting the only Roman place Augustine had visited, Milan. He serves and studies at Alexandria, in Palestine under Jerome, at the royal court of Constantinople. He translates the gospels into Gothic under Wulfia and becomes the tutor of the then royal-familiar, Gaiseric. As a wanderer, he perfects his truest calling, collecting news and gossiping in the kitchens of the great houses and schools from Egypt to Jerusalem to Constantinople, Gaul, Hispania, and, just ahead of Gaiseric's arrival, back in Hippo Regius and Carthage.

Like the friend-of-his-youth, Augustine, he has perfected all aspects of his craft and intellect but allied himself to no one house, to no single creed, to no defined faction, but to knowledge only. He stands in counterpoint to his bishop-employer, perhaps seeing more clearly, certainly more convivially, people up close and society and the world from well-traveled perspective. Given all this, perhaps he sees, too, that which is outside of this world through a sharper lens than Augustine himself.

What more can one ask from a narrator and chronicler?

Fictional Figure

Sequidei, "Daughter of Augustine and Sabina"
c. 389 – c. 460

The service of fiction brings Sequidei to life in the presence of not a shred of historical evidence.

Her conception in Carthage, though, is hardly an affront to Augustine's prominence or importance, but more of a signal of man's weakness in the face of loss of hope, however temporary. Even though Augustine before the time of Sequidei's conception had converted to Christianity, his future as a Catholic churchman, indeed, any conceivable future activities, were less than certain although founding a monastery and school in Thagaste was a distinct possibility. If Augustine were to suffer a lapse in his celibate life (and not the first since dispatching Sabina), within just a couple of years of their parting, the occasion of meeting Sabina whom he tells us he "loved dearly," at the funeral of their only child would certainly be the time.

But what of Sequidei? Being the child of Augustine and a devoted but not overbearing Sabina and having, through her father's and later her mother's generosity, become a landowner, inheriting a part of her grandfather's Thagastan estate, Sequia, using her familiar name, derives a certain independence as well as a clear love for learning from her parents. As we have it here, Augustine, for his own reasons, passes his father's farm to Sabina who when she has raised her daughter and decided to enter the convent, passes it to Sequia.

Like many a woman-precursor in the Christian community, then, Sequidei, though far from rich, remains independent enough to become a mainstay and supporter in local spiritual life which could at that time encompass Catholics, Donatists, Arians, pagans, and Berbers who may have followed their own spiritual paths. That her mother, Sabina, chose the Catholicism of her lover, Augustine, does not bind Sequia to that one faith. After all, though her grandmother was Catholic, her father had once been Manichean, and her paternal grandfather a pagan until on his deathbed. It is entirely possible that her mother had come from Donatist beginnings, that sect having been the largest in Africa at the time of Sabina's birth. So Sequidei is presented as an ecumenical exception in a world of male dominated sectarianism—a clear counterpoint to her father's intransigent heretic-hunting and narrowing of the faith—as an example of true chastity, and perhaps, as the owner of that wish-of-an-orphaned-child: to make whole that which certainly was never one. True for Sequia, perhaps, both of family and of north African society.

Consider her appearance if only to underscore the times and her connection to the Bishop of Hippo. It is likely that her heritage on both sides was Berber, certainly Augustine was one such. It is given us that she highly resembles her dead brother, and thus likely her father. She would be, then, smaller in stature, with desert-darkened complexion, dark brown hair, and luminous eyes, likely brown, perhaps green, and prominently featured [Here, her physical appearance attracts Gaiseric, who forebears ravishing her, for perhaps political, or, maybe, spiritual reasons].

When the story opens, Sequidei is nearly forty years of age, a known celibate and spiritual magnet in the Thagastan area. Despite the intransigence of her father, not acknowledging her existence, it is well known there that Augustine is Sequidei's putative father in no small part by virtue of the land that she owns. She herself knows it very well which shines a most interesting light on her religious activities.

Historical / Fictional Figure

Sabina, "Concubine of Augustine"
c. 356 – c. 435

"Our curiosity about her [Sabina]," Augustine's modern biographer, Peter Brown, says, "is a very modern preoccupation, which Augustine and his cultivated friends would have found strange."[1] One example of this interest is in Jostein Gaarder's *Vita Brevis: A Letter to Saint Augustine*. The novelist and Norwegian intellectual, who writes in the persona of Floria Aemilia, Augustine's concubine, lectures the saint through correspondence. Our scrutiny would be found even stranger had our 21st century sensibilities *not* become preoccupied with this character we know so little about, so very little that we cannot even be told her name.

Here is the bare outline of her life,[2] omitting Augustine's recounting of his feelings: Sabina becomes Augustine's lover and concubine in 372 in Carthage. She bears him a son, Adeodatus, the following year. She presumably moves with Augustine to Thagaste where with his "friend" (our Inno) he teaches in 375, and with him still, back to Carthage in 376. On a summer night in 383, Sabina, Adeodatus, and Augustine slip out of Carthage to avoid confronting his mother, Monnika. They are together in Italy without Monnika until the mother arrives unbidden in Milan in the spring of 385. Within a year of Monnika's arrival, Sabina is dispatched, returned to Africa, and Augustine is set to marry an heiress.

Peter Brown paraphrases Augustine's words about the parting, saying, "this nameless woman will return to Africa, 'vowing never to know a man again,'"[3]although the passage also translates, "vowing never to give herself to any *other* man,[4] "vowing unto Thee never

---

1 Brown, pp 61-2
2 Pine-Coffin, III & IV.
3 Op Cit, p.89.
4 Pine-Coffin, VI, xv. [Emphasis mine, Ed.]

to know any *other* man,"[5] And, so we imagine Sabina several years later in Carthage keeping her vow, having only Augustine as her lover, comforting him in their shared grief over their son's death and conceiving another child, Sequidei.

Further imaginings take root from Karen Jo Toriesen's important study, *When Women Were Priests*, and her relating the spiritualist and political story of fourth-century noblewoman Lucilla's fashioning the rise of the Donatist church in Carthage.

So, then, Saint Augustine's concubine, far from "an obscure victim of high Catholic principles" or "a nameless woman,"[6] becomes a named, well known influence in the local church, both singly and through both Augustine and their daughter, Sequidei. She holds position and a gentle power rooted in love and devotion. She is a woman presbyter in a masculine world, therefore, provocative and disruptive, but steady and faithful at the same time, even in the face of Augustine's ambivalence, trying to decide whether his "heart was crushed to bleeding"[7] at Sabina's leaving or that she was only "a bargain struck for lust, in which the birth of children is begrudged."[8]

Neither Sabina nor her daughter would have agreed with the Vatican's 1976 "Declaration on the Question of Admitting Women to the Priesthood"[9] much less cast off one "dearly loved" for preferment, worldly or spiritual.

Let the story say the rest.

---

5 Pussey, VI, xv. [Emphasis mine, Ed.]
6 Brown, p. 63.
7 Pine-Coffin, VI, xv.
8 Pine-Coffin, IV, ii..
9 see Thorjesen, p. 3.

Adeodatus, b. 370-d. 390
Augustine's and Sabina's son, promising but who died very young.

Africanus
In this case, Gordian a Thysdrian pressed by the revolting citizens to don the purple, the throne of the empire, 238. The town is in southern Tunisia now called El Djem.

Aksil *
Berber trader under Sabina's protection and agent for Innomenatus.

Alans
An asiatic, near-eastern, equestrian people who allied themselves with the Hasding Vandals.

alþingi
The Vandal council. The word taken from Icelandic.

Alypius, d. 5th century
Bishop of Thagaste, long-time friend of Augustine, converted with Augustine in Milan and followed him all his life.

Amazigh
Berbers of north Africa.

Arian
Any follower of Arius (c. AD 256-336) whose heresy centered on the idea that Jesus as son of God did not always exist and was lesser than God the Father. Goths and, therefore, Roman legions of the 4th- 7th centuries were Arians as were most Germanic tribes including Vandals.

Athanasius, c. 296-d. 5-2-373
The patriarch and 20[th]bishop of Alexandria for whose successor, Peter, Inno wrote. Stood firmly against Arianism.

Augustine, b. October 14, 354-d. August 28, 430
Aurelius Augustinus, philosopher and religious writer, Bishop of Hippo Regius (modern Anaba, Algeria). Died 8-28-430 during the siege of the city. Promulgated the ideas of original sin, dependence on grace, and actively promoted a celibate and all-male priesthood and apostolic succession. Notable writings: *Confessions* and *The City of God*.

Beremudus, 4[th]century
Gothic king, father of Pelagia, wife of the Count of Africa, Bonifacius.

Bonifacius, d. 432
Roman general whose abilities and early success in defending Gaul propelled him to high positions under the emperor Valentinian III and his mother-regent Galla Placidia. He took the title Count of Africa for himself and enjoined northern Africa as a realm for himself which he defended at times against Rome.

bucellarii
Literally "biscuit eaters," refers here to a royal guard serving Bonifacius and Pelagia. They were part of the Gothic princess's dowry.

Caelestius, condemned posthumously in Rome, 431
A central figure in the Pelagian heresy. Was denied priesthood in Carthage, c. 411, but was later ordained in Alexandria, then condemned in the east in 418. Opposed Augustine's doctrine of original sin. Argued that Adam's sin harmed only himself and not his progeny.

* Denotes a fully fictional character.

Castinus, active early 5[th]century
> Flavius Castinus quarreled with Bonifacius in Spain and was left alone to subdue the Vandals who, after some early Roman success, defeated him at the Battle of Tarraco. Castinus supported the usurper Joannes and at that emperor's fall faded into obscurity.

christicolae
> Followers of Christ, the name is a Medieval anachronisim.

Comes Africae
> The Count of Africa, Bonifacius's self-proclaimed title.

Darius
> The Roman envoy of Regent Galla Placidia who was sent from Rome to Africa to broker peace between Sigisvultus, an agent of the western empire, and Bonifacius. Fictionally, he is sent by Bonifacius further west to the Vandals to halt the advance at Icosium (modern Algiers).

Donatists
> African Catholics who resisted and withstood Diocletian's persecutions and later objected to the elevation of some who had repudiated their faith in the face of that tyranny. The issues led to a schism in the African church that lasted through Augustine's term as bishop in the 4[th]century and ended in the 8[th]century Muslim conquest. Augustine was a key figure in the Donatist supression.

Ehgil *
> Adult son of Aksil who guides Innomenatus through the maze to the postern-gate.

Eraclius, nominated September 26, 426
> Augustine's designated successor to the bishopric of Hippo Regius. He assisted in the operation of the monastery during his mentor's last years.

Flavius Felix, d. May 430
> The lesser of three Roman generals (with Aeitus & Bonifacius) who here is shown to plot, unsuccessfully, against *Comes Africae*.

foederati
> A special class denoting association or statehood under the Roman umbrella often bestowed on successful mercenary populations.

Gaiseric, d. January 25, 477
> King of the Vandals and Alans who guided his people from Baeteca (now Andalusia in Spain) across the Straits of Gibraltar and conquered Africa Proconsularis (Hippo and Carthage), the Baeleric Isles and Sicily. Late in his reign over the Vandal kingdom of north Africa, he took and sacked Rome, 455.

Galla Placidia, b. 393-d. 11-27-450
> The daughter of Roman emporer Theodosius I, was the mother of Valentinian III and ruled from her son's sixth year as regent of Rome. Between 428 and 430 she was alternatively supportive and suspicious of Bonifacius, pitting him against other strong generals of the time.
> She employed Bonifacius to restrain Flavius Aetis in 432 which cost even in victory *Comes Africae* his life.

Gelimmer∗
> A close ally and cousin to Gaiseric, and a thane of the Vandals. Not to be confused with a later Gelimer active as late as 533.

∗ Denotes a fully fictional character.

Godegisel, d. 406

Father of two Vandal kings, Gunderic and Gaiseric. He notably led the migration to Gaul after the crossing of the Rhine c. 406. He died likely at the hands of the Franks and was succeded by his son Gunderic.

Gunderic, d. 428

Son and successor of Godigisel and half brother to Gaesiric who followed him as King of the Vandals and Alans.

Gunter∗

Kin to Gaiseric. A sub-general and scout-leader.

Hasdings

The Vandal group to which Gaiseric belonged. Not always the leading people of the tribe, but rose to prominence during war in Hispania. Associated with Sillings and Alans, and rivals of the Sueves.

Honoratus∗

The owner of a villa near Castra Nova that was used by Darius to meet with and impress Gaiseric.

Huneric the Elder ∗

An elder thane of the Vandals and advisor to Gaiseric.

Idir∗

An old man, Berber farmer and rancher who shelters Aksil.

Innomenatus Quimortuus

Friend of Augustine who appears unnamed in the saint's *Confessio* first recovering then relapsing and dying of fever. He is here resurrected as the narrator and main actor in Augustine's final years. Known also as Inno, Namlaus (to Gaiseric), and Amicus.

Jerome, c.342-347-d.420

Known as St. Jerome, a scholar and translator of the *Bible*, known later as the *Vulgate*.

Jugurtha, c. 160-104 BC

King of Numidia. Innomenatus claims him as an ancestor.

Julian of Eclanum, b. 386-d. 454

Took up the defense of Pelagius after that man's condemnation and was then Augustine's target (giving as well as he got) in the African's fight against the Pelagians. Julian lost his seat as bishop of Eclanum. Notably, characterized Augustine as the chief goat of the African herd. Here he is a correspondent with Sequidei, Sabina's daughter.

Manicheans

A Christian sect headed by the Persian Mani. Augustine was an adherent during his early years in Carthage. The Manichean idea that evil and good coexisted separately in the world as equivalent powers was later debunked by Augustine. Still, Augustine was accused even in his old age of being a Manichean.

Maximus,

An Arian bishop who served Sigisvultus in Afrrica. Baptised *Comes*'s daughter.

Memorius

An Italian bishop who knew Augustine. Father to Julian of Eclanum.

∗ Denotes a fully fictional character.

Monnika, b. 332, d. 387

Augustine's mother, at whose death, some say, the future bishop became inspired to write his *Confessio.* A Christian married to a pagan, she watched her son's spiritual progress very closely, following after him to Milan, uninvited, working toward his conversion with St. Ambrose.

Nestorius

A one-time bishop of Constantiople.

Nicene Creed

In Latin, the *credo.* Adopted in 325 during the First Ecumenical Council in Nicaea (now Iznik, Turkey). Defines a line between Arian and Catholic Christianity, establishing the Trinity as a single three-personed god.

Pelagia, 4th/5th centuries

Daughter of the Gothic king, Beremudus, and wife to Bonifacius. She was an Arian Christian. She adopted✳ Sabina to her care.

Pelagius, active 390-418

A Celtic theologian, fluent in Latin and Greek, who espoused the idea of free will and denied the concept of original sin, both of which Augustine favored. Humans were quite capable of good acts without a special grace granted by God. Augustine wrote extensively against this ascetic and his later defenders, notably Julian of Eclanum.

Possidius, d. 437

A longtime friend of Augustine and bishop of Calama. Possidius wrote the first biography of Augustine, *Sancti Augustini Vita,* shortly after his friend's death.

Regianus✳

The hapless bishop of Ad Fratres and informer to and victim of Gaiseric.

Sabina

Concubine (unnamed by Augustine in *Confessio*), mother to son and daughter, Adeodatus and Sequidei✳, respectively. The *materfamilias* of a convent in Hippo Regius and a correspondent to Augustine. Founded with her daughter an ecumenical sect in Thagaste and acted as priest in its liturgy. Also known by her Berber name *Tizem*, the Lioness.

Sallust (**Gaius Sallustyius Crispus**)

Roman historian of the 1st century BC. Reported Jurutha's comment on the city of Rome.

scope

After the Old English, storyteller, poet, shaper. [shōp]

Sequidei✳

Daughter of Augustine and Sabina, posthumous sister of Adeodatus. She served as a priest in an ecumenical sect she founded in Thagaste and expanded to Calama and Hippo after her capture by Gaiseric. "Follower of God." Called Sequia, familiarly.

Sigisvultus, active 427-448

A Roman general tasked to bring Bonifacius to heel after he had defeated two previous Roman armies. Sigisvultus succeeded, taking both Hippo Regius and Carthage, though Bonifacius was allowed to range in parts outside those cities. When Bonifacius reconciled with Galla Placidia, his fellow Arian, Sigisvultus, returned to Italy.

✳ Denotes a fully fictional character.

Silings

A Vandalic people who moved along with the Hasdings then joined them after suffering decimation by Goth and Roman forces in Hispania.

Sueves

A Germainic tribe rivaling both Silings and Hasdings until defeated by Gunderic's forces in Hispania.

Tanit

Ancient Punic goddess sometimes worshiped by pagans and desert peoples.

Tizem

Sabina's Berber name signifying "Lioness."

Theodosius, b. 401-d.450

Theodosius II, emporer of the Easterrn Roman Empire, nephew of Galla Placidia, supporter of Valentinian III who was another child-ruler.

Ulfa∗

A thane of the Vandals and opposer of Gaiseric. Resists the African crossing.

Ulfasson∗

Son of Ulfa, rescued in the crossing and adopted by Gaiseric but later betrayed the king.

Ulfilas, c. 311-383

Also known as Wulfilas. Evangelist to the Goths and translator of the *Bible* into Gothic.

Ulman∗

Brother to Ulfa, uncle to Ulfasson, also betrayed Gaiseric in an attempted assassination.

Valentinian III, b. July 2, 419-d. March 16, 455

Western Roman emporer for whom his mother, Galla Placidia, served as regent 425-437.

Valerius∗

A layman and benefactor in Augustine's church at Hippo Regius.

Visita Nocte∗

The night visitor appearing in dreams, especially of Augustine who considers it an alter ego akin to God.

wight

"Man," adapted from the Old English (p.171)

wegas or *gomes*

"Men," adapted from the Old English

Wulfilas

See Ulfilas.

Wulfson∗

A general of Gaiseric at the battle of Calama.

∗ Denotes a fully fictional character.

Ad Fratres
>City in Mauretania Tingitana, now eastern Morocco. (p. 109)

atrium
>The first public room in a Roman house, the *impluvium* being at its center and open to the sky. (p. 40)

Baetica
>Southern Hispania, now roughly described as Andalusia, Spain. (p. 109)

Byzacena
>Roman province due south of Africa Proconsularis. (p. 109)

Calama
>A city in Proconsularis and the Catholic See held by Possidius from which the conquering Vandals conducted Bonifacius's defeat in this story. (pp. 109, 185, 300)

Canaria
>The largest of the modern Canary Islands.

Cartenna
>City in Mauretania Tingitana, now Algeria. (p. 109)

Carthage
>The major city and seaport in Africa Proconsularis (pp. 8, 34, 109, 185), now within Tunis, Tunisia.

Carthago Spartaria
>A major Mediterranean port city in what is now modern Spain. (p. 109)

Castra Nova
>Near Casa Honoratus where Gaiseric and Darius meet. (p. 109)

Cassiciacum
>A villa north of Mediolanum, now Milan, where Augustine, Monnika, Adeaodatus and his mother lived prior to Augustine's betrothal. (p. 8)

Chaouïa
>Specifically a province in what is modern Morocco. Generally refers to a Berber people spread as far as eastern Algeria (Proconsularis).

cohort
>A Roman military unit, 480 soldiers, in use during Bonifacius's time.

Cydamus
>The Roman name for the Libyan town, Gadams, due south of Carthage.

Dacia
>Area defined by Romania and Bulgaria, where Inno translated Luke from Greek to Gothic for bishop Ulfilas. See Nocopolis, p. 8.

Eclanum
>East of modern Napoli was the See of Bishop Julian of Eclanum.

Gaul
>Modern France, especially the south. (pp. 8, 34)

Heliopolis
>A hill town, five miles north of Calama, on the road to Hippo Regius.

Hippo Regius
>Modern Anaba, Algeria, 80 kilometers west of the Tunisian border. In 5[th]century Africa Proconsularis. (pp. 8, 34, 109, 185) Augustine's home from 395 until his death in 430.

Hispalis
>Modern Seville. (pp. 8, 109)

Appendix D
Places

Hispania
Modern Spain. (pp. 8, 34, 109)

Icosium
Near modern Algiers. According to the truce Darius brokered, this is the westernmost point allowed the Vandals to advance. (p. 109)

impluvium
The well of a roman house. (p. 40)

Igligili
A coastal town midway between Icosium and Hippo Regius.

Leptis Magna
A port city in what is now western Libya.

Leptis Minor
City south and east of the southern Proconsularis border. (p. 109)

Lilybaeum
A sizeable city in Sicilia.

Libya
In ancient times all of North Africa. In the narrative, all east of Carthage and west of Alexandria.

Madaurus
A town just south of Thagaste in which Augustine and Innomenatus studied prior to matriculating to schools in Carthage. (p. 185)

Malaca
Modern Malaga. Gaiseric's likely embarcation port to Africa. (p. 109)

maniple
An ancient Roman militray unit, replaced by the smaller, more flexible *cohort* prior to Bonifacian times. Augustine uses the archaic term.

Mare Major
The Black Sea. (p. 8)

Mare Mediterraneo
The Mediterranean Sea. (pp. 8, 34, 109, 185)

Mauretania Tingitana
The area east of the Pillars of Hercules (Gibraltar) toward the modern border with Algeria. (p. 109)

Mauretania Caesariensis
East of Tingitana and Mauretania Sitifensis along the route of the Vandal advance. (p. 109)

Mauretania Sitifensis
A buffer zone between the Vandal foederati established by Darius lying east of Mauretania Caesariensis and Numidia. The westernmost point lies 300 kilometers from Hippo Regius. (p. 109)

Mediolanum
Modern Milan. (p. 8)

Nicopolis ad Istrum
Now in northern Bulgaria, adopted home and workplace of Wulfila and Innomenatus who translated for bishop Wulfila. (p.8)

Numidia
Now in eastern Algeria, bordering Tunisia. (pp. 109, 185)

Ostia
Then, as now, the port city of Rome.

ostium
> In a Roman house, the main entry. Leads to the *atrium*. (p. 40)

Pannonia
> Located in what is now Hungary. (p. 34)

peristylium
> An open well area in a Roman household behind the *atrium* and *tablinium*. (p. 40)

Proconsularis
> Also Africa Proconsularis and singly, Africa. (pp. 8, 109, 185)

Portus Magnus
> A port city in eastern, modern-day Morocco. (p. 109)

Ravenna
> The contemporary capital of the Western Roman Empire, established as such in 402 until the collapse of the western empire.

Seybouse
> The river flowing between Heliopolis and Calama. (p. 300)

Selectum
> A city in northeast Byzacena. (p. 109)

Septem Fratres
> A town near the Gibraltar straits, landing place for the Vandals. (p. 109)

Sicilia
> Contemporary name for Sicily, Italy.

tablinum
> In a Roman house, a room opposite the atrium at the far end of the *peristylium*. (p. 40)

Tacapae
> A Lybian city south and east of Carthage. (p. 109)

Tarrasco
> A port city in *Hispania*, the modern Tarragona.

Thagaste
> Modern Souk Ahras, Algeria. Then a Berber and Roman community into which Augustine was born. He built a school there. The farm of Patricius, Augustine's pagan father, was there, and in this story figures as the home of Sequia, Augustine's daughter, the place of her capture by Gaiseric, and the location of her ministry. (pp. 109, 185)

Tingitana
> Mauretania Tingitana, the seaboard of modern Morocco. (p. 109)

Tipasa
> A Mauretanian city from which refugees flee. (p. 109)

Trinarcia
> The three-legged ancient Sicilian symbol.

Vandalusia
> A name for the Hispanic-Vandal kingdom, speculatively, aka Andulasia.

vestibulum
> The first room at a Roman house entry, leading to the *atrium*. (p. 40)

Timelines

Appendix E
Timelines

4th& 5thCenturies

354 Aurelius Augustinus born in Thagaste, Africa Proconsularis (AP).

354* Innomenatus Quimortuus, Amicus born in Madaurus, AP.

357* Sabina (Tizem) born in Carthage, AP.

368 Augustine studies at Madaurus and Carthage. Returns to Thagaste in 375.

372 Meets Sabina, takes her as a concubine in Carthage.

373 Adeodatus born.

376 The-friend-of-Augustine's-youth purportedly dies.

376* Innomenatus leaves for Alexandria, then to Jerusalem and Constantinople.

376 Augustine returns to Carthage.

381 Innomenatus works translating for Wulfilas in Nicopolis ad Istrum.

383 Augustine sails for Rome without Monnika but with Adeodatus and Sabina.

385 Monnika follows Augustine, joins Augustine in Milan in springtime.

386 Augustine, Adeodatus, Alypius, Sabina, and Monnika at Cassiciacum villa.

386 Monnika arranges a marriage for Augustine. The concubine must go.

387 All return to Milan. Augustine converts, is baptized. Sends Sabina to Africa.

387 Monnika dies.

388 Augustine returns to Carthage, goes home to Thagaste.

390 Adeodatus dies. Augustine and *Sabina briefly join. *Sequidei is conceived.

391 Augustine is ordained a priest.

392 Augustine takes an active role in suppression of heretical thought (Donatists).

395 Augustine named bishop and successor to seat at Hippo Regius

397 *Confessions* written.

399 Pagan shrines shuttered by Imperial agents. Donatists persecuted.

400's A series of Donatist outrages, riots, and incivilities. Pagans riot in Calama.

405 Hasding Vandals begin moving west along the Danube.

406 Germanic tribes cross the Rhine. Vandals included.

410 Rome sacked by Alaric. Pelagius flees to AP, denunciation follows.

411 Vandals scale the Pyrenees and enter Hispania.

411 Pelagius and Caelestius land in Hippo. Are rebuked and move on.

412 Donnatists persecuted/denounced.

415 Pelagius is excommunicated.

419 Julian of Eclanum publishes his first attacks on Augustine and the Africans.

425 Valentinian III, emperor.

425* Innomenatus resident in Hispania. Tutors Gaiseric.

427* Innomenatus sails home to Africa, finds employment with Augustine.

428 Hasding Vandals and Alans victorious in Spain. Gaiseric acclaimed king.

429 Vandals cross into Africa and proceed toward Hippo Regius.

430* The battle of Calama.

430 Vandals in Numidia, siege of Hippo Regius.

430 Augustine dies, August 28.

*Denotes a fictional event.

Narrative Timeline

428 A.D.

Sept

Early-month:
Inno collides with Augustine. Innomenatus to *Casa Bonifati.*
Sabina pictured writing to Augustine.
Gaiseric proclaimed Vandal king.

Late-month:
Innomenatus writes to Gaiseric for Bonifacius.
Sabina travels to Thagaste.

Oct

Alypius and Augustine greet the delegation at the port.

429 A.D.

Jan
Gaiseric plans to cross the strait to Africa.
Inno meets Pelagia, still at *Casa Bonifati.*

Feb

Early-month:
Augustine's first dream.
Gaiseric replies to Bonifacius, accepting the invitation, *foederati.*

Late-month:
Bonifacius discovers the plot of Flavius Felix. Rescinds Vandal invitation.
The Vandals begin massing in Tingitana.

Apr
Word of Vandal movements begin reaching Hippo Regius.

May
Darius / Gaiseric meet at Castra Nova. Vandals are allowed to advance.

Jun
Julian attacks Augustine's integrity. Innomenatus must return to Hippo.
Darius returns and Innomenatus goes to Augustine. Formal truce with
the Vandals.
Augustine reports to Amicus a dream of the *visita nocte* and names
Inno as his chief scribe.

Late-month:
Reports of mayhem at the hands of Vandals increase.
Augustine dreams and visits Amicus late at night. Will move him closer.
Sabina houses refugees. Worries and writes to Sequia. Leads relief
efforts and preaches publicly.

Jul
Innomenatus begins writing to Sabina.

Aug
The Vandals move beyond Icosium.
Sabina meets Innomenatus.

429 A.D. (cont.)

Sept   *Early-month*
Augustine confesses.

       Late-month
Gaiseric captures Sequidei outside Thagaste.
The great sandstorm.
Aksil returns.

Oct   *Late-month*
Augustine confesses more.
Sabina is arrested, jailed.

Nov-
Dec   Vandals take Thagaste.
Pelagia employs Innomenatus, attending Sabina.

430 A.D.

Jan   The Vandals advance on Calama.

Feb   The ransom demand of Sequidei.
Bonifacius confronts the bishop.

       Late-month
Augustine confess again.
Pelagia frees Sabina.

Mar   *Mid-month*
Calama falls to the Vandals.
The public confession of Bishop Augustine.
Aksil leaves for Gaiseric camp.

Apr   *Late-month*
Bonifacius is defeated at Calama.

May   The Vandals appear before the walls of Hippo Regius.

       Late-month
The siege of Hippo Regius begins.

June   *Early-month*
Sequidei is ransomed, enters Hippo Regius.

Aug   Augustine's final confession.

Sept   Innomenatus escapes to Caneria.

Author's Note on Language

My decision to include in this novel the lines of ancient languages was not made lightly. Besides listening to widespread and often eager counsel on both sides of the issue, I referenced novels set in ancient times: Mailer, Vidal, Gaarder—historical novels set in the old Roman world. Perhaps my famous fellow writers had better sense or superior counselors. I have departed from them and chose for my own reasons to use a smattering of Latin, Gothic, and, much less, Greek, this last of which like Augustine, I know little. Each instance is followed immediately be a modern English translation for the convenience, in particular, of the American reader.

The inclusion of the languages will be an embellishment for those who know them and a curiosity, I hope, for those who do not. I trust neither the adornment nor the novelty will engender sighs or stern faces in the reader. I encourage those who wish to skip the foreign sentences going straight to the English to do so freely.

In no way should my use of ancient tongues be taken as a philological excursion. Though I've been at pains to be as correct as possible, there is no wish to enter into or to transgress upon the domain of the linguist. Consider my practice as fair use.

I have stayed exact in passages quoted, but have relied elsewhere on my own study of Gothic and Latin. Where what is known of ancient Gothic did not fit my needs, I relied on Old English, and in one case, Icelandic. I gloss the pronunciation of a few words and names that occur in the text frequently in the interest of allowing the reader to be more comfortable discussing the book, but other than the few I specify on the next page, a common American- or British-sounding pronunciation should do well.

tj

Aksil (ăκ´ səl)[1] exactly as Americans say "AX el."[2]

alþingi (ôl ᴛʜĭɴ´ ᴊē) as Americans would say "all THIN gee."

Alypius (ə ʟĭᴘ´ē əs) as Americans would say " a LIPPY us."

Augustine (ô´ gə-stēn´) is my preference, though my Roman Catholic friends invariably say (ô-gŭ´-stĭn).

Bonifacius (bŏn´ ə fās´ ē əs) as Americans say "bon i FACE ee us."

bucellarii (bōō sə´ lâr ē) as Americans say "BOO sell airy."

Chaouïa (chä´ ōō ē ə) as Americans say "TCH ooey a."

christicolae (krĭst´ ĭ kō´ lī) as Americans might say "KRISTY **coal** eye."

Comes Africae (kō´ māz Ă´ frĭk ī) or say "CO maze **A** fric eye."

Ehgil (Ē´ gəl) just like an American "eagle."

foederati (fĕd´ ər ä´ tē) or as Americans might say "fedder AWE tea."

Gaiseric (gī´ sĭr ĭk) or "GUY sir ick."

Ia (ē´ ə) or "EE a" as in the colloquial "(s)ee ya."

Innomenatus Quimortuus (ĭn nō´ mĕn ä´ təs kwē môr´ tōō əs) or "in NO men AWE tus Kwee MORE to us."

Manicheans (măn ə kē´ ĭnz) or in America "man uh KEY ann's."

Monnika (môn´ ĭ k ə) as in "Santa Monica, CA."

Sabina (sä bē nə) or "saw BEAN a."

scope (shōp) or "Showp" rhymes with "dope." Old English for "shaper."

Sequia (sĕ kwē´ ə) as in "se(t) KWE a."

Sequidei (sĕ´ kwē dā´ ē) like "SE(t) kwe DAY ee."

Thagaste (tô gäst´) like "Taw GHAWST."

weird (Wîrd) say it as in modern "weird." The Old English word means "fate."

---

1 The initial guide follows *The American Heritage College Dictionary*, 2002.
2 Attuned to my Midwestern ear. tj

p. 16 - Peter 2:11, *Vulgate*. http://vulgate.org.
Carissimi obsecro tamquam advenas abstinere vos,
Dearly beloved, I beseech you as strangers and pilgrims, abstain from fleshly lusts, which war against the soul.
p. 23 - Psalm 6:1- 2, *Vulgate*. http://vulgate.org.
Lord, rebuke me not in thine anger, neither chasten me in Thy hot displeasure, . . .
O Lord deliver my soul: oh, save me for Thy mercy's sake.
p. 23/4 - Sabina alludes to *The Gospel of Mary*: 5. See gnosis.org or Barnstone.
Lord, as with your servant, Mary, guide our family to share in openness, bringing your word—for Thy goodness's sake—to your multitudes.
p. 36 - The Wanderer, *Bright's Old English Grammar and Reader*, p. 324.
Weird biþ ful arade.
p. 79 - Nicene Creed, http://www.catholic.org
Credo in Spiritum Sanctum, sanctam Ecclesiam catholicam, sanctorum communionem, remissionem peccatorum, carnis resurrectionem, vitam aeternam. . .
p. 97 - John 3:16, *sic enim dilexit Deus mundum ut Filium suum unigenitum daret ut omnis ui credit in eum non pereat sed habeat vitam aeternam.*
For God so loved the world, as to give his only begotten Son: that whosoever believeth in him may not perish, but may have life everlasting.
p. 97 - *The Apocryphon of James*, I tell you this that you may know yourselves (See Barnstone).
p. 98 - *The Gospel of Philip*, When a blind man and one who sees are both together in darkness, they are no different from one another. When the light comes, then he who sees will see the light, and he who is blind will remain in darkness (See Barnstone).
p. 98 - 1 Corr. 13:13, And of these, love is the greatest.
p. 98 - Mark IV. 11, Unto you is given the mystery of the kingdom of God: but unto them that are without, all things are done in parables. That they may see, and not perceive.
p. 98 - *The Gospel of Thomas*, Seek and do not stop seeking until you find. (See Barnstone).
p. 129 - Psalm 6: 2, 5, 8. *Vulgate*. http://vulgate.org.
Domine ne in furore tuo arguas me neque in ira tua corripias me, . . .
. . . I have grown old amongst all my enemies.
p. 131 - Psalm 6: 2. *Vulgate*. http://vulgate.org.
revertere Domine erue animam meam salva me propter misericordiam tuam.

p. 143 - *doxologia minor.* https://www.preces-latinae.org/thesaurus/Basics/GloriaPatri.html

Gloria Patri, et Filio, et Spiritui Sancto. Sicut erat in principio, et nunc, et semper, et in sæcula sæculorum.

Glory be to the Father and to the Son and to the Holy Ghost. As it was in the beginning, and now, and ever shall be, world without end.

p. 201 - https://penelope.uchicago.edu/Thayer/E/Roman/Texts/Cicero/de_Finibus/home.html.

Rerum principia parva sunt. Big things start small.

Amicus refers to Cicero's *De Finibus Bonorum et Malorum* or simply to a Roman folk saying he'd forever heard.

p. 223 - Augustine paraphrases **Matthew 27:46 and Mark 15:34.**

"*Eli, Eli, lema sabachthani*?"

"My God, my God, why hast Thou forsaken me?"

p. 276 - Psalm 6:6. *Vulgate.* http://vulgate.org.

I am weary with my moaning: every night I flood my bed with tears; I drench my couch with my weeping.

p. 278 - (an anachronism) "Tantum Ergo," St. Thomas Aquinas, 1264 A.D.

Genitori, Genitoque

Laus et iubilatio,

Salus, honor, virtus quoque

Sit et benedictio:

Procedenti ab utroque

Compar sit laudatio.   *Amen*

p. 278 - (English Version) "Tantum ergo." *Wikipedia, The Free Encyclopedia.* "Literal Translation." 7 Jan. 2022. Web. 31 Jan. 2022.

To begetter and begotten

Praise and jubilation

Hail honor and virtue

Be and blessings, too:

From One through Both

Let there be equal praise.   Amen

p. 310 - Attributed to Jurgutha in Sallust, *Bellum Iugurthinum,* The Jugurthine War. "*urbem venalem et mature perituram, si emptorem invenerit,* a city for sale and doomed to quick destruction, if it should find a buyer."

p. 320 - Psalms: 6, 30, 100, and 129. *Vulgate.* http://vulgate.org. *domine ne in furore, in te Domine speravi, misericordiam et judicium, de profundis clamai.*

p. 321 - Psalm 100:1.*Vulgate.* http://vulgate.org. "*misericordiam et iudicium cantabo tibi,* I will sing kindness and judgment to you."

p. 323 - Psalm 23:4. *Vulgate.* http://vulgate.org. *sed et si ambulaver in valle mortis not timebo malum quoniam vos mecum,* for though I walk through the valley of death, I fear no evil for You are with me.

Augustinius, Arelius. *City of God.* [tr] Gerald G. Walsh. Image Books, 1958.

---. *On the Two Cities, Selections.* F. W. Strothmann, ed. [tr] Marcus Dods. Frederick Ungar Publishing, 1976.

---. *Confessions.* [tr] R. S. Pine-Coffin. Penguin, 1970.

---. *Confessions.* [tr] E. B. Pusey. Project Gutenberg, #3296.

---. On Christian Teaching. [tr] R. P. H. Green. Oxford University Press, 2008.

---. *The Trinity.* [tr] Edmund Hill. New City Press, 2017.

Baigent, Michael and Richr Leigh. *The Dead Sea Scrolls Deception.* Touchstone, Simon & Schuster, 1993.

Barnstone, Willis and Marvin Meyer, eds. *Essential Gnostic Scriptures.* Shambahla, 2010.

Brennan, Brian. *Herculaneum, A Roman Town Reborn.* Ancient History Seminars, Australia, 2018.

Brown, Peter. *Augustine of Hippo, a biography.* U of CA Press, 1967.

Cassidy, F. G. and Richard N. Ringler. *Bright's Old English Reader,* 2nd Edition. Holt, Rinehart and Winston, 1971.

Churton, Tobias. *The Gnostics.* Barnes and Noble Books, 1997.

Ercolano Ricostruita. ArcheoLibri, Italy, 2019.

Eusebius. The History of the Chruch. [tr]G. A. Williamson. Penguin, 1981.

Gaarder, Jostein. *Vita Brevis, A Letter to St. Augustine.* [tr] Anne Born. Sara Perkins, illustrator. Phoenix House, 1997.

Gibbon, Edward. *The Decline and Fall of The Roman Empire.* Random House, 2003.

Grant, Michael. The Fall of the Roman Empire. Phoenix Press, 2005.

Heather, Peter J. and John Matthews, translators. *The Goths in the Fourth Century,* Liverpool University Press, 1991.

Hieronymus, Eusebius (St. Jerome). *The Vulgate.* Vulgate.org. Jan. 31, 2022.

Hollingworth, Miles. *Saint Augustine of Hippo, An Intellectual Biography.* Oxford University Press, 2013.

Hughes, Ian. *Gaiseric the Vandal Who Destroyed Rome*. Pen and Sword Books, 2017.

Jacobsen, Torsten Cumberland. *A History of the Vandals*. Westholme, 2012.

Merrills, Andy and Richard Miles. *The Vandals*. Wiley Blackwell, 2014.

Pagels, Elaine. *The Gnostic Gospels*. Vintage / Random House, 1989.

Pine-Coffin, R. S. [tr], *Confessions*. Penguin, 1970.

Possiiuds. *Sancti Augustini Vita*. [tr] Herbert T. Weiskotten. Evolution Publishing, Merchantville, NJ, 2008.

Project Wulfila. Universtiy of Antwerp. http://www.wulfila.be.

Pusey, E. B., (translator). *The Confessions of St. Augustine*, Project Gutenberg, #3296.

Torijesen, Karen Jo. *When Women Were Priests*. HarperSanFrancisco, 1995.

Vidal, Gore. *Julian, A Novel*. Vintage Books, 1992.

---. *Live from Golgotha: The Gospel According to Gore Vidal*. Penguin, 1992.

Vulgate, The. http://vulgate.org.

Warmington, B. H. *Carthage, A History*. Barnes and Noble Books, 1969.

Wikipedia contributors. "Augustine of Hippo." *Wikipedia, The Free Encyclopedia*. Wikipedia, The Free Encyclopedia, 29 Jan. 2022. Web. 31 Jan. 2022.

---. "Bonifatius." *Wikipedia, The Free Encyclopedia*. Wikipedia, The Free Encyclopedia, 7 Jan. 2022. Web. 31 Jan. 2022.

---. "Gaiseric." *Wikipedia, The Free Encyclopedia*. Wikipedia, The Free Encyclopedia, 30 Jan. 2022. Web. 31 Jan. 2022.

---. "Ulfilas." *Wikipedia, The Free Encyclopedia*. Wikipedia, The Free Encyclopedia, 30 Jan. 2022. Web. 31 Jan. 2022.

Wills, Gary. *Saint Augustine*. Penguin Books, 2005.

Acknowledgments

The early chapters of this book were written, looking south over the Mediterranian toward Carthage and Anaba, modern Hippo Regius, at the kitchen table in my apartment high up on the cliffs overlooking the little town of Letojanni, very close to its more famous sister, Taormina where the tourists like to go. I worked there two months in that early Sicilian spring of 2019 and thank Bruno who hosted me and insisted that the book belonged on the apartment bookshelf. And so it does.

A good deal of the story was penned during the pandemic years, beginning January, 2020 at home—looking over the little waters of Lake Merritt in Oakland—but still peering deep into seas that Innomenatus traveled and that Augustine hated and feared.

It is an illusion of writers and their readers that we work alone. Not so. Beside the company I kept with my characters, it was quite crowded at home, sequestered often with the scholars who have written of the ancient days between the deaths of Christ and Augustine, just four centuries!

I mention many of them in the bibliography, but I cannot say which one galvanized my idea that it was inconceivable that the mother of Adeodatus not be present at her son's funderal. And so, among so many admirers of Augustine, at least one thought as I had, that Sabina, as I called her, returned to Africa alone but that her lover soon followed. Sabina's unnamed condition in Augustine's *Confessions* gave birth to her here and also demanded the resurrection of the other Augustine left unnamed, Innomenatus.

Others without whom I could not have completed this work are Carol Squicci, James Richter, Bruce Coyle, John Cox, and Kitty Fassett, my early readers. And again, I thank Carol of CASdesign for her devotion and graphic contributions to this book.